MemoRandom

ALSO BY ANDERS DE LA MOTTE

Game

Bubble

Buzz

MemoRandom

A Thriller

ANDERS DE LA MOTTE

EMILY BESTLER BOOKS

—

ATRIA

NEW YORK   LONDON   TORONTO   SYDNEY   NEW DELHI

ATRIA PAPERBACK
An Imprint of Simon & Schuster, Inc.
1230 Avenue of the Americas
New York, NY 10020

First Emily Bestler Books/Atria Paperback edition December 2015

EMILY BESTLER BOOKS / ATRIA PAPERBACK and colophon are trademarks of Simon & Schuster, Inc.

For information about special discounts for bulk purchases, please contact Simon & Schuster Special Sales at 1-866-506-1949 or business@simonandschuster.com.

The Simon & Schuster Speakers Bureau can bring authors to your live event. For more information or to book an event, contact the Simon & Schuster Speakers Bureau at 1-866-248-3049 or visit our website at www.simonspeakers.com.

Interior design by Kyoko Watanabe

Manufactured in the United States of America

10 9 8 7 6 5 4 3 2 1

Library of Congress Cataloging-in-Publication Data is available.

ISBN 978-1-4767-8806-7
ISBN 978-1-4767-8807-4 (ebook)

For Anette

PROLOGUE

Saturday, November 23

Blue lights . . . that's his first lucid thought after he opens his eyes.

He can't have been unconscious for more than a few seconds, a tiny micropause in his head. But the world seems so strange, so unfamiliar. As if he weren't quite awake yet.

Blue reflections are dancing around him. In the rearview mirror, bouncing off the concrete walls, the roof, the wet road surface, even off the shiny plastic details of the dashboard.

A car. He's in the driver's seat of a car, going through a long tunnel.

The pain catches up with him. He has a vague memory of it from before he blacked out. A brilliant, ice-blue welding arc cutting straight through the left-hand side of his skull and turning his thoughts into thick sludge.

He can even identify the way it smells.

Metal, plastic, electricity.

Something's happening to his body, something serious, threatening his very existence, but weirdly he doesn't feel particularly frightened. He tightens his grip on the steering wheel, feels the soft leather against the palms of his hands. A pleasant, reassuring sensation. For a moment he almost gives in to it and lets go, tracing those smooth molecules all the way back into unconsciousness.

Instead he squeezes the wheel as hard as he can and tries to get his aching head to explain what is happening to him.

"David Sarac."

"Your name is David Sarac, and . . ."

x **Anders de la Motte**

And what?

The car is still driving through the tunnel, and one of the many incomprehensible instruments on the dashboard must be telling him that he's going too fast, way too fast.

He tries to lift his foot from the accelerator pedal but his leg refuses to obey him. In fact he can't actually feel his legs at all. The pain is growing increasingly intense, yet in an odd way simultaneously more remote. He realizes that his body is in the process of shutting down, abandoning any process that isn't essential to life support until the meltdown in his head is under control.

"Your name is David Sarac," he mutters to himself.

"David Sarac."

Various noises are crackling from the speakers: music, dialing tones, fractured, agitated voices talking over each other.

He looks in the rearview mirror. And for a moment he imagines he can see movement, a dark silhouette. Is there someone sitting in the backseat, someone who could help him?

He tries to open his mouth and sees the silhouette in the mirror do the same. He can see stubble, a tormented but familiar face. He realizes what that means. There's no one else there, he's all alone.

The light in the rearview mirror is blinding him, making his eyes water. The voices on the radio are still babbling, louder now—even more agitated.

The shutdown of his body is speeding up. It's spreading from his legs and up toward his chest.

"Police!" one of the radio voices yells. The word forces its way in and soon fills the whole of his consciousness.

Police.

Police.

Police.

He looks away from the rearview mirror and laboriously turns his head an inch or so. The effort makes him groan with pain.

"Your name is David Sarac."

And?

Some distance ahead he can see the rear lights of another car. Alongside them is a large warning sign, an obstruction of some sort, and an exit ramp. The rear lights are suddenly glowing bright red.

He ought to turn the wheel, follow the car ahead of him out of the tunnel. His every instinct tells him that would be the sensible thing to do. But the connection to his arms seems to be on the way to shutting down as well, because all he can manage is a brief, jerky movement.

The obstruction is getting closer, a large concrete barrier dividing the two tubes of the tunnel. The reflective signs are shimmering in the glare of the car's headlights. He tries to look a few seconds into the future and work out whether he's in danger of a collision. But his brain is no longer working the way it normally does.

The shutdown reaches his face, making his chin drop.

The distance to the barrier is still shrinking.

"*Police.*"

The word is back, even more insistent this time, and suddenly he realizes why. *He's* the police; the blue lights are coming from his own car.

His name is David Sarac. He's a police officer. And . . . ?

The pain in his head eases long enough for him to be able to piece together a coherent chain of thought. What is he doing here? Who is he chasing? Or is he the one being chased?

The lights in the rearview mirror are getting closer and closer. Burning into his head.

Fear overwhelms him, sending his pulse racing. The ice-blue pain returns, even stronger this time. His eyelids flutter; all the noise around him fades away into the distance. He tries to remain conscious, fighting the shutdown process. But there's no longer anything he can do.

A brief jolt shakes the car. But he hardly notices it. The

xii **Anders de la Motte**

shutdown process is almost complete and he is more or less unconscious again. Free from pain, fear, and confusion. All that remains is a stubborn, scarcely noticeable signal in his tortured brain. An electrical impulse passing between two nerve cells that refuses to let itself be shut down—not until it's completed its task.

Just before his car crashes into the concrete barrier, the second before the vehicle goes from being an object with clearly defined parameters to a warped heap of scrap metal, the impulse finally reaches its target. In a single, crystal-clear moment he suddenly remembers everything.

Why he is in this car. What it's all about.

Faces, names, places, amounts.

The reason why all of them, every last one of them, must die.

All because of him. Because of the secret . . .

An immense feeling of relief courses through his body. Followed by regret.

His name is David Sarac. He is a police officer.

And he's done something unforgivable.

Friday, October 18

As a child, Jesper Stenberg sometimes got the feeling he could make time stop. It usually involved Christmas or birthdays. Special occasions he'd been particularly looking forward to. In the midst of everything, when things were at their height, it was as if time would slow down. Giving him the chance to suck every little nuance, every euphoric sensation out of the moment he had been looking forward to for so long, in peace and quiet.

He could still recall those occasions of being utterly in the moment, and could describe them in minute detail thirty years later: the color of his mom's dress, the smell of his dad's after-shave, the way the shiny wrapping paper felt beneath his little fingers. It was all fresh in his memory, without the sad patina of pictures in a photograph album.

But the ability suddenly vanished during his early teenage years. For a long time he believed it was because of his parents' divorce. Unless it was simply because he was growing up and losing his childish perception of time. Whatever the reason, special occasions were never the same after that. Graduation from high school, getting his law degree, his first criminal case, when he proposed to Karolina, even their extravagant wedding. It could all be summarized with just one word: disappointment.

He had worked so hard for those moments. Had longed for them, fantasized about how they would feel, taste, smell. Then, all too quickly, everything was over and all that was left were a few fuzzy memories and a nagging sense of dissatisfaction.

He would persuade himself that it would be different next time. If he could just aim a bit higher and pull the bow a bit tighter, he'd be able to feel more. When the children were born, his job in the Hague, membership in the Bar Association, the day when he was invited to become the youngest-ever partner in the prestigious law firm of Thorning & Partners.

But there was always the same feeling, the same inability to live in the moment. As if there were some sort of thin filter between him and reality.

He started to take photographs. Deluged his computer with scalpel-sharp digital images, devoting hours to putting together short films of holidays in the sun, gingham-cloth picnics and Astrid Lindgren moments with Karolina and the children. But no matter how good the resolution of the camera, or how many pixels on the screen, he still didn't feel satisfied. It was as if he had missed something essential in those moments, some tiny, invisible nuance that could make all the difference.

But today everything was different. This was Stenberg's greatest moment to date, the moment he had been waiting for for years, and he didn't need to look down at the Patek Philippe watch on his wrist. He knew that the second hand of the precision-made Swiss watch had just stopped, and that this moment would be just as stylized and perfect as he had always dreamed it would be. All his hard work, all his sacrifices were finally about to pay off. The years of drudgery in the public prosecutors' office: the fraudsters, wife beaters, petty criminals, thieves, and all the rest of the rabble. Then his time in the Hague, admittedly with bigger cases, but where a young prosecutor like him mostly got used as an errand boy. Then the move to Thorning & Partners. High-profile cases, excellent for a young, ambitious defense lawyer who wanted to make a name for himself.

But in spite of the money, the prestigious job, and the increasing media interest in him personally, in spite of the fact that John Thorning had chosen him as his protégé, he had hated being a lawyer. During his first six months there, the first thing he'd do when he got home from the office was have a shower. Changing out of the bespoke suits and expensive

Italian shoes that made such an impeccable impression on television. Scrubbing his skin until it was bright red.

After that he got used to it and adopted a mask, just as Karolina had suggested. A sort of alter ego he could slip into and out of in a fraction of a second. Someone who looked and sounded like Jesper Stenberg, but with whose words and deeds he would prefer not to be associated.

That way he could go on playing the game and keep up appearances. He patiently bided his time, waiting for his moment. *This moment.* And that was why he intended to squeeze every last millisecond out of it. Fix it to his cerebral cortex so he could remember every single detail, every nuance, even in forty or fifty years when the expanse of time that had seemed so infinite to him as a child was approaching its end.

His senses were wide open, feeding him with details. The grain of the wood on the heavy, dark furniture around the conference table. The thick, red carpet under his shoes. The light from the chandeliers reflecting off the silver coffeepots in the middle of the table. The wafer-thin porcelain of the cup in front of him. Everything was just as he had imagined it. But the most enduring impression was still the way the room smelled. A heavy, sweet smell that overwhelmed him. Almost making him feel slightly aroused.

The smell of power.

At the top of the table sat the boss, in toadlike majesty. His subordinates, including Stenberg's own father-in-law, crowded the long sides of the table. Suits, Botoxed foreheads, and double chins. Friendly expressions on most of the faces, but naturally not all. After all, he was an outsider, an upstart who hadn't followed the prescribed path. Someone who could disturb the balance of power.

The men and women around the table were all looking at Stenberg, awaiting his response. He checked his own expression. Humility, with a hint of surprise, he could manage that in his sleep. But an irritating little grin was lurking somewhere, he could feel it tugging at one corner of his mouth. Hardly surprising, really. He had just been asked the Question. His dreams—no, *their* dreams—were about to come true, and everything would be different from now on.

The moment he opened his mouth and transformed that little grin into his best television smile, he thought he could detect a tiny vibration from his watch. As if a new age had just begun.

. . .

Atif opened the cooler, dug about among the cans of soft drinks until he found one that was still more or less cold, and pressed it to the back of his neck. Sweat was running down his back; one of the many power cuts had brought the fan on his desk to a standstill more than an hour ago, and the air in the shabby little room was almost still.

He opened the can, drank greedily, and then went back to his lookout post at the dirty, half-covered window.

Outside, everything was going on pretty much as usual. A dozen parked trucks, all with their rear doors or covers open, between which various goods slowly circulated. Half of the vehicles were military green. Their uniformed drivers were standing by the little café, smoking while the workmen unloaded their trucks. A few scabby stray dogs were wandering about in the shadows between the vehicles. They kept their distance as they occasionally sniffed the air, as if to check whether any of the many crates being unloaded contained anything edible.

By now Atif was very familiar with everything that was going on in this dusty square. What brand of cigarettes the truck drivers preferred, the name of the café owner's sullen daughter, which of the drivers smuggled hash, which one of the mangy animals was top dog. The one the others feared.

The cell phone in his breast pocket began to vibrate. Atif inserted the hands-free earpiece, then raised the binoculars. He zoomed in on the sentry box beside the only real entrance to the square. The man was leaning against a wall, smoking, his Kalashnikov nonchalantly slung over his shoulder.

His cell phone vibrated again and Atif pressed the Answer button.

"Hello."

"It's me. How's it going?"

"Pretty much the same as usual."

"Still no sign?"

"This is where the trail brought me."

"And how long have you been sitting there now, Atif?"

"Almost three weeks."

"Right. You don't think it's time to give up yet?"

"He'll be here."

The line was silent for a few seconds. Atif scanned the rest of the square through the binoculars, then went back to the guard. The man was standing up straight now, stubbing his cigarette out on the red earth.

"A woman called," the voice in his ear said. "From Sweden. Said she was your sister-in-law, she wanted you to call back as soon as you could. Something to do with your brother . . ."

"Half brother," Atif muttered, without taking his eyes off the guard.

The man's body language had suddenly changed. He had taken his gun off and was now holding it in both hands, and all of a sudden he seemed to be taking his duties more seriously. The man let out a whistle and the sound brought all activity in the square to a halt.

A dark-colored car with military registration plates and tinted windows was slowly approaching. The guard raised a hand to his forehead, in a sort of hybrid between a salute and a wave. The atmosphere in the square was transformed in a matter of seconds. The drivers dropped their cigarettes and stubbed them out, and exchanged nervous glances. The workmen quickened their pace.

Even the dogs seemed to realize that something was going

on. They drew back further into the shadows as they warily followed the dark car with their eyes. It stopped and a man in uniform and dark glasses got out. Atif didn't need to look through the binoculars; the reaction of the other people in the square was enough to tell him who it was.

The man he had been looking for.

The top dog.

Atif reached out his hand and picked up the pistol from the wobbly little table and tucked it into the back of his trousers. He tugged his shirt looser to make sure the gun couldn't be seen.

"I've got to go," he muttered into his cell.

"Atif, wait," the voice said. "It sounded important. Properly important. You should probably call home."

Saturday, November 23

The inner city seems to be full of blue lights. They bounce between the facades of the buildings, only slightly muted by the falling snow before reflecting off the dark water under the bridges. Some of the emergency vehicles have their sirens on, but most of them race through the night in silence.

The six students walking north along Skeppsbron are already bored of the commotion. They had stood for a while at a good vantage point up at Slussen, watching the circus down on the long highway bridge. Loads of ambulances, fire engines, marked and unmarked police cars, so whatever it was that had happened inside the tunnel had to be something serious.

A couple of the students had held their cell phones over the ice-cold railing in the hope of capturing some of the action. But when several minutes passed without anything much happening, they quickly lost interest. The intense cold and falling snow persuaded the group to carry on toward the city center.

The snowball fight starts somewhere near halfway along Skeppsbron. One of the boys, it isn't clear which one, stops and picks up an armful of snow from the windshield of a parked car. He quickly forms an uneven snowball and throws it at the backs of his friends, and then everything kicks off. All six of them are running along the sidewalk, dodging one another's snowballs and stopping to make new ones.

The young woman in the red woolly hat is the one who makes the discovery.

"Look, there's someone sitting in here asleep," she cries, pointing at one of the parked cars, from whose windshield she's just swept an armful of snow.

"Hello, wake up! He looks like he's passed out." She laughs as her boyfriend catches up with her. Through the black hole in the snow he can make out a large, fair-haired man. The man is sitting in the front passenger seat, with his head resting on the dashboard. It looks as if he's asleep.

The young man on the sidewalk knocks on the windshield as well, and when there's no reaction he starts clearing the snow that's still obscuring the view. Slowly at first, then faster and faster, until at last almost the entire windshield is clear. He clears the side window as well. The man in the car still hasn't moved.

In the distance they can hear the sound of motors and the pulsing roar of a helicopter approaching. Something makes the others stop their snowball fight and approach the car. Cautiously, as if they're not really sure they want to see who or what is concealed inside. But the girl in the red woolly hat hasn't noticed the change in mood.

"Come on, leave it," she says, with laughter in her voice. "I'm freezing, let him sleep."

She tugs at her boyfriend's arm, trying to pull him with her. But the young man doesn't move. As soon as the snow on the side window is gone he presses his nose to the glass.

"Shit," he mutters.

"What is it . . . ?" Suddenly the girl's voice doesn't sound so amused. More like scared. The noise of the helicopter's rotor blades is getting louder.

"Shit," the young man repeats, mostly to himself.

Frost on the inside of the glass is obscuring the view, and the inside of the car is dark. But the sleeping man is no more than an arm's length away and the young man has no problem seeing enough details. The leather jacket, the embroidered logo on the back, the tribal tattoo curling up from the man's collar like a snake, across his thick neck.

But it's the dark patch at the back of the sleeping man's head that catches the young man's interest. A little hole, full of black ice crystals, each one just a fraction of an inch across, forming a thin pattern of pearls over the stubble at the back of his neck.

The sound of the rotors is deafening, echoing between the buildings and rising to a howl as the helicopter passes straight over them.

"Shit . . ." the young man says, for the third time, without anyone hearing him. Then he takes a long step backward and starts to fumble for his cell phone.

• • •

David Sarac isn't aware of any of the rescue effort going on around him. Not the agitated voices. Not the firemen drenching the car with foam and struggling intently with their hydraulic tools for almost a quarter of an hour before they manage to free him. Not the paramedics who use a curved piece of apparatus to force an oxygen tube into his throat and stop his lungs from collapsing at the last minute. Where Sarac is, there is no pain, no anxiety, no fear. Instead he feels an immense sense of peace.

His body is nothing more than a number of carefully bonded molecules, a temporary union that—like all other solid matter—is on its way toward its inevitable dissolution.

He can hear sounds around him, machines making warning signals, the focused discussions of the rescue team. An unpleasant gurgling sound that he gradually realizes is his own breathing.

But he isn't scared. Not the slightest bit. Because he understands this is the universe's plan. His time to be transformed. To reconnect with the universal stream.

Not until someone lifts one of his eyelids, calls his name, and shines a light directly into his brain does he get scared. Not because of the bright light or the voice calling out to him. What frightens him is the shadowy figure in the corner of his eye. A dark, threatening silhouette on the edge of his field of vision. Sarac tries to keep track of it, but the silhouette keeps evading him. He manages to see a leather jacket, a pulled-up hood whose shadow transforms the silhouette's face into a black hole.

". . . need to get out of here now. The helicopter's just arrived," someone says, presumably one of the paramedics.

But the silhouette doesn't move, it just hovers at the corner of Sarac's eye. Somewhere a cell phone rings. Once, then again.

The sound only exacerbates his fear. It grips Sarac's rib cage, making his heart race and setting off a painful fusillade of fireworks in his head. Then the paramedic lets his eyelid fall and he slips back into the merciful darkness.

Friday, October 18

Jesper Stenberg flushed the condom down the toilet, showered carefully, and then dried himself with one of the thick towels in the bathroom. He inspected his appearance briefly in the bathroom mirror, checking as he always did that there were no telltale signs on his body or face. Then he quickly put his clothes back on before returning to the main bedroom.

It was 9:32 p.m.; his parents-in-law were looking after the children and Karolina had gone out to dinner with her girlfriends. She had offered to postpone it, but he had persuaded her to go. They could celebrate properly tomorrow. His father-in-law had already arranged everything. Dinner at his favorite restaurant, champagne, cognac, expensive wine. And of course his father-in-law would foot the bill and would go on about the future, and the possibilities that lay ahead of them, as long as they played their cards right.

She wasn't lying in bed as he had been expecting. Instead she had poured herself a drink and was sitting on the sofa in the living room. She was still naked, and he couldn't help admiring her body. Small, firm breasts, long, lithe legs, porcelain-white skin, and a toned stomach that suggested diets and an exercise regime he could barely imagine. He was going to miss her body. And the things she let him do with it . . .

But times were changing. From now on everything was going to be different.

"So, Jesper, you've been asked the question," she said.

He went over to the drinks cabinet and poured himself a stiff whiskey in one of the heavy crystal glasses. He shouldn't really have any more to drink if he was going to drive. But he needed a drink; he realized that the moment she opened her mouth.

For a moment he got it into his head that she had already realized this wasn't going to be as hard as he imagined. But her tone of voice instantly dashed any hopes of that nature. Obviously he should have realized she wasn't going to make it easy for him. Sophie Thorning never made things easy for anyone. In that respect she was just like her father.

"Everyone's got what they wanted. You've got your big chance, John gets to pull the strings, and your ambitious little wife and her power-crazed family have finally got themselves a new launchpad." She laughed, a low, mocking laugh that he didn't like.

"And now you want to break up with me, don't you? Minimize the risks, reestablish control?" She made a slight gesture toward the bedroom with her glass.

He still didn't answer her, just turned away and looked out the window. Far below he could see the exit from the parking garage. In just a few minutes he would be down there. In the car, on his way home. Ready to put all this behind him.

"Everyone's got what they wanted. Everyone except me," Sophie went on. "I'm just expected to back down and act like the last few years never happened. Is that what you're thinking, Jeppe?"

He turned around slowly. She knew he hated that nickname.

"Jeppe on the mountain, like the old story." She leered. "An idiot who thinks he's something special. That he's suddenly someone to be reckoned with. But in actual fact he's just a marionette, a puppet who jumps whenever anyone pulls his strings. Does that sound familiar?"

He opened his mouth to tell her to shut up, but stopped himself at the last moment. Sophie knew precisely which buttons to press. He mustn't let himself be provoked.

"Ooh, did that make you cross?" She smiled. "You know what they say—the truth hurts. But you like pain, don't you,

Jeppe? Just like me. You get a real kick out of forbidden pleasures."

She twisted around and crossed her long legs, slowly enough for him to get a good view of her hairless genitals.

"I think we should go back to the bedroom to celebrate your success properly. I've got a few ideas that I'm sure you'd enjoy, things Karolina would never agree to."

Stenberg emptied his glass and put it down slowly on the island unit between the living room and kitchen.

"No, Sophie," he said. "This was the last time. I'm leaving now. From now on we'll only see each other in the office, and any interaction between us will be strictly professional."

He held up his hand before she had time to say anything.

"No, no, I know how the game works. This is when you pull out your trump card, and threaten to tell Karolina or your dad. Maybe even both of them?"

She turned her head slightly and her face cracked into a mocking grimace.

"But you don't seem to have realized that the game has changed," he went on. "You're quite right, other people have helped elevate me. I accepted that a long time ago, and realized it was the only way to get where I wanted to be. And now I'm there." He paused for a moment, collecting himself.

"Sophie," he began, adjusting his tone of voice to show a hint of regret. "A few months ago you really could have spoiled everything. You could have ruined my life. But your trump card lost all its value the moment I was asked the Question."

He gestured toward the telephone on the table.

"Call Karolina if you want. She'd never leave me now, just as my father-in-law would never advise her to."

Sophie's smile had stiffened somewhat, but she still didn't seem to have quite understood.

"John," she said, "Daddy would—"

"Come on, Sophie." His tone was perfect now, a cocktail made up of equal parts concern and condescension. "Do you seriously believe that John would sacrifice me for your sake? Now that his investment is finally about to pay off?"

He nodded toward the phone.

"Please, call Daddy and cry on the phone to him. Tell him everything, be my guest." He smiled, copying her mocking grimace.

Sophie glanced at the phone. She licked her lips once, then several more times. Then she looked down. Stenberg breathed out. The match was over, he had won. All of a sudden he felt almost sorry for her.

"Smart decision, Sophie," he said. "It would have been a shame if you'd had to spend Christmas in the clinic again."

He regretted saying it the moment he heard the words leave his mouth. Bloody hell! The glass missed his head by a whisker, hitting the wall behind him and sending a shower of crystal shards across the oak floor.

"You fucking bastard!" She took a couple of quick strides toward him, her fingernails reaching toward his face. Her knee missed his crotch by a matter of a fraction of an inch.

"For God's sake, Sophie." Stenberg twisted aside and grabbed hold of her wrists.

She went on trying to kick him, wriggling frantically in an effort to break free. He dumped her on the sofa, but Sophie bounced up instantly and attacked him again. She was growling like a dog, and her eyes were black. Her lips were pulled back, as if she were planning to bite him.

The blow was a purely instinctive reaction. Right-handed, with an open palm, but still hard enough to make her head snap back and her body crumple onto the sofa. Shit, he'd never hit a woman before. Not like that, anyway.

Sophie lay motionless on the sofa. Her arms and legs were hanging limp. Something wet was running down one of Stenberg's earlobes and he felt his ear without really thinking about it. Not blood, as he suspected, but a golden-brown drop of whiskey that must have flown out of the glass.

"Sophie," he said in a tremulous voice. She still wasn't moving.

In the oppressive silence he could hear his own pulse thundering on his eardrums. He glanced quickly toward the elevator, then at the inert body. Sophie's eyelids fluttered a couple of times and Stenberg breathed out.

He turned around and was about to go into the kitchen to get some water. But the floor was covered with broken glass. So he went to the bathroom instead and moistened a towel. On the way back he picked up her white terry-cloth robe from the floor.

She was sitting up when he got back, and he passed her both the towel and the dressing gown.

"Sophie, I'm—"

"Get out!" She snatched the towel and pressed it to her cheek. He stood motionless for a few seconds, unsure of what to do. "Didn't you hear me, get the fuck out of here!" Sophie hissed, covering herself with the dressing gown.

He backed away a couple of steps and tried to think of something to say.

"Sophie, I mean—"

Sudden pain interrupted him. A sliver of glass had cut into his left heel and he swore as he hopped on the other leg and tried to pull it out.

Her laughter was shrill and far too loud.

"God, you're so fucking pathetic, Jesper, can't you see it? Pathetic . . ."

He straightened up, tossing the sliver of glass toward the sink. He gave her one last glance before limping toward the elevator, without saying another word.

"I'll do it!" she screamed after him. "I'll kill myself!"

He pressed the elevator button, resisting the impulse to turn around.

"I'll go to the media, do you hear me, little Jeppe!" She carried on yelling as the elevator doors opened. "I'll tell them everything! Everything, yeah? You're finished, your whole fucking family's finished! I'm going to—"

Her voice rose to a falsetto as the doors cut her off midsentence. He heard running footsteps, then the sound of her fists on the elevator doors. He pressed the button for the garage several times, but it wouldn't light up. The hammering went on, growing louder and echoing off the metal walls of the elevator.

Boom, boom, boom, boom . . .

He kept jabbing at the button, until eventually the little light behind it came on. Then he covered his ears with his hands and the elevator slowly nudged its way down toward the basement.

· · ·

Atif took a deep breath and then looked up. The night sky was so different here compared to Sweden. Higher, clearer somehow. Yet at the same time it also felt strangely closer. But of course that wasn't true. Obviously the sky and the stars were exactly the same, it was just that he was looking at them from a different place. A distance of more than two thousand miles had simply given him a different perspective on things. And now he was going to have to switch perspective again.

"Something's happened, Mom," he said, without looking away.

She didn't answer; she hardly ever did. She just sat still in her wheelchair with a blanket over her thin legs as she looked at the stars. But Atif knew she was listening. She really ought to have gone to bed a long time ago. But on starry nights like this the nurses let her stay up. They knew it made her calmer.

He took a deep breath. Time to spit it out.

"I have to go back to Sweden. It's to do with Adnan," he went on. He tried to force his mouth to form the words. But to his surprise his mother spoke instead.

"A-Adnan . . ." Her voice was weak, thin, almost like a child's. "Adnan isn't home from school yet."

Atif opened his mouth again. *Say it, get it over and done with. Tell her what's happened.* But he hesitated a few seconds too long. One of the nurses was heading toward them across the cracked paving.

"Adnan's a good boy," his mother went on. "He's got a good head for learning, he could be anything he likes. An engineer, or a doctor. You must help him, make sure he doesn't end up like, like . . ." She fell silent and looked up at the night sky. Atif bit his lip.

"It's time for bed now, Mom." He leaned over and kissed her on the cheek. "I'll call you from Sweden. Khalti will come and see you the day after tomorrow. She says she'll bring some of those dates you like."

His mother nodded distantly. Her gaze was fixed on the stars again. Atif straightened up and began to walk away. He'd tell her when he got back. That would have to do.

"You've got a good son, to come and see you so often, Dalia," she heard the nurse say. "You must be very proud of him."

Atif quickened his pace. And tried to convince himself that it was the distance that meant he couldn't hear her reply.

• • •

Jesper Stenberg limped toward his car, got in, and then sat behind the wheel for a few moments. His hands were shaking, and his left shoe felt warm and wet.

Fucking psycho bitch. Why the hell hadn't he stuck to the plan, said what he had to say and then left? Fucking her and then dumping her wasn't a very smart thing to do. Not to mention that stupid remark about the private clinic in Switzerland, a subject he should have avoided at all costs. But, as usual, Sophie had managed to unsettle him. To get beneath the skin of his bespoke self-confident image.

Stenberg took a few deep breaths as he tried to pull himself together. It was only ten o'clock. Karolina wouldn't be home before two. Plenty of time to go home, patch himself up, then settle back on the sofa with a whiskey and do his best to forget this sordid little episode. He was pretty good at that. Forgetting, leaving things behind, and setting off toward new goals.

He started the engine and slid the car out of its parking space. The pain in his left foot had turned into a dull throb. At the exit he stopped at the barrier. His pass card was in one of the inside pockets of his wallet, an anonymous white plastic card, obviously not issued in his name. He put the gearshift in neutral and opened the window. The Eco-Drive function instantly shut off the big engine and everything went silent. In the distance he could hear the garage's ventilation system. A dull, ominous sound that made him feel badly ill at ease. The feeling came out of nowhere, and for a few seconds it took over his whole being and made his hands shake.

He had to get out of there, right away!

Stenberg touched his wallet to the card reader. The machine made a vague clicking sound. But the barrier didn't move.

Cannot read card.

He swore silently to himself and tried again. "Come on, come on . . ."

He thought he could hear a noise, something that sounded like a distant scream, and glanced quickly in the rearview mirror. Everything seemed okay behind him. The sound must have come from out in the street.

The barrier started to move, slowly and jerkily. Just an inch at a time, as if it didn't really want to let him go.

Stenberg turned the stereo on and tried to find something to lift his mood. The intro kicked in and the stereo began to count the seconds.

0.01.

0.02.

0.03.

As soon as the gap under the barrier was big enough he sent the car rolling. Relief radiated through his body. He slowed down just before the ramp reached street level. His hands were still shaking, making it hard for him to fasten his seat belt.

The music stopped abruptly, making Stenberg raise his head. The timer had stopped but the play symbol was still illuminated. Odd. Something white fluttered at the corner of his eye, hovering in the air just above the hood of the car.

A plastic bag, he found himself thinking. But the object was far too large. The stereo was still silent, the time on the display static. And all of a sudden Stenberg realized what was happening. He realized where the car was, and what the large, white, fluttering object in the air actually was.

He shut his eyes, clutched the steering wheel, and felt an icy chill spread from his stomach and up through his chest. The timer on the stereo suddenly came back to life and the music carried on. It was only drowned out by the sound of Sophie Thorning's body as it thudded into the hood of the car.

MemoRandom

ONE

Atif leaned back in the uncomfortable chair. In spite of the snow and cold outside, the air in the windowless little room felt stuffy. The smell of burned coffee, various bodily excretions, and general hopelessness was very familiar. You could probably find the same thing in police stations all over the world.

He was hungry, and his neck and shoulders were stiff after the long journey. He hated flying, hated putting his life in other people's hands.

"Name?" the policeman sitting opposite him asked.

"It says in there." Atif nodded toward the red passport on the table between them. The policeman, a fleshy little man in his sixties with thinning hair, who had introduced himself as Bengtsson, didn't reply. In fact he didn't even look up, just went on leafing through the folder he had in his lap.

Atif sighed.

"Atif Mohammed Kassab," he said.

"Age?"

"I'm forty-six, born June nineteenth. Midsummer's Eve . . ." He wasn't really sure why he added this last remark. But the policeman looked up at last.

"What?"

"June nineteenth," Atif said. It had been several years since he had last spoken Swedish. The words felt clumsy, his pronunciation seemed out of synch, like all the dubbed films on television back home. "Once every seven years it's Midsummer's Eve."

The policeman stared at him through his small reading

glasses. The smell of polyester, sweat, and coffee breath was slowly creeping across the table. Atif sighed again.

"Okay, Bengtsson, it's been over an hour since you stopped me at passport control. I flew in from Iraq so you suspect my passport is fake, or that it's genuine but not mine."

He paused, thinking how much he'd like a hamburger right now. The look on the policeman's face remained impassive.

"I'm tired and hungry, so maybe we could do the quick version?" Atif went on. His voice felt less out of synch already, the words coming more easily.

"My name is Atif Kassab, and I was born in Iraq. My dad died when I was little and my mom brought me to Sweden. She got married again, to a relative. When I was twelve he went off to the USA, leaving me, Mom, and my newborn younger brother. But by then at least we were Swedish citizens so we didn't get thrown out."

"So you say." The policeman was looking down at his file again. "According to the National ID database, Atif Mohammed Kassab has emigrated."

"That's right. About seven years ago," Atif said.

"And since then you've been living . . . ?" Bengtsson raised his eyebrows slightly.

"In Iraq."

"Where in Iraq?"

Atif frowned. "How do you mean?"

The policeman slowly raised one hand and took off his glasses.

"Because the Atif Mohammed Kassab who you claim to be has a pretty impressive criminal record." He gestured toward the file with his glasses.

"And?" Atif shrugged his shoulders.

"Well, if you really are Atif Mohammed Kassab, it's in the interests of the police to find out a bit more about you. Where you've been living, what you've been doing, whom you've spent time with."

"I've got a Swedish passport, I'm a Swedish citizen. I'm not obliged to say a fu—" Atif interrupted himself midsentence and pinched the top of his nose. It was almost eleven o'clock in the evening now. Almost ten hours since he last had any proper food.

"If we suspect that there's anything funny going on, we can put you on the next plane back to Iraq. There's a flight first thing tomorrow morning."

The fat little policeman clasped his hands together behind his neck and slowly stretched. The sweat stains under his arms were clearly visible on his shirt.

"Or we could lock you in a cell for a few days," he went on. "While we compare your fingerprints with the database. That sort of thing can take a while, obviously." The policeman grinned.

Atif was on the point of saying something but thought better of it. That last threat was probably a bluff. Even if the fat little cop still doubted that his passport was genuine, he must have realized by now that Atif wasn't trying to sneak into the country illegally. But, on the other hand, he had no wish to end up in a cell. Besides, he had an appointment to keep.

Atif took a deep breath. This whole contest in who could piss farthest was actually pretty pointless. He had nothing to lose by cooperating. Being awkward was mostly just a reflex. But things were different now. He was older, wiser. Besides, he really wanted that hamburger. A supersize meal with loads of fries and a large Coke with ice.

"Najaf," he said. "It's in western Iraq. That's where my family's from. Mom got sick and wanted to move back home. I went as well, to help her, and then I stayed on." He shrugged slightly and decided to stop at that. The policeman nodded almost imperceptibly and jotted something down in his file.

"And what has someone like you been doing with his time down there . . . ?"

Atif paused a couple of seconds, thought about lying but

changed his mind. *Someone like you* . . . He put his hand in the inside pocket of his jacket and waited until the policeman looked up.

"I'm a police officer," he said as he opened the leather wallet containing his ID card and little metal badge and put it on the table.

• • •

For once, Detective Inspector Kenneth Bengtsson wasn't sure what to think. His colleague at the passport desk had sounded one hundred percent certain when he handed the case over. A fake passport, well made, probably a real one with the photograph replaced. The fact that the passport's original owner turned out to be a real troublemaker seemed to support the theory. A genuine Swedish passport was worth several thousand kronor if you had the right contacts. And all the information they had indicated that Atif Kassab had plenty of the right contacts.

But the man claiming to be Kassab wasn't a typical illegal immigrant with the usual staccato sentences learned by rote. This man's Swedish was as good as his. A bit rusty, maybe, as if he hadn't used it for a while.

The only picture they had of Atif Kassab in their files was more than ten years old and hadn't been improved by being sent by fax. Kassab's DNA and fingerprints were obviously on file, but Bengtsson had no great desire to grapple with the ink roller to get prints for a comparison. He often couldn't help laughing when the cops in a television show did a bit of tapping at a computer and managed to bring up fingerprints, addresses, pictures of friends, shoe sizes, and anything else that might be remotely useful. In Bengtsson's world, ink, paper, and manual comparisons with a magnifying glass were still the order of the day. Unless you wanted to wait for forensics to get around to it.

So he preferred to rely on his own personal judgment when trying to identify people. The information in the database was seldom as exhaustive as it was in this case. He had the print-outs in the folder on his lap. He had already ticked off three things.

Age: 46.

Height: 6 feet 5 inches.

Eye color: brown.

But next to the information about build and hair color he had put little question marks. The man in the grainy photograph who was staring arrogantly into the camera had long, slicked-back hair and a little goatee beard that did nothing to hide a serious double chin. He looked just like the trouble-maker his police record suggested he was, even down to the thick gold chain around his neck.

But the man sitting opposite Bengtsson had military-style cropped hair, and the little that could be seen was going gray. But the stubble on his cheeks was still dark, so, after some hesitation, Bengtsson changed one of the question marks to another tick.

And this man wasn't fat, not remotely. He was big, certainly, probably weighed in at around two hundred and twenty pounds. But the word *stocky* didn't really fit. Bengtsson wrote *very fit* in the margin, then changed his mind. The words made him think of the gym-pumped look that bros who'd just finished their national service usually had. Bengtsson wrote *in very good shape* instead and found himself smiling at the description. The man's posture was good, the look in his eyes alert, and even if Bengtsson had eventually managed to wind him up, he had been smart enough to calm himself down.

Bengtsson had noticed that the man's left ear was slightly deformed. A bit of cartilage was missing from the back, and he had a scar stretching from his jaw down to his neck that was almost bare of stubble. The description he had in his lap said nothing about injuries or scars. But, on the other hand, it wasn't difficult to imagine how they might have come about.

Bengtsson inspected the wallet containing the metal badge

from all angles. Looked at the ID card with its picture of the man wearing a uniform.

Sgt. Atif M. Kassab.
6th Army div.
MP. Bat.

It was similar to Bengtsson's own official ID, but the shiny metal badge in the shape of a shield was clearly modeled on the American version. It seemed genuine, but obviously he couldn't be sure.

"Military police, you say . . ." Bengtsson said, putting the leather folder down. He couldn't help smiling to himself. Talk about setting the wolf to watch the sheep.

"And how did you end up in that job, if you don't mind my asking? I mean, with your background?"

"A relative recommended me. The army needed people," Atif said.

"No, no, I get that bit," Bengtsson said. "What I'm wondering is why you chose to take the job? Change sides?" The policeman put his file on the table and leaned forward.

Atif shrugged. He could say that it was his mom's fault. That she refused to let him pay for her little room in the nursing home unless the money had been earned honestly. And what could be more honorable than being a police officer? Besides, he liked his job, he was good at it. But Atif had already revealed more than he had expected to, so this fat little cop would have to go on wondering about his motives.

Silence fell in the room. Atif took a few sips of water from the little plastic cup on the table. Bengtsson went on staring at him for a good while.

"Okay, I believe you," the policeman said, throwing his hands out. "Let's go and get your bag, then I'll take you through to the arrivals hall. Welcome home to Sweden."

He made a short note in the file, closed it, and stood up. Atif got quickly to his feet. He was thinking of the hamburger joint between the terminals. He hoped it was open all night.

"Just one last thing," Bengtsson said.

"Sure."

"Why have you come back? To Sweden, I mean. Why now?"

Atif paused a few seconds before replying. It would be easiest to lie. His former self would have done just that without blinking. Maybe that was why he chose not to.

"I'm here to bury my younger brother," he said.

"Sorry to hear that," Bengtsson said.

Atif made a slight move toward the door, hoping the policeman would do the same. And that he would not ask the logical follow-up question. But he could see from the man's eyes that it was already on its way.

"How did he die?" Bengtsson said. "Your younger brother, I mean. You said you were twelve when he was born, and you're forty-six now, so your brother can't have even been thirty-five?"

Atif stopped. He wished he'd followed his instincts and kept his mouth shut. He bowed his head and looked up at the policeman.

"Adnan was murdered," he said.

TWO

David Sarac is still floating. Sometimes he thinks he's dead, at times he's actually completely convinced that he is. It doesn't bother him. *If this is death, then I daresay I can live with it,* he thinks. But before he has time to laugh at his little joke, the feeling is gone. Vanished into a part of his brain to which he no longer has access.

His body is lying in a bed; he gradually realizes this. But he doesn't manage to make sense of much more than that. Beyond the fact that his name is David Sarac, that he's a police officer, and that he's been in some sort of accident.

Various people come and go in the room, mostly white coats that poke and pull him about, which ought to mean he isn't dead. Not yet, anyway. But sometimes he notices the presence of other people, faceless figures that keep their distance. White shirts and blue uniforms with gold insignia, interspersed with a few dark suits. Most of them are somber and seem a bit lost. As if they're not quite sure what's expected of them.

But the others feel all the more troubling. Their vigor frightens him, but he still can't help looking at them more closely. It was from one of them that he heard the name.

"Do we know anything more about—Janus . . . ?"

Janus.

The name floats in his consciousness, making it impossible for him to rest properly. But no matter how hard he tries to remember, the answer is beyond reach.

"Need to get this fucking mess cleared up," a faceless figure whispered at one point, and, oddly enough, that particular memory hasn't faded. Maybe the remark was addressed directly at him? Is that why his body doesn't want to give up, because he hasn't finished his mission? Because there are still some loose ends?

Things that need to be . . . cleared up?

•   •   •

Atif woke up to find someone prodding him. It took him a few moments to realize where he was. On the sofa in Adnan's apartment. Or, to be more accurate, Cassandra and Tindra's apartment, seeing as Adnan was lying in cold storage at the undertaker's.

He had gone out like a light the moment his head hit the pillow, which was pretty unusual. Someone prodded Atif again and he rolled over.

"What's that?" Tindra asked, pointing at a large scar on Atif's right shoulder. A patch of scar tissue the size of a hand, wrinkled and slightly discolored.

"An old tattoo," Atif said.

"Like the one Daddy's got?" Tindra tilted her little blond head to one side and looked at him.

"Something like that," he replied. "Is your mom up yet?"

Tindra shook her head.

"Not yet."

"But you're already up, all on your own?"

She shook her head again and looked serious for a moment.

"We're both awake, *Amu*." She laughed. She used the Arabic word for uncle, and Atif realized he liked it. He pushed the covers back and sat up.

"So you know who I am?" he said.

This time she nodded.

"Of course I know. Daddy's got a picture of you in his phone. And me . . . but *lots* more of me," she added.

"Of course he has," Atif said. "A pretty girl like you."

Tindra looked different in real life, far more animated than in the digital prints with which he had lined his mother's little room at the nursing home. The girl was wearing a washed-out nightdress with a picture of some cartoon character he didn't recognize. It looked as if she'd tied her hair up in two untidy ponytails herself. *You've got your mom's skin,* Atif thought. *But your dad's eyes.*

"*Amu,* can you make pancakes? Daddy always makes pancakes when he's home. With jam *and* sugar."

Atif got up from the sofa and stroked her cheek. He liked the way she frowned slightly when she asked for something. Adnan had done the same thing when he was little.

"Of course I can, sweetheart. I taught your dad everything he knows." Atif regretted the words as soon as they were out of his mouth.

• • •

Tindra had already eaten three whole pancakes by the time Cassandra appeared at the door of the kitchen.

"Good morning," Atif said.

"Mmm . . ." She bent over and kissed Tindra on the head. Atif glanced at her. He had known Cassandra before she and Adnan started dating. Back then her name had been Malin, someone's plain little sister, slaving away in the city's bars to earn enough money for a pair of silicone breasts and a few other physical enhancements.

Then she had changed her name, appeared in a couple of episodes of some forgotten reality show, and picked up some work as a glamour model. Car shows, VIP events, nightclub appearances, and a bit of associated activity. In those days she had been very attractive, if you liked nightclub blondes. Adnan evidently did. He had been a bouncer at a few fashionable clubs, where he helped fend off drunk jerks who got too handsy. He was good-looking, and every so often had plenty of money. And he was funny. He could entertain a whole room when he was in the mood.

Having a girlfriend whom other men would drool over suited Adnan, and when Tindra was born his world must have looked pretty much perfect. But that was several years ago now, and Cassandra's glitzy glamour had started to fade. Wrinkles at the corners of her mouth from smoking, sallow skin, tired eyes. One of the rectangular false nails on her left hand was missing and the dark roots were clearly visible in her blond hair.

"Sorry we can't offer you anything better than the sofa."

Cassandra came and stood beside him at the stove as she fiddled with a pack of cigarettes.

"No problem. Like I said, I could always check into a hotel instead," Atif replied.

She shook her head, lit a Marlboro, and blew the smoke toward the stove hood.

"Tindra really wanted to meet her uncle."

"How's she taking it?" Atif said, nodding toward the table, where the little girl was setting about her fourth pancake.

"She's only six." Cassandra shrugged. "How much do you remember from when you were six?"

More than I'd like to, Atif thought to himself.

"By the way, I've got a job this evening. Don't suppose you'd be able to babysit for a few hours?"

"Of course," Atif replied. "No problem at all," he added. "Are you managing okay?"

"Money, you mean? Well, what do you think?" Cassandra shrugged again. "Did Adnan ever tell you about the gym he wanted to open up, over in Gläntan? Or the fact that he was plowing all our savings into it?"

Atif slowly shook his head.

"It's been a long time since I spoke to Adnan."

"Well, as usual, he managed to make a mess of it," Cassandra said. "He got impatient that the building work was going so slowly, and borrowed money to speed things up. The gym turned out brilliantly in the end, but by then Adnan had already been bought out. You know what he was like, charming as hell, sociable, but patience was never one of his strong points." She pulled a face that looked almost like a smile.

"Adnan was full of great ideas that never quite happened," she went on. "Always on his way toward something, without ever really getting anywhere, if you know what I mean?" Her voice was hard, or at least harder than it needed to be. "But I've got my own income, and we've got friends who can help us, so we're okay."

"I see. Are there many people coming tomorrow?"

"Of course, that's what I was going to tell you." Cassandra dropped her cigarette in a half-full cup of coffee on the draining board, in which other yellow butts were already floating. "We had to push the funeral back a couple of days. To begin with, the cops didn't want to release the body. Then the undertaker had other bookings and it clashed with my work. I did try calling you, I spoke to that guy Faisal again, your boss. But you'd already left.

"You're welcome to stay," she went on. "But it's okay if you need to get back. Like I said, we're managing." She pulled out another cigarette and offered him the pack. Atif shook his head.

"You've given up?" she said.

Atif didn't answer. He was thinking of his return ticket, the job he'd been forced to leave unfinished, his neat little house, and the starry sky above his small garden.

Tindra was humming a song as she struggled to finish the last of the pancake. Atif looked at Cassandra again, thinking that he didn't like her tone of voice when she talked about Adnan. The way she said *the body*. He wondered what sort of friends were helping her.

"It's okay," he said. "I can always change my ticket."

$\bullet\ \bullet\ \bullet$

Atif was on his way back to the building when he saw it. A big, dark-colored Audi, parked a bit farther up the street, but it set his alarm bells ringing straightaway. He hadn't been out long, ten minutes max. He'd locked the front door securely and hadn't even bothered to put his jacket on.

He had tucked Tindra up in bed about an hour ago, kissing her forehead gently before switching on the old CD player and pressing Play for all of her favorite story, just as he had been instructed to do. Then he had settled down in the living room and zapped through a number of television channels, full of commercials, before realizing that the bag of paperbacks was still in the rental car over in the parking lot. He didn't think it would take more than five minutes to fetch it. Tindra was fast asleep, and Cassandra wouldn't be home before midnight.

The cold was biting into him, making him hurry even more. But when he saw the dark Audi parked there he slowed down and almost stopped. The car hadn't been around when he came out, he was quite sure of that. There was no way he would have missed it.

It could be a surveillance car, but both the model and the shiny, outsized wheel trims made him doubt that. This car was too expensive and too ostentatious to be a cop car. But it was still parked in a perfect position for someone to keep watch over the entrance to their building. The engine was switched off but there was someone sitting inside, probably more than one person, judging by the steamed-up windows.

He really ought to ignore it. Jog back across the street, just as he had planned, lock the door behind him, and settle down with his books. There must be fifty apartments on the block, so it was hardly likely that whoever was in the car was interested in him. Even so, he still couldn't help going closer.

He stuck to the far edge of the sidewalk, setting one foot down in the snow on the grass to stay out of the cones of lights beneath the streetlamps as best he could.

When he was about thirty feet away he heard a noise. An electric whirring sound followed by a little click as one of the windows was opened slightly. He didn't stop, just looked down at the sidewalk and carried on. He could make out movement inside the car now. The outline of someone sitting in the driver's seat, then someone else who seemed to be moving between the front seats. Fifteen feet, ten, five . . .

He passed the car and glanced cautiously inside it. He heard someone groan through the gap in the window and realized all of a sudden that this was something quite different from what he had thought at first. He carried on toward the door, almost grinning to himself.

But then he realized that the woman in the car seemed familiar. The jacket, tight leather pants, the long, platinum-blond hair that could do with having its dark roots bleached.

Suddenly he wished he hadn't been so damn curious.

THREE

Sarac could see the white-coated woman's mouth moving. He could make out the occasional word and realized that he was nodding in agreement, as if they had been talking for a while. His head felt strange, as if it had been filled with sludge. Heavy heartbeats in his chest. Fear. Who was this woman? Where the hell was he? This last question was easily answered. Gray plastic floor, textured yellow wallpaper, speckled plaster tiles on the ceiling. The distinctive smell of hospital, impossible to disguise, no matter how hard anyone tried.

"We've met several times now, David. Do you remember?" the woman in the coat said.

Sarac's head went on moving up and down. He stared at the woman, trying to focus. High forehead, long, graying hair, dark-framed glasses, a tiny scar on her upper lip. Probably about fifty years old. Her appearance looked familiar, but he couldn't locate a memory to match it against. His thoughts were still sluggish, as if he had been fast asleep and had just opened his eyes.

"Do you remember my name, David?" the woman asked.

"N-no, sorry," he said.

The words sounded clumsy, as if he were sounding out each letter instead of joining them together.

"My name is Jill. Jill Vestman, and I'm a senior consultant in the neurology department here. Do you remember why you're here?"

"Er . . . no."

His body was still out of reach, but he managed to perform a brief check. His rib cage ached; his left arm was hanging limply in a sling. His chest and stomach felt tight, as if they had been strapped or sewn up. And then there was the headache. A rumbling, pulsing headache, the like of which he had never experienced before. It was making his thoughts fuzzy.

Dr. Vestman pulled a stool over and sat down beside the bed. She took a small notebook out of one of her top pockets.

"You suffered a minor stroke almost two weeks ago now, David. A hemorrhage in the left side of your brain. You were driving at the time and lost consciousness. You had a crash, in the Söderleden Tunnel."

Sarac tried to straighten up but his body refused to obey him. What the hell was she saying? A stroke? No, no. Strokes happened to old men. Christ, he was only . . . only? His headache got worse, muddying his already hazy thoughts. The doctor seemed to note his reaction.

"The impact was severe," she said. "You'd probably have been killed if you hadn't been wearing a bulletproof vest and weren't already unconscious."

"Drunk driving," Sarac said out of nowhere, without really knowing why.

"What do you mean, David?"

He had to stop for a few seconds to think. He tried to trace the train of thought back from his mouth and up into his foggy brain.

"Drunk drivers almost always survive," he said slowly, tasting each word. His voice still sounded odd. As if it weren't really his. Dr. Vestman nodded.

"That's right, relaxed muscles don't get damaged the same way tense ones do. It's interesting that you remember that." She made a note in her book.

"H-how?" Sarac muttered. "I mean, when . . . ?"

Things ought to be getting clearer now, but instead everything seemed to be going the wrong way. He was feeling sick, and his headache was getting worse too. And he was starting to feel frightened.

A stroke—a brain hemorrhage.

"Like I said, it was almost two weeks ago," Dr. Vestman said, but stopped when Sarac tried to say something. Then she went on when he didn't actually speak.

"When you came in you were in a very bad way, David. We kept you sedated for over a week to stabilize your condition. To start with we concentrated on the most acute problems, releasing the blood and easing the pressure inside your head. Then we dealt with your other injuries. You've broken your left collarbone and ruptured your spleen. Several of your ribs are cracked and you've got severe bruising. But, considering how bad the impact was, you've actually been extremely fortunate."

She paused and looked down at her notebook, as if to give Sarac a few seconds to digest the information.

"On Monday we performed another operation on your head," she went on. "We removed the remaining blood clots. You and I had our first conversation the day before yesterday." She smiled at him, a gentle, sympathetic smile that she probably learned when she was training and had been refining ever since.

What the hell was she talking about? Awake, for three fucking days! He shook his head, harder this time, as if to shake that irritating smile out of it. His anger came out of nowhere.

"No way," he snarled, and tried to sit up again. A fierce, burning pain made him put his hand to his head instinctively. His pulse was pounding in his temples. His right hand slid about, unwilling to do what he wanted it to. A double layer of gauze bandage, tightly wrapped around his skull. His hair! They'd shaved off all his hair. He must look terrible.

"The swelling in your brain is slowly subsiding, David," the doctor said. "But it's likely to affect your short-term memory for a while. That's why you don't remember the last few days. It's not unusual, and in all likelihood it will improve." Dr. Vestman fell silent and opened her notebook again, as if to let him take in what she'd just said.

He had questions, so many questions. An infinite number of

questions. Like, for instance . . . Fuck, fuck, fuck! He had to try to calm down and get a grip on his brain before his headache succeeded in crushing it against his skull.

"I was thinking of asking a few questions, mostly to see where we are in the healing process. Don't worry if you can't answer some of them at the moment," the doctor went on.

Sarac still couldn't manage to say anything. He nodded instead, as he tried to slow his pulse down. It seemed to be working, at least partially.

"Do you know what month it is, David?

"How about what time of year?" the doctor added when he didn't answer.

He was trying but couldn't find the words. Instead he tried to conjure up images in his head. A calendar, the date on a newspaper, the screen on his cell phone. Snow, he suddenly re-membered. Heavy, wet flakes covering the tarmac, settling like a blanket on the car windshield. Headlights reflecting off the snow. Blinding him, sticking into his head like knives.

"W-winter," he said.

"Well done, David, that's right."

Sarac leaned his head back on the pillow. He felt suddenly relieved. At least he wasn't completely gone. If he could just calm down a bit, if only this bastard headache could let up a bit, everything would become clear.

"Do you know what year it is, David?"

"Of course," he said. "Two thousand eleven."

Doctor Vestman said nothing, just made a small note. But something in her body language had changed.

"No, no, sorry! Two thousand twelve. Obviously, I meant 2012," he quickly corrected himself.

She looked up. Smiled again, the same irritating, sympa-thetic smile as before.

"It's December 2013, David."

"W-what?"

"It's Thursday, December twelfth, 2013."

"Impossible. I mean . . ." Sarac struggled once more to sit up, trying to push back against the mattress with his feeble right hand and almost losing his balance. He slumped back against the pillow instead. His headache shifted up a gear, then another. He screwed his eyes shut a few times. Then he slowly opened them. The fluorescent lights in the ceiling were flaring.

"Can you tell me about your last memory, from the time before the crash, David?"

"Of course," he muttered. "No problem," he added after thinking for a couple of seconds. But it wasn't true. It didn't even come close.

The time before the crash . . . His heart was suddenly galloping in his chest.

A stroke.

Car crash.

The time before . . .

December 2013.

The time before the crash . . .

December.

20 . . .13!!

Fucking hell!!!

"It doesn't matter, David," Dr. Vestman said, putting a hand on his shoulder. "Let's rewind a bit," she went on. "That often helps. Try telling me what your name is."

"David Georg Sarac," he said quickly. The words helped ease his panic slightly.

"And how old are you, David?"

"Thirty-five!" He breathed a short sigh of relief. It worked when he didn't try to think. If he just let the answers come out automatically.

"Where do you live?"

"Birkastan. Rörstrandsgatan, number 26. Third floor."

"Family?"

"Mom and Dad are dead. My twin sister, Elisabeth, lives in Canada." He paused.

"Ontario," he added, and suddenly felt much calmer. He wasn't some fucking vegetable, as he'd begun to suspect. His brain was sluggish, sure, but he wasn't completely gone. All this would soon be over, and everything would fall back into place.

"A number of your friends and colleagues have been to see you. A lot of people care about you, David. Could you tell me something about your work?"

"I'm a police officer," he said.

"What sort of police officer, David?"

"The Intelligence Unit. I handle confidential informants, CIs . . ." He suddenly broke off. New feelings were suddenly running through him. It took him a few seconds to identify them. Discomfort, shame. A growing sense of danger.

His headache instantly redoubled its efforts, forcing him to close his eyes. For a few seconds he thought he was going to be sick. The words broke free and bounced around inside his head.

What.

Sort.

Of.

Police.

Officer?

"And what does that involve?" the doctor asked. "Handling informants, I mean." Her voice sounded very distant all of a sudden. What was her name again? Dr. . . . ?

You've had a stroke, you crashed your car in the Söderleden Tunnel, and you're in the hospital. Today is Thursday, December 12, and the doctor's name is . . . something beginning with V. He suddenly felt incredibly tired, could hardly keep his eyes open.

"It's okay, David, there's no rush. You've already made very good progress. Get some rest and we'll carry on tomorrow."

He heard the stool scrape as the doctor stood up. He could feel himself slowly slipping into sleep.

"Secrets," he muttered when she was almost at the door. "I collect secrets."

FOUR

The young man groaned cautiously, but the sound from the cinema screen drowned him out. The scarf that the young blond woman had tied around his eyes a short while before meant he was missing the film, but to judge by the expression on his face, he didn't seem to mind.

Natalie Aden, who was sitting in the row in front, turned around and leaned over the back of the seat, zooming in on the man's face with the camera on her cell phone. She made sure the blindfold was clearly visible and waited until she could get a picture where he didn't look quite so happy before pressing the button. Satisfied with the result, she silently got up. The blonde looked up from the man's lap, not that that meant interrupting what she was doing, and Natalie gave her a curt nod. On her way out of the cinema she glanced at the time. Quarter past three in the afternoon, an hour and twenty minutes left of the film. Plenty of time. Hötorget was full of market traders and people aimlessly wandering about. It took her a while to reach the café, where she ordered a latte and settled down at one of the window tables. She got her laptop out of her rucksack, plugged in her cell phone, and transferred the picture she had taken in the cinema. She had written the message in advance, so attaching the image and sending the whole thing off took fewer than thirty seconds.

An hour and eight minutes left until the film was over, and around about . . . *now*, the message ought to have reached its recipient. Her chat status was green, so she was sitting in front of her computer at her pretend job. Her long lunch with her girlfriends would have ended an hour ago, the wine buzz would be fading, and it was still a bit too early to head home. Regardless of the money, Natalie couldn't understand how anyone could bear to live that sort of fake life.

She opened another tab on her browser and logged into a Western Union account. The balance was showing as zero, but that would soon change. She reached for her latte and leaned back in her chair, wondering about getting something to eat. She knew she shouldn't. She had already exceeded her ration of points for the week. Maybe time to try the 5:2 diet instead?

Her phone buzzed. A number she didn't recognize. She inserted her hands-free earpiece.

"Hello," she said in a clipped tone of voice.

"Hi, Natalie!"

The man on the other end of the line sounded amused, as if she had already said something funny. *Telesales manual, page one, heading "customer contact."* She was about to hang up.

"How did you catch him? Facebook? Instagram? Some other social network for the young and rich?" the man said.

"What?" Natalie was taken aback.

"Hans Wilhelm Sverre Wettergren-Dufwa, or Wippe to his family and friends."

Her brain locked for a couple of seconds, then her pulse started to race.

"Side parting, Canada Goose jacket, Burberry scarf, final year at Östra Real high school," the man on the phone went on. "Registered as living at the family's simple four-room pied-à-terre at Karlaplan. Daddy good for a few hundred million. And right now, little Wippe's got his cock in your friend Elita Brogren's mouth, over at Filmstaden."

Natalie leaped up from her chair and closed her laptop. She had to warn Elita, tell her to get out of there at once.

"How much were you hoping to take Wippe's mom for?" the man said in her ear. "Two hundred, two hundred and fifty thousand? Or have you raised the rate?"

Natalie grabbed her jacket and felt along the hands-free cord for the disconnect button.

"Sit down, Natalie!" The voice in her ear was suddenly very stern.

She stopped and looked around quickly. The man was watching her from somewhere nearby. Maybe he was even inside the café. A cop, a private detective, maybe even a victim out for revenge? Whoever the man was, he liked playing games. Her heart was pumping like mad in her chest. She glanced at the exit.

"Please, sit down, Natalie," the man said, somewhat more gently. "If I'd wanted to harm you, I'd hardly call to warn you in advance. All you have to do is listen."

Natalie hesitated. The most rational thing she could do was get out of there. But there was something in the man's voice that told her she wouldn't get very far. She pulled her chair out and sat down.

"Good," the man went on. "The fact is, we're impressed by you, Natalie. This whole idea is brilliant. You track down rich people's children through social media, and use a fake profile to insinuate yourself into their network. Then you can just take your pick. You google the parents and have a word with your little admirer in the Tax Office until you find a suitable victim."

The amused tone was back in the man's voice again. Natalie looked around cautiously, trying to figure out where he might be. And what the whole of this little game was about.

"Rich but absent father, overprotective mother with too much time on her hands. Ideally the victim should be an only child, or at least the youngest. Mommy's little darling, isn't that right?"

Natalie didn't answer, just pressed the hands-free earpiece tighter into her ear as she tried to focus on the other people in the café. A man at the far end seemed to be talking on his cell phone.

"You're very careful with your choices," the man went on. "No celebrities or politicians, no Wallenbergs, H&M heirs, or anyone else who might be *too* rich and powerful. No, you focus on the ones just beneath them. Once you've identified the right victim, you get sexy Elita to pick him up. Hormones raging, the young man skips school to go off to the cinema one afternoon. After a bit of preliminary petting, Elita says she wants to spice things up a bit. She blindfolds him, and by this point the poor guy is practically bursting out of his Calvin Kleins, so he's hardly going to protest. While he's moaning in the dark with the blindfold on, you take a few pictures of his face."

Natalie looked around, but the man she had seen seemed to have hung up.

"And while the lad's dreams are all coming true in the cinema, you e-mail his mother. You tell her that her darling has been kidnapped, attaching a grainy picture of the crown prince wearing a blindfold, and tell her she's got one hour. *Pay up, or he gets hurt. Don't call the police, we're watching your every move*, and all the other kidnap nonsense she's familiar with from cop shows on television."

The man sounded amused, but Natalie wasn't having any difficulty not laughing. Where was he, who was he, and how the hell could he know? She glanced toward the door again and wondered what would happen if she got up and left anyway. But the man seemed to know all about her. Trying to run might buy her a bit of time, but what could she do with it?

"Obviously Mommy calls her little darling," the man went on. "But of course he doesn't answer, because Elita's made sure he's switched his cell phone off. Then Mommy calls the school and finds out that Junior isn't there. She's starting to panic now, and she calls her husband, but he's away on business and probably isn't the sort who answers when his wife calls. Time is running out, the deadline is approaching, and panic has really set in now." The man paused for a moment and Natalie realized she was holding her breath.

"Then, all of a sudden, Mommy realizes that the amount you're asking for isn't actually that much. That she can buy her way out of this unpleasant situation in one go. The sort of people you pick on are, after all, used to solving all manner of problems with their wallets. And what's a few hundred thousand on the Amex card when the crown prince's life is at risk? So, within an hour, Mommy transfers the money to an anonymous Western Union account whose number you've given her. And after she's sat there biting her nails for a good long while, the film ends and finally her little darling replies to one of her many anxious messages. She's beside herself with relief. It takes her quite a time before her emotions settle down and she realizes that she's actually paid for her naughty little boy's very expensive afternoon blow job." The man chuckled again. "No one wants to make a fool of themselves in public, so after Daddy and the family lawyer have had a talk, everyone agrees to leave this unfortunate little incident behind them. No report to the police, no publicity, nothing." The line fell silent.

"What do you want?" Natalie's voice wasn't anywhere near as calm as she had been hoping it would be.

"Open your laptop," the man said.

"No way!"

"Just do as I say, Natalie."

She hesitated at first, then reluctantly did as he asked.

"What now?"

"Check your inbox!"

The icon for a new e-mail was lit up. No message, just a link to a web page.

"Click the link," the man said.

She did as she was asked. The page loaded. A dull gray background, covered by black text and a 1970s-style logo. It took her a few moments to realize what she was looking at.

GENERAL POLICE REGISTER
CRIMINAL RECORD

Name: *Natalie Aden*
Date of birth / ID number: *19850531-2335*
Eye color: *brown*

Hair color: *red*
Height: *5 feet 3.5 inches*
Build: *large*
Distinguishing features: *tattoo, left calf—butterfly*
09-19-2010—minor drugs offense (fined)
02-02-2011—theft, minor drugs offense (conditional sentence)
10-12-2012—fraud (dropped)
07-14-2013—fraud (dropped)

"Not very pleasant reading, is it, Natalie? You're on your way to becoming a doctor, then you get picked up in a car with the wrong crowd and a joint you'd forgotten about in your pocket. You might have got away with that, but then you were stupid enough to steal from the pharmacy at the hospital where you were doing your training, and that was that. Little Natalie with her lovely grades, who was going to be a doctor just like Daddy. And unlike him you'd have a Swedish degree so you wouldn't have to clean floors. But with two separate entries in your criminal record, that opportunity has gone. So instead you make a living from fraud, like this one. You put a bit of money into your Mom's account every now and then, in an attempt to ease your conscience. I'm guessing you and Daddy haven't spoken for a while. You must have been such a disappointment to him."

She opened her mouth and yelled at him to shut up and shove his criminal records up his ass. Then she hung up and stormed out of the café. Well, that was what she ought to have done. Instead, she sat there paralyzed, not saying a word as he went on.

"Your boyfriend admitted responsibility for everything. Very good of him, I must say. He did that so you'd get off with a conditional sentence." The man lowered his voice to a whisper. "But both you and I know that the pills weren't for him. It's tough having to carry the weight of everyone's expectations on your shoulders. Mommy and Daddy's, and your family's, and—

not least—your own. It's hard to unwind. Hard to get your head to relax, isn't it, Natalie?"

Natalie swallowed the lump in her throat.

"What do you actually want with me?" she muttered.

"I want to employ you. A task that would be a perfect match for your training, your intelligence, and your . . . special abilities."

"What do I get in return?" she said.

"What do you say about a fresh start? A chance to begin again?"

Natalie thought for a moment. A police officer, the man had to be a police officer. How else could he know so many details about her?

"And if I refuse? Will you arrest me?" she said.

The man laughed quietly. Outside the café a large black car with tinted windows pulled up. And stopped right outside her window. One of the rear doors opened but no one got out.

"Get in and we'll discuss it," the man said. "I'm confident we can find a solution that will satisfy both of us. By the way, you can call me Rickard."

FIVE

"We now commit Adnan Kassab's remains to eternal rest."

The funeral director knelt on the mat surrounding the little hole and carefully placed the urn inside it. Down there threads of roots stuck out here and there, like narrow hairy fingers groping out of the earth and reaching toward the weak winter light.

They must have used a digger to break through the frozen ground, Atif thought. One single scoop in the ground, that was all it would have taken. Adnan had hardly been of a religious persuasion, so using a priest or an imam would have felt strange. Better like this. Cremation, a short ceremony, and then down with the urn. He glanced toward Cassandra, who was standing next to him. She hadn't wanted Tindra to attend the funeral, said she was too young. A six-year-old shouldn't have to confront death, at least not yet. There hadn't been much he could say to that. But one thing he definitely didn't agree with was the large wreath on the other side of the grave. An overblown affair, presumably the largest you could order, and it made all the others look insignificant.

Never forgive, never forget was written in ornate golden letters on the silk ribbon. The men who had in all likelihood sent the wreath were all standing in the group just behind Atif. A couple of dozen people, almost all men. Most of them were wearing sunglasses even though the sun had barely risen above the pine trees. Several of the men had nodded to Atif as he and Cassandra hurried past in the chapel. There were a few familiar faces, but most of them were unknown. In Adnan's world, friendship was often a perishable commodity.

In a short while he would have no choice but to talk to them. Shake their hands, accept their condolences. He wondered whether any of them drove a large Audi with shiny wheel trim. But that was really none of his business. Cassandra wasn't the sort who liked living alone; she needed a benefactor. Someone to take care of her. Her and Tindra, he corrected himself. The thought of the little girl made him feel slightly brighter. But the feeling vanished when he looked down into the grave again.

He was hardly in any position to stand in judgment over Cassandra. If it hadn't been for him, Adnan might have stood a chance. Might not have ended up as a five or six pounds of ash in a cheap urn before he had even turned thirty-five.

Money, respect, recognition—that was what it was all about. Adnan had followed in Atif's footsteps, the way he used to in winter when he was little. Adnan had followed the path marked out for him, not reflecting on where it was going to take him. Or on the fact that he was actually walking around in a large circle and would end up back where he started sooner or later. Atif had tried to make his little brother understand—at least that was what he tried to tell himself afterward. Had tried to persuade him that the only way to get anywhere in life was to dare to take a step into unknown territory. But clearly he hadn't sounded convincing enough.

After the move to Iraq they only spoke a few times a year. Christmas and birthdays, little more than that. They had mostly talked about Tindra or their mother, never about work—his own or Adnan's. But Atif had still got the impression that Adnan knew he had changed sides. Maybe their mother had mentioned it, before she disappeared into her own memories. She and Adnan had always been close. He was the youngest, Mommy's little boy.

During the early years there had been vague talk of Adnan moving down to join them. They talked about setting up their own business, a security firm, something like that. When their mother got worse Atif even bought a plane ticket for his brother. But a week before he was due to leave, Adnan was arrested for taking part in the robbery of a security van and locked up for two months. The trip was never mentioned again after that. It had never been more than idle talk, Atif thought. Adnan would never have left Tindra. The same would have applied to him if it had been his daughter.

Atif looked around at the rows of snow-covered gravestones. He hated Swedish cemeteries. He hated the smell of box hedging, which even the snow was unable to hide. The day after tomorrow he would be leaving and going back to the heat, to his house and garden. Leaving all this behind him, for good.

A gust of wind caught the dark pines, making a dull, rumbling sound that drowned out the funeral director's concluding words. Beside Atif Cassandra shivered and pulled her coat tighter.

Sleep well, little brother, Atif thought.

· · ·

"So, how are you feeling, David?"

Sarac gave a little shrug. "Bruised, sore, a bit confused. Apart from that, not bad." He was clutching the piece of paper in one hand, keeping it under the covers, out of sight of the thin-haired man in the visitor's chair.

"The doctor said something about gaps in your memory?"

Sarac tried to force a smile, then glanced down at the note that the nurse had written for him.

You've had a mild stroke.

You were involved in a car accident in the Söderleden Tunnel on November 23, 2013.

Your doctor's name is Jill Vestman.

The gaps in your memory are . . .

"Temporary," he said quickly. "That'll improve as soon as the swelling goes down a bit."

At least Sarac had no trouble remembering Kjell Bergh. He

had recognized his balding, overweight boss the moment he walked through the door. Bergh was the sort of man who could never be taken for anything but a police officer, even though he didn't wear a uniform. There was something about the way he held himself and his weary but watchful eyes. Almost forty years in the force had left their mark.

"So how much do you remember?" Bergh adjusted the vase of flowers he had just put on the bedside table. There was a note of tension in his voice.

"The accident and the days leading up to it are a bit of a jumble," Sarac said. "The weeks before too. But all that's only—"

"Temporary." Bergh nodded. "Yes, you said."

"The car accident. Can you tell me what happened?" Sarac said.

Bergh shrugged his shoulders and pushed his thin glasses up onto his forehead.

"You drove straight into one of the concrete barriers in the Söderleden Tunnel. Next to the exit for Skanstull. Head-on, no rubber on the road to suggest that you braked, according to the traffic unit. Molnar's group got there just after the accident and managed to put the fire out. I heard that a couple of the guys were in tears, it looked so bad."

Sarac nodded and gulped.

Bergh leaned closer to the bed. Sarac suddenly noticed the dark patches under the man's eyes.

"We had to open the safe," Bergh said in a low voice. "It's standard procedure when a handler . . . I mean, we weren't sure if you were going to make it."

Sarac nodded, trying to work out why he didn't want to tell his boss the truth about the gaps in his memory. His sense of unease began to grow again. It made him clutch the piece of paper even tighter.

"Kollander was there, as head of Regional Crime. He and I used our codes, all according to protocol," Bergh went on, pulling a face. Sarac's heart immediately began to beat faster. "Your envelope was empty, David." Bergh's voice was so low now that it was almost a whisper. "No backup list, no names, nothing."

Sarac slowly shook his head. He could feel the headache gathering strength in his temples. Suddenly there was the sound of voices out in the corridor and Bergh glanced quickly over his shoulder. Then he leaned even closer to Sarac, so close that it was possible to smell the garlic on his breath.

"I managed to get the head of Regional Crime to hold back on filing an official complaint. Or at least wait a few days, until we'd had a chance to talk to you. None of us want Dreyer and the Internal Investigation team snooping about the department again." Bergh licked his lips. "Kollander's wetting himself. Says we might have a mole in the department. Someone selling information. It's only a matter of time before he goes running to the district commissioner, and you know what that would lead to."

Sarac gulped again and tried to moisten his lips. But his tongue felt as if it were glued to the roof of his mouth.

"Forty years in the force, only three left to retirement. None of that would count for anything when it comes to Operation Clean Threshold. Just look at what they did with the Duke. The district commissioner has set her sights on becoming the next national police chief, and nothing's allowed to spoil her pitch. Nothing!" Bergh's face was now bright red, and his tired eyes looked worried. Almost frightened.

"Well, I, er . . ." Sarac tried to say something but his voice cracked. He cleared his throat, once, then several more times. He suddenly noticed that his right hand was cramping. He slowly forced it open and glanced down at the crumpled piece of paper.

"I trusted you, David," Bergh said. "I didn't ask any questions, I let you run your own race." A little drop of saliva flew out of his mouth and landed in front of Sarac. "Up to now the results have been fantastic, but now you've got to explain what's going on. The missing list, and your crash. That can't be a coincidence. Someone's after you, David. And after your CI."

Sarac swallowed again, trying in vain to moisten his mouth and lips.

"Do you remember what job you were working on?" Bergh hissed. "Was it weapons, drugs? What instructions had you given your CI? Who was he targeting? For Christ sake, you must remember something?!"

More voices in the corridor, closer this time. Bergh spun around toward the door.

The scrap of paper in Sarac's hand gradually unfurled. He could see some of the writing. But it wasn't the nurse's even handwriting he could see. There was something written on the back of the paper. Jagged capitals that looked as if they had been written with a lot of effort.

EVERYONE IS LYING
DON'T TRUST ANYONE!

Bergh turned back to Sarac, who quickly slid his hand back under the covers. The voices in the corridor were clearly audible now. One of them belonged to Dr. Vestman.

"You have to hand him over, David," Bergh hissed in his ear. "I can protect him, you—the whole department. But you have to give me Janus!"

SIX

The smell of perfume lay heavy in the little entrance hall to the chapel. About fifty people in total, Atif estimated. Considerably more than he had thought at first. A seventy-thirty split between men and women. Almost all of them were younger than he was; a few of them didn't look like they were even twenty-five. More than half the men had gym-pumped bodies and a swaggering walk. They were also relatively smart and well turned out. There were a couple in tracksuits and a few more in jeans and hoodies, with T-shirts underneath with gang symbols on them. But most of them were, like him, dressed in cheap black suits from Dressman. Diamond earrings, gold necklaces and bracelets—all the predictable gangster accessories. Atif didn't recognize any of the men, but he still knew exactly who they were. Or rather, who they were trying to be.

Did I used to be like that? Did you, Adnan? Silly question . . .

They had all shaken his hand, fixing their eyes on him and giving it a good squeeze. To show that they didn't back down for anything, never showed any cowardice. But at least half of them had had sweaty palms and not even their overwhelming aftershave could hide the smell of fear. The first of them had made the mistake of attempting some sort of ghetto hug. But Atif had been prepared; he locked his lower arm, and stopped the man halfway. He had given him a quick look, which the man had been smart enough to pick up. The rest of them figured out the rules, even the women.

It was different with Cassandra; she hugged them all and took her time over it. She let them kiss her on both cheeks and seemed to enjoy being the center of attention in her role as the grieving widow.

He had exchanged a few words with Cassandra's parents and some of the older guests. Naturally they had all said nice things about Adnan. How pleasant and considerate he was, how much he loved his family. Atif had listened, knowing full well that they weren't just the usual funeral clichés. Adnan had been an easy person to like, he always had been. Open, cheerful, funny, loyal. He could think of a whole heap of adjectives.

Atif slid over to the coffee machine in one corner of the hall, put in a ten-kronor coin, and waited as the machine set to work. He tried to force his mind to change track. Soon he would be sitting on the plane.

A plastic mug slid out, then the machine squeezed out a thin brown trickle. The mug filled slowly, as if the huge machine were really doing its best to produce some liquid.

"Atif, my friend."

With the plastic mug in his hand he turned around. He had identified the hoarse, rasping voice before he saw the familiar face. He couldn't help smiling.

"Abu Hamsa!"

He leaned forward and let the fat little man kiss him on both cheeks. Abu Hamsa was an old friend. Atif's mother had worked in one of his bars a long time ago. Atif, and later Adnan, used to hang out there after school. Running small errands in exchange for the occasional bar of chocolate or can of cola. Hamsa was one of the old guard. He owned a couple of neighborhood bars, a few exchange bureaus, and loaned out money—no champagne orgies or luxury villas, no overblown signs of success. Nothing to attract the attention of the police, or anyone else, for that matter.

"Envy, boys . . ." he used to say in his hoarse but simultaneously slightly shrill voice. "Envy is fatal. If you make too much of a show of success, people will want to take it from you!"

Hamsa was content with what he had, the status quo suited

him, with its calmness and balance. For that reason he was also a popular mediator, someone everyone trusted. He must be close to seventy now, yet there wasn't a single gray hair on his head. He probably dyed both his hair and his little mustache. The rug on his head also looked suspiciously thick: Abu Hamsa had always been rather vain.

"I'm truly sorry for your loss, my friend," he hissed in Arabic. "Your brother was a fine young man. He deserved a far better fate than this."

"Thank you, Abu Hamsa," Atif said as he blew on the scalding-hot coffee.

"How long are you staying, my friend?"

"I'm going back the day after tomorrow."

"Ah, so you're not looking for work?" Abu Hamsa smiled.

Atif shook his head, which seemed to make the little man's smile even wider.

"Wise decision. Things aren't what they used to be. The consultants are taking over, even in our business. Everything is being opened up to competition, there's no honor anymore, no loyalty. High time for people like me to get out. Let younger talents take over, inshallah."

Abu Hamsa made a small gesture toward the ceiling. Atif couldn't help looking over at the young men who were still flocking around Cassandra. A couple of them were glaring in his direction. He drank some coffee without looking away.

"You can hardly blame them." Abu Hamsa seemed to have read his mind.

"How so?"

"You still have a certain . . . reputation, my friend. There was a lot of talk when you left. Some people really weren't happy, and even suggested that you were letting everyone down."

"Like I said, I'm going back first thing next week," Atif said, still without looking away from the young men. "And whatever a load of snotty kids think about that, well—" He broke off, realizing that his tone of voice was getting harder. "You must forgive me, I didn't mean to sound unpleasant," he said, and looked back at the little man.

"No problem, my friend. I understand. Not an easy situation, this. Your brother, his little girl. What's her name again? I'm starting to get old, I was at her naming ceremony and everything . . ."

"Tindra," Atif said, noting how his voice softened as he said it.

"Little Tindra, yes, that was it. Losing your father so young, in that way . . ." Something in Abu Hamsa's voice made Atif frown, and the little man noticed. "I . . . I assume you know what happened?"

Atif nodded. "Cassandra told me."

"And you know the details?"

"The boys were unlucky," Atif said. "An unmarked cop car saw them driving away from the security van. Evidently one of them hadn't taken his balaclava off in time, so the cops followed them and called in backup. The rapid response unit went in just as they were changing cars, and shots were fired. Adnan and Juha were killed, and Tommy was left a vegetable."

"Sadly that's all true." Abu Hamsa nodded. "I just wanted to be sure that you knew all the details. Sometimes stories take on a life of their own, people talk so much. You know how it is." The little man held out his hands. "By the way, you don't have to worry about Adnan's family." Hamsa tilted his head toward Cassandra. "There are a lot of people supporting them, people who are angry with the police. Perhaps you heard that the rapid response unit was cleared of any suspicion of using excessive force, and that the whole thing was regarded as self-defense seeing as Adnan fired first? Things looked very unsettled for a while afterward. Cars set on fire, stone throwing, all the usual."

Atif nodded slowly and drank his cooling coffee.

"And I myself will keep an eye on Tindra and her mother. For the sake of old friendship," Abu Hamsa added. The little man glanced at Atif, evidently expecting some sort of reaction.

"Thank you, Abu Hamsa. I know Adnan would have appreciated that," Atif said.

Abu Hamsa went on looking at him, then broke into a smile.

"You seem different, my friend. Calmer, nowhere near as angry as you were before. You look much healthier, and your Arabic is much improved. You did the right thing in leaving. If your brother had done the same, or me too, for that matter, who knows how things might have turned out? But it takes great courage to do what you did, leaving everything behind. Starting again from scratch. Courage that most of us don't have." Abu Hamsa gestured toward the ceiling again.

"Well, my friend, I shall let you finish your coffee," he said. "It was lovely to see you again, even if the circumstances could obviously have been better. Please, convey my condolences to your mother. How is Dalia, by the way?"

"Alzheimer's," Atif said quietly. "She's living in a nursing home. But I promise I'll tell her. She remembers things from the past fairly well. The present is more of a problem."

"I understand." Abu Hamsa nodded. "I myself have come to the painful conclusion that I have forgotten considerably more things than I remember. My doctor says that it's all there in my head, and that I've just forgotten how to find it. Like a path in the forest getting overgrown. Maybe she's right, unless she's just saying that to cheer me up." The little man patted Atif on the shoulder. Tenderly, almost cautiously, in a way that made Atif smile slightly without knowing he was doing it.

"Farewell, dear friend. Now I must convey my condolences to the beautiful young widow," Abu Hamsa said. "But if there's anything you need, I hope you'll be in touch. Cassandra has my number, you only have to call. No matter what." Abu Hamsa gave him an emphatic wink.

"Really, I thought you were going to retire?" Atif said.

"Inshallah!" the little man said, bursting into a hoarse laugh. "If it is God's will. Have a safe journey home, my friend!"

SEVEN

He had to make sense of things. Get his weak, pathetic body out of this damn hospital bed and force his head to make the right connections. Try to work out what was going on. Why he had lied to his boss about the gaps in his memory, why he was scribbling cryptic warnings to himself, and why that name made his pulse race out of control.

Janus. Clearly a code name for a CI, and a very important one, to judge by Bergh's questions and paranoid behavior. The problem was that he couldn't remember any code names, he couldn't actually remember a bloody thing. Well, that wasn't quite true, he wasn't Jason Bourne. He could remember loads of things, just nothing that could help him make sense of what had happened. It was as if the stroke had sliced through his brain, cutting off all connections to the part where events of the past few years were kept. The only thing that seemed to bridge the gap was an indefinable, creeping sense of unease. Something was wrong, considerably more wrong than just a weak body trying to recover from an accident, or even a gash in his brain and migraines from hell. What was it Bergh had said about his crash? The words hadn't wanted to fall into place properly.

Sarac snorted and tried to hold his breath for a moment to stifle a sob. The mood swings were hard to get used to. He was being tossed between anger, grief, and fear, and occasionally a euphoric sensation that felt almost like happiness. The whole process made it much harder to make sense of everything.

Damn it! He grabbed a couple of tissues from the bedside table and blew his nose. It would get better, it had to get better.

One of the nurses put her head around the door.

"Can you handle another visitor, David? It's the man with the beard," she whispered with a smile.

"Hmm." Sarac tried to sound as if he knew who she was talking about, but didn't succeed.

"About forty, six three, suntanned, very fit. He's been to see you most days."

"Sure." Sarac nodded, feeling relieved. He recognized the description and his mood improved at once.

The nurse walked into his room, followed by the man with the neatly trimmed beard.

"Hi, David!" The man smiled broadly as he pressed Sarac's hand between both of his. He went on holding it in a way that made a lump start to grow in Sarac's chest. "Good to see you looking brighter today."

Sarac nodded, then held his breath for a few seconds to get this new surge of emotion under control. Peter Molnar was one of his best friends, and also something of a mentor to him, but bursting into tears the moment he saw him was definitely not Sarac's usual reaction. What the hell was happening to him? He swallowed a couple of times and managed to force a smile.

"Fucking good to see you, Peter," he muttered. Then suddenly wondered when he had started to swear so damn much.

The nurse's description of Molnar was pretty accurate. The only thing she had left out was his short, blond hair, with a slightly raised side part, and the chewing gum that was constantly on the go between his square, white teeth, spreading a smell of mint around the room.

"I brought some roasted nuts from that place you like on Södermalm." Molnar tossed a ziplock bag, filled to bursting, onto the bedside table.

"I mean, he is allowed nuts, isn't he, nurse? There aren't any rules about that, are there?" He winked at the nurse, who was adjusting Sarac's drip, and rounded it off with a dazzling smile.

"You don't seem the type to be too bothered about rules."

She smiled back. "Ten minutes, maximum, or you'll have me to deal with."

The nurse left the room, slowly pulling the door shut behind her as she gave Molnar one last look. The man pulled up a chair, sat on it the wrong way around, and rested his arms on the back.

"Nice!" He grinned, nodding toward the door. "I can see why you'd want to lie here and get looked after while the rest of us work our backsides off. We did a raid on that heroin case last night—more than two pounds. Your information was correct, as usual." Molnar was still smiling, and Sarac realized that he was doing the same, almost without noticing.

"Like I said, good to see you, Peter," he said, trying to match his relaxed tone, but mainly just sounding a bit maudlin. The happiness he had felt just now was gone. He couldn't remember the case Molnar was talking about, couldn't actually remember a single case they had worked on. And this strong, suntanned man in front of him only emphasized his own wretched condition. His collarbone and the bandages around his head and stomach. The mood swings, not to mention the lack of energy. He must have lost at least fifteen pounds of muscle while he'd been lying there, if not more. Molnar seemed to notice the change in his mood, because he hurried to break the silence.

"The boys say hello. They wanted to come as well, but I told them to wait a bit. Thought you probably needed a chance to recover first. After everything you've been through." He pulled a face.

Sarac nodded and unconsciously put a hand to his head.

"I bumped into Bergh. He said you had a few gaps in your memory," Molnar said.

Sarac took a deep breath, trying to muster his thoughts, but the headache kept getting in the way.

"Well . . ." he said. He cleared his throat to make his voice sound more steady. "It's not like it is in films. I know who I am, where I live, what my parents' names were, where I went to school, how to tie my shoelaces, all that sort of thing." He waved one hand, trying to find the right words. "But everything feels so distant, it's like I'm not really . . . present. Like I'm looking on from the sidelines, if you see what I mean?"

Molnar nodded slowly. His clear blue eyes were looking straight at Sarac, as if he were saying something incredibly interesting. Peter was good at making people feel that they were being noticed, appreciated.

"What about the crash, do you remember anything about that?" Molnar said in a low voice.

Sarac shook his head and decided to tell the truth. "To be honest, I can hardly remember anything about the past couple of years. After 2011, all I've got are random fragments floating about in my head.

"But that'll pass," he added quickly. "The doctor's sure that things will become clearer as soon as the swelling has gone down. It's just a matter of time."

This last bit wasn't entirely true. Dr. Vestman was far too cautious to promise anything like that. But no matter. Sarac had made up his mind. He was going to get better, completely better, in both mind and body, and in record time.

His headache was on the move, gradually unfurling its spidery legs.

"So when precisely do your memories stop? You started in the Intelligence Unit early in 2011. I was the one who recruited you," Molnar said.

Sarac nodded. "Yes, I remember that, no problem."

"Do you remember any specifics about what you were working on?" Molnar leaned forward slightly.

"Of course. I recruit and handle CIs. Tip-offs, secret sources, people who might be useful to us."

Sarac put his hand to his forehead. The spider's legs were all around his head, laying siege to his brain. A faint buzzing sound that he thought at first came from the fluorescent lights in the ceiling started to fill his head, making Molnar's words indistinct.

"And you're very good at it, David. In fact you're the best handler I've ever come across. Myself included. Professional, ambitious, loyal, always reliable. And you know exactly how to read people. It's actually a bit uncanny. You seem to have a sixth sense for how to find a way in, how to get people to trust you with their deepest—"

Secrets.

Something suddenly flashed into Sarac's head. A brief glimpse of a parked car. A dark color, a BMW, or possibly a Mercedes?

"I left the Intelligence Unit in early 2012 when I was offered the job of being in charge of Special Operations. But you and I carried on working together closely. You did my old job better than I ever did. Your CIs were the best, and there's no question that they gave us the best information."

Molnar's words were blurring together. The image in Sarac's head suddenly got clearer. He's sitting inside the car, at the wheel, or possibly in the backseat? His perspective keeps switching, seems to change the whole time. A thickset man with a shaved head gets into the front passenger seat. He brings a smell of cigarette smoke with him into the car, and something else as well. The smell of fear.

"It was after that operation that Bergh and, indirectly, Kollander, basically gave you carte blanche to do as you liked. You really don't remember any of this? It was all over the papers, Kollander and the district commissioner even appeared on television to bask in the glory."

Sarac didn't answer. All he could manage was a little shake of the head.

"Then you started work on a top-secret project. With one particular contact."

"Janus . . ." Sarac mumbled.

Molnar didn't respond, unless Sarac's headache had affected his hearing. Suddenly everything was completely quiet, a perfect, dry absence of sound, with the exception of his own heartbeat. He tried to conjure up the image of the man in the car. Tried to see his face. But the only thing that appeared was a pattern, a snake in black ink, curling up from beneath a collar. A faint sound, growing louder. The car's chassis buckling, protesting in torment. Then a sudden collision.

Sarac jerked and woke up. "Th-the accident," he muttered. "Tell me . . ."

Molnar was silent for a few moments. Ran his tongue over his even front teeth.

"Please, Peter. I need to know." Sarac put his hand on Molnar's arm. Molnar bit his bottom lip and seemed to be thinking.

"You called me from your cell," he began. "Your speech was slurred and you weren't making much sense. You wouldn't tell me what was going on, just that something bad had happened and that you were in trouble. We dropped everything and set out to meet you. But when we got to the meeting place, all we could see were the taillights of your car."

Molnar's voice drifted off again.

". . . impossible to catch up. You were driving like you had the devil himself in the back of the car."

Sarac was back in the parked car. The ink snake on the man's neck suddenly came to life, moving in time with the man's voice. "I was thinking of suggesting a deal." His hands are rough but his voice surprisingly high. Almost like a child's.

"Your secrets in exchange for mine." The man grins, trying to sound tough even though he reeks of fear. His leather jacket creaks as he turns his body. "Well, what do you say? Have you got a deal?"

Outside it's started to snow. Heavy snowflakes, falling thickly. Settling on the windows like a dense white blanket until the buildings of Gamla stan are hidden from view. Suddenly Sarac gets the impression that there's another person in the car. Someone hiding in the darkness of the backseat. He catches a glimpse of a familiar pair of eyes in the rearview mirror, stubble, and a raised hood that shades the face. The devil himself.

A sweet, chemical smell fills the car. The smell is very familiar; it's easily recognizable. Gun grease.

He catches sight of the pistol, sees it raised to the back of the man's head, where the snake is still slithering. He holds his breath as . . .

•   •   •

The bang made Sarac open his eyes. Molnar was leaning over him, his hands about an inch in front of Sarac's face.

"David, can you hear me?!" He clapped his hands in front of Sarac's nose, forcing him to blink. Sarac opened his mouth and swallowed a mixture of saliva and air. He coughed and gasped for air as his heart raced in panic. A machine was bleeping close by, and there was the sound of running in the corridor.

"You blacked out." Molnar's voice sounded shaky. "Your face went all blue, you scared the shit out of me, David." He put his hand on Sarac's shoulder and gave it a gentle squeeze.

"You're not thinking of dying on me, are you? Not after all the work we did cutting you out of the wreckage." Molnar's tone was joking, but there was a hint of anxiety there too.

Sarac grabbed hold of his hand. "J-Janus," he stammered. "Everything's fucked." The lights in the ceiling flickered. He gasped for air again. Terror was clutching at his chest, and the spider's legs had hold of his head. "We've got to find him, Peter," he panted. "It's all my fault . . ."

The hospital staff came storming in, three or four white coats. Maybe more. Sarac felt Molnar being pushed aside, then an oxygen mask was placed over his nose and mouth. Everything started to blur and the room became a mass of pain and colors.

". . . a severe migraine attack, but we can't rule out a further hemorrhage," Dr. Vestman's voice said. "We need to get him back to Intensive Care."

The bed started to roll, a peculiar feeling. Various figures hovered above him, slipping in and out of his clouded field of vision. White coats, green ones. Faces covered by masks. He thought he could hear a voice. A whisper, close to his right ear, so faint he could hardly hear it.

Protect the secret, David. You promised!

The voice blurred into the background. And fell silent.

After that . . .

Nothing.

EIGHT

It's all about attitude, Jesper Stenberg thinks. If you just have the right attitude and focus on the right things, you can get through pretty much any challenge.

He had a framed quotation by Robert Kennedy on the wall. A moving-in gift that Karolina had persuaded the caretakers to put up immediately above the huge desk, just in time for his first day at the department.

No society can function without a democratically controlled, fair, measured, and powerful justice system. Bobby Kennedy hadn't hesitated to do what was required of him. He didn't let himself get distracted by political intrigues. Instead he focused on doing as much good as he could for society. He had aimed at a higher goal.

Stenberg thought he had made a similar choice. Either he was someone who had driven his fragile lover to suicide, or he was someone who was no longer subjected to the warped whims of a demonstrably sick person. Someone who just happened to be in the wrong place at the wrong time.

Sophie's suicide had been unavoidable. If it hadn't been for the happy pills, it would probably have happened a long time ago, without affecting him. But instead she had chosen to kill herself in a fiendishly calculated way, literally trying to take him down with her. A frontal attack on him, his family, and their shared future. The measures he had taken were therefore no more than a form of self-defense. Sophie had tried to destroy him, but he had withstood the attack, even if it had taken almost all of his strength of will.

He had reversed back down into the garage with Sophie's body on the hood of his car. He had done his utmost not to meet her gaze on the other side of the shattered windshield. He parked in the darkest corner of the garage and covered the hood with a tarpaulin he took off a sports car that had been covered up for the winter. Then he had forced himself to leave the scene calmly, resisting the temptation to run for his life.

He had made the call half an hour later. It took him three attempts before his fingers managed to find the right number in the phone book. Then he had followed instructions, getting a taxi home and disposing of all his clothes, before downing half a bottle of whiskey and falling asleep on the sofa.

During the days that followed he had felt okay, but the nights were worse. As soon as he shut his eyes Sophie's shattered face appeared in his head. Staring at him with an accusing look in her eyes, making him wake up with a scream. He had blamed everything on his new job, and the tension of recent weeks. As usual, Karolina was a rock. She listened and comforted him, made him chamomile tea and left her self-help magazines on the kitchen table. It was in one of them he had read that the more the brain got stuck in a particular track, the harder it was to break out of. In other words, you had to make a conscious choice about how you wanted to think about things, and what thoughts you no longer wanted to entertain. And, just a couple of days later, once the shock had subsided, he had decided what thoughts he wanted to have. After that, the nightmares had almost disappeared altogether.

The police investigation had actually made him stronger. He had read every last line but skipped the photographs of the scene of the accident and the autopsy. Everything was basically true, none of the essential facts were missing. At least nothing that had any effect on the end result.

In the end she had been found by someone delivering papers. Her body had gone through the windshield of a Volvo that had been parked illegally below the window of her study.

Her iPad was on her desk, containing her suicide note. Just a couple of lines about how she couldn't bear it anymore, that she didn't want to go back to the clinic. The note had been sent to her father's work e-mail that same night, just minutes before she was found. Her penthouse apartment also contained plenty of pharmaceuticals, prescribed by doctors both in Sweden and abroad. A chair was found next to the open window, and the front door was locked. The autopsy more or less confirmed what was already clear: death caused by massive trauma, her stomach full of a mixture of pills and alcohol.

Naturally, Stenberg had called John Thorning to convey his condolences. He had practiced for hours so that the words came out right, in a calm tone of voice, before he dialed the number with trembling hands. But the whole thing had been a huge anticlimax. The call was forwarded to John's secretary, who told him that Sophie's father wasn't taking any calls, even from him. He felt extremely relieved, and almost burst out laughing. After that, his letter of condolence practically wrote itself.

Our deepest sympathies for your tragic loss . . .

The funeral had been a quiet affair, with only the closest family present. Suicide wasn't something that the Thorning family wanted to make a public show of.

Karolina had naturally organized a tasteful wreath. Lilies to symbolize innocence, white narcissi for friendship and closure. An almost perfect choice.

And, as always after something ended, new opportunities presented themselves. His plan was already in motion. The need for it was obvious, and discussions were already under way. All they were waiting for was for someone to take the initiative. Someone who had the courage, will, and energy to dare to lead the way.

The judicial system was hopelessly old-fashioned, a product of the 1950s that had been patched up as time went on, and which stood no chance of meeting the challenges and threats posed by the twenty-first century. You had to look at the situation as a whole and deploy your resources where they could give the greatest reward, instead of spreading them thinly. It was a matter of getting in synch with reality and delivering concrete results that the general public could understand and accept.

The first move was already made. He had brought in his old colleague Oscar Wallin. He had recruited him and a few hand-picked officers from National Crime to conduct a "special investigation for the Ministry of Justice." Wallin and Stenberg had worked together in the Hague and were comfortable with each other. They shared the same goals.

In actual fact, Wallin's task was simple: Identify the best working practices in the country and bring in the most competent officers. Find out what works in a new, modernized organization, and which people are happy to go along with it. And which ones aren't.

He would make enemies, he was perfectly aware of that. The judicial system was full of desk jockeys and filing clerks. Police officers, prosecutors, and judges with smart titles, expense accounts, and large mortgages, but whose contribution to the system was questionable, to say the least. Plenty of them would see an abrupt end to their career paths and would find themselves out in the cold.

Attitude, he thought once more. It was all about attitude. Seeing the whole picture beyond the details, and not hesitating to make unpleasant decisions.

The phone on his desk rang. Calls usually went via his secretary, but this was his direct line. It must be Karolina.

"Stenberg."

"Good afternoon, Mr. Stenberg," the dry voice said.

Stenberg stood up sharply, glancing quickly at the door.

"Y-you mustn't call me here. All calls are logged."

"Don't worry, this call can't be traced, I can assure you of that," the man on the other end of the line said.

Stenberg gulped and tried to gather his thoughts. "What do you want?"

"To start with, I'd like to congratulate you on your new job, Minister of Justice. According to the media, your future prospects look very bright."

Stenberg didn't respond.

"I thought it might be time to discuss recompense for our services. I presume everything was to your satisfaction, Minister? The case has been closed, after all. A lonely, unhappy woman who chose to end her own life."

Stenberg took a deep breath. He had been worrying about this call since the week after Sophie's death, but when a month passed without a word he had almost convinced himself that it wasn't going to come. Stupid, of course. The man on the other end made his living from providing services of this nature, after all. Stenberg sharpened his voice, trying to sound calm.

"How much?" he said.

"Oh, we're not after money, Minister."

Stenberg waited, closing his eyes for a few seconds. Sophie's shattered face was back in his mind, and he quickly opened his eyes again. He had to get this out of the way, as soon as possible. Otherwise he would never be able to move on.

"So what do you want?" he said.

"Oh, nothing much. Just something that the country's Minister of Justice, the head of the entire Swedish police system, would surely find simple to achieve."

"And what might that be?" Stenberg found he was holding his breath.

"A name," the man on the other end of the line said. His voice sounded almost amused. "The name of the person concealed behind the code name Janus."

NINE

Atif had said his good-byes. He had dutifully kissed Cassandra on the cheek before handing her the envelope full of dollar bills. The cost of his mother's nursing home ate up most of his salary, so it wasn't much. And from the look on Cassandra's face he could tell that she certainly didn't think it was enough, regardless.

He had hugged Tindra for so long that her little knuckles had left marks around his neck. He realized that he didn't actually want to let go.

"Why do you have to go, Amu?"

He had struggled to find a good answer and failed. Cassandra had come to his rescue.

"Your uncle has to go, darling. He has to go home and look after Grandma. But you can e-mail him if you like. And you can send him one of the lovely drawings you do on your iPad."

The thought of the drawings seemed to help, because Tindra had let go of his neck. Then she stood in the window and waved until he was out of sight.

He realized he was going to miss her. The intense look in her eyes, the way she put her little hand in his. The way she tilted her head when she disagreed with something. Just like her dad had done at her age. Maybe he should have offered to stay for longer. To spend more time with Tindra. But what sort of example could he be to her? He was pretty sure Cassandra could help him provide an answer to that question. The same example he had been to Tindra's father. An example that vanished when he was needed most.

The gym looked pretty smart. It was on the edge of an industrial estate just ten minutes from the suburban station. Judging by the thirty or so cars in the parking lot, it also seemed to have plenty of members. Mostly 4x4s, Honda CR-Vs, various models of Volvo XC, and a few other fairly pricey cars. Almost all of them were typical mom cars, presumably from the well-to-do residential areas just a mile or so away. Much smarter than targeting the young lads in the suburbs who couldn't afford the membership fees. And much less trouble too, of course. Nice and peaceful, a steady income, that was presumably what Adnan had been thinking.

Atif didn't really know why he had decided to come this way. Actually, that wasn't quite true. Even if it wasn't particularly far from the cemetery, he had no desire to go back there again, so this would have to do as his final farewell to Adnan. The dream his brother never managed to achieve. In some ways it was a fitting place for a good-bye.

He steered the rental car into the lot. He tried to look through the big panoramic windows, but the sun filters meant he couldn't see much. It didn't really matter. He parked in a vacant space, switched off the engine, and looked at the time. He sat there for a minute or so, forcing himself to think about Adnan.

He tried to persuade himself that he'd done all he could. Adnan had lived his own life, made his own decisions, and paid the price for them. Besides, they were very different, not just in age but in all manner of other ways. Unlike him, Adnan had been good at school, was liked by everyone, the favorite child. He had had opportunities that Atif had never had. Atif was grieving for his little brother, of course he was. But there were clearly also more emotions than grief alone. Guilt, that one was easy to identify. Anger too. He was also able to put his finger on a vague desire for revenge, even if he was keeping that under control. But there was another feeling there as well, one he was ashamed of, and would prefer not to put a name to, even in his thoughts.

He started the engine and did a circuit of the building. At the back, next to the Dumpsters, were a row of expensive parked cars. One of them was a familiar Audi with shiny wheel trims. Atif drove around the next corner and found himself close to the exit from the parking lot. He paused for a few seconds and looked at the time. Three hours and thirty-five minutes left until the plane took off. Plenty of time. The question was, what for? Why not just head out to the airport right away? Leave all this behind him, the way he had planned?

∙ ∙ ∙

The reception area had a black slate floor and had to be at least fifteen feet high. Rhythmic bass music was pumping from the far end of the building, and behind a frosted glass window he could see bodies moving.

To the left, behind another glass panel, there were rows of gleaming machines. A pair of gym-pumped guys were doing bench presses in there, but they were concentrating so hard on what they were doing that they didn't even look in his direction. There was no one at the reception desk, but a large arrow marked with the word *Café* was pointing toward a closed door in the far corner of the atrium.

Atif strolled toward the closed door. On the way he noticed the security cameras. Expensive ones, with night vision, not the sort of thing you usually found in gyms. He didn't really know why he'd come in, it had mostly been an impulse. The gym, the Audi, and its owner, Cassandra—none of them had anything to do with him. Besides, he already had a fair idea of who owned the car. But he still hadn't been able to resist the temptation to come in and get proof of whether he was right.

Next to the café door was a solitary folding chair, and on top of it a half-full plastic bottle containing something pink. The sign on the door said *closed*, but Atif could still see movement behind the frosted glass panel. He could hear Abu Hamsa's familiar voice and reached out for the door handle, but an unknown voice made him hesitate. Had he heard wrong? Atif stood there for a few seconds, listening for more sounds from inside the room.

"You've got nothing to worry about, my friend, nothing at all," Abu Hamsa was saying. "I've known him since he was a boy."

The other voice grunted indistinctly: ". . . cause problems?"

"No, no, he swallowed the official version," Abu Hamsa replied. "Adnan Kassab is dead and buried, and no matter how much our opinions may differ, we have to stay focused on getting hold of the traitor before he costs us everything we've built up."

Atif felt his heart beat faster. He took a cautious step closer to the door to hear better.

". . . going with the inside man?" another voice said.

"The lawyer's working on it," Abu Hamsa said. "But apparently there's some sort of problem. Crispin is convinced it's only temporary, then we'll soon be back on track."

"We'd better bloody hope so, after what we've paid," a voice said in a singsong Eastern European accent.

"That's hardly fair, Crispin's insider has been a huge help, which means we've been able to compensate at least in part for all the damage the traitor's caused. The fact is that without the insider, we wouldn't even know that Janus really existed," Abu Hamsa said.

A sudden hush fell inside the room, an uncomfortable silence that went on far too long. Atif realized immediately what had caused it. The name that Abu Hamsa had just mentioned: Janus.

"Allow me to point out once again," a dry voice said, "that according to the instructions you have been given, Janus is to be handed over to me at once. Alive, and unharmed. No one is to talk to him until I do."

"Not a problem for me," the indistinct voice grunted again. "There's no way he's one of my boys. We don't have a rodent problem here.

"Big words, Lund. It would be a shame if you had to take them back," someone said.

Atif started. He had heard correctly a short while before, no doubt about it. That voice belonged to another old friend. Although *friend* probably wasn't the right word. The last time they had met, the man had held a pistol to his head and sworn to kill him.

"The fact is that the rat bastard could be sitting in this room right now. With the exception of the consultant here, we're all equal suspects, aren't we?" the familiar voice said. "Everyone in here could be Janus."

"That's why you should leave the cat-and-mouse stuff to me and my team!" The dry voice again, clipped, almost military in tone. Presumably it belonged to the man who had been called the consultant.

Atif remembered that Abu Hamsa had said something about consultants at the funeral. He must have had this man in mind.

"We're experts in investigations of this sort, and we don't have to pay attention to anything that might spoil our concentration. Finding and eliminating Janus is our job, our only priority, and the best thing you can do is stay out of the way," the dry voice went on.

Once again, mention of the name brought conversation to a halt. As if none of them wanted to be the first to speak after the name had been uttered.

The sound of a toilet flushing just a few yards away made Atif jump. He turned his head and saw that the dial above the lock on one of the doors was showing red. Someone was moving about in there and was likely to open the door at any moment. But there was another door, on this side of the toilet. He took two long strides and tugged at the handle. The door was unlocked and led to a small cleaning cupboard. Atif slipped inside and closed the door behind him just as the toilet door swung open.

He peered through the crack in the door. A gorillalike man lumbered past, picked up the bottle, and sat down on the folding chair next to the door, just a yard or two from Atif. The man was shorter than he was and had dark cropped hair and a diamond ring in one ear. His chest muscles were so pumped up that his arms stuck out at an odd angle. A tattoo stretched out from one sleeve of his T-shirt, covering his skin all the way down to the wrist. Atif recognized him at once: it was one of the men from the funeral. Dino, something like that.

The man gulped down the rest of the protein drink, then belched loudly. He took out his cell phone and started fiddling with it. It took a few seconds for Atif to realize that Dino was sitting there for a reason. It was his job to make sure that the men in there could talk undisturbed. Not that he was a particularly attentive guard.

Atif looked at his watch. Three hours and twenty-five minutes left, still no real hurry. He looked cautiously around the little room. The floor was only about ten feet square square, and obviously there was no window. The smell of ammonia and disinfectant was already making his eyes water.

Dino belched again, then came a groan and the sound of a long, wet fart. Atif peered through the crack in the door and saw the man squirm in his chair. Suddenly he flew up and took a couple of quick steps, reaching out his hand toward Atif. But before Atif had time to react, the man disappeared from view and a moment later the toilet door slammed shut again. He heard the toilet lid being lifted, then a loud splash followed by a groan of relief.

Atif slipped silently out of the cleaning cupboard, hurried across the reception area, and left the premises the same way he had come.

* * *

He found a good lookout post on a neighboring plot. In the middle of a row of parked trucks, with a wire-mesh fence that didn't really impede his view but would make his car almost invisible. Three hours and nineteen minutes until his plane left. The drive to Arlanda would take an hour, so he still had plenty of time. He leaned his seat back and tried to stretch out as best he could. He wished he had his army binoculars with him.

His window of time had shrunk by another twenty-five minutes before anything happened. Abu Hamsa emerged first, lit a fat cigar, then jumped into the Audi. Atif had guessed right. The tone of voice the old man had used when he spoke about Cassandra had given him away. His promise to look after the family and the fact that Cassandra had his cell number just made things clearer. The only question was how long the old man had waited after Adnan's death before taking on the role of Cassandra's protector. Or had he already done so before Adnan was killed? But Atif reminded himself once again that it was none of his business. Cassandra made her own decisions, and maybe having an affair with Abu Hamsa was a cheap price to pay for having her family looked after.

The bowlegged man who emerged after Abu Hamsa was big, and considerably more lardy than gym-pumped. Leather waistcoat, long goatee, blond hair in a plait down his back. Swedish biker thug, model 1A. Atif recognized him as Micke Lund: seven years ago he had just been appointed sergeant at arms in the Hells Angels. By now Lund must be close to fifty. A padded jacket hid most of his leather waistcoat, but Atif could make out red lettering on a red background. Still with the Hells Angels, then.

The lard-ass stopped to insert a dose of chewing tobacco, waiting for the man following him out. Another biker, one who evidently didn't feel the cold, wearing a waistcoat in the yellow and red of the Bandidos. Short hair, younger, fitter than Micke Lund, and far less the blond, blue-eyed stereotype. But the two men no longer seemed to have anything against each other. They stood and chatted for a few minutes as two more men came out to join them. They were wearing tracksuits and had

closely cropped hair, with broad foreheads and defined cheek-
bones. Typical Eastern Europeans, probably Russian.

The two tracksuits lit cigarettes and offered one to the
Bandidos biker, while Micke Lund made do with his chewing
tobacco. The men stood and talked for a few minutes, stamping
in the snow. When another man with a face like a death's head
emerged from the door the four of them exchanged glances,
then quickly shook hands with one another and slid away to
their respective cars.

The death's head stood still as he lit a cigar. The man gave
a suitably mocking wave to the others' cars, then strolled over
to a big Porsche Cayenne. Atif studied the man and concluded
that he had heard correctly inside the gym. His appearance—
bald head, hook nose, and sunken eyes—was unmistakable. It
was his old friend and colleague Sasha. A war hero from the
Balkans, capable of anything, a man with no inhibitions. On
their first job together Sasha had cut off a man's fingers with a
pair of garden shears. He carried on until only the forefingers
were left, even though the man had long since crumbled and
told them what they wanted to know. Violence was one thing,
but Sasha was a full-blown sadist, and eventually Atif had
asked not to work with him any longer. Evidently this information had found its way back to Sasha, and as thanks he had
held a gun to Atif's head in the middle of a nightclub. He had
told him that the next time they met he was going to pull the
trigger, no matter how many witnesses there might be. Shortly
after that Atif's mother had fallen ill. And once Atif accompanied her back to Iraq, the matter had seemed irrelevant. But to
judge by the conversation in there, and the looks the bikers and
Russians had exchanged out in the parking lot, Atif wasn't the
only one who had a problem with Sasha. His presence at the
meeting, his suit, and the expensive car clearly suggested that
he had risen through the ranks. And was now someone to be
reckoned with.

Two different biker gangs, some Eastern Europeans, Abu

Hamsa, and Sasha. The discussion he had overheard had been a top-level meeting. The gangster version of Who's Who.

The last man didn't emerge until after Sasha had left. About thirty-five, suit, overcoat, short, dark hair, and a wary look in his eyes. It was impossible to see more from a distance. The man moved smoothly and exuded more genuine self-confidence than the others, more control. He was also considerably calmer than the men who had come out before him. Considerably less nervous.

In all likelihood, this was the consultant Abu Hamsa had talked about. Although the man actually looked as if he was in the military. Or the police.

The consultant stopped outside the back door for a moment and put on a pair of aviator sunglasses. Then he walked slowly toward a dark Range Rover as he let his eyes roam across the surroundings. The man stopped beside his car and for a few moments Atif was sure he was staring straight at him. But then the gym door opened again and Dino, or whatever the lunk was called, came out. He said something that made the consultant turn around and waved his short arms excitedly in a way that looked almost comical. The consultant said something in reply, then the two men hurried back inside the building.

Atif wondered about the security cameras in the gym, and how easy it was to rewind the recording just a matter of minutes. A couple of mouse clicks and he'd be there on the screen.

He turned the key in the ignition and put the car in gear. Just fewer than three hours before his plane took off.

TEN

When Sarac woke up he noticed two things immediately. First: it was pitch black. Not even a tiny light on a monitor, nothing to focus on. So he wasn't in his usual room. Second: there was someone else there in the darkness. He could sense movement of some sort, and then someone taking a deep breath.

"Can you hear me, Sarac?" a low male voice asked.

He turned his head toward it as he searched his memory for something to match to the hoarse voice. A name, a place, anything at all. But he couldn't find anything.

"You're not an easy person to get a little chat with, Sarac. There are lots of people keeping an eye on you. A lot of people worried about what you might reveal."

Sarac tried to raise himself to a sitting position, but got tangled in the tubes sticking out of his body.

"You know who I am, don't you?" the man said.

"N-no . . ." Sarac said. But that wasn't entirely true. They had met, he was almost certain of that. He just couldn't remember where and when. His eyes were gradually getting used to the darkness, and the man began to appear as a dark shadow just ten feet away away from him.

"We had an agreement, you and me, remember?" the man said.

Sarac shook his head, once again without really managing to convince himself. Was this all a dream, a hallucination playing out in his head? He clenched his hands tightly under the covers. He felt the back of one hand touch something. A plastic object connected to a cable. The alarm button.

The man came closer and stopped right next to the bed. He smelled strongly of tobacco. Sarac could make out a furrowed face, the mouth a black hole in which a gold tooth glinted. His sense of unease slid into fear, making Sarac's heart race. He fumbled for the alarm, but his hand slipped off it.

"An agreement is an agreement. You know what the consequences will be if you break it," the man said.

Sarac shut his eyes, screwing them shut as hard as he could, and pressed the alarm button. Once, twice, again . . .

"Get out!" he roared. "Go to hell!"

There were voices in the distance. Then steps as someone approached along the corridor. Any moment now the door would open.

"You can't hide forever," the man hissed in his ear. "You're going to stick to our agreement, do you hear?"

Sarac went on shouting, yelling out loud until the door opened and the light was switched on. He blinked against the sudden glare and saw the woman in white who was gently shaking his arm.

"David, how are you feeling?" she asked.

He blinked again, then rubbed his eyes in an effort to see better. Apart from the nurse, the room was empty. But in one corner was an empty chair. Its padded seat looked slightly compressed, as if someone heavy had recently been sitting on it.

* * *

The plane took off on time, at 8:35 p.m.. It climbed about seven hundred feet before retracting its landing gear and starting a long bank toward the east.

Atif leaned back in his seat and shut his eyes. He tried to fit the pieces together as best he could.

1. Adnan and his gang rob a security van.
2. By coincidence, they happen to encounter an unmarked police car.

3. The cops follow them and call in the rapid response
   unit, which strikes when the gangs are switching cars.
   Shots are fired. Adnan and Juha are killed. The third
   bloke, Tommy, is left a vegetable.

A perfectly consistent story. No matter how thorough your
preparations, the odds weren't always on your side. Adnan had
been lucky up to then. This time the pendulum swung the other
way.

Atif had made a conscious choice and accepted the chain of
events exactly as it was explained to him before he had arrived
in Sweden. He had decided not to ask any unnecessary questions. Not to find out any more than he had to. But he couldn't
shake off Abu Hamsa's words:

Envy is fatal, boys . . .

Even though Adnan made his living the way he did, and
even though his little brother had a remarkable ability to turn
gold into shit, Atif had envied him. Envied him all the qualities
that he himself didn't have. His charm, his family, and their
mother's unconditional love.

Could someone else in Adnan's vicinity have felt the same?
And have wanted to take something or someone from Adnan?
Was this about Cassandra? Atif seriously doubted it. No matter what the motive was, someone had ratted on Adnan and
indirectly caused his death. Possibly the same person whom the
gangsters in the gym were now terrified of.

Janus. The Roman god with two faces. The lord of beginnings, transitions, and conclusions, the god who started all wars
and made sure that they all ended. Associated with doorways,
gates, doors, time, and, not least, journeys.

Atif opened his eyes and looked up. The plane had become
a tiny point of light that was slowly disappearing into the dark
evening sky. In a minute or so it would be gone. He turned the
key in the ignition, put the car in gear, and pulled out of the
airport parking lot.

ELEVEN

Peter Molnar looked out the window, down at the meticulously gritted yard of Police Headquarters. He put a piece of chewing gum in his mouth, then glanced at his expensive diver's watch. That asshole Kollander was five minutes late, as usual.

The head of Regional Crime's little power games were as predictable as they were irritating. He ought to do what Bergh did and take care always to arrive late himself, just to even things out. And stick a discreet finger up at Kollander.

"You can go in now, Peter," Kollander's secretary said, and at that moment the head of the Intelligence Unit appeared in the doorway.

"Morning, Peter!" Bergh exclaimed as he pushed his glasses up onto his forehead. "Do we know why?" Bergh said in a low voice as he nodded toward their boss's door. Molnar shook his head.

"Not exactly, but I saw Oscar Wallin in the corridor a little while ago."

"Oh shit," Bergh muttered.

"Well, it was only a matter of time before Golden Boy showed up. Shall we find out what's on his mind?"

As if we didn't already know, Molnar thought. Bergh knocked on the door and opened it without waiting. Staffan Kollander was seated behind his very large desk. As usual, he was impeccably dressed in a smart, well-pressed white shirt with heavy cuff links that matched the gold of his epaulets.

Molnar and Bergh exchanged a discreet glance. Neither of them was in uniform, nor was the fourth person in the room. A fair-haired man with a boyish face, who was leaning with just the right amount of nonchalance against a low filing cabinet over by one wall.

"Good morning, gentlemen," Kollander said. "You both know Deputy Police Commissioner Wallin, don't you?"

"Of course, absolutely. Hello, Oscar!" Both Molnar and Bergh nodded to Wallin.

Wet-combed hair, clean-shaven, wearing a three-piece suit, Molnar noted. A bit of a difference since they worked on patrol together. But that was, what, ten, twelve years ago? Shit, he was starting to get old. If he wasn't careful he'd end up like Bergh, gray and overweight, with a beer belly so big he could hardly see his cock when he went for a piss. Molnar straightened up unconsciously and tensed his taut chest muscles. Well, there was no immediate danger.

Oscar Wallin had made good use of the intervening years. He had been through senior-officer training and had done some extra courses at university. Then a stint at the International Court of Justice in the Hague, before ending up in the Intelligence Unit of National Crime. It was hardly surprising that Minister of Justice Stenberg had handpicked him; they were cut from the same cloth. Ambitious high achievers, media-savvy, and sufficiently ruthless to get wherever they wanted.

Molnar already had an idea why Wallin was honoring them with his presence.

What goes around comes around . . .

"Sit yourselves down." Kollander gestured to the armchairs opposite him. "Deputy Commissioner Wallin and I have been having a very rewarding discussion. His investigative task sounds very interesting, and I've told him that we here at Regional Crime in Stockholm are naturally looking forward to a fruitful collaboration."

Kollander turned to Wallin, who was still leaning against the filing cabinet.

"Oscar, would you like to say a little more?"

"Of course, Staffan."

Wallin straightened up, took a couple of steps forward, and then sat down on the corner of Kollander's desk. The head of Regional Crime's upper lip twitched, a fleeting microsecond of disapproval. Molnar had to make a real effort not to grin.

"Minister of Justice Stenberg has given me a very clear task," Wallin began. "The idea is to gather all manner of key competencies under one shared roof. A national knowledge center where resources are exploited fully rather than being spread out around the country. We can't afford to have several parallel organizations doing their own thing."

"And what do you want from us, Wallin?" Bergh interrupted.

For the second time in less than a minute Molnar came close to breaking into a smile. Fucking Bergh! He may be a desk jockey these days, but every now and then the street cop in him still shone through. Bergh had been a tough bastard in his day. Seriously tough.

Wallin gathered his thoughts quickly.

"Intelligence management," he said curtly. "You are doubtless aware that other departments in the county have their own CIs. Cityspan, the licensed premises division, the narcotics squad, and plenty more besides. Not to mention my own former workplace, the Intelligence Unit of National Crime."

Wallin smiled toward Bergh, but the look in his eyes was icy. The older man squirmed slightly but was wise enough not to respond.

"Sometimes the same CI reports to a number of different handlers, without their being aware that this is the case. This means that erroneous information from one CI risks being accorded far too much attention because the information is confirmed by several different police units, when their source is actually one and the same. And our intelligence material becomes less reliable as a result, as I'm sure you would agree, Bergh?" Wallin went on staring at Bergh for another couple of seconds, waiting until he gave a curt nod before turning toward Molnar.

"Apart from this, it sometimes happens that certain handlers withhold valuable sources. Some of whom could be exploited more efficiently."

This time it was Molnar's turn to try to appear unconcerned. He adopted a different strategy than Bergh and met Wallin's gaze head-on. Without giving any sign that he would back down.

"Two of my coworkers will be coming over tomorrow," Wallin continued. "They have the highest security clearance and I expect you to cooperate fully with them. We need the names and contact details of all of your CIs, without any nonsense. All of them. I hope I've expressed myself sufficiently and clearly?"

He paused and seemed to be waiting for a response from Molnar, who still didn't move a muscle. Instead it was Kollander who interjected.

"Of course," the head of Regional Crime said, and cleared his throat before going on. "As I said earlier, we're all looking forward to our upcoming collaboration, Oscar."

• • •

"Well, that's that," Kollander said when Wallin had left the room. "What do you both make of all this?"

"Well," Bergh said, casting a quick glance at Molnar. "We had a feeling that something like this was in the offing. Our work with our CIs is second to none, and our results speak for themselves. As you no doubt remember, Wallin tried to muscle in when he was up at National Crime. Now he's got enough influence to demand things instead of having to beg for them, cap in hand."

"Mmm, I was thinking roughly the same. Our new Minister of Justice appears to have a lot of new ideas. We'll have to see how things develop in the future." Kollander straightened up slightly. "District Commissioner Swensk and I agree that the best strategy for the time being is to cooperate. But we don't have to give them everything on a plate. In advance of a big holiday like this, perhaps now might be a good time to take a look at which members of staff have put in too much overtime, and give those who need it a few weeks off?" Kollander gave the two other men a pointed grimace.

Bergh nodded.

"I've got a few guys who need to go on a course. Ethics and Equality, the district commissioner's favorite subject. What do we think?"

"Authorized," Kollander said. "Get the papers sorted at once and backdate them a week or two and I'll sign them." He drummed his fingers on his blotter. "Now, on to our next subject: David Sarac. Have we heard anything from the hospital?"

"I spoke to his doctor this morning," Molnar said. "Things are progressing, he's up and moving about. But he still has big gaps in his memory. He doesn't remember anything about the crash or what he's been working on recently."

"I see. Well, that's unfortunate, to put it mildly." Kollander laced his fingers together in front of him. "What does the doctor say?"

"That Sarac will certainly get better, but that there are no guarantees about how much better. Some memory gaps might well turn out to be permanent." Molnar cast a quick glance at Bergh.

"And the CI? Janus?" Kollander turned to Bergh, who shook his head.

"We haven't heard anything from him since the accident. He's probably lying low, seeing as he can't contact Sarac. Waiting for someone to get in touch via the usual channels. Those are certainly the instructions Sarac ought to have given him."

"I understand." Kollander drummed his fingers on the desk again. "So we don't appear to know why Sarac's envelope in the safe was empty? Nor why we have no information at all about the true identities of his CIs, either Janus or anyone else?"

"No, I'm afraid we don't," Bergh said.

Kollander went on tapping. "Then we don't have much

choice. We shall have to make a formal report and hand the matter over to Internal Investigations. I daresay Dreyer will want to take charge of this case himself. But before we do that I have to inform the district commissioner about what's happened."

As if you haven't already done that, Molnar thought. Operation Clean Threshold was probably already on the starting blocks.

"Well, we'll have to be prepared to be questioned about what we know about Sarac and his working methods," Kollander added. "Which is, of course, very little in my case. The way I see it, Sarac appears to have ignored a large number of the rules governing our work. And chose to see his successful results as some sort of carte blanche to do pretty much as he liked. Perhaps we've already given some thought as to his suitability and future here at Regional Crime? Documentation that might support a discussion of that nature?"

Kollander looked at Bergh. Molnar noticed that the older man's eyes seemed slightly unsteady. Shit, he had been wrong. Operation Clean Threshold was actually already under way, and Sarac was going to be its first victim.

"Well then, gentlemen!" The head of Regional Crime patted his desk gently a couple of times to indicate that the meeting was over. Molnar took a deep breath, then straightened up and made an effort to appear as calm as possible.

"There's one other possible explanation for why we can't get hold of Janus. A scenario that we certainly ought to consider," he said.

"And what's that, Peter?" Kollander leaned across his desk.

"Janus hasn't heard from Sarac for three weeks, so he must have realized something's happened. He may even have pieced things together after reading in the papers about a police officer being badly injured in a car crash. Either way, he'll have worked out what's going on by now."

"I'm not sure I follow, Peter," Kollander said. "Worked what out?"

"That there's no backup. Sarac's his only contact in the police. The only person who knows his secrets." Molnar ran his tongue over his perfect teeth. "Think about it," he said. "Janus is high up in the criminal hierarchy, we know that much. The information he's given us has led to the biggest seizures we've made in the last ten years, which have done serious damage to organized crime. In other words, there are plenty of people who'd like to see him dead. Everyone around him, basically." He paused for a couple of seconds to let what he was saying sink in.

"I know from experience that you don't recruit that sort of CI with the crap money the force will pay, so the only way Sarac could have recruited him is by getting some sort of hold over him. A secret that Janus would do anything to hide. Something that means he'd rather risk his life as a CI for the police than have the secret revealed."

A light lit up on Kollander's desk telephone, but he didn't seem to notice.

"But whatever Janus's secret is, Sarac has kept it to himself," Molnar went on. "He hasn't shared it with anyone, hasn't even written it down anywhere. Not as far as we know, anyway. I think Janus might have worked that out, and has decided to exploit the situation. Maybe he was doing just that before Sarac's car crash."

"You mean . . . ?" Kollander frowned.

Molnar nodded, and Bergh joined in.

"We have to consider the possibility that Janus simply doesn't want to be found. That he's prepared to go to great lengths to protect his secret. He might even be prepared to walk over dead bodies."

TWELVE

Sarac opened the door cautiously. The guard was hanging around by the reception desk over by the elevators, at the other end of the corridor. He was talking to one of the nurses, saying something that made her laugh. Gray-green uniform, a Securitas beret on his head. Radio, baton, and handcuffs in his belt. Presumably there to protect him. But, if so, from what? From whom?

He unfolded the crumpled note again and read the new message on the back.

YOU'RE NOT SAFE HERE!!!

Just as with the earlier message, he couldn't remember writing it. The past few days were hazy; he had been slipping in and out of consciousness. He had vague memories of being out of bed to go to the toilet, and of someone giving him an injection. But the rest was foggy.

He had dreamed about the snow-covered car again, and the man with the snake tattoo. He had felt the man's fear, heard his voice and then seen him die, over and again as the bullet hit the back of his head. But no new details had emerged, nothing that could help him understand what the hell was happening. Or who the man with the pistol was. The devil in the backseat.

Was it the same man who had been sitting in his darkened room, whispering about agreements and smelling of tobacco? Had that even actually happened, or was it just a migraine-fueled hallucination? He was inclined to think it was, but he couldn't be sure. Not here.

Sarac looked at the note again. His migraine attack, absurdly, seemed to have helped a bit. He felt better, his head clearer than before. He had taken off the sling and freed his left arm. His shoulder was still tender but usable. His right leg, on the other hand, slid about of its own accord, and he couldn't rely a hundred percent on his right arm either. But at least he could move about with the help of the aluminium crutch someone had left beside his bed.

He opened the tall, narrow wardrobe and pulled on the clothes he found inside. The jeans had been washed, no sign of the accident. The same with his socks and boots. There was no sign of his top or jacket, and he guessed the paramedics had been forced to cut them to shreds, so he had to keep the white hospital shirt on. He tucked it into his trousers in an effort to make himself look less like an escaped patient.

His keys and wallet were on the little shelf at the top, but not his police ID. One of his colleagues was probably looking after it for him—Bergh, perhaps? That seemed logical.

He couldn't find his cell phone either, which actually troubled him more than his police ID. His phone contained all his contacts. Information that could help him remember. He would have to ask Molnar about it, call him as soon as he got home and had safely locked the door behind him.

Sarac heard the elevator ping and looked out into the corridor again. Two men in dark suits got out, and one of them started talking to the guard.

Somber faces, neither of them remotely familiar, but he still guessed they were talking about him. Sure enough, the guard pointed toward his door. Sarac felt his pulse quicken. He didn't know who the men were, who they worked for, or what they wanted with him. Nor why their appearance should make his heart race.

The only thing he knew for certain, the only clarity that had emerged from the wretched haze of the past few days, was that somewhere inside his ravaged brain lay the answers to all his questions. Why he was here, what had happened in the hours leading up to the accident, and the reason for the ever-more-tangible feeling that he was in danger. Imminent danger.

I collect secrets . . . The question was, whose secrets?

The men in suits started walking straight toward his door, with the guard right behind them. Sarac took a deep breath. The message on the note had been right, he needed to get out of there, immediately!

He looked around the room, then stared at the window. There was a fire escape outside, he'd already spotted that. Six stories down on steep, snow-covered metal steps and frozen railings, leading down to a narrow alleyway.

He could hear the voices getting closer in the corridor. Realized he had to make a decision. He grabbed one of the sheets from the bed and opened the window. Ice-cold night air hit his face, making him gasp with shock. He glanced down quickly into the darkness. It was just about possible. It had to be possible!

. . .

The door flew open and the two suited men walked into the room, closely followed by the uniformed guard. The men looked around, saw the empty bed, then the wide-open window.

"Shit!" the shorter one hissed. "He got out."

The man ran over to the window and stuck his head out. Far below he could see something white flapping in the darkness.

"The fire escape," he shouted over his shoulder. "I'll go this way. Cut him off down in the alley!"

He swung his leg over the windowsill and climbed out as the guard and the other man spun around and started to run toward the elevators.

A minute or so later Sarac carefully opened the wardrobe door and laboriously slid out. He stifled a groan as his body protested. He grabbed the crutch, forcing the fingers of his right hand to grasp the plastic handle, then peered cautiously out into the corridor.

Empty, apart from one nurse at the far end by the reception desk. She had her back to him and seemed to be busy on the phone.

He crept out slowly and set off toward a glass door farther along the corridor.

Ward temporarily closed, a handwritten sign announced.

Sarac felt the door: unlocked—probably in case of an emergency evacuation. Thank God for Swedish health and safety regulations! He slipped quickly inside and limped along a narrow passageway that led to another, similar glass door.

The next ward looked much like his own, with the only difference that the lights were all switched off. The only light in the corridor leaked in through the windows or came from the emergency exit signs. It was also completely quiet. No voices, no telephones ringing, no machines humming, no alarms ringing. Just a ghostly silence that was broken a few seconds later by an ambulance siren. He needed to hurry; by now the men must have found the sheet on the fire escape and realized he'd tricked them.

Sarac limped off toward the elevators as fast as he could, struggling to get his body to cooperate. Sweat was already pouring down his back. Strange how something as easy as walking in a straight line could suddenly become so fucking difficult.

When he was just a few yards from the elevators one of them pinged. The up arrow on the wall lit up and a narrow strip of light rose up between the doors. Someone was about to get out. Someone who would wonder what he was doing there, who would probably ask questions he couldn't answer. Sarac looked around, saw the nurses' little reception desk, and ducked down behind it. He pulled the crutch closer and tried to ignore his body's protests. On the floor of the corridor just a few feet or so away he saw a rapidly growing rectangle of light as the elevator doors opened. In the middle of the patch of light was the dark silhouette of a man.

Sarac held his breath and waited.

The man got out of the elevator and stood still for a few seconds, as if to get his bearings. His shadow covered most of the rectangle of light from the elevator, making him look enormous. Sarac felt a stab of pain and his pulse rocketed. He pushed back against the reception desk. His body ached, his head was thudding. A memory flickered past and vanished before he could grab it. Flashing blue lights, shadows playing on a tunnel wall.

He heard footsteps as the man went past. Sarac caught a glimpse of a green operating gown and a pair of broad shoulders. Most of the man's head was obscured by a little green cap and a breathing mask.

Sarac leaned out carefully into the corridor and watched the man as he walked away, heading toward the door that led to his own ward. A doctor taking a shortcut. Nothing strange about that. But his gown was stretched tight across his back, as if it didn't really fit. His sleeves and trousers looked too short as well. It could have been an illusion, caused by the shadows and the poor lighting, but would a doctor really wear black boots when he was visiting a ward?

The man seemed familiar, his smooth, measured movements, the creeping way he walked. All of a sudden he was convinced. Just like the men in suits, this man was after him. But why? Who was he?

The memory was back. Voices, flickering shadows. A dark silhouette right at the edge of his field of vision.

Sarac gulped unconsciously. It sounded louder than he had expected, as if his gullet had got hold of his larynx. The man stopped just before the door. He turned his head slightly in Sarac's direction and seemed to be listening. Sarac quickly pulled his head back. He pressed against the reception desk and tried to blend into the darkness. He bit his top lip to help him hold his breath.

Silence. The lack of oxygen was threatening to make Sarac black out. His heartbeat pounded against his eardrums. Between its beats he could suddenly hear voices.

Your secrets are mine.

Get this fucking mess cleaned up!

The devil himself . . .

A heavy sole squeaked against the plastic floor. Then he heard the door at the other end of the corridor slowly open.

THIRTEEN

Naturally, Atif could have rung. Could have booked a meeting and they could have sat down like old friends. But the element of surprise was always better, especially if you were after the truth. If that was even possible.

The fact was that he had met plenty of people who thought they knew the truth. But when it came down to it, and no matter what means of persuasion were applied, all they ever managed to deliver was a subjective interpretation. The truth, objective truth, remained unattainable. The best you could hope for was to get as close to it as possible.

Abu Hamsa was sitting at his usual table, reading a newspaper. A thickset man with cauliflower ears was sitting a few tables away, fiddling with his cell phone, but the moment he caught sight of Atif the man stood up and blocked his way.

"What do you want?" he growled.

The man was a head shorter than Atif, five nine or so, but he puffed himself up as much as possible to seem bigger. Lowered his head, tensed his thick neck. Waited for Atif to say something, either back down or give him a reason to attack.

But Atif had played this game plenty of times. Instead of saying or doing anything, he ignored the man and carried on toward Abu Hamsa. The gorilla's eyes flickered; Atif could almost hear the cogs turning in his head as he tried to work out what to do.

"Didn't you have a plane to catch, my friend?" Abu Hamsa croaked, lowering the paper. The little man shook his head toward the gorilla, who, red-faced, had begun fumbling inside the back of the waistband of his trousers.

Atif carried on walking toward Abu Hamsa's table, pulled out a chair, and sat down.

"You never used to need a bodyguard," Atif said.

Abu Hamsa shrugged. "Times have changed. It's not so easy to know who you can trust." He paused for a moment as he gave Atif a long look. "So, what can I do for you, my friend? I don't suppose this is a courtesy call?"

"Janus," Atif said. "How is Janus connected to my brother's death?"

Abu Hamsa did his best to maintain his mask and actually almost succeeded. Thirty or forty years in gambling dens had given him a good poker face. A little twitch at one corner of his mouth that made his mustache quiver, that was all. He folded his paper, then looked around slowly.

"My dear Atif," he then said, grimacing as if the words he was about to say tasted unpleasant. "If you really want to talk about that subject, I must first take certain . . . precautions, if you understand my meaning?"

"You think I'm wearing a microphone?" Atif said.

"I didn't say that," the little man said. "But you appear out of nowhere after seven years and start asking questions. Questions about very serious things, things you definitely shouldn't know about. Besides, as you know, there are a number of rumors about you in circulation. Some suggest that your loyalty"— Abu Hamsa made a little gesture with one hand, as if he were searching for the right words—"is open to question."

Atif sat still. If anyone had spoken to him in that way seven or eight years ago . . . But that way of thinking was purely hypothetical—no one had dared talk to him in that way back then. Not even Abu Hamsa.

Atif stood up and took his jacket off. "Okay, go ahead!"

Hamsa went on looking at him for a few seconds, then turned to the bodyguard.

"Eldar, please search our guest. And do it nicely," he added.

The bodyguard took his task very seriously. Checked every

pocket, peered under Atif's T-shirt, even pulled his trouser legs up, the whole time trying his luck in a staring contest. He glared angrily at Atif, trying to get a reaction out of him. Get him to say or do something that would give him the chance to redeem himself in front of his boss.

But Atif just ignored him, pretending he was one of the little lizards that used to stare at him in his bedroom back home. A little reptile who didn't deserve his attention.

"He's clean," the bodyguard eventually grunted.

"Thank you, Eldar," Abu Hamsa said. "Could you fetch us some coffee, please?"

The bodyguard gave Atif one last glare, then lumbered off.

Abu Hamsa gestured to Atif to sit down again, then leaned over the table.

"You should have gone home, my friend. That's what a wise man in your position would have done."

Atif shrugged his shoulders. The old man was right. But he wasn't wise. He was who he was.

"What you're asking of me is no small thing, my friend," Abu Hamsa went on.

Atif didn't respond.

"But, for the sake of old friendship, and out of respect for your brother's death, I shall do my best to oblige you. You should know, however, that this sort of knowledge has a price."

Atif made a small movement with his head that could be interpreted as a nod.

"Good, then I'll get straight to the point." Abu Hamsa took a deep breath and appeared to think before going on. "For the past year or so, I and many of my business contacts have had a growing problem. It looks as if someone we trust, someone in our immediate vicinity, is actually working for the police."

"A rat?" Atif shrugged his shoulders. "It can't be the first time?"

"No, that's true." Abu Hamsa stroked his mustache. "But this time it's different. We're not talking about some ordinary little rat, but a senior associate. Someone we all know and trust. An infiltrator who is exploiting his position and knowledge to cause us serious damage. Extremely serious . . ."

Abu Hamsa leaned even further across the table. "The police are extremely protective of their infiltrator and have never acted in haste. The last thing they want is for him to become known and have to stand witness in court, so they lie in their reports. Hide the true source of their information and cover it up so well that we can't trace it back to any specific individual."

He paused for a moment.

"Obviously it's all illegal, Swedish law forbids the use of infiltrators. We've put our lawyers on the case, but unfortunately nothing can be proved as long as we don't know the infiltrator's identity. All we've managed to find out is his code name."

"Janus," Atif said.

Abu Hamsa nodded.

"That's more or less all we know. Janus really is top secret. His true identity is known only by a very small number of people. Our usual sources in the police are no use at all. Most of them have never even heard of him."

Abu Hamsa frowned.

"This cancer has cost us a lot of money, as a result of police raids, but even more so because of lost opportunities. Anxiety is spreading, and hardly anyone dares to do business. Even old friends no longer trust each other, and you only have to mention Janus for people to get cold feet. No one wants to take the risk of being in any way associated with him; that would be fatal."

Atif thought for a few moments.

"Was it Janus who told the police about Adnan?" he finally asked.

Abu Hamsa ran the back of his forefinger over his mustache. "What do you think? The idea that experienced guys like Adnan and his gang would have forgotten to take off their balaclavas during the getaway doesn't sound particularly credible. Besides, the pattern of events doesn't match the police description."

"No, that's what I thought too," Atif added. "The suggestion that plainclothes cops could get a heavily armed rapid response unit in place within ten minutes doesn't make any sense."

Eldar returned with a tray, which he put down on the table between Atif and Abu Hamsa before returning to his previous post.

"Janus has a great deal on his conscience," Abu Hamsa said. "Far worse things than your brother's tragic death. He is basically a threat to our entire operation, which is why we are devoting a lot of resources to finding him. We are unanimous on this. All means are permissible, and no cost or sacrifice too high."

The little man sipped his coffee cautiously.

"I understand," Atif said.

Abu Hamsa shook his head slowly. "No, I'm rather afraid that you don't, at least not completely. But now that you know what this is all about, it's my turn to ask you for a favor."

"What?"

"You need to keep out of the way, don't ask any more questions, and, above all, don't mention that name to anyone else."

Abu Hamsa paused and seemed to be waiting for a response. But Atif just sat there in silence.

"We have an opening," Abu Hamsa went on in a low voice. "A very good chance of solving the problem once and for all. But right now the situation is sensitive. Extremely sensitive. There's far too much at stake to . . ."

The little man gestured with his coffee cup.

". . . take any unnecessary risks," Atif concluded.

"I'm glad we understand each other, my friend." Abu Hamsa nodded.

"Was that why you didn't tell me? At the funeral?"

Abu Hamsa shrugged.

"I didn't think I had a choice. Like I said, where the search for Janus is concerned, no sacrifice is too small. The truth would hardly have made your loss any smaller, or brought Adnan back to life. But naturally I regret that I was forced to keep anything from you."

Atif turned his coffee cup as he reflected.

"So now you want me to go home to Iraq?" he said. "And forget about all this? The man who betrayed my brother and sent him into a trap. The man who basically caused his death."

"I'm all too aware that my request might be difficult to swallow." Abu Hamsa grimaced gently. "But, like I said earlier, this sort of knowledge has a price. I have told you everything you wanted to know, without even asking where you heard that name. What you do now is obviously up to you."

The little man leaned forward over the table and lowered his voice until it was almost a croak. "But you must understand, my friend. A man with your reputation who starts asking questions about things he shouldn't know about causes anxiety and attracts unnecessary attention. A man like that would constitute a risk. A risk that we sadly can't afford."

FOURTEEN

Sarac got no farther than the hall before he realized that something wasn't right. As if the whole energy of the apartment was wrong. There was a stale smell, a mixture of garbage, decay, and something else. Something familiar but simultaneously troubling.

He fumbled across the wall and found the light switch, but for some reason decided not to turn it on. Instead he waited until his eyes had got used to the gloom. The floor was covered with mail. Newspapers, letters, and advertising leaflets, all mixed up.

How long had he been gone? About three weeks, give or take. But a lot of this mess seemed older than that. There was probably a logical way to find out how much older. But right now logic wasn't his strong point. He felt exhausted. Getting all the way down to the ground floor of the hospital, then into a taxi and up into his apartment, had pretty much used up his reserves. His breathing was labored, the headache was still thudding away, and his hospital shirt was like a wet sail on his back.

He shuffled slowly into the living room, still not turning on any lights. Only a bit later did it dawn on him that this was exactly the right move if he didn't want to let the entire street know that he was home.

He stood in the middle of the room for almost a minute, letting his eyes get used to the darkness, while his brain tried to absorb what he was looking at. The blinds were closed, the floor covered with pizza boxes, newspapers, and clothes. All the sofa cushions were standing on end and it looked as if someone had split them open with a knife. The same went for the frame of the sofa, where foam rubber and sawdust were spilling out of the long gashes. The coffee table was covered with bottles of spirits and overflowing ashtrays, and in the middle of the table was a transparent glass pipe containing a sticky black substance. Methamphetamine, his brain concluded happily, as if it were pleased with its achievement and didn't actually realize what the discovery meant.

The stench was even worse in the kitchen. The draining board was overflowing with dirty dishes, and on the stove was a plastic container with the remains of a ready meal that was furry with mold. There were more improvised ashtrays in there, and a bucket that stank like hell. But he didn't smoke, did he? Unless perhaps he did?

His head was pounding like mad and he was having trouble keeping his eyes open.

In the bedroom the mattress had been dragged onto the floor and he saw from the long cuts in it that it had received the same treatment as the sofa. All the drawers in his bureau had been pulled out and their contents scattered over the floor. The same thing with the clothes in the wardrobe. Sarac sat down on the edge of the bed, trying in vain to take it all in. It took him several minutes to see the message that had been scrawled on the bedroom wall in jagged, bloodred letters. And beneath it a symbol, two *J*s turned to face each other.

PROTECT THE SECRET!

W

. . .

The men weren't even trying to hide. Atif only had to peer through the blinds of his spartan hotel room to see their car. A dark 4x4 parked a little way down the street. One of them was standing on the pavement ten feet away from it, smoking. Jeans and a military jacket, the sort with loads of pockets that plainclothes police officers tended to like. The man had a Palestinian scarf wound around his neck a few times, and a woolly commando hat pulled down to his eyebrows. He was stamping his feet in the cold.

Atif wondered who they were. The car and the man's clothing reeked of the cops. He remembered Bengtsson, the fat little policeman who had questioned him when he arrived. He'd probably made some sort of notes after their conversation and made sure they found their way into the police database.

Even if the airport hotel was shabby, they had still demanded some form of ID, and he had obediently handed over his passport and waited while the receptionist tapped his details into the computer. Perhaps that had been enough?

But it was more likely that the men had been sent by Abu Hamsa. The bodyguard had taken plenty of time to get their coffee. All he had to do was make a quick call. Make sure someone was tailing the rental car when Atif left the restaurant.

He hadn't noticed anything, so presumably the guys out there were rather better at surveillance than they were pretending to be right now. The alternative was that they had attached something to his car, a little GPS tracker or something like that; you could probably buy them from Clas Ohlson these days.

Cops or gangsters? Maybe both?

The man outside the gym, the one they'd called the consultant, had definitely had an air of police about him. The others at the gangster conference were pretty representative of their business. A couple of bikers, Eastern Europeans, his old sociopathic friend Sasha, and Abu Hamsa himself, who as usual was probably representing one or more groups. They had all been playing it cool, as if they were in complete control. But he had still detected the fear in their voices and seen it in their hasty, wary glances out in the parking lot.

All those men were hardened criminals, with several lives on their consciences. Men who didn't usually shy away from anything. But they were all scared, nonetheless. After what Abu Hamsa had told him, he understood why. The men were terrified of what might happen to them if Janus the traitor turned out to be one of their men. Someone they had trusted, someone they had vouched for, maybe even confided in. Fear was seeping out of their pores, stronger with each passing day. It was affecting their judgment, their capacity to make decisions. Sooner or later others would pick up on it, interpret it as a sign of weakness and react accordingly.

The men's only chance of survival was to cooperate. Temporarily forget all their differences and set to work putting the puzzle together, while simultaneously keeping a wary eye on one another. Waiting for the decisive piece of the jigsaw to turn up, the one that would lead them to Janus. They were all perfectly aware that as soon as that happened, the game would change completely, and all their promises and agreements would disintegrate.

Janus could obviously also be used as a weapon, a well-honed blade to strike at the heart of whichever organization he belonged to. It was hardly surprising that the men at the gym had been nervous. This was a game with extremely high stakes.

The only one who hadn't seemed so anxious about the situation was the consultant. He had nothing to fear and, just as the man himself had pointed out, in many ways that made him a better hunter. But who was he? The registration number of his Range Rover hadn't led anywhere, it was leased from a limited company with a postal address out in Stuvsta. The model and color were roughly the same as the car out in the street. So what did that mean?

The man outside dropped his cigarette, stubbed it out, and then stood there for a few moments, looking up at Atif's window. Then he opened the passenger door and got back in the vehicle. The light inside stayed off, which suggested at least that they weren't amateurs. The feeling Atif had had when he first caught sight of the car was getting stronger, and becoming more of a certainty. The men in the car wanted him to see them, wanted him to understand.

A risk we can't afford . . .

The lights of Arlanda's runways were clearly visible above the treetops, and a movement in the night sky made him look up. Another plane coming in to land. The roar of the plane's engines made the blinds shake gently under his hand.

• • •

Sarac must have dozed off, falling asleep on what was left of his bed. The sound that had woken him was still going on. A rattle from the front door, followed by a metallic clicking sound. Someone was opening the door, someone who had a set of keys. Maybe the same person who had searched the apartment and ripped open his furniture.

He struggled to his feet, feeling his heart race in panic in his chest.

Coming home had been a mistake; obviously it was the first place they'd look when they realized he was gone. He should have got out at once when he saw the state the apartment was in. Instead had fallen asleep. Stupid fucking bastard dickhead!

The crutch was lying on the floor and it took him a real effort to reach it. He needed to get out of there, at once.

The rattling from the hall was interrupted by a small thud. Then it was completely silent. Whoever was outside must have got the door open and discovered that the security chain was on. And realized that he was in there.

Sarac staggered out into the hall. His footsteps were clearly audible; the crutch made a metallic clicking sound, but he didn't care. Panic had taken a firm hold of him, and all he could think about was escape.

The hall was still quiet. The person out in the stairwell was probably wondering what to do next. The safety chain was held in place by only two little brass screws. If anyone kicked the door hard enough they'd give way, he knew that from experience.

So who was it? The men in suits from the hospital, the man in the tight surgical gown? Or someone else entirely?

He reached the kitchen and pulled the drawers open, looking for something to defend himself with. He found a sturdy carving knife that he gripped in his left hand. Not exactly ideal, but better than just standing there clinging to his crutch.

Sarac looked out into the hall. The door was ajar but the lights in the stairwell had gone out. He was still sure there was someone standing out there, someone who wanted to get in, to get at his secret.

A gloved hand suddenly reached in through the gap in the door and started feeling for the security chain. It tugged at it, as if to test how firmly attached it was.

Sarac acted on instinct. He limped through the hall, raising the carving knife. He took aim at the middle of the back of the hand. Just as he was about to strike the hand pulled back and the door slammed shut. Sarac was left standing there with the knife raised above his head. Waiting.

The other person must have heard him coming and changed tactic. He heard sounds in the stairwell that he couldn't identify at first. A squeaking noise, like a rubber-soled shoe on a stone floor. Then padding footsteps. After that everything was silent for a long time.

Then came the sound of a key in the door again. Sarac got ready with the carving knife. The door opened again and, just like before, was caught by the security chain. Sarac took a step forward, angling the knife. He could see movement through the gap in the door, saw a face, and jabbed the knife at it. He realized too late that the lights in the stairwell were now lit.

The knife missed the gap in the door by fewer than two inches, hit the frame, and almost slipped from his grasp.

"What the hell?!" he heard a woman's voice say.

FIFTEEN

"Hello, Mom? It's me, Atif."

"Hello?" He could tell from the tone of her voice that this wasn't one of her better days.

"How are you, Mom? Are the nurses being nice to you?"

"Oh yes. Everyone's so nice here."

"Good. Listen, I'm going to be staying in Sweden for a bit longer. There's something I need to take care of. But I'll be back soon."

"Have you found him?"

"Found who, Mom?"

"Your little brother! Adnan hasn't come home from school yet. You promised to find him." Her voice suddenly sounded different. More alive.

"I'm going to find him. Don't worry."

"Promise me, Atif. Promise you'll find him!"

The line went dead before he had time to answer. She did that sometimes. For a while he had thought it was because she was angry. But gradually he had realized that his mother had simply forgotten who she was talking to and didn't want to humiliate herself by having to ask.

He slipped his cell phone back into his inside pocket. It was early in the morning, and the darkness made it impossible to see in among the tall conifers. The lights from the city were staining the sky, turning it into a milky, impenetrable haze. He missed the desert, the clear, starry sky. But he tried to convince himself it was still up there. That he would soon be back.

He took the little stone from his pocket. It had been polished by the desert sand over tens of thousands of years, all rough edges removed until all that remained was a velvet-smooth, warm surface. He had packed it in his case, pretending it was a present for Tindra. But part of him had already known, suspected what he would have to do. Because he was who he was.

Atif laid the stone on the frozen ground, then took a step back. The hole made by the digger had been filled. The headstone wouldn't be erected until the ground had thawed out.

"I promise . . ." he mumbled to himself. "I promise to find him for you."

.   .   .

"Are you mad, David?! Why are you walking around with a knife?"

The woman stared at David as he just stood there in the middle of the mess in the hall. He must have looked like a lunatic. Health service shirt, big bandage around his head, and a crutch in one hand. Not to mention the carving knife he'd just tried to stab her in the face with. He was holding it behind one leg, unwilling to let go of it until he knew whether she was friend or foe. But once the woman had got over the initial surprise, the knife didn't really seem to bother her.

He had opened the door, mostly to stop her from shouting or calling the police. And she had somehow maneuvered them both back into his hall.

The woman seemed distantly familiar. Red hair and freckles, a nose stud, somewhere between twenty-five and thirty. Neither tall nor short. Her build was verging toward stocky, exacerbated by the heavy padded jacket she was wearing. She was wearing woolly Lovika mittens, not black gloves. So she wasn't the person who had tried to get in the first time around. But why was this woman here, and why did she have the keys to his apartment?

"W-who are you?" His fingers clutched the knife behind his leg.

"Natalie," she said, waving a laminated ID card on which

Sarac only had time to notice a company logo. But there was something about the woman's energy and charisma that had already made him calm down slightly. The way she spoke to him, the openness in her voice. She reminded him of Dr. Vestman, but without the sympathetic smile.

"I'm your care assistant, David. We met the other day at the hospital," she said.

Sarac smiled uncertainly, not entirely sure what reaction was expected of him. Care assistant. Well, that seemed to fit her behavior. And he couldn't deny that she looked familiar, even if he couldn't quite remember that they had actually met.

The woman looked at him, then pulled a folded sheet of paper from her inside pocket.

"We talked to Dr. Vestman," she said. "Went through your rehabilitation program. You signed it here."

Sarac took the paper and discovered that there were actually several pages. At the top was the same logo that was on the woman's ID card. Beneath it were loads of words that overwhelmed his brain. Paragraphs about services, responsibilities, timetables, keys.

"At the bottom of the third page," the woman said.

Sarac leafed through the sheets and found a series of signatures. He saw his own, slightly shaky, but still perfectly recognizable. Next to his name was another signature.

"Natalie Aden," he muttered.

"That's me. According to the doctor, you weren't going to be discharged until next week at the earliest. I was going to get things ready. Do a bit of cleaning and shopping, that sort of thing. I like getting up early."

She frowned and pulled a tube of ChapStick from the pocket of her jeans and ran it across her lips.

"You don't remember that we've met, do you?" she said.

"N-no, I'm afraid not."

Sarac suddenly noticed that the front door was still open. The lights in the stairwell had gone out.

"Did you see anyone?" he muttered.

"Where?"

"On the stairs, on your way up. Did you see anyone?"

Natalie looked at him and seemed to be trying to work out what he meant.

"No," she said. "Has someone been here? Is that why you're holding that knife, David?"

Sarac didn't answer. Natalie seemed to understand.

"Paranoia is a fairly common side effect after a stroke," she said gently. "That's because the brain is interpreting things differently. It throws up images that you can't quite match with reality."

Sarac looked at the open door, the darkness in the stairwell. For a brief moment he thought he could hear noises from the floor above. A squeak, maybe a rubber sole on a stone floor.

"Have you got a car, Natalie?"

• • •

Sarac was fiddling with his wallet, trying to pull out the pass card that was tucked behind his driver's license. He almost dropped his crutch on the floor when the plastic card wouldn't cooperate. Even though he had pulled his woolly hat down over his forehead to hide his bandaged head, the guard seemed to recognize him. The man pressed a button and opened the disabled entrance. Sarac hesitated for a moment, then chose the easy option. He made an effort to give the guard a friendly nod as he went past. At least he ought to be safe in here, even if he wasn't sure who from.

"Morning," the guard said. "The early bird catches the worm!"

Sarac went over to the elevators, but once he was standing inside one of them he felt suddenly uncertain. What floor did he work on? Obviously he could lean over and read the labels next to the buttons. But instead he closed his eyes, then opened them quickly and pressed the first button his finger found. It turned out to be the fourth floor. The mirror in the elevator gave him a quick glimpse of his face. The blue eyes were the only things that looked right. Everything else, the prominent nose, the dimpled chin, even the mouth and teeth, seemed odd. As if they actually belonged to a stranger, a skinny, hollow-eyed doppelganger.

The elevator doors opened. *Regional Crime—Intelligence Unit,* a sign said on a door a couple of yards away, which put him in a slightly better mood. At least he hadn't forgotten where he worked. He thought about Natalie, the woman who had driven him here. How could he have forgotten that he had a care assistant?

The reader accepted his pass card without protest and he found himself in a dimly lit corridor. A long, beige plastic mat led off between rows of identical brown office doors. The corridor was utterly silent, which probably wasn't that strange. It was barely half past five in the morning. He had felt he had to get out of the apartment. Away from whoever it was who was after him.

The short car journey had given him time to think, and he was feeling increasingly certain. It seemed credible that the man who had been dressed up as a doctor had just tried to get into his apartment. But who was he? What did he want? Was it the same man who had turned his apartment upside down and written the message on the wall? The man in the stairwell had had keys, so it seemed logical. And that symbol, the two *J*s facing each other, what the hell did that mean? And what secret was the man referring to?

The answer ought to be along this corridor, in his office. All he had to do was look through his desk and everything would be bound to fall into place.

He took a few cautious steps forward. Closed doors on both sides. Little white signs with blue lettering. The names were familiar and conjured up faces.

He almost felt he could see through the doors, see people sitting in their offices, even hear their voices. All different, but with roughly the same tone: collegial, respectful.

The illusion vanished as quickly as it arose. The silence and the dim lighting in the corridor suddenly made him feel ill at ease.

A sign marked *Detective Superintendent Kjell Bergh—Head of Unit* made him stop. He felt the handle tentatively, but the door was locked. The same applied to the following doors. People in here were careful to protect their . . .

Secrets.

The whispering voice made him spin around, and his heart began to race. But the corridor was empty. There was no one there. Just a figment of his imagination, served up by his unreliable brain.

When he was almost at the end of the corridor he instinctively turned left and stopped in front of the last door. There was no nameplate, but he was still sure it was his door.

He took out his key ring and found the right key on the first attempt. He looked over his shoulder before putting his hand on the door handle. The room was small, no more than thirty square feet. A desk along one wall, an office chair, a window with the blinds closed, that was all. Evidently he hadn't made any effort to decorate the place. Not a single photograph, picture, or memento, none of the usual things people accumulated.

The room still looked very familiar, and felt familiar too. The air was still. Just a faint smell of linoleum. One of the fluorescent lights flickered a few times, then buzzed feebly before suddenly going out. Something popped into his head, another flash of memory.

Three people in this room, one of them himself. Whispering voices, indistinct faces. Just as with the sequence in the snow-covered car, the perspective kept shifting, letting him see things from a different angle. From outside, as if he had actually been a spectator.

"Someone up here is leaking information, we can't trust anyone," one of the voices whispered; it sounded a bit like Bergh. "We have to protect Janus, at all costs."

A ringing sound made Sarac jump. A gentle, digital burble from the phone on the desk. He stared at it. Saw the little red light flashing. The phone rang again, then once more. He walked over to the desk, hesitantly reached out his hand, and picked up the receiver.

"H-hello?"

There was no reply, but he knew there was someone there at the other end of the line.

"Hello?" His voice still didn't sound the way it ought to. It was tremulous, uncertain, pretty much the way he felt.

Still no answer, but there was definitely someone there. He even got the impression he could hear someone breathing. Deep, slow breaths. He pressed the receiver to his ear, trying to hear more. But all he could make out was a gentle hum of static.

"Hello!" he said for a third time, more firmly. "This is Detective Inspector David Sarac. Who am I talking to?"

No response. The name was suddenly back in his head, forcing its way in, blocking any other thoughts. In the end it forced its way out of his mouth.

"Janus? Is that Janus?"

A faint sound, a dry snort, almost a laugh. Then the line went dead.

SIXTEEN

Sarac looked up and slowly straightened his back. The clock on the desk said 08:15. He had fallen asleep again. Just like that, across the desk, and he'd been out for more than an hour. Not that strange, perhaps, seeing as he hadn't slept much that night. His neck and shoulders felt stiff, and he had drooled on the desk. But when he straightened up he suddenly remembered something. Something important.

He bent over and pulled out the bottom drawer of the little filing cabinet under the desk. Empty! He pulled out the drawer above, then the next. All four drawers were empty. Not even any pens, Post-it notes, or spare coins for the coffee machine. He stood up and pulled out one of the many identical box files from the shelf. He didn't even need to look, just feeling the weight was enough. He dropped it on the floor and pulled out the next one, then the next. He carried on until he had emptied the whole shelf. His pulse was racing, making his chest heave and sweat pour down his back.

He looked more closely at the walls and discovered some small nails he hadn't seen at first. Pale rectangles on the textured wallpaper, small scratches and marks on the shelves of the bookcase. It finally dawned on him what it all meant. He wasn't a minimalist after all. Someone had cleared his room out. All his files, photographs, and belongings, even the nameplate on the door. Everything had gone, down to the very last detail. Everything that could have helped to jog his memory. But who had done it, and why?

His anger flared up out of nowhere, overwhelming him

and giving him new strength. He grabbed the empty bookcase and pulled it over. Then did the same with the office chair. He yanked the door open and staggered out into the corridor. His heartbeat was pounding in his head.

Almost all the office doors were open now, and a couple of people were standing by the glazed door at the end of the corridor, talking. They fell silent when they caught sight of Sarac.

"What the hell have you done! What the fuck have you done, you bastards!" The words came out by themselves, he couldn't stop them. More people looked out from their rooms and seemed to stop in their tracks when they saw him. He took a few steps forward. The crutch felt sturdier now, as if the adrenaline in his body had fixed it to his right arm.

"David?" Bergh said, half running out of his office.

"My things!" Sarac yelled. "Where the hell are all my things?"

"Take it easy, David." Bergh was looking around anxiously. "Come into my office and I'll explain."

"David Sarac?" The voice came from behind him, and he spun around. Two men in dark suits had emerged from one of the rooms. Sarac recognized them, the men in suits from the hospital, the ones he had managed to lose.

"Why?!" he snarled. "Who the hell are you?"

"My name is Odhe. We work for Deputy Police Commissioner Oscar Wallin. He wants to talk to you, right away."

"Go to hell, you clown!"

David didn't really know why he said that. His anger seemed to be dictating both his speech and actions. The pressure in his temples was getting worse and worse. Threatening to split his head open. He turned back toward Bergh and opened his mouth to say something. The next moment everything went black. He stumbled and managed to reach one of the walls for support. He slowly slid down it until he was sitting on the floor, and he had to make an effort not to throw up. Someone grabbed him under the arm and seemed to be trying to lift him up off the floor.

"L-let go of me, for fuck's sake!" Sarac tried to pull free. But his anger was draining away, taking all his energy with it. All the sounds around him were blurring, he heard the door at the end of the corridor open, then loud voices from several different directions. He retched and vomited a mouthful of saliva and bile onto the plastic floor.

"For God's sake, can't you see he's ill," a familiar voice said. "He should be in the hospital, not dragged off to be interrogated."

"Molnar, our orders are to—"

"Look, Odhe, you can take your orders and shove them up the Bekaa Valley. We're going to take Sarac home, right now, and it would be fucking unwise of you or your colleague to try to stop us. In-traction-for-a-month unwise. I hope I'm making myself clear?"

Sarac looked up. Peter Molnar was standing right in front of the man in the suit, so close that the tips of their noses were almost touching. Behind him were a couple of muscular men in dark military jackets and Palestinian scarves. The pent-up force they exuded overwhelmed Sarac, and he lowered his eyes again.

Odhe, the man in the suit, took a couple of steps backward. "You've seriously lost it now. I'll be contacting . . ." Odhe muttered something inaudible to Bergh. Molnar crouched down beside Sarac and passed him a handkerchief.

"We're going to take care of you, David, okay?" he said in a low voice. Sarac nodded and wiped his mouth and cheeks.

"Are you strong enough to stand up?"

Sarac managed to nod again, slightly more firmly this time. Molnar helped him get slowly to his feet and passed him his crutch. The two suited men had moved a little way down the corridor. The man who had introduced himself as Odhe was holding a cell phone to one ear. Neither of them was saying anything, but Sarac could clearly see the hostility in their eyes. Beyond them he could see more faces, all staring at him. Faces that had once looked at him with respect and admiration. Now all he could see was pity. They could all fuck off, the whole lot of them.

Sarac straightened up, made sure the crutch was in the right place, then nodded at Molnar a third time.

"Ready," he mumbled.

"Okay, David," Molnar said. "How about getting the hell out of here?"

· · ·

The elevator carried them all the way down to the garage beneath Police Headquarters. Their vehicle was big and black, with chrome-plated steps on both sides. Molnar carefully helped him into the backseat and got in beside him. One of the military jackets, Sarac had an idea his name might be Josef, jumped into the driver's seat and drove off without waiting for the third man.

Josef put his foot down as they drove through the garage, and the wheels shrieked on the smooth concrete as he turned into the long tunnel that led up to ground level. He switched the flashing blue lights on and the noise of the engine echoed off the tunnel walls and turned into an intense buzzing sound inside Sarac's head.

A memory popped into his head. It resembled the one that had appeared in the hospital. Tunnel walls, car headlights, flashing blue lights all around him. And something else as well, something important.

But before he managed to grab hold of the memory they emerged into the daylight at Fridhemsplan. The traffic lights were red, but Josef switched the siren on and pulled straight out into the oncoming traffic. Only now did Sarac notice that Molnar was watching him. He leaned his head back against the seat, shut his eyes, and swallowed a couple of times.

"That wasn't particularly smart, David," Molnar said a few seconds later. "You weren't supposed to be discharged until next week. We were about to go and visit you in the hospital. Damn lucky we decided to look in at work first."

"Who were they?" Sarac interrupted without opening his eyes. "The guys in suits. Odhe, or whatever his name was? They were up at the hospital last night."

"Oscar Wallin, you remember him?" Molnar pulled a face as if the name left a bad taste. "Very ambitious, used to be based in National Crime, a real pain in the ass. He tried to get us to collaborate a while back. Wanted to know absolutely everything without giving anything in return. He got really pissed off when we rejected the offer. Now our new Minister of Justice has given him a mandate to take whatever he wants instead of asking nicely for it. His guys are basically scooping up all the CIs they can find in the department."

"And now he wants to get hold of Janus?" Sarac said.

Molnar didn't answer.

"You said he was top-secret. That no one else knew."

"It's impossible to keep anything completely quiet, David."

Sarac remembered the flash of memory inside his office. Bergh had been talking about a leak. Same thing when they met in the hospital a few days before. He opened his eyes and slowly shook his head. "I don't remember him."

"Wallin? Floppy fringe, looks like a little kid," Molnar began, then fell silent as Sarac went on shaking his head.

"Janus," Sarac said. "I don't remember anything. Just that something's gone wrong, terribly wrong."

"Yes, so you said up at the hospital, before they wheeled you out. But you couldn't remember what had happened. No details." Molnar looked at him. And ran his tongue across his perfect front teeth.

"It's all just a huge mess," Sarac said. "A mass of fragments flying around inside my head. I thought it would help if I saw my office. At first it looked like it was going to work, then I realized all my stuff was gone. That someone had emptied my office."

Molnar grimaced. "Kollander has embarked on Operation Clean Threshold. District Commissioner Swensk has set her sights on becoming our next National Head of Police, and nothing's allowed to get in the way of her plans. An internal investigation of her own crime unit would look bad, not least because it was investigated a few years ago when the Duke was forced to leave. So you've been moved out. Kollander probably got Bergh to backdate the files to make it look like the transfer happened before the car crash. Before they discovered that your backup list was missing from the safe. Whatever happens now, they can blame a single officer who exceeded his authority. Someone whose competence was already in question and who therefore no longer works for Regional Crime." Molnar shook his head.

"Where . . . ?" Sarac cleared his throat. His voice wasn't doing what he wanted. "Where have they moved me? Where are all my files?"

"The property store," Molnar said. "I went down and checked. The only thing there is half a packing crate containing your personal possessions. Nothing to do with work, not even a single Post-it note. It's all missing."

Sarac bit his lip, suddenly feeling almost on the verge of crying. He leaned forward and covered his face with his hands. Molnar put a hand on his shoulder. They sat in silence for a while as the driver skillfully maneuvered the heavy vehicle through the traffic.

"Listen, David, if it's okay with you, we're not going to drive you home. Wallin's people would be at the door the moment we left. Same thing with the Internal Investigation team. Superintendent Dreyer would love to take you in for questioning and search your apartment. We're thinking of taking you somewhere you'll be safe. Give you a chance to lie low and get some rest."

Sarac opened his mouth to protest. But then he thought about what happened during the night. The man who appeared to have keys to his apartment.

"Sure." He couldn't be bothered to ask what Molnar had in mind and wasn't that interested in finding out either. Anything had to be better than that dump right now. His adrenaline rush was exhausted. His body felt heavy, and even the slightest movement took a huge effort.

"Good," Molnar said. "Try to get some rest, we've got a fair way to drive."

Sarac shut his eyes and leaned his head back. He gave up fighting his tiredness but didn't actually fall asleep, at least not properly. Something was holding him precisely on the boundary between sleep and wakefulness. There was something he ought to remember, something to do with his office. All his files.

"Terrible to see him like this," he heard Josef say from the driver's seat. "My uncle had a stroke a year or so back. He's still a vegetable, can barely find the toilet these days. Sometimes he pisses in the wardrobe."

"Leave it, Josef." Molnar muttered something else inaudible.

The sound of the engine and their voices faded into a blur as Sarac sank deeper into real sleep. Images flitted past in his head.

A small room and a whiteboard full of photographs. Some of the portraits stern, staring darkly into the camera. Their names on small labels underneath. Others taken surreptitiously, people getting in or out of cars. Names written in, along with numbers, presumably phone numbers. Red lines everywhere, arrows linking the people in the pictures. Weaving them together into a pattern, a huge spiderweb. And, in the center of a large circle, two *J*s facing each other.

He imagines he can see movement, a brief reflection in the shiny surface of the whiteboard. The outline of a figure with a hood pulled over its head. The impression only lasts a fraction of a second and is gone before he manages to make out any details. But he has other things to think about. Because now he can see it. In the middle of the little desk along one wall. A black notebook that he recognizes very well. The book is open;

he can see lines of writing covering the pages. But for some reason he can't read them, he can't put them together to form anything intelligible. Or can he? Because when he looks at the text for a while he imagines he can make out a pattern. Some of the letters seem to stand out more than others. Suddenly he realizes that he knows what the words mean, what secret they are hiding. All the information he's looking for exists inside that notebook. Hidden among words that are becoming ever clearer. All he has to do is interpret them and write them down more clearly.

But just as he's about to go on reading, someone grabs him by the shoulder and drags him out backward. He reaches out his arms, trying to grab the notebook, take it with him out of the dream. In the distance he can hear a voice calling him.

"David! David, we're here." Molnar was standing outside the car, gently shaking Sarac's shoulder. Waiting patiently as he came around.

"Good place to lie low, don't you think?"

SEVENTEEN

"Atif, sit yourself down, man!"

The bowlegged little man, whose name was Bakshi, cleared some of the magazines and cat toys from the big leather sofa and gestured to Atif to sit down. But instead of doing as he was told, Atif went over to one of the overblown armchairs and lifted it slightly to get rid of the scrawny, hairless cat lying across the cushion. The animal landed softly on the floor, gave him a long stare, then strolled off into the kitchen.

"My girlfriend's cat, she's called it Missy Elliott," the little man grinned. "Missy Elliott, get it? What a fucking name."

Atif nodded. And thought that there were two sorts of rats. The usual blabbermouths despised by everyone, who almost always ended up in plaster or buried in an abandoned quarry. Then there were the others, the exceptions who proved the rule. People who were still accepted, even though everyone knew they talked, for the simple reason that they were useful. Sometimes there was good reason to tip the cops off about what your competitors were doing. Level the playing field a bit. That was where people like Bakshi came in. They stopped you from having to go directly to the police and becoming a rat yourself. You could tell Bakshi a secret, any secret, and he would run straight off to the cops with it. As untrustworthy as he was predictable. Everyone knew it—and everyone exploited the fact.

Bakshi grinned uncertainly at Atif, stroked his thumb across the screen of his cell phone, checked the display, then put it down on the coffee table.

The apartment smelled of fresh paint and leather. Big, Italian designer furniture, not the usual Ikea stuff. In the middle of one wall of the living room was a massively oversized flat-screen television hooked up to an expensive-looking sound system. The apartment seemed to have recently had a complete makeover, as had its owner. Nice, even teeth, a couple of shades too white, a spray tan, and a ridiculously neat beard along his jawline that must take at least half an hour to trim.

The last time he had met Bakshi, he had been a slimy little rat who scuttled along close to walls. Now he had been up-graded and cleaned up. A silk shirt, not tucked into his designer jeans, his hair greased and combed back, and his pale pink hairline had to be several inches closer to his brow than before. Bakshi evidently noticed him looking.

"Nice, eh?" He pointed to his hair. "Had it done a month ago. They take hairs from your neck, roots and all, and trans-plant them into tiny holes in your forehead, one at a time. Hurt like hell and cost a fortune. But it was worth it. The girls love it." He grinned at Atif, but he didn't smile back. The two men stared at each other.

"Jesus, it's been a while, Atif," Bakshi said, thumbing the screen of his cell phone again. The screen was locked, but Bak-shi tapped in the code almost without looking. "How long has it been, six, seven years?"

"Something like that," Atif said.

"Fuck, time flies, man. Back then I was just small-time. A bit of a difference now, eh?" Bakshi gestured toward the over-furnished apartment. "I run a couple of beauty parlors: nails, bikini waxing, spray tanning, the whole works. I've got sixteen Thai girls working for me, and there's more on the way. Thai girls are clever, hardworking. No Swedes, too much like hard work, you know?" Bakshi grinned, and his fingers reached to-ward his phone again.

But you're still a little shit with big ears and an even bigger mouth, Atif thought.

"So, what can I do for you, Atif?" Bakshi repeated the trick with his phone a third time as he leaned back into the sofa. He adjusted his position slightly before spreading his legs, as if something was pressing against the small of his back. *Knife or pistol,* Atif thought. Probably the latter. One way of greeting an old friend. And probably the reason why it had taken him a while to open the door.

"Adnan," Atif said bluntly. "I want to know who ratted him out."

Bakshi pulled a face. "Yeah, awful, what happened to your brother." He scratched his head with exaggerated caution.

"But as far as I know, the boys were just unlucky. They ran into some plainclothes cops." He smiled, trying to look like he was being completely honest. He wasn't fooling anyone, least of all Atif.

"Who talked?" Atif asked again. His voice harsher this time. "Who's Janus?"

He could see the cogs turning in Bakshi's head. He was still fiddling with his cell phone, although he hardly seemed aware he was doing it. His fingers were tapping the code almost of their own accord, like a tic: 2558.

"Janus is a ghost," Bakshi said. "Everyone's scared of him, no one even likes saying his name out loud. A lot of people have been put away because of him, and he's probably sent a few to their graves as well."

"Adnan?" Atif wondered.

"That's one of the rumors," Bakshi said. "But I don't know any more than anyone else."

"So what do you know about Janus?"

Bakshi revealed his freshly whitened teeth again. "Janus has a price on his head. If I knew anything about him, I'd have said so long ago. And bought a house in Thailand, where it's always summer."

Bakshi paused, evidently detecting that Atif didn't believe him. He changed strategy and went on the offensive instead.

"Anyway, what makes you think you can just march into my

home and start asking a load of questions, just like that? You clearly have no idea who I work for! The last things I heard about you really weren't very flattering. You fell out with Sasha and fled abroad with your tail between your legs."

Bakshi grabbed the pack of cigarettes that was lying next to his phone, tapped out a Marlboro, and lit it. He took a couple of deep drags, blowing the smoke out toward Atif as his other hand went back to fiddling with his cell phone.

"Everyone said you'd changed, that you'd lost your edge. Even your little brother joined in." The man was staring at him, waiting for his reaction.

Atif got up slowly from the armchair. Bakshi was on his feet fast. He dropped the cigarette on the table and fumbled at the small of his back with his other hand. His put-on self-confidence crumbled and fear oozed from every pore.

"I see. Sorry you weren't able to help me, but thanks for your time." Atif stood there looking at the little man. He waited until Bakshi began to grin uncertainly before calmly walking toward the door.

"No problem, sorry I couldn't help," Bakshi said nonchalantly as Atif pulled on his coat and boots. "But you know how it is. Times have changed."

"Yes, so they say."

Atif left the apartment and walked down the stairs. He heard Bakshi lock the door behind him. He glanced at his watch and stood for a while in the hallway. Outside the door a little orange tractor was busy clearing the snow from the pavement.

Atif thought about his house, and the fragrant old mulberry tree in the back garden. He shut his eyes and tried to imagine the starry sky above him, but didn't really succeed. Precisely ten minutes later he went back up to the apartment and rang the doorbell.

"Sorry, forgot my hat. My ears are cold as hell," he muttered when Bakshi opened the door in some surprise.

"Sure." He turned around to check the hat rack and Atif took the chance to slip into the hall. The hairless cat was sitting in the middle of the marble floor next to its food bowl, licking its paws. When it noticed Atif it looked up, curled its top lip slightly, and showed its teeth.

Atif took two quick strides, grabbed the cat by the back of the neck, and held it up in the air. The animal spat and stuck its claws out.

"What the fuck are you doing?!" Bakshi said behind his back. Atif turned around.

"Now, listen very carefully, Bakshi. This cat is considerably smarter than you are." Atif could tell his voice had changed and had a completely different resonance now.

"W-what? What the hell are you talking about?" Bakshi looked confused. One hand was fumbling behind his back again.

"Do you know what sets cats apart from other hunters, Bakshi?" Atif didn't wait for an answer and lowered the cat until it was level with his face.

The animal was still hissing, trying in vain to reach him with its razor-sharp claws.

"Catch!" He threw the cat right in Bakshi's face. The man raised his hands in reflex. But not fast enough. The animal clawed frantically for a foothold, digging its claws into Bakshi's face and pink hairline. The man howled with pain but fell silent instantly when Atif kicked him in the groin.

Bakshi collapsed and ended up lying in a fetal position on the shiny hall floor. One foot was twitching spasmodically. Atif leaned over him and pulled out the pistol that was tucked into the waistband of his trousers. A rusty old Zastava with duct tape wrapped around its handle, probably an import from the Balkans. There had to be at least a twenty percent chance that it would explode in your hand if you fired it. Atif pulled out the cartridge, then slid the gun away across the floor. Then he discovered a clip sticking out of one of Bakshi's trouser pockets and fished out a dangerous-looking switchblade. A pistol and a knife. It was no wonder that the little rat dared to be a bit cocky.

"You see, Bakshi," he said, standing astride him, "sometimes cats kill just for the fun of it, because they enjoy it. Same thing with some people."

He grabbed hold of Bakshi's thin hair and opened the long, curved blade.

"That's just how they are. It's in their nature."

He shook the man's head, waiting for him to come around. But instead Bakshi started shaking. His eyes were rolling, his jaw cramping. Shit. He'd seen it happen a couple of times before. Perfectly healthy people who suffer severe pain or shock could end up having something like an epileptic fit. Atif let Bakshi's head drop to the floor. He used his pink shirt to wipe the blood and strands of hair from his fingers. He watched for a few seconds as the attack got steadily worse and Bakshi's body began bouncing about on the marble floor. Then he went back into the living room.

The cell phone was in the same place as before. He tapped in the number 2558 and looked up the most recently called numbers. If Bakshi knew anything about Adnan's death, he was bound to have called his contact and told him about Atif's visit, boasting about how he had coolly stared down Adnan's big brother. How tough he'd been when it came to protecting their secret.

The number at the top of the list belonged to someone Bakshi had named E.J. He had called the number just three minutes ago. In fact, Bakshi had tried to call the same number several times in a row during the past ten minutes. When Atif pressed Redial, he realized why.

"Hello, you have reached Erik Johansson's cell phone, please leave your name and number . . ."

So E.J. was Erik Johansson. Sounded like a perfectly ordinary guy.

Atif scrolled through the address book and soon realized

that almost all the contacts were listed by their initials. None of them meant anything to him. So he had a look at Bakshi's e-mails instead and read the last few messages. Most of them were from various women and were about practical matters concerning the beauty parlors. But there were a couple of exchanges with different girlfriends that consisted mainly of sexual innuendo. He typed in the name *Erik Johansson* and got one result immediately. An e-mail sent two days ago to the address Pitbull8U.

Yo Pasi

Hope the girls in Patpong are looking after you ☺ Say hi from me.

I had a bit of a look and what Erik J's mate told you is right. False alarm, in other words, so you're okay to come back home.

Business as usual.

Bfn,
B

Atif pulled out paper and pen from one of his coat pockets and wrote down Erik Johansson's phone number and the address of the e-mail in which his name had cropped up. Then he deleted all traces of his activity from the cell phone, put it back on the table, and went back out into the hall.

Bakshi was still lying on the floor. His body was still shaking, but not as violently as before. Little trickles of blood had run down over his face from his hairline, and the hairless cat was slowly and happily licking them off. The animal was so absorbed in its meal that it barely looked up when the front door closed behind Atif.

EIGHTEEN

"Mr. Thorning, the lawyer is here to see you."

"Okay, thanks, Jeanette! Ask him to wait a couple of minutes, then show him in."

Jesper Stenberg got up from his chair, took his jacket off the coat stand behind the door, and pulled it on. Time to get this out of the way. He had already got Jeanette to cancel his last two meetings with John Thorning. Playing at power politics, to show him that their roles had switched.

The day had started well, an interview with a lifestyle magazine about the challenge of combining life as a father, husband, and Minister of Justice. About Karolina's duties as the supporting wife. He always felt rather guilty whenever her career was mentioned. Or rather, the career she had given up for his sake. So that he could make their dreams come true.

Then, after the interview, a meeting with his press secretary and an update about social media. More than a hundred new followers every day, and more on the days when he posted or tweeted something. He needed to get better at that.

After that he was straight back to the Stone Age with a meeting with the National Head of Police. He hadn't even had to try. Old Rosengren wasn't stupid. He had realized long ago that his term wasn't going to be extended next year. He was already muttering about wanting to cut down on his workload. Spend more time with his grandchildren, go fishing, play a bit of golf, blah, blah, blah . . . Stenberg felt inclined to let the old man get away with it and couldn't see any immediate advantage in leaking the fact that Rosengren was actually being given the sack. Either way, next year he would be able to appoint someone of his own choosing to the top post within the national police force. Someone who, unlike Rosengren, had what was needed.

Well, one thing at a time. For the next half an hour, he had to concentrate on his meeting with John Thorning. His old boss and mentor seemed to have got over the tragedy of his daughter's suicide. Time for the obligatory visit where John Thorning would tactfully imply the importance of keeping on good terms with old friends, and offer him the benefit of his knowledge, experience, and contacts.

There was a short knock, then his secretary walked in.

"Mr. Thorning, Minister." She smiled and held the door open for the older man.

"John, good to see you! How are you?" Stenberg smiled his broadest heartfelt-but-still-professional smile. All of a sudden he felt inexplicably elated.

"Jesper. Karolina and the children are well, I hope?" The handshake was dry and firm, as always. But the expensive suit didn't fit as well as usual. John Thorning had lost weight, fast, and not in a good way. His shirt collar was loose, revealing folds of skin, his face was gray, and there were dark bags beneath his thin, rimless glasses. His steel-gray hair could have done with a trim a few weeks ago as well. The difference from the man's usually imposing appearance was striking.

"Sit yourself down, John!" He gestured to one of the arm-chairs on the other side of the desk. "So, how are you and Margareta?" Stenberg opened, in his most sympathetic tone of voice. But John merely shook his head.

"You're a busy man, Jesper, so we can skip the small talk and get straight down to business."

Stenberg was taken aback. "Er . . . of course, by all means."

"I want the investigation reopened."

"I'm sorry? I'm afraid I don't follow you, John."

John Thorning grimaced irritably. "The police investigation into Sophie's death. I want it reopened, as soon as possible."

Stenberg cleared his throat, trying to buy himself a couple of more seconds' thinking time. His brain had shifted into top gear.

"W-well, John, you know as well as I do that it doesn't work like that," he began. "A Swedish government minister can't simply—"

"With respect, Jesper, that's complete bullshit!"

John Thorning leaned over Stenberg's desk and jabbed a bony index finger at the polished mahogany. "You're the most senior lawyer in the country, Jesper. Head of the entire justice system. Do you mean to say that you can't get a tiny little police investigation reopened, without a lot of fuss about exceeding your authority?"

"Erm, well . . ." Stenberg was perfectly aware of how uncertain he sounded. Damn, this discussion really wasn't turning out the way he had expected. But he was saved by the gong.

"I've brought you some coffee," his secretary twittered with exaggerated cheeriness as she slowly put the tray down on the desk.

"Do you take milk and sugar, Mr. Thorning?"

The lawyer muttered something in response, clearly annoyed at the interruption. Then he leaned back in his chair and took the cup from her.

Stenberg shot Jeanette a look of gratitude. Her timing was perfect, as always. Almost as if she could hear the discussions going on in his office.

Jeanette handed him his coffee. Black, with just a teaspoon of milk, exactly the way he liked it.

"The cake is homemade," she added. "I hope you like it. If you need anything else, I'll be right outside." She addressed this last remark to Stenberg. He gave a short nod of thanks.

"I apologize for my little outburst, Jesper," John Thorning said the moment the door was closed. "I've been having trouble sleeping. Margareta is down in Marbella with some friends. The house is far too quiet."

He took a sip of coffee, then put the cup down on the delicate saucer.

"It's like this, Jesper." John Thorning took a deep breath. "The police officer who investigated Sophie's death made things very easy for himself. He got the prosecutor on his side early on—agreeing that they were dealing with a clear case of suicide. But there were several lines of inquiry that were never investigated properly. A neighbor heard raised voices earlier that evening, for instance."

John Thorning leaned forward slightly. "Not to mention the suicide note that was sent to me from her iPad. I must have read it a thousand times, and I can't escape the feeling that it was written by someone else. Little things, words that Sophie wouldn't have used. And the fact that she called me John rather than Daddy in the e-mail."

Stenberg was fighting hard to look neutral and even managed to squeeze out a couple of sympathetic nods. That fucking e-mail, he had sensed it was a step too far when he read the police report.

"But in spite of that," John Thorning said, tapping on the desk again, "the whole thing was written off as suicide. It's eating me up from inside, Jesper." He threw his arms out. "You knew Sophie, you worked together for years. She could certainly be a bit unstable. But suicidal?"

Stenberg realized he was expected to say something here. His old mentor was clearly in complete denial. Time for a small, tentative reality check. He took a deep breath and made an effort to sound thoughtful and sympathetic. It took a lot of work.

"John, obviously you have my very deepest sympathies. But, as you once said to me, it's never a good idea to let your feelings get in the way of your judgment. Sophie had problems, we both know that. All the facts indicate that—"

"Stop it, Jesper!" The older man held up his hand. "You forget who you're talking to, so stop tilting your head to one side and pretending to quote me. You're a father too, try to imagine if something happened to one of your girls. Wouldn't you do anything to make sure that justice was done?"

It was a clever trap, one that Stenberg had used many times in court. No matter how you answered, you were caught, so it was better not to say anything. Which was exactly what he did.

After a few endless seconds John Thorning stood up, put his hands on the desk, and leaned forward.

"You're clearly not going to make things easy for me, Jesper. Well, there are obviously other ways to get some clarity in this matter. I know a former police officer who runs his own security company. I could ask him to investigate the case for me. But then an interesting little problem arises."

Stenberg sat up straight.

"As you know, I'm also general secretary of the Bar Association, and generally regarded as your mentor," John Thorning said. "Someone who's part of Team Stenberg. Imagine the reaction if it leaked to the media."

He paused.

"That my faith in the police, the organization for which you are ultimately responsible, is so low that I choose to initiate a private investigation into my daughter's death." John Thorning smiled at Stenberg, a cold smile that was little more than a twitch at the corners of his mouth. Then he sat down and folded his arms.

Stenberg did his best to look unconcerned, as if the threat didn't really bother him. But the old bastard was right. It would harm his reputation if one of his most ardent supporters was seen to be dissatisfied. It would give rise to unnecessary speculation, maybe even lead others to reevaluate their support. And the Bar Association was a very influential body, capable of shaping opinion. He would need its support in the future. But political considerations were really secondary. It was considerably more troubling that an external investigator might end up snooping about in the case. All it would take was one witness whom the previous investigation had missed. Someone who

had spotted Stenberg down in the garage or out in the street, or
had seen his registration number or something else that could
link him to the scene.

In some ways the old man had done him a favor by coming
to see him first. It gave him an opportunity to take control of
the situation. Stenberg closed his eyes and discovered that his
heart was beating a bit faster. The way he had felt in the garage
came flooding back. The sense of sharpness. Of being completely in the moment.

"I hear what you're saying, John," he said slowly. "Naturally,
I want to help you. But a Swedish government minister isn't
permitted to intervene directly in operational matters. I'd risk
being called in by the Standing Committee on the Constitu-
tion. Anything of that sort wouldn't do either of us any favors."

John Thorning's expression hadn't changed.

"What I might be able to do is ask one of my more trust-
worthy colleagues to take a judicious look at the case. Go
through the investigation again and follow up any loose ends,
and hopefully that could give you the answers you think you're
missing," Stenberg went on.

He left his mouth open for a moment, waiting until the old
toad leaned forward.

"But in that case I would have to impose certain conditions,
John."

Stenberg leaned across the desk as well, his face barely a foot
and a half from his former mentor's. John Thorning nodded
almost imperceptibly. He thought he'd got his way, the way he
usually did. That he was still the one pulling the strings. He
hadn't realized that things had changed.

"Firstly." Stenberg held up his thumb. "You have to leave
everything to us. No private detectives running around compli-
cating matters, not now, and not later. Is that clear?"

Thorning went on nodding, slightly harder now.

"Secondly." Stenberg held up his index finger as well. "No
leaks. If I see the slightest hint in the media that some sort of

secret investigation is under way . . ." He paused long enough to be interrupted.

"Of course not, Jesper, this stays between us."

Bait taken, hook in mouth. Now to make sure the barbs were secure.

"Excellent. There's just one more condition, John, and it's nonnegotiable. I suggest that you think it through very carefully before replying."

"I'm listening, Jesper."

Stenberg stood up from his chair, walked around the desk, and sat down on one corner of it. He suddenly realized that he was enjoying the tension of this game. His heart was thudding in his chest, and the sense of being in the moment was almost total.

"If my people reach the same conclusions as the previous investigation," he said. "If all the evidence indicates that Sophie committed suicide, you have to accept that. Put the matter behind you and move on, no matter how painful it might be."

John Thorning opened his mouth to say something, but Stenberg was quicker.

"To put it plainly, John: no private investigations, no long interviews in the Sunday edition of *Dagens Nyheter*, no teary appearances on daytime chat shows. Nothing of that sort. None whatsoever. I want you to give me your word on that!"

John Thorning's lips narrowed to form a thin line. His eyes became slits. Stenberg was unconsciously holding his breath and felt he could almost taste the tension in the room.

"And if the reverse happens." The old man cleared his throat. "If you do find something to suggest that Sophie . . ."

Stenberg swallowed a barely noticeable hint of nervousness, looked John Thorning in the eye, and held out his hand for a firm handshake.

"If anything crops up, any evidence to suggest that someone else was involved in Sophie's death, I guarantee that we will identify that person and bring them to justice. You have my word on that, John."

NINETEEN

Sarac took a couple of cautious steps across the snow-covered cul-de-sac. He looked up at the wooden building, shading his eyes with his hands so as not to be blinded by the sharp sunlight. He must have slept like a log; he hadn't even noticed them getting onto the car ferry.

The air was crisp, the silence almost total. Just a few magpies calling from the tall pines around the old house. Nothing but snow and trees in all directions, with the exception of the little drive winding off toward the road no more than six hundred feet away. The house was one of the oldest on the island, a big, yellow archipelago villa, two stories, built in the early 1900s. There was a glazed veranda facing the garden, with leaded windows and plenty of ornate woodwork. The plot was huge, stretching all the way down to the water and the private jetty on the other side of the wooded hillock.

Molnar went up the steps to the porch, kicking away some of the snow before raising a loose plank. He fished out a key, unlocked the door, and went inside. Sarac slowly followed him. He was taking small steps to stop himself from slipping. Josef kept close behind him, ready to catch him if anything did go wrong.

Sarac stopped in the porch and inhaled the familiar smell of old wood and dampness. A torrent of memories overwhelmed him. Images of idyllic summers with Elisabeth and her children. Cloudless skies, trips in the rowboat, hammocks in the shade, and Evert Taube on the transistor radio. He longed intensely for those moments. But could they really have been as perfect as he remembered them? As beautiful and faultless? It was impossible to say.

"Come in, David." Molnar came back to the door. "After all, it is your house. Cold as hell, but I'll get the wood burner going. It'll soon warm up. You don't happen to know if there's any oil in the tank?"

"No idea," Sarac muttered.

"No, of course not, sorry." Molnar made a little apologetic gesture. "Can you sort some wood out, Josef?" he called over Sarac's shoulder. "The woodshed's around the back of the house." Molnar closed the front door behind them.

"Is this okay with you, David?"

Sarac nodded mutely.

"I was just thinking that this is a perfect place to lie low for a while. It's registered in your sister's name, and she's in Canada, so there's no link to you on any database," Molnar said. "Wallin and Dreyer's people aren't likely to find their way here for a while."

Nor anyone else either, Sarac found himself thinking.

They went into the large hallway. The staircase to the first floor swept up one of the walls. They turned left and followed the scrubbed wooden floor into the spacious rural kitchen. It all looked exactly as Sarac remembered, from the blue wooden panels along the bottom half of the walls to the stripes of the rag rug. Maybe his happy memories of this place weren't too inaccurate after all?

Molnar knelt down and started to fiddle with the big iron stove. He opened and closed the cast-iron doors at random, without really knowing what he was doing.

"There's some wood in that white box at the back, on the wall," Sarac said. "Just press that button on the side."

Molnar did as he was told and there was a rumble as a couple of blocks of wood fell into place. He tore up some newspaper and pushed it in through a hatch. He fiddled for a while with a long brass lighter, swearing out loud.

Sarac carried on through the kitchen into the next room, where the walls were all lined with built-in bookcases. Two worn velvet armchairs and a small table were the only pieces of furniture in the room. The room smelled of textiles, dust, and old books. Of Grandma. He resisted the temptation to sit down in her chair and turned right instead, into the big living room, which led to the veranda. The winter sun was shining in through the windows and he could see Josef's powerful frame moving about over by the little outhouses that lined one side of the property.

The snow-covered lawn was about a hundred and fifty feet long and sloped gently down toward the forest. Halfway down stood the rusting base of a flagpole, and at the far end of the lawn he could make out a few old fruit trees that almost blurred into the woods. The whole place was astonishingly beautiful, and he stood there just looking at it for a long while.

"Right, the stove's lit now." Molnar rubbed his face, inadvertently smearing a small speck of soot across his cheek. "I'll try the boiler in a bit. Shall we go back to the kitchen, or would you rather . . . ?" He gestured toward the large sofa that stood against one wall.

Sarac barely noticed him. He was having trouble taking his eyes from the view. There was something about the shadows at the edge of the forest that was absorbing his attention, but he couldn't put his finger on what it was.

"David?"

"The sofa," Sarac replied.

"Here you go." Molnar put a cell phone on the coffee table between them. "It's pay-as-you-go; the number's on the back. I programmed my cell as quick-dial number one, Josef's as two. Call if there's anything you need, no matter what. We'll make sure the fridge and freezer are full before we leave, same with the wood."

He gestured toward the outhouses. "And if Wallin and Dreyer ask, obviously we dropped you off at your apartment and have no idea where you went after that." Molnar smiled and winked at him, and Sarac did his best to return the smile.

"The most important thing right now is for you to take things easy and get some rest," Molnar went on. "Have you got enough drugs?"

"Hmm," Sarac muttered, not really listening. His eyes kept wandering back to the edge of the forest. The shadows down there seemed almost to have a life of their own. He suddenly remembered the room he had dreamed about. The photographs, the harsh expressions on the men's faces, the spiderweb linking them together.

"I think he's looking for me," Sarac said vaguely.

"Who?" Molnar said. "There are quite a few to choose from."

"Janus. I think he's trying to get hold of me." He heard the words come out of his mouth. Even so, it was like listening to a stranger.

"You're going to have to be a bit more specific, David." The new, sharper tone in Molnar's voice made Sarac wake up.

"Er, of course." He took a deep breath, trying to get his thoughts in order. "Well, someone tried to get into my apartment last night. Someone who had keys."

"Did you see who it was?"

Sarac shook his head. "The security chain was on; all I saw was an arm through the gap in the door."

"But you think it was Janus? And that he's got keys to your apartment?"

"Mmm," Sarac mumbled. He could hear how uncertain he sounded. "And someone had searched the apartment as well, it was a hell of a mess."

"And what makes you think it's Janus?" Molnar said. "Your address isn't listed anywhere; we never tell our sources where we live. Never, ever, that's one of the most basic security regulations. You'd never disregard that, would you?"

Sarac tried to think. He wondered about mentioning what had happened at the hospital. The tobacco man who had talked about an agreement, the man in the tight surgeon's gown taking a shortcut to his ward. The well-used meth pipe he'd found in his own apartment. Something about the look on Molnar's face told him that wouldn't be a good idea. Not until he himself was sure about what was going on. About what was real, and what was just nonsense cluttering up his damaged brain.

Paranoia is a fairly common side effect of a stroke. Who'd told him that, Dr. Vestman? No, it was his care assistant, what was her name again? Damn!

Sarac suddenly realized he felt ashamed. Ashamed of his confused chatter, his hopeless physical condition. And other things, things he couldn't really remember.

"Peter, I really don't know. Sorry, everything's a bit of a mess right now." He closed his eyes and pressed his fingertips to his eyelids as if to push back the headache. Molnar studied him carefully and seemed to be thinking about something.

"Okay, I understand. You've been through a terrible time lately, the sort of thing that would break most people. You really don't have to apologize. I'll get a couple of men watching your apartment from this evening. We're extremely keen to get hold of Janus as soon as possible."

Sarac nodded and tried to think of some way to change the subject of conversation. He had questions, loads of questions. He had pretty much two years' worth of memories to try to reconstruct. But he didn't know where to begin. All of a sudden everything felt so huge, so overwhelming.

"The car crash," he finally said. "Bergh seemed to think it wasn't an accident. That my crash was somehow connected to the missing backup list. Was that why there was a Securitas guard at the hospital?"

Molnar nodded. "Considering what's at stake with the Janus affair, Bergh probably just wanted to err on the side of caution. But, like I said, we got there just after you crashed. There wasn't anyone else in the tunnel."

"What about my cell phone, then?" Sarac said. "What happened to that? It wasn't in my locker at the hospital. You said I called you from the car just before it happened."

Molnar shrugged.

"Missing. It was probably somewhere inside the car. The wreckage . . ." He paused and rephrased what he was about to say. "The car was totaled, there was hardly anything left of it. We were sure you . . . Well, things didn't look good. Your phone was the last thing it would have occurred to us to look for."

"The list of calls, did that come up with anything useful?" Once again Sarac was surprised at himself. The question was entirely logical, but he had no intention of asking it until it popped out of his mouth. Some parts of his brain seemed able to function perfectly well on their own.

The same thought seemed to have occurred to Molnar, because one corner of his mouth twitched.

"Yes, we got the list. The last call you made was to my cell, like I said. Before that you called a whole load of pay-as-you-go numbers that we haven't managed to identify."

"Can I see it? The list of calls, I mean. I might recognize some of the numbers."

Molnar frowned. "Sure, but do you really think now's the right time for that? Wouldn't it be preferable for you to concentrate on getting better?"

The feeling came out of nowhere, without the slightest warning. Sarac couldn't identify what had triggered it. The look on Molnar's face hadn't changed, and as far as he could tell his tone of voice was exactly the same. Even so, Sarac couldn't shake the feeling, and it was growing stronger with each passing second. There was more information, something connected to the crash and his cell phone. Something Molnar didn't want to reveal.

TWENTY

"Wallin, Jesper Stenberg here. Have you had a chance to look at what I was asking about?"

"Minister of Justice, good morning! Oh yes, the matter was investigated by the crime unit of the City Police, just as I thought. But I've asked a colleague to take a closer look at it, and to come up with a good reason that shouldn't raise any suspicions. I'm expecting to get a report between Christmas and New Year's."

"Good. We can rely on his discretion?"

"Hers . . ."

"Sorry?"

"Her discretion. It's a woman, Detective Inspector Julia Gabrielsson. She's currently training to be a senior officer and has just done a six-month exchange with the FBI. Young, ambitious, exactly the sort of colleague you tend to like. And reliable as well."

• • •

Detective Inspector Julia Gabrielsson stood in the hall as she slipped the key ring back into her jacket pocket. Apart from the faint sound of traffic in the streets below, the apartment was completely silent. She had read the report of the preliminary investigation that morning. Nothing particularly odd. A woman with a documented history of mental problems and a bathroom cabinet stuffed full of antidepressants decides to open a window and jump out. Suicide note written on her iPad and sent by e-mail, all very 2013.

The postmortem identified a mass of injuries that were fundamentally all consistent with a fall from a considerable height. And no injuries that weren't. The stomach contents were the usual farewell cocktail of strong spirits and tablets.

There had been nothing odd at the scene either. The door of the apartment was securely locked, no signs of a break-in, nor anything else to indicate that anyone else had been present. One of the neighbors had apparently heard agitated voices from the apartment, but because the man had, by his own admission, drunk at least a whole bottle of wine and four shots, his statement was hardly very solid. He had also seemed a bit too talkative, the sort of person who might well adjust his memory to be amenable to the police.

There was really only one conclusion: if Sophie's dad hadn't been one of the most well-known lawyers in Stockholm, the case would have been buried and forgotten and she could be getting on with considerably more important matters. But Oscar Wallin wanted to do John Thorning a favor and had called her in. Obviously she had said yes; Oscar was aiming high, right for the top, and she was thinking of tagging along.

"All you have to do is take a look. See if there's anything odd. I'd really appreciate it. No rush at all, you can have a look next week." But of course she hadn't wanted to wait that long. It was just as well to get going.

She pulled a couple of blue shoe covers from her jacket pocket and put them on. Then she put on a pair of thin, black latex gloves and took a short walk around the apartment to get her bearings. Hall, kitchen, living room, two bedrooms. All furnished in the same minimalist, impersonal, and presumably incredibly expensive industrial style. Polished gray concrete floors, tubular steel furniture, the occasional photograph. Most of them showed the apartment's former occupant herself in various exotic locations. All the pictures were black-and-white, not a hint of color anywhere.

At the far end was the study, where Sophie Thorning had

climbed over the railing of the French balcony. The chair was still there. Julia resisted the temptation to go over to the window and look down at the street, and went back to the front door instead. No signs of a break-in, just like the preliminary investigation said, which was hardly surprising. The door led directly to the elevator shaft, and there were only two ways of getting up to Sophie's apartment. You could either do what she had just done and insert the right key under the appropriate name inside the elevator, or ring the bell and be let up by the occupant of the apartment.

Julia went into the larger of the two bedrooms. She stood for a while before opening the door to the walk-in closet. Row upon row of clothes, arranged with minute precision. A whole wall of nothing but shoes. Louboutin, Jimmy Choo, Manolo Blahnik. Expensive labels for a spoiled little girl. One section of wall was covered by drawers, and she started from the bottom. Underwear, tights, various other accessories, nothing out of the ordinary. Even the sex toys in the fourth drawer were hardly a shock. A couple of dildos, handcuffs, a set of straps and belts, and a few other bits and pieces. Slightly more advanced than the average housewife's *Fifty Shades* collection. Sophie Thorning evidently like playing rough. Presumably not the sort of thing she ever mentioned to her doting daddy.

The huge bed looked freshly made. Black sheets, gray duvet cover. Six big pillows, the same color as the duvet, arranged at the head of the bed. Something about the way the bed had been made caused Julia to frown. She ran a hand over the fabric. The cover and sheets were stretched tight, not a single crease. The fold from the mangle ran neatly across the duvet cover. Perfectly straight lines, military precision.

Julia took hold of the duvet and lifted one corner, then bent over and sniffed the fabric. It smelled freshly laundered. She pulled the duvet off, turned the pillows upside down. Nothing, not the slightest little strand of hair or flake of skin, which ought to have been very visible on the black sheet.

Julia went back into the closet and carried on into the spacious bathroom. Thick towels were hanging next to the washbasin and on the drying rack over by the shower. They were all smooth and clean and showed no sign of having been used.

The linen basket was in a discreet alcove in one corner, hidden behind a curtain. Next to it was a set of basket drawers. She pulled everything out and found a bit of dirty wash, but no towels, and no bedclothes. Not that it necessarily meant anything. Sophie Thorning probably had a cleaner, so maybe laundry and bed making were part of the deal? But Sophie had died on a Friday night, and how often did anyone have cleaners over the weekend? She made a mental note to call and check. There were a couple of more details that were even easier to check.

She left the bathroom and went out to the large, open kitchen. The sink was empty, no unwashed glasses or cutlery. Hardly unexpected, considering how tidy and minimalist Sophie seemed to prefer things. The dishwasher was concealed behind one of the white kitchen cupboards. She opened it and pulled out the two baskets. Empty, both of them. So how often did that ever happen? Usually you managed to build up a few things that hung around waiting on the countertops. A couple of glasses, some cutlery, the sort of thing you then put in the machine as soon as you'd emptied it. At least that was how it worked for her and Nilla.

She opened the kitchen cupboards and studied the even rows of differently sized glasses. One deviation caught her attention. There were two whiskey glasses missing. One of them was in the inventory; it had been on the desk in the study. Analysis had shown that it had contained the same sort of whiskey that was found in Sophie's stomach. But where was the other glass? She sniffed the air. That faint, slightly acrid smell could very well be whiskey. A dropped glass, perhaps?

Julia took out her flashlight and shone it past the kitchen cupboards. She discovered some tiny yellow stains on one of the polished walls. She had a look in the trash can, but that too was empty.

The vacuum cleaner was in one of the hall cupboards, and after a bit of effort she managed to get the lid off. The bag was brand-new, but whoever had changed it probably wouldn't have bothered to change the filter. She carefully loosened it, then shone her flashlight at it from the side. A faint shimmer from tiny fragments of crystal made her break into a satisfied smile.

She returned to the kitchen, lay down flat on her stomach, and shone the flashlight across the smooth, gray concrete floor. There was a light, even layer of dust on the floor, which was only to be expected. The apartment hadn't been cleaned since the death. But apart from that there was nothing, not even the tiniest crumb. Except . . . Something stood out against the light. An uneven little deviation in one of the cracks in the concrete under the island unit. She wriggled closer, careful not to take her eyes off it. She couldn't help smiling when she realized she had been right. A tiny splinter of glass, or crystal, to be more accurate. A splinter that, unlike the rest of the glass, hadn't been sucked up by the vacuum cleaner and which had therefore not been removed from the apartment along with the trash, towels, and used bedclothes.

She got up from the floor. She couldn't be sure, not until she had checked the cleaning company's timetable. But her gut feeling told her that she was onto something.

The apartment had been cleaned, carefully and methodically, by someone who knew exactly what he or she was doing. Probably the same person who had been in the bed, used the towels, and drank from the shattered glass. The same person the neighbor thought he had heard earlier that evening. The only question was, who?

She held the splinter of glass carefully between her thumb and index finger and shone the flashlight on it from all angles. There was a hint of color in the reflection. A tiny touch of red, barely visible without a magnifying glass.

It looked like blood.

TWENTY-ONE

Atif had rung the doorbell, peered through the mail slot, and tried to detect any sign of life from inside the apartment. But all he had been able to make out were a dark hall and a stale, slightly acrid smell that was hard to identify. There was no one home and, to judge by the heap of mail on the hall floor, it had been a while since anyone had been there.

Bakshi had grown nervous when he had raised the subject of Adnan and the robbery. He had leaped at his phone and called Erik Johansson the moment the door had closed. But he hadn't got through. So, why was he calling? Presumably because Erik J. was involved, and Bakshi wanted to warn him, or boast about how cool he'd been, staring down Atif and not giving anything away. No matter which, the trail pointed in one direction—toward Erik Johansson.

The cell number had been a dead end. No results in any search engine, which either meant that the number was un-listed or that it was a pay-as-you-go phone with no registered owner. He'd tried calling the number a few times from his own pay-as-you-go phone, but kept getting Erik's voice mail. According to the telephone directory, there were more than three hundred Erik Johanssons in Stockholm alone, which was hardly a number he could work with.

So instead he had followed up the e-mail in which Bakshi discussed Erik J. with someone called Pasi. He had googled the e-mail address, Pitbull8U, and had discovered that it belonged to a one-man business registered to a Pasi Arvo Lehtonen, who was supposed to live behind this very door at number 62 Roslagsgatan.

Atif would have preferred to dig out Bakshi again and squeeze him until he revealed what he knew. But Bakshi was gone, probably hiding at one of his girlfriends', with his pistol under his pillow. Or else he'd left the city. Either way, his apartment was dark and shut up.

So right now Pitbull-Pasi was Atif's best lead, but judging by the available evidence, the man hadn't had time to act on Bakshi's advice that it was okay to come home. So what was Pitbull so worried about that—judging by the e-mail—it had made him leave the country? Did it have any connection to Adnan's death? There was only one person who could answer that.

Atif stood up and brushed the dust from his knees. A little farther down the corridor the door to another apartment slowly opened. An elderly woman emerged, pushing a check-patterned shopping trolley. When she caught sight of Atif she stopped and seemed to be considering going back inside.

"Police," Atif said quickly, pulling out his ID and holding it in the air. The woman was more than six yards away and, from the look of her thick-lensed glasses, would hardly be able to see any details beyond the little sleeve and shiny badge. He was right; the woman relaxed at once.

"Oh, what a relief," she said. "I thought you were one of them, Officer . . ." She nodded toward the door behind him.

"That's actually why I'm here. I was hoping to have a word with your neighbor, Mr. Lehtonen," Atif said.

"Yes, I can understand that," the woman said. Her voice was surprisingly melodic. "There's a lot of coming and going in that apartment. Funny people."

"Hmm." Atif made an effort to sound polite and respectful. "You don't happen to know if he's at home, madam?"

"No, he's probably away for Christmas, like most young people these days. My grandchildren usually go to Thailand, but I could never do that. Christmas without snow and cold wouldn't be the same."

Atif nodded. He put his hand in his pocket and took out a pen and a piece of paper. "Could I possibly ask you for a small favor, madam? You see, I really would like to get hold of him, ideally as soon as he reappears."

· · ·

Sarac was already feeling better. Even though he was spending all his time indoors, it was as if the air out on the island was making his head feel clearer. He had slept on the sofa in the living room, curling up in the green sleeping bag Molnar had left. A whole night of unbroken, dreamless sleep.

He would much rather have gone out and tried to get down to the edge of the forest to see what it was down there among the trees that held such a strong attraction for him. But he realized that in his current state he was hardly going to be able to wade through the snow. Instead he had gone for a walk inside the big house. His most recent memories of the place were probably from two summers ago. Elisabeth, Jeff, and the children had come over from Canada, and they had tried to work out what to do with the old house. Jeff had suggested in his usual tactful way that perhaps they ought to sell it, because the cost of renovating it would be too high. But he had managed to persuade his sister to wait, and said he could do most of the work himself and that it wouldn't be too expensive. After all, the house was part of their childhood. The last thing they had left.

The upstairs was exactly as he remembered it. There was a large open landing at the top of the stairs, facing the entrance hall down below. A corridor with two small bedrooms on either side led to the upper floor of the veranda. But the roof of the veranda and some of the windows were covered by large tarpaulins, which combined with the dirty windows made the whole upper floor seem dark and gloomy. The veranda was full of building materials. Sawhorses, rolls of insulation, tar paper, a couple of large gas cylinders, and a saw. The stack of planks had turned yellow and seemed to have been sitting there for a while.

Sarac opened one of the bedroom doors. He found a neatly made bed, a ribbed chair, and a little bedside table. The smell of damp fabric was unmistakable. In one wall there were two small doors with brass catches instead of door handles. One turned out to conceal a small wardrobe, the other led to a little bathroom.

Sarac turned on the tap in the basin. He felt the metal vibrating in his hand before it started to jerkily spit out discolored water. He let it run for a while until the water was clear and constant. Molnar seemed to have got the boiler going in the basement, because the water gradually heated up, or at least became tepid.

He turned the tap off and went back to the landing. He looked down toward the front door. The feeling was getting stronger with each passing second, strengthened by the peeling walls and damp-stained ceiling. The whole of this imposing old building was in an inexorable state of decay.

His stomach was rumbling and he suddenly remembered that he hadn't eaten any breakfast. Josef had stocked the fridge up and he pulled out a few things at random. He sat down at the kitchen table while he waited for the coffee to filter through. He put his right hand on the table and wiggled his fingers. They felt better now, considerably less spongy than before. His right leg too, even if he still needed to use the crutch. If it carried on like this, he'd soon be ready to go back to work. The moment he thought that, it occurred to him that he no longer had a job, at least not properly. The property store was a final stop, somewhere you dumped people you couldn't put anywhere else. People who were no longer fit for good, honest police work.

He gulped and carefully scratched his woolly hat. The bandage was gone; the only thing he'd kept was the plaster covering the hole in his skull. He had touched it, gingerly feeling his way to the edge of the bone. Underneath, his brain was still more or less unprotected. But he still didn't seem to be able to get at the things it was hiding. He had to try to make sense of things. Find a way to fill in the gaps and show that the people trying to push him out of the way were wrong.

He hadn't yet managed to shake off the flashes of memory that had arisen in Molnar's car. The room, the men with the harsh looks on their faces. The red lines that linked them, like a spiderweb with that symbol in the middle. A pattern that both scared and intrigued him. But another feeling was starting to develop. He had felt it back in his hospital bed, but his conversation with Molnar had made it accelerate. Shame. He was ashamed of something, not just the pathetic state he was in or the fact that he was being left out in the cold, but something else. Something he had done, something unforgivable.

Who was the man in the snow-covered car, the one whose death he had witnessed? Who had fired a bullet into the back of the man's head in cold blood like that? Someone he knew, someone he worked with? Maybe even Janus? Was that why Molnar hadn't wanted to show him the list of calls, because he didn't really trust him? Did he doubt Sarac's objectivity?

The unmistakable sound of a car door closing roused him from these circular thoughts. He twisted around and looked out through the window, and saw a little red Golf with some bad patches of rust parked out in the drive. He hadn't heard it arrive, presumably because the snow had muffled the sound of the engine. It looked familiar, but he couldn't quite place it.

He could see the driver's back heading toward the front door. Sarac stood up, his heart racing. No one but Molnar and Josef knew he was here. So who was the person outside the house?

He pulled the kitchen drawers open, trying but failing to find some sort of weapon. There was a knock on the door, firm, decisive, as if the person outside had no desire to be kept waiting. Sarac crept into the hall, pressing against the wall and trying to peer out the window to the porch. But all he could see was a thick padded jacket. In the corner, just behind the door, he discovered a baseball bat with long, sharp spikes hammered into it. Was it his? He didn't recognize it. What would have made him construct such a terrifying weapon?

There was another knock, harder this time. Sarac hesitated for a moment. Then he snatched up the baseball bat, turned the lock, and yanked the door open. The person on the porch didn't seem surprised and slowly looked him up and down. Then pointed at the spiked club in Sarac's hand.

"We have to stop meeting like this, David." Natalie smiled.

"W-what the hell are you doing here?!" Sarac tried to hide the baseball bat behind his back.

"What you really mean is: Thank you, Natalie, for waiting outside Police Headquarters for three hours yesterday, all for no reason. And thanks for going back home and tidying up my squalid junkie's apartment while you were waiting in vain for me to show up. And a particularly big thank-you for coming out to the archipelago to deliver my medication." Natalie smiled again and waved a bag from the drugstore.

Sarac shook his head. "H-how did you find your way here? I mean, who, the house . . . ?" His thoughts were getting tangled up.

"I smell coffee," Natalie said, pointing toward the kitchen. "If you invite me in for a cup, I'll tell you."

      •   •   •

"Nice place, must have cost a fair bit." Natalie looked around the kitchen, clearly impressed.

"It belonged to my grandmother. My sister and I inherited it," Sarac muttered as he fumbled with the coffee cups. To his own surprise, he realized he was pleased to see Natalie. A normal person in the middle of the nightmare surrounding him.

"Elisabeth Matilda Sarac, now Wilson. Emigrated to Canada in 2001. The house is in her name, not yours. Wise move if you want to avoid capital gains tax." Natalie dug about in the bag from the drugstore. "You medication was on the kitchen table in the apartment, so when morning came and you still hadn't shown up I started to get worried. There was a key ring hanging in the hall with the word *Skarpö* written on it, so I guessed there was a summerhouse out here. My friend in the Tax Office did a bit of looking. Your records are confidential, so at first he didn't find anything. Then he tried looking for other people with the same surname."

"And you found my sister, and then this address?" Sarac noticed how his words suddenly sounded rather slurred.

"Yep, all I had to do was find the number of a talkative neighbor and ask if there was any smoke coming from the chimney, and bingo!"

Sarac sat down at the table and gently pinched the bridge of his nose, then his lips. His face felt strangely numb.

"When did you last take your migraine medication?" Natalie said.

"Yesterday, I think," Sarac mumbled. "Unless it was the day before yesterday . . ."

TWENTY-TWO

There was a glint of light from the peephole, then Atif heard the rattle of the security chain. He noted that she had used all the locks.

"Come in!" Cassandra said. She was trying to make her voice sound firm, but he immediately noticed the fear that lay hidden beneath her composed exterior. As usual, he could smell it, right through the heavy cloud of her perfume.

He stepped into the hall and closed the front door behind him.

"Lock the door!"

Atif did as he was told, then waited for her to invite him further inside the apartment. But instead they remained standing in the hall.

"Tindra?" he said.

"She's asleep."

He nodded, trying not to show his disappointment. He waited for her to tell him what this was about. Then he realized that she was going to make him ask.

"You wanted me to come around as fast as I could. Well, here I am." Atif shrugged his shoulders.

He had called Cassandra a couple of days before, to tell her he was staying in Sweden for a bit longer, and had given her his number. She hadn't sounded pleased, and pointedly hadn't invited him to spend Christmas with them, as he might have hoped. But, little more than an hour ago, she had called and asked him to come around. She'd said it was urgent.

Cassandra put her hand in the back pocket of her jeans,

pulled out a folded piece of paper, and waved it in front of his face.

"What the fuck is this, Atif? Huh?!" Her voice had risen almost to falsetto.

He took the piece of paper. A Christmas card with a cheerful Santa Claus on the front. Someone must have dropped it on the ground, because there was a clearly visible shoe print on the back. The marks from a heavy sole that reminded him of his own military boots. Inside the card was the usual printed greeting, *Merry Christmas and Happy New Year,* and beneath it some handwritten lines in black ink.

> *Hello Tindra.*
> *Hope you've been a good girl this year. Because you know what happens if you aren't good, don't you?*
> *Just ask your Uncle Atif!*
>
> > *Best wishes,*
> > *Santa*

"It was on her shelf," Cassandra hissed. "On her fucking shelf at preschool. Get it? She was over the moon, thought the card really was from Santa. That he'd written to her and her uncle. I didn't know what to say."

Atif nodded; he knew exactly what had happened. He could see it in front of him. The doors of the preschool were usually left unlocked; you could just walk in. Don't ask the staff, ask one of the kids which way to go. Children always knew all about one another and were useless as witnesses. The rest was easy. Just leave a little greeting. It didn't really matter what, the message would be clear enough. *We know where the most valuable thing in your life is, and we can get at it whenever we want to.*

But for the first time in his life he was on the other side. He ticked the feelings off, one by one: fear, anger, impotence, desire for revenge. Then he forced himself to set them aside. Someone had made a mistake, someone who was so afraid of his involvement that they had chosen to get at him through Tindra. All in good time; whoever it was would pay for that mistake.

"It's all your fault, Atif!"

He didn't answer, just stood there quietly and calmly while she went on shouting at him.

"We'd just got away from all that shit. We'd started to live a normal life."

He could see she was thinking of saying something else but bit her lip instead. Then she took a deep breath and seemed to calm down slightly.

"Do you even know what a normal life is, Atif?" She pulled a face. "It's a life where your cell phone doesn't ring in the middle of the night, a life where the police don't kick your door in every time a security van has been held up. Where you don't have to lie to your six-year-old about what Daddy really does."

Atif said nothing.

"A normal life is where you don't have to feel scared the whole time." She stared at him, seemed to be waiting for him to say something.

"Is that the sort of life Abu Hamsa's offering?"

"W-what?" Her anger had melted away, replaced by uncertainty. Maybe even a bit of shame. But she soon recovered.

"I don't know what you're talking about," she said. She almost made it sound as if it were true.

"Tell me about the gym, Cassandra."

She closed her lips tight and glared at him for a few seconds.

"Like I said before, Adnan and his friend Dino were going to open the gym together. Then Adnan messed things up, like he always did. He ended up in a load of debt and needed money fast. Dino bought him out, actually did him a favor. But that's not how Adnan saw it. So when the gym opened and started to do well, he caused a big row, claiming Dino had defrauded him. He stormed in one day waving a pistol."

"So it was war?" Atif asked.

Cassandra shook her head. "No, thank God it never got that far. Adnan and his guys walked around armed the whole time, they even had plans to pick Dino up, which was fucking ridiculous. Dino's got plenty of friends, the sort of people you don't pick fights with."

"So what happened?" Atif asked.

"Abu Hamsa intervened and negotiated a deal. Adnan and his men agreed to do that holdup. His cut of the takings was going to buy back his share of the gym, for the same amount he got from Dino."

"But instead Adnan ended up in the mortuary," Atif said. "Killed by the police because someone ratted on him. Someone who told them what was going on."

Cassandra said nothing and started pulling the cellophane from a pack of cigarettes instead. Atif looked at the Christmas card again, turning it over and examining the boot print.

"Adnan and I had already pretty much split up." She lit a cigarette. It took her several attempts. "After things went wrong with Dino he hardly ever slept at home. When the cops turned up to tell me he was dead, I hadn't seen him in over three weeks." Her voice suddenly sounded sad.

"I know it sounds mad, but the fact is I almost felt . . ." Cassandra bit her lip.

Relieved, Atif thought. *You felt relieved that Adnan was dead, but just like me you can't bring yourself to say the word, because you know it's wrong. That it makes you a bad person.*

"Don't get me wrong, I loved Adnan." Her voice resumed something of its earlier harshness. "But no matter how much we tried, it just wasn't working anymore." She took a deep drag and blew the smoke toward the ceiling. "I didn't want to tell you when you arrived. I thought it didn't really matter how things were between us toward the end. Adnan was still dead."

"I understand," Atif said. And realized that he actually meant it.

He was suddenly struck by how tired Cassandra looked.

Tired and worried. She was still pretending to be tough, but recent events were taking their toll.

"So what happens now? About that . . . ?" She nodded toward the Christmas card.

"I need to get hold of someone," he said. "As soon as that's done, I'll be gone."

"Is this about Adnan?"

Atif didn't answer, but she seemed to realize it anyway.

"And what do Tindra and I do in the meantime?" she asked.

"Is there anywhere you can go? Some relative, anyone like that? Somewhere no one would think of looking for you, at least not immediately?" Atif said.

Cassandra thought for a moment.

"My aunt. She's got a farm outside Leksand with her new husband. She's been going on at me about visiting," she said.

Atif nodded.

"Leksand sounds good." He felt in his inside pocket and pulled out his wallet. He took out eight smooth five-hundred-kronor notes and put them on the little hall bureau.

"That's all I've got on me," he said. What he didn't tell her was that it was also the last of his savings. From now on he'd have to use his credit card to cover expenses.

Cassandra snatched up the money. He quickly put his hand over hers and held it down.

"Cassandra," he said in a low voice. "It's probably a good idea not to let Abu Hamsa know about this."

TWENTY-THREE

"Here's my report." Julia Gabrielsson put the blue folder down on the table between them. Oscar Wallin left it where it was. He tried to go on eating his lunch.

"I imagine he'll be pleased," she added with a smile.

"Who?" Wallin said.

"John Thorning. He's the person we're doing a favor, isn't he?"

Wallin looked down, cut a piece of beef, and popped it in his mouth. He chewed it slowly, then wiped his mouth with his napkin.

"And exactly what do you mean by *pleased*, Julia?"

"It looks very likely that there was someone else in the apartment that evening. Someone who either had their own keys or who was let in by Sophia Thorning." She paused, waiting for his question.

"And how do we know that?"

"Good, honest police work. The sort of thing the first detective ought to have done." She couldn't resist a smile. "All the towels had been changed, the bedclothes too. There were no dirty dishes, not so much as a single used glass. Even the bag in the vacuum cleaner was brand-new."

"So what?" Wallin shrugged. "Sophie Thorning must have had a cleaner. They could have changed the sheets and towels while they were at it."

"Nope!" Julia held a thumb in the air. "One: against all the odds, little Sophie seemed to want to take care of her own dirty laundry herself. The cleaning company didn't do that."

She added her forefinger. "Two: her apartment was last cleaned on the Tuesday of that week. As you know, Sophie died on the night between Friday and Saturday. There's nothing to indicate that she slept or showered anywhere except at home. She even had a visit from her younger brother that week. He says he's sure Sophie was sleeping at home. He even remembered using the towels in the bathroom. Blue, not the white ones that are hanging in there now."

Julia paused to let her words sink in.

"In other words, someone's cleared the whole lot out," she went on. "Someone who made a real effort to remove all traces of their own presence."

"Hang on a minute, Julia." Oscar Wallin put his knife and fork down. "I seem to recall that I asked you to take a discreet look at Sophie Thorning's apartment, not start phoning members of her family and questioning them."

Julia shrugged.

"Seeing as it was Daddy Thorning who wanted the case looked at again, I didn't think it would do any harm. Besides . . ." She paused again, keen to drag the moment out a little longer.

". . . I know who the mysterious visitor was. Or I soon will," she added.

"I'm listening," Wallin said tonelessly.

"There was one whiskey glass missing," Julia said, trying to work out why he didn't sound anywhere near as impressed as he should. "And I found tiny pieces of crystal in the filter of the vacuum cleaner. Broken glass. After a bit of crawling about on the floor, I found a splinter of glass with blood on it in a crack in the floor. I sent it down to the National Forensics Lab in Linköping this morning. Sadly it doesn't work the way it does on television, and it's the holidays too, so we'll have to wait a couple of weeks for the results."

She stopped and waited for him to say something. But Wallin just sat there looking at her, nowhere near as impressed as she had expected he would be. She was starting to get the impression that she'd done something wrong.

"I mean," she said, mostly to fill the silence, "obviously it could easily be Sophie Thorning's own blood." She detected a hint of doubt in her own voice and cleared her throat to get rid of it. "But I'm almost one hundred percent sure that it isn't—" She broke off midsentence, before her insecurity had time to reappear. By now Wallin ought to have been doing a Mexican wave in his delight at her findings. Instead he was just sitting there, cold as a fish.

"Of course a bit of blood obviously doesn't mean that some-one killed Sophie Thorning," she went on, rather too quickly. "But there's every reason to investigate the matter further. Even the sleepwalkers at the City Police ought to able to manage that. DNA tests of people in Sophie's vicinity ought to be enough. Friends, family, workmates."

• • •

Sarac hadn't managed to get out of bed for two days. He lay rolled up like a larva inside the sleeping bag on top of one of the musty beds upstairs as he tried to ride out the migraine.

Every so often Natalie would bring him a tray of food, but whenever he tried to eat anything he ended up clutching the toilet, listening to the echo of his own retching on the porcelain.

He spent most of the time asleep. Although sleep wasn't really the right word for it. It was more like a strange state be-tween dozing and being awake.

He could hear the creaking of the old house as the heat of the radiators and chimney made its wooden fibers dry out and contract—twisting in torment, the way his brain was. It was al-most as if the house were trying to tell him something. Sounds from the ground floor made their way up through the flues, following the warm air from the stove up through the house. They echoed through the old ventilation pipes and eventually emerged as barely audible whispers from the little rectangular air vent in the floor by his bed. Voices from the transistor radio in the kitchen. Music.

I owe everything
Debts I can't escape till the day I die.

He let himself be rocked along with it. Drifted in and out.

"It's all about confidence, David," someone whispered right next to his ear. The voice made him open his eyes. His heart was suddenly beating faster. He tried to raise his head and look around the dimly lit room. But his head felt as if it were made of concrete; he couldn't move it. Then he noticed a faint movement. The room had slowly, infinitely slowly, started to rotate counterclockwise. Then faster. It made him feel suddenly weightless. He stared at the air vent, trying to see beyond the dusty grille. Down into the darkness.

"Everything has a price," the voice down there whispered. "A secret wish, a fear, or a desire so strong that we're prepared to betray absolutely everything we hold sacred. If someone confides their deepest secret to you, you can make them do almost anything."

The room was spinning faster now, and the floor and ceiling had swapped places. He grabbed hold of the edge of the mattress, trying to cling on. Part of him wanted nothing more than to close his eyes and spare his brain all these impressions. The music came back.

But he went on struggling, trying as hard as he could. He knew there was more. If only he listened hard enough.

"Like a spiderweb," the voice went on. "Tiny silken threads, each one a work of art in itself. Together they make up something incredibly beautiful. And deadly. But you need to be careful, David. Sometimes you can get too far into the web and forget who you are."

The room was rotating faster and faster, the movement so violent that he felt his legs lift from the mattress. Then his stomach, and his chest, until in the end he was sticking straight out from the bed. Ceiling, walls, window, everything was spinning wildly, making him lose sight of the air vent. He felt his grip on the mattress loosening and screwed his eyes tightly, tightly shut. He was thrown out into the darkness.

I owe everything
Debts I can't escape till the day I die.

Far away he could hear Bergh's voice. "I can protect him, protect you . . ." Then the man in the hospital, whose gold tooth was glinting in the darkness. "An agreement is an agreement, David," the man said, as the smell of cigar smoke spread through the room. "You know what the consequences will be if you break your side. Your job, your career, your whole life, everything will be taken from you. You won't be able to hide forever."

The darkness turned into images, showing him the whiteboard covered in photographs, the hardened faces, the lines forming a spiderweb. The symbol of the conjoined *J*s.

Then suddenly something completely different. Swaying trees, rows of snow-covered gravestones. Beside them a skinny little man with a downy mustache, wearing shiny tracksuit trousers and a padded yellow jacket that was far too big for him. The man opened his mouth to say something but was interrupted by a phone ringing. He smiled apologetically and pulled his cell phone from his pocket.

"Hello, Selim here," the man said. He paused while the person on the other end said something. Then his face cracked into a broad smile.

"Hey, Erik J., long time no see!"

TWENTY-FOUR

They had to use a net to get the body out of the water. One of the firemen was new and made the mistake of trying to pull the corpse by its arms, with the result that one of the arms came detached from the shoulder joint and bobbed around loose inside the yellow padded jacket.

Two of his colleagues laughed and made fun of the color his face had turned until their commanding officer told them to shut up.

"This man has been in the water for about a month, maybe two," he explained to the new fireman. "You can tell from the color and swelling."

He pointed at the dead man's swollen, gray-blue face, where a downy little mustache had turned into a stiff, black brush.

"They can almost double in size if the water's warm, like Michelin Men." The officer inserted a dose of chewing tobacco before going on. "The water loosens the skin and other tissues. That's why we use the net and never pull on any of their limbs, if you see what I mean?"

The new man nodded and gulped a couple of times. He glanced down into the net at the padded yellow jacket and shiny tracksuit bottoms straining against their jellylike contents. Then they both helped the two men in the police van to transfer the swollen body into an extra-large body bag.

"Well, the winter darkness is already starting to show in the suicide figures. Third body in the water this month," one of the men said, sighing. "There'll be more after Christmas."

It wasn't until much later, when the bloated body was on a table in the Forensic Medical Center and the pathologist had stretched out the skin, that anyone noticed the thin metal wire that had been noosed around the man's neck.

•   •   •

"Hello?" Stenberg said.

"Good afternoon, Minister, and Happy Christmas!" the dry voice said down the line.

"Is this line secure?" Stenberg asked.

"Of course! How can I help you, Minister?"

"It's about that service you provided."

"Yes, Minister?"

"You didn't keep your part of the bargain."

"How do you mean, Minister?"

"I'm not going to go into details, all I can say is that you didn't do the job properly. You were sloppy. You assured me there wouldn't be any loose ends. Nothing that could link me to the scene." Stenberg bit his lip. He was making an effort to sound professional rather than worried.

"Yes," the man at the other end of the line said.

"But now there's a loose end," Stenberg said.

"I thought the police investigation had been dropped, Minister?"

"It has. Well, I mean . . . the police took another look and found some inconsistencies. And I have to say, that damn e-mail to her father was quite unnecessary. It only made him suspicious. Sophie wasn't exactly the letter-writing type, you should have asked me . . ."

"You weren't exactly talkative, Minister," the man said. "We made the best of the situation. How come the police are looking at the case again? If it's already been closed, I mean?"

"That's irrelevant!" Stenberg said sharply. "The problem is that despite your guarantees there was still evidence there. Evidence that could lead—"

"Let me stop you there, Minister," the man said. "If I can summarize the matter, you're unhappy with the result of our services?"

"To put it mildly," Stenberg growled.

"In spite of the fact that you haven't actually done anything in return?"

"As I explained, it isn't that simple." Stenberg immediately recognized the defensive tone in his voice and cursed silently to himself.

"Of course not, Minister. I wouldn't have had to ask you for the favor if it had been a simple matter. Just get hold of the name and you'll see that everything sorts itself out."

The conversation came to an abrupt end. Stenberg switched off the cheap pay-as-you-go cell phone and fought an impulse to throw it into the lake. This whole situation was at risk of slipping out of his control. All because Wallin's "reliable" colleague hadn't understood what was being asked of her. All she had to do was take a look at the apartment and confirm that the original report was accurate. Just as Wallin and he had agreed. So he could pull out the trump card that would make John Thorning dance to his tune.

Instead she'd played at being Sherlock Holmes, even sending samples to the National Forensics Lab. Oscar Wallin had taken his eye off the ball, thereby exposing Stenberg to an unacceptable risk. Perhaps Wallin was getting a bit too comfortable in his role, taking things too much for granted? In which case it was high time to turn up the temperature. Stenberg waited for his dog to pee, then walked a thousand feet along the path before getting out his own cell phone.

"Wallin, Stenberg here." He had been aiming for a suitably irritable tone but overshot the mark badly. "How are we doing with Regional Crime in Stockholm?" he went on, slightly more reasonably.

"Good morning, Minister! Well, we're making progress. We've been there a week now and expect to have it under control by early January. The head of Regional Crime, Kollander, has been largely cooperative."

"Good! And what about that handler, what was his name?" Stenberg paused on purpose so as not to seem too keen. Wallin took the bait at once.

"Do you mean David Sarac, Minister? I'm afraid he's disappeared from view at the moment." Stenberg noticed a slight shift in nuance in Wallin's voice, as if he were trying to sound more composed than he really was.

"And what are you doing to find him?" Stenberg made sure his own voice remained measured.

"We've got his apartment under surveillance, and we've got people up at his office," Wallin said. "Dreyer has instigated an internal investigation up there, and he's also very keen to get hold of Sarac. As you know, Minister, Dreyer investigated the whole issue of how CIs are handled once before, after that unfortunate business with Eugene von Katzow, or the Duke, as he's also known."

Stenberg didn't reply; he had only a vague memory of what Wallin was talking about, and it really wasn't relevant right now.

"Bergh is claiming that Sarac was moved to the property store the week before the accident, because his competence was under question," Wallin went on. "If you ask me, that's a bit of retroactive tidying up. A way of them distancing themselves from Sarac and his working methods, probably ordered by Kollander or someone even higher up."

"Okay, Wallin, listen very carefully now." Stenberg paused. Time to raise the temperature to "grill."

"I had lunch with the district commissioner of Stockholm the other day," he went on. "Eva Swensk made it abundantly clear that she's aiming for the post of National Head of Police. There are plenty of people within the party who'd like to see a woman in that position, instead of yet another man. There may even be enough of them for me to have to listen to them, in spite of my earlier reservations."

Stenberg paused once more as he let Wallin absorb what he had said. He nodded as another dog walker passed him on the path.

"This Sarac," Stenberg continued before Wallin had time to say anything. "I've got a feeling that there's a reason why he's disappeared. That he's sitting on something big that could well end up staining the district commissioner's lily-white blouse. Do you understand what I'm getting at, Wallin?"

"Absolutely, Minister, I'll see that the matter is given top priority." Wallin cleared his throat before going on, but Stenberg had already stopped listening. The tone of Wallin's voice was enough to tell him the message had hit home. He found himself smiling happily.

• • •

Natalie had gone through the whole of the old wooden villa. She had spent several hours each day searching while Sarac slept off his migraine attack. She started with the building materials on the upper floor of the veranda, then worked her way down to the damp cellar, just as Rickard had told her to do. But, just as in the apartment, she hadn't found anything of interest. Sarac's permanent home had already been methodically searched. The furniture pulled apart, drawers pulled out of chests and kitchen units. Whoever had searched the apartment had been in a hurry, or had been in a fucking bad mood. Both, perhaps.

Out here there was no sign of anything of that sort. But she had found little traces in the dust on the shelves and window-sills. As if things had been moved and then put back, in almost the same place. Of course it could have been Sarac poking about, but she couldn't quite shake the feeling that someone had got there ahead of her again. Unless it was just her own frustration trying to make excuses.

Rickard hadn't been happy. A month had passed since they agreed on their deal, and so far she hadn't managed to come up

with anything of interest. His happy tone in their early conversations had been replaced by something considerably more
uptight. He sounded stressed but also something far worse—he
sounded disappointed.

Rickard had hit the nail on the head the first time they
spoke. He had found her sore point, the wound that wouldn't
heal because she kept picking at it. He had offered her an
opportunity that she didn't think existed. Clearing her record
and giving her the chance to rehabilitate herself in the eyes
of her parents, family, friends. But, perhaps most of all, in her
own eyes. She wanted to become a doctor, wanted to be someone who saved lives. Working with Sarac had actually only
strengthened that ambition. For the first time since she had
been forced to break off her medical training, she had a patient.
If she hadn't turned up with his medication, Sarac would have
passed out sooner or later, and may even have suffered another
hemorrhage.

She pulled her ChapStick out of her jeans pocket and ran
it over her lips.

The fact was that she had no idea whether Rickard would
keep his part of the bargain. They didn't exactly have a written
contract, and he never said anything about himself or his working methods. Despite that, she had still allowed herself to be
convinced that he could be trusted. Rickard seemed to be the
sort who could achieve pretty much anything. She wasn't about
to disappoint him.

.   .   .

Sarac managed to get out of bed halfway through Christmas
Eve. His migraine had subsided, along with the nausea. His
thoughts were slowly getting clearer; it was as if he were adjusting the focus on a pair of binoculars.

Natalie had put up Christmas decorations. She had found
a couple of electric candelabra that she must have got from the
boxes in the cellar, and had even managed to sort out a ragged

little Christmas tree that, to judge by the strong smell, must have come straight from the forest outside the house.

"Good morning," she said as he stumbled into the living room. "There's rice pudding in the kitchen if you'd like some. Ham too. Happy Christmas, by the way." She held out a small, flat parcel.

"Thanks." The Christmas present made him feel stupid. Obviously he didn't have anything for her.

"Open it." She nodded eagerly.

He fiddled with the paper, feeling her watching him. A DVD. The cover showed five men standing in a lineup. His eyes slid away, toward the old fruit trees at the edge of the forest.

"My favorite film," Natalie said. "I found it in the bargain bin in the Co-op, of all places. Cost about as much as three liters of milk."

He forced himself to look away, trying to get his brain and mouth to cooperate.

"Thank you, Natalie," he said with as much emphasis as he could muster. "I really appreciate it. I mean, not the film. Well . . . not just the film," he mumbled.

"No problem, just doing my job." Natalie shrugged her shoulders. "Look, I was thinking of heading off to see my family now, I just wanted to make sure you take these."

She put a glass of water and some pills in front of him. Sarac did as he was told. He forced the pills down, suppressing the urge to gag with a serious gulp of water. Then he lay back on the sofa and closed his eyes. He realized all of a sudden that he felt a bit disappointed that Natalie was going away so soon. Leaving him on his own out here. But of course she had better things to do on Christmas Eve than sit in the forest on some damn island keeping him company. He would just have to deal with his sudden craving for social interaction the way everyone else who was on their own did: by watching television.

Besides, he had made up his mind about something. As soon as he had gathered enough strength, he was going to go down to the old orchard and find out what was so special about it. He had a feeling that whatever was down there was something he ought to keep to himself.

TWENTY-FIVE

"Hello, *Khalti*, it's Atif."

"Atif," his aunt said. "It's good to hear from you."

"I just wanted to hear how Mom is. I've been trying to call, but she's not answering."

"Dalia's fine, Atif. I think there's some problem with the phones again. The power cuts seem to knock out the exchanges."

A few moments of silence followed.

"She has a right to know," his aunt said in a low voice. "Even if she has trouble distinguishing times and places, she still has a right to know. Adnan was her youngest son, she talks about him all the time."

"I know, *Khalti*," he said.

"Do you want me to tell her? It might even be easier if it came from me," his aunt said.

"No." The sharpness in his voice surprised him. "No, thank you, *Khalti*," he said, rather more gently. "I'll tell Mom as soon as I get back."

"And when will that be, Atif? I thought you were only going to be gone a few days. That's why I agreed not to say anything."

"Soon," Atif said. He understood from his aunt's silence that he was expected to say something more. "I'll be home soon. There's just something I need to take care of first."

"What sort of something, Atif? Is it anything to do with Adnan?"

"No," he lied. Even he could hear how false it sounded. But he couldn't tell the truth. Couldn't say that his only defense against his mother's accusations was the thought of a dead man. The thought that Janus would be held to account for what he had done to her, to Cassandra and Tindra. To him.

A beep on the line warned him that he had a call waiting.

"*Khalti*, I'm afraid I have to go now. Someone's trying to get hold of me."

. . .

Atif cautiously nudged the mail slot open. The apartment was dark, just like last time, and the pile of mail was still on the hall floor. It had only taken him thirty minutes or so to get there. His new hotel was much closer to the city and the cheap car he had bought from a less-than-fastidious dealer out in Barkarby was running like clockwork. Yet he couldn't quite shake off the feeling that he was too late.

There was a rattle from a door farther along the corridor and Mrs. Strömgren looked out.

"Isn't he there?" she whispered.

Atif shook his head. "It's all quiet and very dark. You're sure it was him you saw?"

"As sure as I can be, Constable. He was wearing a short, shiny jacket with a colorful dragon across the back and sides. It's visible a long way off, even if you can't see well. I called you as soon as I found the note with your number."

Atif nodded.

"Well, I'll wait a while longer. If he doesn't turn up this time, I'd be very grateful if you'd call again, Mrs. Strömgren."

The woman nodded, then closed her door.

And opened it again.

"Perhaps you'd like to wait in here, Constable? I've got some coffee ready."

Atif thought for a moment and realized he hadn't eaten any breakfast. He could just as easily wait in her apartment as out in the stairs.

"Thank you, that's very kind of you."

The apartment smelled of heavy furniture and a lonely old person, pretty much like his mother's little room in the nursing home. Otherwise it looked more or less exactly as he had expected. Walls and tables covered with ornaments, pictures, and photographs. Mrs. Strömgren as a young woman beside a man in glasses, presumably Mr. Strömgren. The same couple a few years later with a baby, then a chubby little girl and another little bundle. Then a long series of school photographs, confirmation pictures, graduations, weddings. Four lives documented neatly in chronological order. At one end of the wall was a little table with a solitary picture of Mr. Strömgren and a candle. A short pause before life went on once more.

More photographs, more lives. Grandchildren, great-grandchildren. Birthdays, Christmases, holidays. The sequence was repeated until it almost reached the end of the wall.

"Oh yes, Constable," Mrs. Strömgren said when he'd drunk his coffee. "It occurred to me that he might have gone to collect his dogs. He's got two horrible creatures. Sven and I had a dog before Maj-Lis was born. A cocker spaniel. A lovely little thing, she wouldn't hurt a fly."

She refilled Atif's empty cup.

"But these are very different. I've met them on the stairs several times. Square heads and mean little eyes. Sometimes he even lets them run loose between the basement and his apartment. They've never hurt me, but the look in their eyes makes me shiver."

Atif raised the cup to his lips, the flower-patterned porcelain so fragile that he had to hold it between his thumb and fingertip.

"Have you been down in the basement, Constable? He's got a storeroom down there. Big sacks of dog food that smell absolutely awful. I've had to complain to the residents' committee about it."

Atif almost dropped his cup and caught it at the last moment in his left hand. A little splash of hot coffee landed on his jeans. He shook his head.

"No, I haven't been down there. Do I need a key?"

. . .

The sound hit him the moment he opened the door to the basement. In actual fact it wasn't noise but a faint pressure hitting his eardrums, the reverberations of something bouncing off the stone walls down there until all that was left was a lingering vibration. The smell was the next thing he noticed. A cloying, suffocating smell that must be from the dog food. But there was something else as well, something sharper.

He carried on down the steps, following the old woman's instructions and turning right into a narrow little corridor. He could still feel the pressure in his ears. He recognized it, put his hand in his pocket, and closed his fingers around Bakshi's switchblade. The smell was getting stronger, almost overwhelming. He thought he could detect several familiar smells: sulphur, iron, adrenaline. The metal door wasn't properly shut; the lock seemed to have caught. He took the knife out and opened the blade. He held it facing downward so he could attack someone with it if he had to. Then he cautiously nudged the door open.

The room was big, maybe five hundred square feet, and the far wall was only just visible. Just inside the door was a wall of steel mesh, and beside it sacks of dog food stacked almost the whole way to the ceiling, obscuring the view of the rest of the room. He turned right and followed the wall of sacks. Enough light was filtering through from the fluorescent lamp in the middle of the room for him to see where he was going. In the distance he could hear a faint whimpering, followed by a metallic rattling sound. He stopped and sniffed the air again. He was sure now. It was gunpowder he could smell.

He peered around the end of the wall of sacks. There were metal cages lining the walls, like the one he was peering out from behind. They were all closed, and he could make out storage racks inside them. Most of them were full of sacks, boxes, and large plastic tubs.

In the center of the room there were four folding chairs and an old-fashioned wooden table that looked as if it had been found in a Dumpster. Its worn top was covered with drink cans and an ashtray.

The whimpering was still going on, along with the metallic clanking. Atif noticed movement in the cage in the far right corner. Then a short yelp.

He stepped cautiously into the middle of the room. The smell of powder was stronger now, catching in his nostrils. But there were other smells there too. Animal smells: rage, urine, blood.

He found an explanation when he looked inside the last metal cage. Two burly dogs, one dark, one slightly paler, growled at him. Shaking their square heads and making the chains around their necks rattle as they licked their red noses. Atif was reminded of the wild dogs in Iraq. But these were different. Shorter legs, bigger jaws, and considerably more muscular bodies. As he got closer they curled their top lips back, revealing rows of sharp white teeth.

The man was lying on his back further inside the cage. He was suntanned. His eyes were staring up blankly, and the bomber jacket with the dragon pattern was open. In the center of the chest of his white T-shirt there were two dark patches, the same blackish-red color that was slowly creeping across the concrete floor under his body.

The dogs were walking about in the blood. The smell seemed

to make them a bit high, aggressive. The lighter one barked and snapped at the other one. Then it spun around on the spot and seemed to bite at its own rear end before suddenly pissing itself. The darker dog went on growling, staring at Atif. He moved a bit closer, trying to see more detail. He jumped when the darker dog suddenly leaped at the mesh.

The other dog seemed to be venting its frustration on the dead man. It sank its teeth into the padded jacket and shook its head, spreading a cloud of stuffing into the air. The darker one turned and joined it. The two dogs tore at the corpse's clothes, growling and snapping at each other as they ripped the fabric apart.

Atif stood there watching them. The man in the cage was obviously very, very dead, and he couldn't think of a single good reason to venture in there. Not until one of the dogs tore open the inside pocket of the man's jacket and a cell phone fell out onto the floor.

Damn it!

Obviously the smart option would be to get out of there at once. There was no way he wanted to be found down there with a steaming-fresh murder victim. The sound of the gunshots was still hanging in the air. He'd heard the outside door close as he was heading down the steps to the basement, so he must have missed the killer by a matter of seconds. He wondered whether anyone had called the cops.

With his criminal record he could end up locked away for months, probably years, for something like this. It was bad enough that he'd left his name and fingerprints upstairs in the old woman's apartment. Anyone smart would have left by now and been on their way toward Arlanda.

But the cell phone by the wall in there was unquestionably his best lead. Possibly even his only chance of making any progress and finding out more about Erik Johansson and whoever was responsible for Adnan's death. Of tracking down Janus.

He quickly went through the other cages. Five different sorts of dog food, a few boxes containing leashes, muzzles, the studded collars that most suburban warriors chose to dress their dogs up in. One cage containing dietary supplements, protein powder, and various other gym accessories. The man seemed to have made his living importing a variety of goods.

In one box he found a heap of cheap T-shirts. He pulled out a bundle and wound them around his left arm. He used a roll of packing tape to hold them on. Then he turned the table in the middle of the room upside down and kicked off one of its carved legs. Weighing it in his hand, he went back to the cage.

The two dogs bristled the moment he approached, showing their sharp, red-stained teeth. The cell phone was on the far side of the body, almost tucked in against the wall. It may well not give him anything. This whole line of inquiry might be one big dead end, with no chance of leading him anywhere else. But without the phone he would never know.

He opened the door of the cage and took a step back. He'd been hoping the dogs would make a run for it, perhaps toward the food bowls in the far corner. But instead the animals remained where they were, beside the body.

Atif looked at his watch; time was running out. He bit his lip, then stepped cautiously inside the cage. The dogs stared at him with bulging eyes and curled their lips back so far that he could see the pink flesh of their gums. Atif held out the table leg, trying to push the dogs back ahead of him, away from the body. He succeeded reasonably well. The dogs carried on growling, launching quick attacks at the end of the table leg.

The phone was just a foot or so away from him now, right next to one arm of the body. Atif crouched down slightly, all the while trying to maintain eye contact with the dogs. He stretched his left arm out slowly toward the phone. He took his eyes off the dogs for a moment. He saw movement but didn't have time to react as the paler of the dogs threw itself at him and sank its teeth into the bundle of T-shirts wrapped around his arm. The pain took him by surprise, almost making him lose his balance. The dog was clinging on, refusing to let go. He could hear the fabric creak. Unless the sound was actually from his arm itself?

The darker dog leaped forward too and snapped at his leg, missing by about an inch and making Atif stagger back. Shit, there was no way he could let himself end up on the floor with these beasts on top of him.

His back hit the wall of the cage and he regained his balance. His left arm was hurting badly, one of the dog's sharp canine teeth seemed to have penetrated the layers of cotton, and the pressure from its powerful jaws was crushing his lower arm. It was probably a five, possibly a six on a pain scale of one to ten. The animal was gurgling and rolling its eyes, showing their ghostly whites. The blood around its snout was staining the white fabric. It wasn't showing any sign of letting go of his arm.

Atif straightened up and angled his body so the paler dog was blocking any attack by the other one. The pain was getting worse, and he had to get the dog off him somehow, at once. He held out the arm with the dog attached to it, then swung the table leg as far back as he could. Then he brought it down on the animal's back with all the force he could muster.

There was a cracking sound, like a tree branch snapping. Then the pressure on his arm eased.

Atif shook the dog off and saw its legs twitching much as Bakshi's had done. The dog was gurgling, and a steady stream of shit was dribbling out of its rear end. The smell seemed to spur the other dog on. It started to bark loudly as froth dripped from its mouth. It lowered its head, getting ready to attack. It was staring at the no-longer-white bundle of T-shirts around Atif's left arm.

"Nice doggy," Atif hissed through his teeth. Then he slowly raised the table leg.

TWENTY-SIX

Sarac was back on his feet and actually felt pretty okay. The migraine medication was doing its thing, although the improvement was probably just as much due to the fact that he was moving about again. Short goes on the exercise bike in the basement. Very slowly, with the lowest resistance. Yesterday he had tried a few push-ups for the first time. He had managed five before his arms buckled. Sit-ups were only marginally better. But doing a bit of exercise was already beginning to show results; he could now spend up to half an hour at a time on the bike. He could give his brain a rest while he concentrated on getting his feet to push down on the correct pedals.

But it was only a temporary respite. As soon as he got off the bike the questions were back. Who was Janus? Where was he at the moment? Was he hiding somewhere, waiting to hear from his handler? Or was he so cool that he was pretending nothing had happened, trying to maintain his facade in spite of the anxiety that must be gnawing away inside him? That his secret might no longer be safe. If that was the case, it really wasn't difficult to imagine that it actually was Janus who had been in the hospital, and who later showed up at the door of his apartment. The man wanted to get hold of him, to make sure that his secret was still in safe hands.

Sarac only had a vague recollection of what Janus looked like. A dark shape, a glimpse of a pair of eyes in a rearview mirror, an unshaven face hidden by a pulled-up hood. Little more than that.

And the rest of it: the man with the snake tattoo, the missing backup list, his car crash? The man who stank of tobacco, the one with the gold tooth up at the hospital who had talked about an agreement. Was that Janus in another disguise? Somehow it all fit together, he just didn't know how. All he knew for certain was that he had far more questions than answers. And the only person who could help redress the balance was a man whose face he couldn't remember.

As he showered Sarac took the chance to check his body. His left arm felt pretty okay now, apart from a slight stiffness. His collarbone seemed to have healed as it should. The wound across his stomach had already grown some pink scar tissue. His right leg was still a bit unresponsive, making him limp. But he had swapped the clumsy crutch for a neat little stick with a silver handle that had belonged to his grandfather, which made him feel less like an invalid. And the last time he had felt anything of the migraine was several days ago now. Natalie had left a red box with little compartments containing his doses of medication. She had even marked what time of day he needed to take them.

All in all, he felt better than ever. Or at least better than he could remember feeling. It was time to get going, to start finding a few answers instead of just collecting even more questions.

Out on the porch the air was bright and clear, and the first few breaths stabbed at his chest until his airways got used to the temperature. He went down the steps and walked slowly along the wall of the building. Natalie had cleared a path, which made progress easier. But when he went around the corner things immediately got more difficult. There was a path leading to the woodshed that Josef had cleared the day they left him here, but something like eight inches of snow must have fallen since then.

Sarac struggled on, trying to raise his feet as high as possible in order to not have to push through any more snow than was strictly necessary. But his right leg didn't seem to want to cooperate. In places he was forced to drag it through the snow, which quickly used up his energy. By the time he had reached the woodshed his T-shirt was drenched with sweat and his heart was pounding. He had to lean against the wall for a while to catch his breath.

There were at least another one hundred fifty feet to the edge of the forest, one hundred fifty feet where he would have to plow through far deeper snow. It might even be a foot and a half deep in places. But he wasn't about to give up, not when he'd got this far. The feeling that there was something important over there, something that could help him remember, was getting stronger and stronger.

He waited until his heart rate had settled down again before going on, trying to take small, tentative steps in order not to tire himself out as he crossed the lawn. Obviously, in hindsight, he should have skipped his exercises and saved all his energy for this. And he should have stuck with the tried-and-tested crutch rather than relying on the damn stick. But he hadn't imagined how hard it could actually be to push his way through the snow. It was far deeper than he had expected, knee-deep in places.

He reached the base of the old flagpole in the middle of the lawn and stopped for a while, leaning against the peeling metal. His jeans were soaked now, like his T-shirt. In spite of the sunshine it had to be fifteen degrees. If he stopped for too long he'd start to get a serious chill.

He looked behind him. The snow had already collapsed into the trail he had made, and all he could see was a long, unsteady line of uneven snow running across the lawn. Not much use for the walk back.

About sixty feet left, then he'd be in among the fruit trees. From there it was roughly the same distance again to the edge of the forest. Maybe it would be sensible to turn back. Make a fresh attempt in a couple of days, better equipped and better prepared?

He had just persuaded himself that this was the thing to

do when he noticed something on the ground in among the fruit trees. The shadows must have prevented him from seeing it before. He took a couple of deep breaths and carried on. His wet trousers had already started to go stiff.

Thirty feet left, fifteen feet . . . Made it!

He stopped and leaned against a gnarled old apple tree as he caught his breath. Ten feet in front of him was an area of about ten square feet where the snow had been trodden down. Beyond it was a pronounced dip that led away through the trees, passed between the two abandoned cement gateposts that marked the end of the garden, and then continued on up the slope and into the forest.

Deer, perhaps, looking for frozen windfalls? It was a possibility. He leaned forward, trying to clear some of the snow. He tried to find an area where the snow was so tightly compacted that there might be prints on it, but he failed. Just as with his own footprints, the snow had collapsed and covered any tracks.

A sudden chill made him shiver. He turned and looked up at the glass veranda. The shadows and overhanging branches of the old trees made the spot he was standing in difficult to see clearly from the house. But from the old orchard, on the other hand, you had a good view up toward the house. An excellent view, in fact.

The idea came out of nowhere, strong enough to convince him it was right instantly. Someone had stood here watching him. A dark, hooded figure, someone who wanted to know whether his secret was still safe.

A sudden gust of wind made the tall trees on the hillock beyond the gateposts sigh. Sarac shivered again. The cold spread through his body. The conviction had passed and now felt almost ridiculous. The tracks must have been made by deer.

It took him almost an hour to get back up to the house. His outing had been a big failure. He still hadn't managed to work out what it was about that particular place that kept catching his interest. But he simply didn't have the energy to carry on beyond the old gateposts and head up the steep slope. Besides, the weather had turned and the sun had disappeared.

By the time he reached the corner of the house he was both exhausted and frozen. The sky was covered by heavy clouds, and a few wayward little exploratory snowflakes had started to fall. Soon there'd be many more, erasing all tracks left by man and beast alike.

Sarac squatted down cautiously and rested his back against the wooden wall as he tried to muster his remaining strength. He half closed his eyes.

Suddenly he thought he could see a figure out of the corner of his eye. He snapped his eyes open at once and tried to get to his feet. A man in a dark military jacket and heavy boots was approaching. Sarac's stomach clenched in fear. Then he suddenly recognized the man. It was Josef, Molnar's right-hand man, the one who had driven him out here.

"There you are!" the man said. "We were starting to get worried."

"Hi, Josef," Sarac said, as nonchalantly as he could. He managed surprisingly well, considering the way his heart was pounding. "Just taking a walk. I needed to stretch my legs."

More people came around the corner of the house. Molnar and a couple of other men, whose faces also looked familiar. Something shifted in Sarac's head, unleashing a torrent of information. Names, ranks, and serial numbers.

"David, holy shit!" someone exclaimed. "So you're up and about. God, that's quite a relief!"

Sarac grinned and shook his head a couple of times to get his brain to calm down. He could remember them, he remembered them all. Not just their names but what sort of food they liked, the names of wives, girlfriends, lovers, everything. His team, his men. Several hands were slapping him on the back. Broad smiles in all directions.

"Good to see you, guys." Sarac grinned. And for a brief, fleeting moment, he felt genuinely happy.

TWENTY-SEVEN

Atif was back in roughly the same place as before. The battered old car was parked among the trucks in the neighboring plot with its front bumper nudging the fence, facing the gym. He had a pair of binoculars in his lap and Mr. Pitbull's cell phone on the seat beside him.

For what had to be at least the fifth time in an hour, he pulled up his left sleeve and inspected his injuries. The pain was okay, something like a two now. The bruises made by the dog's bite had already spread, forming yellowish-green patterns on his lower arm, and the wound where one of the teeth had broken the skin was itching in a slightly alarming way. If it didn't get better within a couple of days, he'd have to find a doctor and get a tetanus injection, which was hardly an attractive idea.

He had made a mistake; it had been a stupid idea to give his real surname to Mrs. Strömgren in Roslagsgatan. Not to mention leaving a set of fingerprints all over her best china, so presumably there was already a warrant out for him. Two mistakes out of two. But, in his defense, even an oracle would have had trouble predicting that things would turn out the way they had. One man shot, the name and fingerprints of a known thug, and a witness tying him neatly to the scene at the time of the murder. To the police it must look like a straightforward case. Solved the moment they got hold of him.

It had cost him five hundred kronor to crack the code of the cell phone, but it had been worth it. Cell phone logs were an excellent tool when it came to mapping out a person's movements, and Pitbull Pasi was no exception. He had used his phone sparingly over the past month. He had probably picked up a cheap cell phone in Thailand to avoid the roaming charges. But, in contrast to Bakshi's phone, the phone book in this one included first names and sometimes even surnames, which made things much easier.

Atif found a record of a call received from Erik Johansson's number, late in the evening of Saturday, November 23. The conversation had lasted about a minute. Immediately afterward Pitbull had made a call to Thai Airways, so whatever Erik J. had told him had made Pitbull run for his life.

On November 24, 25, and 26, Pitbull had called Erik J. a total of eleven times. All the calls were around twenty seconds long, suggesting that they had gone straight to voice mail. After that Pitbull's cell had been completely dead for almost three weeks, until the day he received Bakshi's e-mail. Then he started making calls again. First Thai Airways, to book a flight home. Then a boarding kennel in Frescati. A third call to an unlisted number that, according to the cell phone, belonged to someone called Rico. Then, finally, he had called here, to the gym. Adnan's old place.

Barely a day later someone executed Pitbull with two shots to the chest and left him as dog food, so presumably they hadn't just been discussing the price of protein powder. At least that was what Atif was hoping, because he was running out of leads.

The mysterious Erik J. wasn't answering his phone, and Bakshi was still in hiding somewhere. But Atif's gut feeling had brought him out here, and it was usually right. He raised the binoculars and looked at the back of the gym. No cars this time. No gangster conference as far as the eye could see.

He thought about Cassandra, hoping she had taken his advice not to tell Abu Hamsa where she and Tindra were. But he wasn't confident. For Cassandra, Abu Hamsa probably signified security. Financial stability. Someone who could look after both her and Tindra. But Hamsa hadn't got where he was by being some cozy old uncle. He may prefer to avoid conflict because it wasn't good for business, but when it was necessary the little man could be even more ruthless than most of the others.

A movement by the back door of the building made him raise the binoculars again. But it was just the protein junkie, Dino, probably coming out to have a cigarette. Atif watched the man for a few seconds as he shivered and pulled out his lighter. A cigarette would have been nice right now, would have helped him stay sharp.

The knock made him jump.

The man he recognized as the consultant was leaning over and peering in through the window of the passenger door. He was grinning and looking at the door handle with a questioning expression.

Atif glanced quickly in the rearview mirror. A black Range Rover glided slowly up behind his car, blocking his escape. He put the binoculars down and tucked Pitbull's cell phone out of the way. He slid Bakshi's switchblade into the door pocket as he opened the passenger door.

The consultant slid into the passenger seat, bringing cold air and a faint smell of aftershave with him.

"I had a feeling I'd find you here." He smiled. "Perhaps we should introduce ourselves. Frank Hunter, security consultant."

Atif ignored the outstretched hand, which didn't seem to bother the man in the slightest.

"Your name is Atif Kassab. Your brother Adnan was killed by the police after a failed raid on a security van a couple of months ago, and now you want to know who gave him away. Entirely natural, even understandable." Hunter smiled again. Atif remained silent.

"I saw you here a couple of weeks ago," Hunter said. "We kept an eye on you for a while. One of my business partners tried to persuade us that you could be reasoned with. That you could be controlled." Hunter shook his head. "I always thought that was nonsense. A man like you. If it had been my brother . . ." He shrugged.

"Well, as you've doubtless already been told, not everyone is happy with you stirring up trouble. Bakshi is making a hell of a fuss. He's demanding that you be disposed of. Apparently that little shit is a decent source of income for people."

"Is that why you're here, Hunter?" Atif nodded toward the car behind them. "Because you listened to Bakshi?"

Hunter said nothing and seemed to be thinking of how to express himself.

"I think you misunderstand me, Atif. I really only wanted an opportunity to have a quiet chat with you. But I realize now that I might not have chosen the right way to go about it."

He took a radio transmitter out of his jacket pocket and held it to his mouth. "You can go, it's okay," he said. The speaker buzzed twice, then the Range Rover behind them slowly drove off.

"There," Hunter said. "Perhaps now we can continue our conversation on slightly more relaxed terms."

Atif didn't respond. The situation surprised him more than he was prepared to admit. But it never did any harm to listen. Hunter. A striking name, probably an alias. The man neither looked nor sounded like he was American, nor British, come to that. But on the other hand, he didn't look much like the security experts Atif had encountered in Iraq either. More like an ordinary businessman.

"The men you saw coming out of the gym—Abu Hamsa, the bikers, and the others—are all regarded as fairly heavy players. But in relative terms they're pretty small. They've all got bosses, who in turn have bosses. The organizations have different names, but the money, the really serious money, always flows upward, toward the top."

He gestured toward the roof of the car.

"But Hamsa and the other little potentates also have something else in common. They have a problem. A big problem," he went on.

"You mean the infiltrator, Janus?"

"Precisely." Hunter nodded. "Janus is ruining their business. Making them all suspect one another. And if business isn't working, then—"

"The money stops flowing," Atif said.

"Exactly!"

"So where do you come into the picture, Hunter?" Atif tried to sound less curious than he really was.

"I'm a sort of problem solver," he replied. "Someone who gets called in when an impartial outsider is required. My job is to see that the problem disappears in a way that creates as little anxiety as possible. You see . . ."

He twisted slightly in his seat.

"If any of the other involved parties finds Janus first, one of two things would happen." He held up a finger. "If it's his own organization that finds him, Janus would vanish without a trace. No one would breathe a word to the others because of the risk of being linked to Janus's treachery. So the whole thing would drag out, with the various groups always looking over their shoulders, and business would go on suffering. Or—"

"Another organization finds Janus," Atif said before Hunter had time to hold up a second finger. "And they'd use him as a weapon and disrupt the balance of power."

"I see that you understand the problem," Hunter said. "My task is to find Janus first. Find out exactly what damage he has done, and if anyone else is involved. Once Janus has been debriefed, I am to deliver a report to my employers."

"The bosses' bosses," Atif said. "Who are . . . ?"

Hunter smiled and shrugged his shoulders gently. "You're probably aware of some of them, but you'd never have heard of most of them," he said.

"And you're sure you're going to find him first? Hamsa sounded convinced that his people were close," Atif said.

Hunter shook his head slowly. "Are you aware of the Wallenda Effect, Atif? No? It's about focusing entirely on succeeding instead of worrying about what might happen if you fail.

My team and I have nothing to lose, so we don't have to waste time and effort contemplating the consequences of failure."

He reached out his right hand and wound the window down slightly, to let out some of the moisture in the car that was starting to mist the windows.

"Anyway," Hunter said. "Once everything is over my employers will ask me to make sure that Janus disappears, for good, and without the slightest trace." He paused.

"And that's actually why I wanted to talk to you, Atif. You see, my men and I all have police or military backgrounds. Obviously, we do whatever is required in the heat of battle. But neither they nor I are particularly comfortable with more cold-blooded . . . solutions of this sort."

"You're not the type to execute a defenseless man, chop his body up, and burn the remains beyond all recognition?"

"Well, no." For the first time Hunter looked slightly less self-confident. But he quickly recovered. "You see, Atif, my mother's family is from Bosnia. A number of my relatives died in the war. Murdered by people who used to be their neighbors, their friends, even. Because I speak the language, I spent several years working in the region for the war crimes tribunal in the Hague. We tracked down people who had participated in atrocities, made sure they were brought to justice. Monsters, you might think. Sick bastards . . ." He shrugged again.

"But in actual fact almost all of them were perfectly ordinary people. Full of excuses but without any real explanations for why they did what they did. It became obvious to me that everything is about morals. Establishing clear boundaries for yourself, and never, ever crossing them."

He wound the window down a bit more and breathed out a plume of steam.

"And as you doubtless know, once you cross that line, there's—"

"No way back," Atif muttered.

Hunter closed the window.

"And that's where I come into the picture," Atif said. "You need to outsource the disappearance, make sure that Janus vanishes without a trace. And you think I'm the right person for that sort of job?"

"I'm glad we understand each other, Atif." The man's mood seemed to have improved again. "I thought that a man in your situation might appreciate a chance to take revenge on his brother's murderer. To restore the honor of his family. And, as I understand it, you've carried out similar tasks before."

Hunter paused, waiting for Atif to say something. Atif wondered who the man had been talking to. He guessed it was probably Abu Hamsa, or possibly even his old comrade Sasha. No matter who it was, he seemed very well informed.

"Besides," Hunter said when Atif didn't say anything, "as part of my team no one would dare to touch you. Neither old enemies nor new, but you would also have to follow my instructions to the letter."

Atif slowly shook his head. Then he took a deep breath.

"I've already got a job," he said.

"Of course, yes, your job. I almost forgot that." Hunter smiled again. "I spoke to your boss the other day. Major Faisal of the military police battalion of the Sixth Army Division. He had a lot of good things to say about you. Said you were one of his best men. Wondered when you were going to be back. I told him it would probably be a while." Hunter winked at Atif. "Contacts, Atif, that's alpha and omega in my branch. It's hard to imagine that a man like you could change sides. I guess there aren't many people here who know about that?"

Atif looked at Hunter, meeting his amused gaze. The man had an irritating smirk on his lips, as if this were all just a game. Who had said anything about Atif's job? Cassandra had spoken to Faisal over the phone, so she could have leaked his name and number. It had to be her. Shit!

"Well, perhaps you could think about it?" Hunter said. "Like I said, we could certainly use a man with your . . . talents on our team. Here's my number." He put a business card in the compartment just above the gearshift, before pulling the radio transmitter from his pocket.

"In the meantime, Atif, I'd advise you to be careful."

The Range Rover appeared in Atif's rearview mirror again. The passenger door was opened from the inside, revealing an empty seat.

"Look after yourself, and get in touch if you change your mind."

The car door closed behind Frank Hunter. Moments later both he and the black vehicle were gone.

TWENTY-EIGHT

"And just as the guy landed on the grass, David tackled him. Hit him so fucking hard he shat himself. Seriously, he actually shat himself. We had to wrap him up in a plastic sheet when we drove him back to the station!"

The laughter that followed was so loud that Sarac almost covered his ears. But he stopped himself in time and laughed along with the others instead, until he was literally crying with laughter.

They were all sitting in the living room. The excursion to the edge of the forest, his contradictory feelings, and, not least, the loud voices around him had left Sarac feeling completely exhausted. But he still didn't want it to end.

Molnar was telling stories, talking about various cases they'd worked on together. Crooks they'd caught, sources they'd recruited. Sarac could actually remember most of it, at least when he was reminded of their work. Or else he was so keen to remember these events that he was turning them into real memories. It was impossible to say where the boundary was.

"Do you remember that gypsy, David? What was his name? Tallrot, something like that. We stopped him on Sveavägen and checked his car, and he said that all seven of his brothers were crooks. All of them but him, obviously. Do you know what David called him?" Molnar turned to the others in the room. There was total silence. "The white sheep of the family!"

The salvo of laughter was even louder than before, overwhelming Sarac's ears, and this time he couldn't stop his hands. He pressed his thumbs into his ears and covered his face with his hands. All sounds blurred together, then stopped abruptly.

"Are you okay, David?"

He tried to nod. He could feel the fingers covering his eyes getting wet.

"We should probably . . ." Someone pulled out a chair and the scraping sound hid the rest of the sentence. Sarac rubbed his eyes, then wiped his hands on his jeans.

"I-it's okay," he said. His voice sounded shaky again. "I'm just . . . just a bit tired. You don't have to . . ."

But they were already all on their feet.

Sarac caught a glimpse of his own reflection in the glass door to the terrace. His fragile body, bald head, the plaster on his scalp. Then he noticed the way they were looking at him, with the same pity as the men in the corridor up in Police Headquarters.

For a short while he had almost managed to convince himself that everything was back to normal. That he was still one of them. But the man they were talking about no longer existed. All that was left was a stumbling, mumbling wreck who couldn't even manage to go for a walk in his garden.

Tears were still seeping out and he covered his face with his hands again. A sudden pressure in his chest was making his breathing uneven, almost gasping. He heard them leave the room and could hear them talking in low voices as they pulled on their coats and slipped out the front door. Then the muffled sound of car doors closing and a large diesel motor slowly driving away.

"Here you go, David." Molnar put a glass of water on the table in front of Sarac and sat down on the sofa.

"Look, I'm sorry," he said. "It's my fault. The guys were so keen to see you, now that it's Christmas and everything. I thought it might cheer you up. But we should have waited." He ran his tongue over his teeth.

"N-no, it's fine, Peter." Sarac drank a few sips of water. Got his voice back under control. "It was good to see everyone. Really. I'm just frustrated that . . ."

He gestured toward his head. And took a couple of jerky breaths.

"That my head's still so fucking sluggish."

"You have to give yourself a bit of time, David. The doctor said—"

"I don't give a shit about any fucking doctors!" His anger took him by surprise, giving him fresh energy. "I don't want your fucking pity. I'm sick of it. Anyway, it's really only relief that it's me rather than any of you guys who's been turned into a fucking gurgling wreck."

He gulped down the rest of the water, knocking the glass against his teeth so hard that it hurt.

"Look, David." Molnar cleared his throat a couple of times. He didn't seem to know what to say.

"You don't have to stay, Peter. I'll be fine." Sarac leaned his head in his hands.

"Okay." Molnar stood up but didn't move. "There was something else. But maybe this isn't the right time."

"What?" Sarac took a deep breath. Tried to pull himself together.

"We managed to get something from the car. Something that belongs to you."

Sarac straightened up. "What?!"

Molnar put a ziplock bag, the size of a sheet of A4 paper, on the table in front of Sarac. Inside it was a flat object that was clearly visible through the plastic. A battered black notebook.

For a couple of seconds Sarac got the impression that the notebook had landed on the table with a loud slap. Then he realized that the sound had come from inside his own head.

TWENTY-NINE

The notebook smelled of burned plastic. The bottom right corner was scorched and curled, and the paper had turned yellow in places. But the book seemed largely intact. Sarac kept turning it over and looking at it, the sound of his heartbeat almost drowning out Molnar's voice.

"I found it in the wreckage. I've been sitting on it for a while. Thought that was the best thing to do."

Sarac nodded distractedly. This was his book, with his notes, his reminders. The thing he dreamed he had seen in that strange room on the way to the island. Now that he was holding the book in his hand, he couldn't believe it had ever slipped his mind. This book was his whole life, his anchor in the world.

He leafed through it, delirious with joy. Almost every page was covered with writing, a mixture of words and numbers. Clues that could help him make sense of things. And find his way back to himself.

It took a fair time before he realized that he couldn't actually understand all the notes.

Meeting with Jupiter 14.00 at 781216.

"Do you remember the code?" Molnar asked eagerly. "Jupiter's a CI, and the number beginning with seventy-eight is probably a place."

Sarac opened his mouth and swallowed a couple of times. Then slowly shook his head.

"Try the first page, then," Molnar said. "Look at that symbol, those *J*s must mean Janus, surely?"

Sarac leafed back to the first page. The same symbol he had

seen on the wall of his apartment, then on the whiteboard in his dream. Two *J*s, the first one reversed so that the tails were facing each other. This version was even more ornate than the one on the wall. And at last he realized what it meant. The letters formed a two-headed symbol—two faces looking in opposite directions. A Janus face. The god who could see both the past and the future. The realization almost made him cry out in delight.

Instead he just nodded eagerly at Molnar as he ran his index finger down the page. Beneath the symbol there were five ten-digit numbers spread out across the lined paper.

The first one was *9728444477*.

Sarac stared at the number and realized that he and Molnar were both holding their breath. The numbers and letters drifted together, briefly forming a pattern. Then they broke apart again.

"I . . . ID numbers," he said.

"Are you sure?" Molnar sounded disappointed.

Sarac nodded. "Fairly sure."

"We've already checked that, of course," Molnar said. "Only one of the numbers works. It belongs to a woman in Umeå, a librarian. She's not in any of our databases, and she hasn't got any relatives or anything else linking her to either you or Stockholm. Kristina Svensson, does that name mean anything to you?" Molnar was pointing at the number at the bottom of the page. Sarac shook his head. It wasn't ringing any bells at all.

"What about the other four?" he said.

"They don't work," Molnar said. "Just look at the first one, 9728444477. Ninety-seven is okay as a year of birth, but the forty-fourth day of the twenty-eighth month?"

Sarac saw the problem and couldn't understand how something so basic had escaped him.

"I think they're bank accounts," Molnar said. "And that they tie in with how you paid Janus. If you could just remember which bank it is, maybe we could get hold of a bit more information. A bank card that he's using, maybe even security camera footage that could give us a face. Can you remember anything to do with banks or account numbers?"

Sarac was still shaking his head. For a few seconds it had felt as if things were shifting, that everything was about to become clear. But instead he was just feeling even more confused. The disappointment was on the point of sinking him altogether. Molnar seemed to notice.

"Don't worry, David. It'll turn out all right. We're going to find him, I promise." He put his hand on Sarac's shoulder. "Sleep on it, then have a proper look at the notebook tomorrow. The pieces are bound to fall into place sooner or later."

"Okay," Sarac mumbled. "T-thanks, Peter. Thanks for all you're doing for me. For being so patient," he added.

"Don't mention it. We're friends, you'd have done the same for me, wouldn't you?"

Sarac nodded. "H-how are things at work? With Wallin and the Internal Investigation team?"

Molnar gave a crooked smile. "Well, they all want to get hold of you. They keep turning up at your apartment at regular intervals. They don't seem too happy about the fact that you're not home. But so far they've got their hands full with other stuff. The internal investigators need to question loads of people before they can work out what's been going on and can formulate any sort of formal suspicions. And that's proving to be rather difficult, because half of Bergh's department are away on an equality course. Wallin's boys have also been afflicted by unexpected absences, so I imagine we've got a couple of weeks before everyone figures out exactly what they think they're going to get you on."

He patted Sarac's shoulder.

"Get some rest now, David, your memory's bound to improve. We've still got enough time to get things sorted out and tie up all the loose ends. Try to concentrate on those bank accounts, and call me if you think of anything, okay?"

"What about Bergh, what do we do with him? He seemed

a bit paranoid up at the hospital. Wanted me to hand over anything to do with Janus to him."

Molnar bit his lip gently.

"Leave Bergh to me. He's not quite—"

A sound from the hall interrupted him. A faint squeak, as if someone was cautiously trying a door handle to see if a door was locked. Molnar stood up fast, pushed his shirt away from the holster on his belt, and took a few quick steps out into the hall. Sarac got to his feet as well.

"Are you expecting anyone?" Molnar hissed over his shoulder.

Sarac shook his head. There was a dark shadow through the porch window. Molnar put one hand on his pistol, the other on the lock on the door.

"Ready?" Molnar whispered. Sarac nodded. He was thinking about the patch of trampled snow down among the trees. The feeling that someone was watching him.

Suddenly there was a loud knock on the door.

"It's me, David, open up," a woman's voice called.

Molnar looked at him quizzically.

"M-my care assistant," Sarac muttered.

Molnar pulled a face. "I thought you were going to lie low?"

Sarac opened his mouth to explain that it was Natalie who had found him but realized it would take too long.

"I needed my medication," he said instead. "I thought it would be okay. She's hardly going to tell anyone where I am, she's probably under oath not to. Besides, I need her help."

There was another knock. Molnar took his hand off his gun.

"Of course, David, no problem. I should have thought of that myself." He looked at Sarac for a few seconds, then slapped him on the shoulder and opened the front door.

"Hello!" Natalie gave Molnar a long glance. "I was wondering whose car it was out in the driveway."

"Hi! I'm Peter Molnar. Work colleague, and a good friend of David's." Molnar smiled his broadest smile.

She shook his hand. "Natalie," she mumbled. "Care assistant."

"Of course," Molnar said, without letting go of her hand. "Say what you like about the Swedish health service, but sometimes it really does work. Do you work for the council, then?"

"Adelfi Care," Natalie said.

Molnar nodded, still holding her hand. "And you come all the way out here, to Vaxholm archipelago, to pay a home visit? Not bad."

Natalie shrugged her shoulders. "We go where our patients are."

She pulled her hand away and picked up the bag of groceries she had put down on the steps.

"I'll put these in the fridge, David," she said over her shoulder as she undid her jacket. Molnar watched her for a few moments, then looked at his chunky diver's watch.

"I've got to go, I'm going to try to catch the six o'clock ferry. We've got a job on tonight. It's a relief to see that you're in good hands."

He pulled his padded jacket on and lowered his voice slightly.

"Call me at once if you remember anything about those account numbers! And keep that notebook to yourself."

"Of course, Peter."

"Good, speak soon, David!"

Molnar winked at Sarac, then pulled his car key from his pocket and went out the front door.

"Nice to meet you, Natalie," he called toward the kitchen. She flashed him a brief smile, almost as if she were pleased to see him. But of course that could have been wishful thinking. A bit of old-fashioned projection.

As soon as the door closed Natalie came back out into the hall.

"Food will be ready in a bit. I'm just going to have a quick cigarette first," she said, digging in her coat pockets.

• • •

The old garage was almost completely burned out. The roof was gone, along with the windows, internal walls, and doors. All that remained were the white, soot-stained outer walls and piles of charred wreckage. Even though two months had passed, the place still smelled of smoke.

Atif stopped in the doorway, shading the sun with his hand and glancing toward the roofs of the run-down buildings opposite. It wasn't hard to imagine what had happened.

The place where they hold up the security van is only a two-thirds of a mile or so away. The drive here takes four minutes at most. Adnan and his two men pull into the garage in the getaway car and close the door behind them. Inside is car number two, clean, one that hasn't been reported stolen. They transfer the takings to the new car, probably in a couple of big sports bags, something like that. Then they take off their overalls, gloves, and bulletproof vests and throw everything into the first car. One or more of them pours gasoline all over the seats and sets fire to it. The car would be ablaze in less than a minute.

The boys jump into the new car. They're all grinning with relief; they feel as if they've won as the door opens again. The money's in the trunk, all the evidence is going up in flames in the other car, and all they have to do is drive home nice and quietly. Adnan is sitting in the front. Maybe he's thinking that everything might work out after all. Soon he'll be part owner of a successful gym. He can offer his family a normal life.

The car pulls out onto the road. The cops are up on the rooftops. The snipers have already identified their targets. No one knows who fires the first shot. According to the cops it's Adnan, but what else are they going to say? No matter who starts it, the whole thing is over in thirty seconds. Adnan and Juha dead, Tommy seriously injured.

And all because someone ratted. Someone on the inside. Abu Hamsa had said the tip-off came from Janus, which ruled out Bakshi. The little rat definitely wasn't a master infiltrator, and everyone knew he talked too much. But Abu Hamsa had also said that Janus's tip-offs were smart, they could never be traced back to one particular person. So there had to be more links in the chain, links that weren't necessarily aware of one another. Pitbull Pasi appeared to have an indisputable connection to the gym. Maybe he had heard about the secret deal between Dino and Adnan that Hamsa had negotiated, and then blabbed about it? And Janus had been listening . . .

Then, once the men had been mown down in the alleyway, Pitbull had worked out what was going on. He realized what he was caught up in, got scared, and fled the country, terrified of being uncovered as a traitor working in league with Janus. He had lain low in Thailand, until Erik J.'s mysterious friend called to tell him things were okay and that no one was blaming him. Just to be on the safe side, Pitbull e-mailed his old friend Bakshi, a man with ears as big as his mouth, to get confirmation.

Pitbull had been back in the country no more than a matter of hours before someone shot him. No sign that anyone put him under any pressure and tried to squeeze information out of him. Two shots to the middle of his chest and, to judge by the look of surprise on his face, Pitbull hadn't even had time to work out what was going on. That he had become a risk factor, evidence that had to be got rid of.

For a while Atif had toyed with the idea that Erik J. was Janus. But that seemed far too simple. Janus would never have been in direct contact with people like Pitbull or Bakshi. Erik J. was really just a sort of go-between, someone whose role he hadn't quite managed to work out yet. Janus was further in, deeper inside the web.

But he had made some progress. If his theory was correct, it ought to have been Janus who got rid of Pitbull down in the cellar, to wipe out the evidence behind him. In which case Atif had missed him by just thirty seconds or so. He had even heard the outside door closing behind him. But there the trail had gone cold.

Bakshi had vanished, Erik J.'s phone was still switched off, and coming out here to this burned-out garage hadn't exactly given him any new leads. There was one way to make life easier for himself. He could accept Frank Hunter's offer, then sit back and wait until Janus was delivered, sooner or later, straight into his hands. The only question was, was he prepared to do what Hunter required of him? The quick, short answer was no. Sorting out Janus was something he needed to do for himself, not something to be dealt with for someone else. Those days were long gone.

Atif was so lost in his thoughts that he didn't hear them coming, not until the slightly shorter one stumbled over some debris. Three men, all heavily built. Two the same height as he, the third, the one with a beard, a bit shorter. Atif put his hands in his pockets, then realized that the switchblade was in the door compartment in the car.

"Atif Kassab?" the beard asked.

"Who wants to know?"

"We've got a little message for you." The man grinned.

The other two men had split up, trying to cut off his escape routes. The beard grinned again, then extended a telescopic baton with one hand. Atif took a deep breath and lowered his shoulders. If the men had been professionals, they would be all over him already. Making the most of the element of surprise, as well as their numerical advantage, to inflict maximum damage. Which meant that they were just three tough guys, presumably not particularly used to working as a team.

One of the two taller men took a couple of quick paces forward. The kick was hard and surprisingly high considering the man's size, but Atif had no trouble dodging it. The other, slightly heavier man realized that the fight had started without him. He lowered his head and charged like a bull straight at Atif.

Atif knocked the man's arms away, pushed back against the

wall, then, at the precise moment of collision, he pushed the fingers of his left hand into the man's face and let him impale himself. He felt something soft give way beneath his middle finger and heard the man roar with pain.

The other man, who was holding his arms in front of him, Muay Thai style, raised his leg for another kick. Atif shoved the heavier man straight at him.

The kick struck Atif on the shoulder, then slid up and hit his left ear. Something white exploded inside his head.

He heard the sound of bodies hitting the ground and staggered forward, blinking hard to get his sight back. He saw movement on the ground and stamped on it with full force. He felt something crunch beneath him.

The baton hit him across his left shoulder blade. The pain rose to a six. Hard, but not enough to knock him out of the game. Atif angled his arm up to protect his head. The second blow came lower but hit his back and ribs rather than his kidneys. A weak seven. Atif moved out of range of the baton.

The Thai boxer was getting to his feet. Atif aimed a kick at the man's temple. He misjudged the distance and hit his nose instead. The man fell backward, pulled his legs up, and rolled out of the way.

For a couple of seconds everything stopped as they all looked at one another. The only sounds were heavy breathing and the sniffs and groans of the fattest one as he tried to crawl away. One down, two left.

Atif decided to switch strategy. Instead of waiting for another attack he charged straight at the man with the beard. The maneuver took the man by surprise, and he couldn't decide whether to use the baton or jump out of the way before Atif rammed him in the chest.

They fell to the floor. Atif felt hands clawing at his face, trying to get at his eyes. He grabbed the man's hair, pulled his head up, then slammed it down against the ground as hard as he could. Once, twice. He felt the man's body go limp.

He didn't see the kick coming, just felt it as it hit his head. He fell to the side, the room lurched, the sky and concrete floor changed places. Atif curled into a ball, protecting his head as best he could. He made sure he rolled to the right, toward the wall. That bought him a couple of seconds' breathing space. He saw the Thai boxer raise his leg, then pushed off against the wall, rolling straight at the man's foot. His leg buckled and he fell backward.

Atif got to his feet. His left arm was practically useless, and he was still seeing double. The pain was rising to an eight. He needed to bring this to a conclusion.

He felt something round under his foot and thought at first that he was standing on someone's finger, then saw that it was something else entirely. The Thai boxer was wiping his face with the back of his hand to get rid of the blood pouring from his nose, and Atif seized the chance to bend down and pick up the object behind his back.

He clutched the handle, then let his useless left hand hang down by his body as he raised his chin.

The Thai boxer took the bait. He stood up on his toes, then gracefully raised his right leg. Atif was waiting for the kick. When it came he swung the baton around in his right hand and brought it down as hard as he could on the man's shinbone. The Thai boxer fell flat on the floor. Atif was already halfway toward the door when the man started to scream.

THIRTY

"Minister, how good of you to come. And so nice to meet you again, Mrs. Stenberg."

"Your Excellency," Stenberg said to the ambassador as they shook hands.

"I hope we can dispense with formalities. After all, we have known each other a long time now, even if it's been a while." The tall, thin-haired man in a dinner jacket smiled warmly.

"Of course." Stenberg smiled. And now you're going to babble about what a talented colleague I was."

"As you know, Mrs. Stenberg, Jesper was one of my very best prosecutors at the tribunal. It was already very obvious that he was going to go far."

"That's lovely to hear." Karolina took the elderly man under the arm. "Do tell me more, Your Excellency. Jesper and I really do miss those days in the Hague. The Netherlands is a wonderful country. Perhaps we could start by getting something to drink?"

Stenberg gave his wife a grateful look as she carefully steered the talkative old man toward the bar. He was good at this sort of occasion. He could do the small talk, he knew all the little codes, how to work a room. But Karolina was in a different league altogether; she was a full-blooded professional. He had learned all he knew from her. Her grandfather had been foreign minister, after all, and no doubt her dad, Karl-Erik, would end up as an ambassador, just like all the other loyal old servants of the party.

Stenberg looked toward the door and received a short nod

from the Security Police officer who had accompanied him to the embassy, but didn't bother to respond.

"Minister?" He moved forward, shaking hands, nodding amiably at passing faces. He threw in one of his patented Stenberg smiles, but without making the slightest move to stop. The trick was to keep moving the whole time, and not get bogged down in nonsense discussions that didn't lead anywhere.

Wallin ought to be here somewhere. The embassy usually invited people who had served at the War Crimes Tribunal to its New Year cocktail party. Stenberg looked around and thought he could see a glimpse of a familiar profile in one corner. But just as he started to move in that direction someone took hold of his elbow.

"Jesper!" It was John Thorning.

"John, good to see you. Are you on your own?"

"Margareta stayed at home. She wasn't feeling very well. This sort of thing"—he indicated the overcrowded room—"tires her out."

And evidently not just her, Stenberg thought. John Thorning looked worn-out. The bags under his eyes were even bigger than last time, and his face now had a couple of red patches on it.

"I understand, do give her my very best, John. I'm afraid I must . . ." He released his grip of Thorning's hand, but the old man kept hold of his.

"How are you getting on, Jesper?"

"How do you mean?" Stenberg glanced around quickly for Karolina.

"With the investigation. It's been over two weeks now. You said—"

"I said you'd hear more after the holidays. But probably not until someway into January."

"But you must have heard something?!" John Thorning was still clutching his hand. His voice was a little too loud, making the people around them look in their direction. Jesper went on smiling as he smelled the alcohol on the other man's breath.

"This isn't the right place for this sort of discussion, John."

"Please, Jesper!"

More and more faces were turning toward them. Far too many for comfort.

"Come with me to the bar, John, and I'll tell you." He pulled the older man after him, and after a couple of paces Thorning finally let go of Stenberg's hand. The old man padded obediently after him like a puppy, and the expression on his face was just like their little dog, Tubbe, when it wasn't allowed out with them. Old John certainly wasn't his usual self. Stenberg had to say something, anything, just to get rid of him.

Stenberg stopped and waited until everyone else turned away. He took a deep breath. John Thorning looked as if he might collapse at any moment. He had to give him some crumb of comfort, something that at least sounded encouraging.

"It's like this, John," he said close to the man's ear. "We've found certain . . . things. The sort of thing that requires a closer look. I mean, nothing conclusive," he added quickly when he saw the man's reaction. "But we're doing what we can. Wallin has put one of his best . . ." Stenberg bit his tongue. Fuck! He should have kept Wallin's name out of this. "Like I said before, John, you'll get a better idea early in January. We'll speak then."

John Thorning nodded eagerly. "Of course, Jesper, I understand! I really do appreciate . . ."

Stenberg smiled his sufficiently modest smile.

"Don't mention it, John. And remember, we're just taking a closer look at a couple of things. That sort of thing happens all the time, it doesn't necessarily mean there's anything wrong."

John Thorning didn't seem to be listening and was squeezing Stenberg's arm instead. The expression on his face suddenly looked almost happy.

"Thanks, Jesper, thanks a million. You've no idea."

When Stenberg glanced over his old mentor's shoulder he noticed his wife looking at them curiously.

• • •

Sarac noticed the smell on the stairs. Cigarette smoke. He had slept soundly, dreaming an awful lot of things, none of which he could remember when he woke up. The only exception was that song.

> *I owe everything,*
> *Debts I can't escape till the day I die . . .*

"Odds and Evens," he thought it was called. He'd have to google the lyrics when he got a chance.

He came down into the hall, followed the smell into the living room and out into the glazed veranda. Natalie was standing just outside the door. The cigarette smoke was swirling around her head, seeping back into the house through the drafty windows. Sarac realized he was pleased to see her.

He tapped gently on the glass. She turned and smiled at him, then took a last drag before flicking the butt out across the snow-covered lawn.

"Have you been here long?" he said as Natalie closed the glass door behind her.

"About an hour. I really do like this place. How far does the plot extend?" She gestured down toward the forest.

"All the way down to the water on the other side of the hill," he said.

"Nice. Is there a jetty?"

"A jetty and a boathouse, but they're both pretty run-down. Like the rest of the place." Sarac threw his hand out. "I was planning to do it up, but a few other things seem to have got in the way."

Natalie nodded, pulled her ChapStick from her pocket, and ran it over her lips.

"Yes, I saw the tarpaulins and building materials upstairs. So you're the DIY type, David?"

"Not really." Sarac shrugged. "But the alternative is selling up. Getting builders in would cost too much. Neither my sister nor I have got the money."

Natalie pulled a face that was hard to interpret.

"By the way, there was something I wanted to ask you," Sarac said. "When you cleaned up my apartment, did you notice if there was anything written on the bedroom wall?"

"Like what?"

"Well . . ." Sarac looked for the right words. "Some sort of message. Something about a secret?"

Natalie shook her head. "It looked like a war zone. But the walls were okay. Why?"

Sarac nodded, then looked out toward the orchard. "Oh, it was just something I got into my head. I must have imagined it. Maybe I dreamed it."

Natalie was studying him and looked as if she wanted to ask something.

"Do you want something to eat?" she said instead. "I can make you some bacon and eggs."

"Sure."

He stayed on the veranda while Natalie went into the kitchen. He peered down toward the fruit trees again and for a brief moment thought he could see movement down among the trees. But then he realized that it was just the wind, making the shadows down there move.

"*Debts I can't escape till the day I die,*" the voice in his head sang. The song was back again, and all of a sudden he remembered the group's name. The High Wire.

"David, I found this in the hall. Are you keeping a diary or something?"

"Er, what?"

Natalie was standing in the doorway. She was holding his notebook in her hand.

Damn!

"Oh, i-it's nothing special," he said, taking a few quick steps toward her. "Just a few things I jotted down."

He held out his hand. He had left the book in his bedroom, he was sure of that. He'd put it under . . . under . . . ? Fuck!

Natalie handed him the notebook.

"Did your friend Peter bring it? Has it got something to do with your work in the police? Secret sources?"

Sarac clenched his jaw. Natalie noticed his reaction.

"Don't worry. I don't want to pry. It was he who told me."

"Who, Peter?"

Natalie nodded.

"He bummed a cigarette off me the other evening before he left. Nice guy, maybe a bit too self-aware for my taste. Besides, I don't really like men who have those neat little goatees. Anyway, he told me what line of work you were both in. No details, nothing like that, just that it was important that you got your memory back soon. Very important, even."

She smiled, and once again that uncomfortable feeling crept up on Sarac. That nothing was the way it seemed.

• • •

The man down in the orchard was barely moving. He stood still as he watched the house through his binoculars. He saw the man and woman talk for a while out on the veranda, then she went back inside the house. For a moment he thought the man had seen him, that their eyes had met in spite of the distance and the shadows hiding him. But obviously that was just paranoia. He was a phantom, a figment of the imagination, impossible to see.

The man lowered the binoculars, took a half-smoked cigar from one of his jacket pockets, and turned away as he lit it. Then he held it inside his cupped hand to hide the angry red glow at its tip. He ought to stop, he knew that. Just not quite yet. Not until he knew that the secret was safe. That *he* was safe . . .

He looked up. The man had gone back inside the house. He took another puff on the cigar. Then turned around, slid back out between the two snow-covered old gateposts, and vanished into the forest.

THIRTY-ONE

Five sets of numbers, spread out across the page. Four of them written in the same black felt-tip pen. But the top one had been scribbled using what looked like a fairly useless standard-issue ballpoint. Molnar was right, only one of the numbers worked as a possible ID number. The rest were clearly something different.

He had at least worked out that there were two distinct sections in the notebook. The majority of it was full of what looked a bit like a diary. Dates followed by code names, and a code that presumably indicated a location. The first date was almost two years old, the most recent dated October 3, involving a CI named Bacchus. None of it meant anything to him.

There was nothing about any meetings with Janus, so how and when they had met must be documented some other way. Unless it wasn't documented at all. But the page with the five numbers under the Janus symbol was the one that felt most interesting. His first impression had been that they were ID numbers. In which case he must have encrypted them somehow. And, if they were ID numbers, and related to five different sources, why had he listed them without giving their code names? Maybe the answers had been on the pages that had been torn out. The glue had come loose in places, and he could see traces of paper both before and after the page containing the list and the Janus symbol. There was nothing about any meetings after October 3. Why not? What was he trying to hide?

He thought about Janus again, wondering where he could be. What he was doing right now. There was a knock on his bedroom door and Natalie popped her head in. "I was just wondering if you'd like some coffee? Food's going to be a while yet."

"Yes, thanks, I'll be right down," he replied, and realized he was smiling in a way he didn't quite recognize. Then it dawned on him that it was because of Natalie.

The smell of tobacco on her clothes made its way across the room, making Sarac think of the man up in the hospital. Did he actually exist, or was he just a product of his imagination? A hallucination brought on by his migraine, like the ones he'd had the other day? He had hoped that was the case, but sadly it probably wasn't. The man felt real, as did the talk of an agreement.

• • •

"You look wiped out," Natalie said when Sarac came into the kitchen. "Can I ask what your job involves, or is it a state secret?" She smiled and raised her pale eyebrows slightly.

"I have a confession to make," she said, nodding toward Sarac's notebook. "The book was lying open on the floor when I found it. I couldn't help looking."

Sarac opened his mouth.

"You don't have to say anything." Natalie held up a hand. "I know it was wrong of me, but in my defense, I had no way of knowing that there'd be secret police stuff in it."

Sarac swallowed, feeling his attack of anger subside. The fact was that she was right, it was actually his fault for not taking better care of his things. Fucking stupid shitty brain!

"It's okay," he said. "I need to learn to look after things better."

Natalie shrugged her shoulders.

"Well, if it's any consolation, confusion is one of the most common side effects of a stroke," she said.

"H-have you had many patients like me? People of my age who've suffered a stroke, I mean?"

She looked at him and nodded. "A couple."

"And what happened to them? Did they ever become them-selves again? The people they had been before?"

She tilted her head and bit her lip slightly.

"No. They didn't," she eventually said.

Sarac gulped and felt his tongue stick to the roof of his mouth.

"But, on the other hand, they got something that plenty of other people would like," Natalie said.

"W-what?"

"A new chance," she said. "A chance to become the people they wanted to be."

Sarac sat in silence, then he nodded slowly.

"Can I help at all, David? I've got my laptop if there's any-thing you want to check." She nodded toward the notebook on the table.

Sarac thought for a moment. Then he suddenly remem-bered something Natalie had said the first time she had shown up.

"Didn't you say you knew someone who worked in the Tax Office?"

•   •   •

"Okay, thanks for your help, Freddie!" Natalie ended the call and turned to Sarac. "What your friend Molnar said was right. The only ID number on the list belongs to a woman in Umeå. Kristina Svensson, she lives on Fältvägen."

Sarac frowned unhappily.

"The rest of the numbers don't work, but we already knew that."

Sarac looked down at the floor. Tried to focus. Maybe Molnar was right after all, and the numbers really were bank accounts. But for some reason that didn't feel right. The num-bers seemed to be connected to people, he was pretty sure about that.

"Listen . . ." Natalie began.

He looked up and saw that Natalie was studying the first page of his notebook. He thought he should probably close it. But what difference did it really make? The numbers meant even less to her than they did to him. He saw her frown; she seemed to be thinking.

"Okay, I've got some numbers in my computer that I'd rather keep a bit confidential. My hard disk is encrypted, but I'm still a bit worried someone could get hold of it and get into it. If that happened, I could end up with serious problems."

Sarac said nothing and tried to imagine what *serious problems* could mean for a care assistant, or why she had any use for a contact in the Tax Office. He didn't succeed terribly well.

"So I checked out the whole business of codes and ciphers," Natalie went on. "I realized that if it was going to work for me, I'd have to be able to decode things quickly and simply."

"And?" Sarac straightened up.

"I use a simple Excel spreadsheet. A few lines between the numbers, to make it nice and easy to read. But there's another reason. Between the lines, so to speak."

Something clicked inside Sarac's head. That piece of music was suddenly back. It started slowly, like a whisper, then grew quickly louder.

I owe everything
Debts I can't escape till the day I die.

"Take a look at this!" Natalie pointed at the open notebook. "The first number, 9728444477, starts on the second line. The next one on the third line. One line between them. Nice and neat. But look at the third number, it's suddenly two lines below, and the gap before the fourth one is even bigger, do you see?"

Sarac nodded. The music in his head was getting louder.

"In my Excel spreadsheet I add the number of the row to each number," Natalie went on. "So if the number one thousand is in row five, the real number is actually one thousand five. If you used a similar system, then the first number would be the figure on the second line, plus two."

She took out a pen and wrote the numbers down on the back of an old newspaper. She left a space and added two to the number.

"No, that isn't right. That only changes the last digit in the number. Or possibly the last two, but the rest stay the same; 9728444479 still isn't a proper ID number. Shit!"

She stared at the paper.

"Okay, I know. What if you add two to every digit, like this: 9728444477—nine plus two is eleven, so, one. Seven plus two is nine, two plus two is four."

She wrote all the numbers down. Then stared at the result.

194066-6699

"Er . . ." Natalie said, and rubbed the back of her neck. "Well, it would be a very old person, born on the sixty-sixth day of the fortieth month in 1919. Crap!"

She crumbled the sheet of paper up.

"Forget it, I thought I'd come up with something clever."

Sarac closed his eyes. The music was echoing in his head, almost drowning out his thoughts. Something in the song's title . . .

He picked up the pen and wrote the numbers down again.

9728444477

"Odd lines minus. Even lines plus," he muttered, almost without thinking about it.

He deducted the number of the row from each digit, then leaned back.

750622-2255

"Shit," Natalie said. "I'll give Freddie another call right away."

• • •

Atif carefully wound the bandage around his left hand, pulling it as tight as he could. His index and ring fingers had swollen up like sausages, and his wrist and lower arm were bluish-yellow and stiff. He probably had a hairline fracture in the bone, or possibly, in the worst case, had actually broken it. At least the dog bite looked a bit better, although that was scant consolation in the circumstances. The left side of his chest was blue as well, and hurt like fuck when he took deep breaths. He guessed that one or more ribs were broken. He also had the headache from hell, which not even four acetaminophen seemed able to touch. All in all, a pain level of a strong five. An irritating nuisance, but at least it was surmountable. He was planning to rest for a couple of days and lie low over the New Year.

Besides, he needed to do some thinking and figure out his next move. Maybe it was time to accept Hunter's proposal after all? At least that way he'd avoid any further undesirable incidents. No one would dare touch him. Or he could give up on the whole thing and just go home. Put all this behind him. But he knew that wasn't going to happen. He'd never let anyone get away with anything before, and he wasn't about to start now. Above all, definitely not Janus.

His phone started to ring, interrupting his thoughts. It made him think of Tindra and Cassandra. He rushed over to the door and dug his phone out from his jacket pocket. The pain was making his temples throb. But the screen was dark.

There was a second ring, and he realized that the sound wasn't coming from his phone but Pitbull's. He found the right pocket, opened the phone, and pressed Answer. Number withheld.

"Hello?" he said.

But the person at the other end had already hung up.

THIRTY-TWO

"Freddie's typing the numbers in now." Natalie held her hand over the phone as she turned toward Sarac.

The code was actually childishly simple. Deduct the line number from all the digits on even lines and add it to the digits on odd lines. And hey, presto, the numbers turned into ID numbers. People born between 1968 and 1981.

"Okay, are you ready, here comes the first result," Natalie said in a tense voice. "Brian Hansen, born 1975 in Bromma. Details confidential."

She wrote the name down, her pen scratching on the cheap paper. The scraping sound made him think of falling snow. Sarac's eyes flashed. A face, a thickset man with cropped hair, a snake tattoo. A voice that was surprisingly high-pitched.

I was thinking of suggesting a deal.

The man in the snow-covered car. Brian Hansen! He felt his heart pound, pumping adrenaline faster and faster through his body.

"What exactly does 'details confidential' mean?" Natalie said into the phone. "That your records aren't shown in public registers," she repeated, looking at Sarac.

"Can anyone have that?" she asked.

There was a short pause while the man on the other end answered.

"On appeal, if there's a clear threat. Abused women, politicians, some police officers," Natalie summarized. "But most people whose records are confidential are—"

"Criminals," Sarac said, pinching the bridge of his nose.

"That's right." Natalie looked at him. She was frowning slightly.

"So that's all? We can't get anything but his name?" she said to the man on the other end. He said something that made her expression change. She looked much more serious. "Ah, okay. No. We won't get much further there, then."

"Why not?" Sarac said.

Natalie held the phone away from her mouth and looked at him before she replied.

"Because Brian Hansen's dead. He died on November twenty-third. The same night you—"

"Crashed," Sarac said. He shut his eyes again.

"Does it say how he died? He was only, what? Not quite forty," Natalie said into the phone.

Sarac thought he knew the answer, but obviously he couldn't say anything. Nor, apparently, could the Tax Office computer.

"Oh well, forget him then," Natalie said impatiently. "Try the next number instead. Selim Markovic, born 1978 in Spånga." She made a note of the name, giving Sarac a quick sideways glance.

He took a deep breath, then leaned his head in his hands. He could see a thick yellow padded jacket in front of him, and inside it a twitchy little man with a downy mustache, talking on a phone. The man from his dream.

Hey, Erik J., long time no see!

"And he's dead too?" Natalie asked. "Just last week," she added, looking at Sarac. "He was even younger. This seems really weird. Shame it doesn't say how they died. Hang on a bit, Freddie, I'll call you back!"

She ran out of the room, over to her rucksack by the door. She returned with her laptop.

"Let's see. November twenty-third, criminal, man, dead, Stockholm."

Natalie typed the information into the search engine and pressed Enter. She read the screen, then clicked on something with the mouse.

"Here," she said. "It's from the *Aftonbladet* website the same night."

She turned the screen so Sarac could see.

Criminal found murdered in Gamla stan.

The picture showed a snow-covered car that he recognized instantly. The back window was covered in an orange health service blanket. A short distance away on the sidewalk he could make out the backs of what looked like a group of young people.

"It's impossible to be certain, but all the details fit."

Sarac said nothing. All he could think about was Brian Hansen. His high-pitched voice, the smell of his fear. The bullet throwing his head forward against the dashboard.

"Let's try the other date." Natalie typed the details in. It took considerably longer this time.

"Okay, this one's harder. There's nothing that resembles what happened in Gamla stan. But Freddie said it's the day someone is declared dead that counts as the date of death. In which case this might fit." Natalie turned the screen toward Sarac again.

Dead man found in water by Riddarholmen.

The picture showed a dark-colored van and some firemen lifting a bright yellow bundle onto a stretcher. One of the firemen seemed to be looking away, as if he'd rather not be there.

"Well, I don't know," Natalie said. "But at least the date fits."

"It's him," Sarac said.

"Are you sure?" Natalie's voice sounded excited. "How can you know?"

"I just do, okay?" he snapped.

They fell silent. Sarac massaged his temples, trying to fit the pieces of the puzzle together. And failed utterly.

How can you know? That was the million-dollar question.

"Shall I call Freddie about the other numbers?" Natalie was looking at him.

"Sure," he muttered. He was trying to get rid of the mental image of Markovic's downy face. He had to move on, get hold of more pieces of the puzzle, try to put them together. There was a bigger picture here, far bigger than two dead men. Something he couldn't quite grasp yet. What he needed was a corner piece, something he could work outward from. But right now he couldn't see anything like that.

"Hi, it's me again. Can we run through the rest?" Natalie said into the phone.

Her pen scratched on the paper.

"Number three is a Pasi Arvo Lehtonen, born 1981. No protected address this time. Lives at number 62 Roslagsgatan.

"Or rather, lived," she added, glancing at Sarac. Holding the phone between her ear and her shoulder, she typed something into her laptop. Then turned the screen toward Sarac without saying anything.

Man murdered in Vasastan

A 33-year-old man has been found murdered in a basement at number 62 Roslagsgatan. The man was already known to the police for a number of petty offenses. The police have not yet released any details, but a source close to the investigation has told *Aftonbladet* that they are looking for a large man in dark clothing who was seen leaving the scene.

Sarac shut his eyes and tried to conjure up an image of Lehtonen, but didn't manage as well as with the other two. An image of a dragon came into his head. Then something about dogs. He leaned back into the sofa. His eyes wandered toward the veranda window. Out to the garden, across the snow-covered lawn, and down toward the shadows.

• • •

Atif woke up midbreath. The cheap sheets were sticking to his body, and his arm and chest were throbbing with pain. He had been dreaming about Adnan, and Tindra. He had dreamed that someone had taken her, snatching her out of Cassandra's arms without his being able to do anything to stop it. A man with two faces . . .

"It's all your fault!" Cassandra had screamed at him in the dream. Now, in hindsight, he realized that the voice wasn't quite right. It sounded more like his mother's voice.

He felt a wave of nausea rising through his body. He just made it into the little bathroom before he threw up.

Damn, he really shouldn't have held back from getting medical treatment. He could have come up with some story and got a dose of penicillin, maybe a tetanus jab as well. He coughed and felt it stab in his chest. He cleared his throat and spat. Blood. Not much, but enough to worry him. He needed to get hold of a doctor, and soon. He'd just have to risk it.

Pitbull's cell phone was on the little desk in the hotel room, plugged into a pirate charger Atif had picked up cheaply. The screen was dark, but when he touched it a message appeared.

From: **Rico**
I'm on my way home. Green light?

Atif weighed the phone in his hand, thinking. Pitbull had called Rico from Thailand, just hours after Bakshi had given him the all-clear. Because the number belonged to a pay-as-you-go phone he hadn't been able to trace it. Instead he had focused on the gym, but that hadn't led him anywhere.

He looked at the screen again. And decided to set a trap.

Green light. Have you heard from Erik J's mate?

He pressed Send. The answer popped up after something like thirty seconds.

Not since he rang.

Atif felt his pulse rate increase. Rico, whoever he was, knew both Erik J. and his mysterious friend. He could lead him deeper into the web, closer to Janus. All he had to do was get hold of Rico.

He fought the impulse to call the number. And did some more thinking instead.

Ok, call me when you're back in the city, got more to tell you.

Rico's response came even quicker this time.

OK c u soon!

THIRTY-THREE

"Okay, the Tax Office VPN has let him in again at last. Freddie's dug up the last two numbers."

Natalie waved her cell phone toward Sarac before returning to the conversation. They had been waiting almost three hours. Natalie had made lunch, but neither of them had been able to do it justice. Three names on the Janus list were ticked off, all of them dead, and none of them from natural causes. Two names remained, two people who, unlike the others on the list, might be able to provide some answers instead of just more questions. Maybe even the corner piece he needed to be able to make sense of the puzzle.

Natalie put her pen down and stood up. She took a few steps out into the hall as she muttered something that, to judge by her tone of voice, was private. She was probably thanking him for his help and promising some sort of favor in return. Sarac turned away and made an effort not to eavesdrop.

Natalie returned a minute or so later.

"They both seem to be alive," she said, and Sarac found himself feeling relieved.

"The first ID number belongs to an Erik I. Johansson. Anyone you remember?"

Sarac sat in silence, waiting for his brain to find the right pathway. Show him a face. But nothing happened. What appeared instead was a strong sense of unease. He shook his head. "No address?"

"No, his details are protected as well. All that's there is an ID number and a name. No other information, other than the fact that he was born in this country and hasn't been declared dead. Can't even find out what the *I.* of his middle name stands for. According to Freddie, Erik Johansson is a combination of two of the most common first and last names in Sweden, so this guy really is pretty anonymous."

Sarac looked away. For a moment he thought he could feel that indistinct buzzing in his head. But Erik I. Johansson's face remained hidden.

"What about the last name, then?" he muttered.

"Erico Sabatini, lives on Södermalm. Still alive and well, like Johansson, at least according to the computer."

This time a face popped up straightaway. Thin hair, pointed nose, and alert eyes. But it didn't stop there. Sarac realized that he knew Erico Sabatini fairly well. Family, leisure interests, private matters. All of a sudden Sarac was struck by a new realization, as if something important was close to revealing itself to him. Five names, three of them already dead. Two still alive. Erik I. Johansson and Erico Sabatini.

"I have to go over there. Right away. Can you give me a lift?" Sarac said.

"Shouldn't you call someone? Your friend Peter?" Natalie said.

Sarac shook his head. "I need to go on my own. He only trusts me. Can you give me a lift or not?"

"Sure." Natalie shrugged her shoulders. She was trying not to seem too enthusiastic. "There's a ferry in ten minutes, we can make it if we hurry."

• • •

"Okay, that's that, then." The doctor stood and held out his hand to Atif. "The injection I've given you ought to stop any infection, and you can pick up the prescription at the nearest drugstore. But if you start to feel worse, go to the emergency room at once."

Atif cut across the little snow-covered parking lot. He

hadn't been followed, he was sure of that. Just to be sure, he had checked the car. In spite of the pain he was in, he had made himself crawl underneath it to make sure no one had attached a GPS tracker to it.

The acetaminophen was keeping his fever under control, the pain was hovering around a five, and the penicillin the doctor had prescribed would hopefully stop him from coughing up blood. All this—health center, doctor, and drugstore—was a risk. His ID number would show up in one or more computer systems. For that reason he had picked a health center a long way from the shabby hostel he had moved into. If he got everything out of the way quickly enough, no one would be able to spot him before he was back in bed. As soon as the medicine started to work and he had time to recover a bit, he was thinking of resuming the chase.

He heard his phone start to ring the moment he closed the car door. He fumbled through his coat pockets, but his feverish brain made him get out his own cell phone rather than Pitbull's.

1 missed called from Rico, the screen said when he finally pulled it out. Damn!

Atif sat there for a few moments, considering his next move. Phoning back was a bad idea, he had no idea what Pitbull's voice sounded like, and it was pretty likely he'd be uncovered before he managed to find out anything. Instead he wrote another text message.

Can't talk now, are you back?

Atif pressed Send, then looked at the time. Almost forty minutes had passed since the nurse typed his ID number into the computer. High time he got away from there.

The cell phone buzzed. Rico was quick to reply.

Central Station. I'll call when I get home.

Atif put his seat belt on. It was at least a thirty-minute drive to the Central Station, there was no way he'd get there in time. Besides, he had no idea what Rico looked like. Better to wait, pick up the prescription from the drugstore, and try to figure out where the guy lived. He was about to turn the key in the ignition when Pitbull's cell phone began to ring noisily.

Rico calling.

Goddamn it, he'd only just texted!

Atif stared at the phone, then at the time. The fever was making his head throb and the tinny noise of the phone wasn't helping. He picked it up to reject the call.

A large man in a beaver-skin hat and a thick winter coat was walking across the parking lot. He was holding a small boy by the hand, and something about the pair's movements made Atif's feverish brain click into action. The boy was struggling, trying to pull loose. Pitbull's cell phone was still ringing, but the sound suddenly seemed very distant.

"But I don't want to!" he thought he could hear the boy say.

"You're not well, Adnan, and when you're not well you have to go to the doctor's," Atif mumbled. "I promised Mom . . ."

The ringing stopped abruptly. The boy and man passed. Atif gulped, then looked down at his hand. The screen was illuminated, the line was open. He must have pressed the wrong button. Damn it!

He ought to hang up and go back to texting. But instead he put the phone to his ear. Waited.

No one said anything.

All he could hear was a faint scraping sound, then a heavy thud. Somewhere in the background was the rumbling sound of indistinct voices. It took a few seconds before Atif realized he was listening to a call made by mistake. Rico must have put his phone back in his pocket after the first call and managed to press the Redial button.

He pressed the phone to his ear, trying to make out as much as possible as he looked at the time once more. High time to get going. But he couldn't drive off now. The sound of the engine would make it impossible to hear anything going on on the other end of the line. The muttered conversation at the other end was still going on, only interrupted by more scraping sounds, presumably as the phone bounced around in Rico's pocket.

In the distance Atif could hear a siren, and at first he thought it was coming from the phone. Then he realized it was coming from outside and was getting louder. He put his hand back on the ignition key. His heart was pounding faster in his chest, making the fever feel even worse.

The sirens were getting closer. If he was the one they were after, they'd fall silent any moment. They never kept their sirens on all the way, because obviously they didn't want to scare off whomever they were after. He looked around and discovered the entrance to a narrow bike lane at the other end of the parking lot. A loud crackle on the phone made him hold it away from his ear. The sirens were getting even closer.

Atif took a deep breath, then turned the key one notch. The voices over the phone were suddenly clearer, as if someone were taking the phone out of the pocket. He pressed the cell phone to his ear. He thought he could hear a car door closing.

". . . ergsgatan 48," he managed to catch. Then another voice repeating the address. He guessed it was a taxi driver. There was another scraping sound, and the line went dead. At that moment the sirens fell silent.

Atif started the engine, put the car in gear, and pressed his foot to the floor. There was a barrier blocking half the bike lane, a metal post bent into the shape of a large letter P. Atif had seen that sort of barrier before and had an idea that they were designed to give way if the fire brigade needed to get through. He clutched the steering wheel and hoped he was right.

The left wing of the car hit the barrier, the wheel jolted, and he was through. The bike lane led straight into a residential area and ran along a line of neatly trimmed hedges before emerging into a park. Beyond some trees he could see a main road.

Atif put the car in a lower gear, twisted the wheel, and drove straight out across the snow-covered grass. The worn tires struggled with the snow, making the car slide sideways. He felt the car slow down and changed gear again, trying a higher one instead. If he got stuck here he was finished, he was in no condition to run. But the car kept on moving, foot by foot. Atif glanced in the rearview mirror. He thought he could make out blue flashing lights reflecting off the houses.

The main road was getting closer as the park began to slope upward. The car was losing more speed now, and the spinning wheels were making the needle on the speedometer tremble. Thirty feet to go.

Fifteen.

The car had almost come to a standstill and was jerking rather than rolling forward now. It broke through a bank of snow and lurched out onto a bike lane where the wheels got a better grip. Atif twisted the wheel, changed down to a lower gear, put his foot down on the floor, and followed the bike lane until he had built up a bit of speed. Then he spun the wheel left and burst through another bank of snow. He crossed another thirty feet of snow-covered grass before crashing through some bushes, mowing down a low wire fence and emerging straight onto the main road.

A couple of cars blew their horns at him but he ignored them. He tucked the car in behind a truck, eased his foot off the accelerator, and went with the flow of traffic.

About two hundred yards farther on two marked police cars raced past with their lights flashing. Neither of them so much as slowed down as they passed.

THIRTY-FOUR

They rolled onto the ferry last and were shown where to park. Natalie hardly had time to switch the engine off before the ramp was raised behind them. The flat, open deck wasn't even half-full, just fifteen cars or so, arranged in three lines.

"I'm just going to have a quick smoke." Natalie opened the car door and let in a gust of cold wind from the sea. She hurried over to the metal construction on one side that contained a waiting room and a small smoking area. Sarac remained in the car and tried to gather his thoughts.

Erico Sabatini's name had opened a new pathway in his memory. He could still see the man in front of him, a small, wiry, talkative man. Not a big fish, probably a small-time dealer, but even people like that could be useful. He tried to remember what sort of information Sabatini had given him, and who he and the other men had informed on. But there he hit a brick wall. Why had he listed the men together? And where did the fifth one, the extremely secretive Erik I. Johansson, fit into the picture?

Sarac massaged his temples. The answers were in there somewhere, and maybe a talk with Erico Sabatini could make things a bit clearer. So far he had been fumbling for information, but now he was suddenly sitting with plenty of pieces of the puzzle, and no idea of how they all fit together.

The piece that troubled him most was Brian Hansen. He could remember the man's death down to the smallest detail, even the way the car had smelled just before the shot was fired. Until he managed to fit that piece of the puzzle into place he couldn't share his progress with anyone, not even Molnar. He hoped Hansen wasn't associated with the feeling he had woken up with in the hospital. A feeling that was still getting stronger. That he had done something unforgivable . . .

The air inside the Golf suddenly felt stuffy and hard to breathe. Sarac was about to open the window, but where the handle should have been there was only a black bolt. So he opened the door instead, picked up his stick, and took a couple of cautious steps out onto the green-painted deck.

The lights of Vaxholm were approaching ahead of them. He made his way between the cars, trying to get to the far side to find some shelter from the wind. When he went around the corner of the two-story cabin he almost collided with Natalie. She had a cigarette in one hand and her cell phone in the other. When she saw him she started slightly. The fleeting expression on her face was almost imperceptible. But for a brief moment Sarac could have sworn that what he saw in her eyes was . . . fear.

• • •

All investigations consist of methodical work, intuition, and a bit of luck, Atif thought. In his case, something as simple as a call made by accident. Rico, whoever he was, seemed to be in roughly the same situation as Pitbull. For some reason he had chosen to get out of the city for a while. Perhaps he was mixed up in Adnan's death, unless the reason for his flight was something else entirely? No matter what, he was a link to both Erik J. and his secret friend.

The building Rico lived in was big. Three stairwells, six floors, plus the ground floor, which was occupied by a mixture of shops and offices. For a brief moment Atif had the feeling he was looking for a needle in a haystack, then he noticed that one of the businesses was a gym. That could hardly be a coincidence. He parked the car where he had a good view of the building and settled back to wait. He didn't really know what for. He had no idea what Rico looked like, and without a surname there was no point snooping about the stairwells. All he could do was keep watch and hope that the good fortune that had led him there wasn't going to let him down.

He pulled out the blister pack of acetaminophen, popped out a couple of pills, and swallowed them dry. He was already feeling a bit better, probably thanks to the injection the doctor had given him. The pain in his arm and chest was under control now, but he leaned the seat back slightly to ease the pressure on them.

After about fifteen minutes a taxi pulled up outside the building and a man and woman got out. Atif thought the woman looked vaguely familiar, then realized that she reminded him of Cassandra. Pouting lips, bleached hair, oversized silicone breasts that were visible even beneath her fur coat. He really should have called them, to make sure everything was okay up in Dalarna. He promised himself he'd call as soon as he was back in his hotel room.

The couple went into the gym. Atif felt his cell phone vibrate in his inside pocket and had a bit of a job extracting it.

Cassandra calling.

Speak of the devil . . . Had something happened? He hesitated, gazed out across the empty pavement, then pressed Answer.

• • •

"Here it is! Sabatini's is the middle door," Sarac said.

"Okay, I'll just try to find somewhere to park," Natalie said.

The drive had taken almost an hour. He had been immersed in thought and Natalie had kept to herself. She hadn't said a word until they were approaching the city. She had asked a question that he hadn't been expecting at all: how common was it for a handler to lie to his source? He had replied in line with regulations, that it was forbidden to lie or make a promise you couldn't fulfill. But he still got the impression that she had worked out what the real answer was. Of course you lied. Lying was a tool, a way to get quick results. The sources presumably realized this fairly often, yet they chose to go on working for him. Perhaps because they so dearly wanted what he was saying to be true. And as long as they didn't see through his bluff, at least they were still in the game. They had a chance.

Natalie drove around a corner, found a loading zone, and parked the Golf. She got ready to get out.

"Er, it's probably best if you wait here," Sarac said. "I mean, I hope you're not offended?"

"No, no." Natalie sounded almost relieved. "Of course not. I'll stay here, call if you need my help." She pulled out her ChapStick and ran it over her lips.

Sarac got out of the car, fastened his padded jacket, picked up his stick, and walked back toward the corner.

• • •

It was Tindra calling, not Cassandra. She must have got hold of her mother's phone and looked up his name. Her bright voice was bubbling in his ear, putting Atif in a slightly better mood.

The couple from the gym came back out onto the sidewalk. The man lit a cigarette for the woman, then one for himself. Over the phone Tindra was chattering about rabbits.

"Tindra, listen to me now. Amu's got to hang up. I'll call you this evening and you can tell me more. Okay?"

The woman spun around and gave the man the finger.

"And it's going to be called Snowball," Tindra went on.

In the distance, at the other end of the building, another man came around the corner. Padded jacket, woolly hat pulled down over his forehead, a stick in one hand. He was walking rather stiffly, as if one leg wouldn't do as he wanted. The man seemed to be aiming for one of the entrances. Atif ended the call, reluctantly cutting off Tindra's description in the middle of

a sentence. He promised himself that the next time he saw her
he'd take her to a pet shop and let her choose her own rabbit,
to make up for it.

He opened the car door and put one foot down on the
tarmac, trying to slip his cell phone back into his pocket at
the same time. His swollen finger slipped and he dropped it
on the seat instead. By the time he straightened up the woman
had just started screaming.

• • •

When Sarac was thirty feet away from the door, it opened and
a man came out. Sarac recognized him at once. It was Erico
Sabatini. The man ran straight into a couple who were standing
smoking on the sidewalk. He wasn't wearing a coat or hat, just
a red-patterned T-shirt and jeans. At the same moment the
woman started to scream Sarac realized that Sabatini didn't
even have any shoes on.

• • •

Atif saw another man come out. His hair was sticking up, he
had no coat on, and he wasn't wearing any shoes. Something
he'd said or done had made the woman start screaming. She
was pointing at the colorful pattern on the man's T-shirt.

Atif went to cross the street, waiting to let a car go past. The
man with the stick was getting closer as well. The woman was
still screaming. The sound echoed between the buildings.

The man with no coat grabbed hold of the woman's hands,
but the man who was with her quickly pushed him away. He
knocked the man off balance and he fell to his knees. The
woman held up her hands, still screaming. Atif suddenly realized what was on her hands . . .

• • •

Blood, Sarac managed to think just before Sabatini collapsed
onto the sidewalk. He had thought the man's T-shirt was just

brightly patterned. But it had actually been white to start with. The woman's screams were echoing through the street, sending flashes of lightning through his head.

He fell to his knees and tried to lift Sabatini's head. The man's eyes were half-open, his eyelids fluttering. The whole front of his T-shirt was covered in blood.

"Shut up," he heard someone bark, and the woman fell silent instantly. She and the man with her backed away ten feet. They stood there staring, without making any move to help.

A large man with cropped hair sank to his knees beside Sabatini and pulled up his wet T-shirt. Sarac started and almost let go of Sabatini's head. Then he realized that the man didn't match any of his memories. Dark red blood was seeping from two stab wounds in the right-hand side of Sabatini's stomach, just below his ribs.

"His liver," the large man growled. "Stop your fucking filming and call an ambulance!" This was aimed at the couple, both of whom had started fiddling with their cell phones.

"Give me your scarf," the man said to Sarac.

The large man rolled the scarf into a ball and pressed it to Sabatini's stomach. The fabric became soaked through and dark almost immediately.

"Y-you . . ." Sabatini had opened his eyes. "Fuuuck!" He grabbed Sarac's arm.

"The ambulance is on its way," Sarac said. He suddenly realized he had tears in his eyes. "It's going to be okay, Erico." He took the man's hand and squeezed it.

"Who stabbed you?" the big man muttered.

Sabatini didn't answer, just went on squeezing Sarac's hand. His breath was coming in shallow pants.

"T-this wasn't supposed to h-happen. H-he promised . . ." In the distance they could hear sirens getting closer.

"Who promised, Erico? Who stabbed you? Was it Janus?" Sarac noticed the big man's reaction.

Sabatini grabbed at the front of Sarac's jacket. "It's all his fault! All . . . Erik . . ." Sabatini's speech disintegrated into a terrible gurgle. The sirens were getting louder, bouncing off the buildings. Sabatini let go of Sarac's jacket. His face was ashen, his jaw clenching and cramping.

"He prom . . . isssed."

. . .

Atif realized the man was finished when he saw where he'd been stabbed. The liver was full of blood, and if it got punctured it was really just a matter of time. Spilled blood always looked much worse than it really was, but Atif guessed there was almost a liter on the sidewalk and soaked into the scarf and his clothes. And probably the same amount inside the man's torso.

He stared at the man who was holding the victim's hand. A thin, angular face, pointed nose, sunken blue eyes. He didn't look particularly well either. The man had called the wounded man Erico and had asked about Janus, which obviously had to mean that this was Rico bleeding to death on the sidewalk. Rico had said something to the other man, something he hadn't heard properly. More than anything Atif felt like yanking the other man to his feet, dragging him into his car, and then quietly persuading him to explain all he knew about Erik J. and Janus. But the sirens were getting closer and closer. In a minute or so the place would be crawling with cops and paramedics.

He glanced over his shoulder and realized he didn't have time to get back to his car. What the hell, it was pretty much fucked anyway after what happened at the health center. He could always get another one.

He straightened up and took a couple of steps back. He saw that the couple on the sidewalk had ignored his instructions and were filming what was going on with their cell phones. Slowly moving in on the dying man for a close-up, like hyenas on prey! With a bit of luck they'd only caught his back on camera. If not, he'd be under suspicion of two murders. There wasn't much he could do about that. He took a few lumbering steps and aimed for the nearest corner.

. . .

Natalie heard the sirens getting closer. She quickly stubbed out her cigarette and pulled her phone from her pocket. No missed calls, no messages. Shit!

Rickard had simply absorbed the information. He had barely even thanked her before he hung up. So what the hell was she supposed to do now? Run after Sarac? A police car raced past, then another one. The sirens fell silent abruptly. Whatever was going on, it was very close, just around the corner.

She took a couple of steps in that direction, then stopped. Maybe it was smarter to curb her curiosity for a few minutes and just see whether Sarac showed up. But what if something had happened to him? What if the sirens were because of him?

A tall man in a dark padded coat came around the corner ahead of her. He was half running, almost lurching in a rather odd way. One of his trouser legs had a dark red stain on it. Something about the look in the man's eyes and the fixed expression on his face made Natalie turn around after him.

She frowned. And thought about the description from the murder in Roslagsgatan. *A large man in dark clothing.* Could this be the man Rickard was looking for? The one known as Janus? In which case she'd just drawn the winning ticket. The thought of Rickard's reaction made her pulse speed up. She raised her cell phone and let out a loud whistle. When the man turned around, instinctively she took a couple of quick pictures of him, then started running toward the corner.

. . .

Sarac was sitting on the sidewalk. He was holding Sabatini's hand, feeling it getting colder in spite of the paramedics' frantic work. In the end he had to let go as they lifted Sabatini into the ambulance.

The police were already cordoning off the area, stretching out their blue and white plastic tape and sealing off almost the entire block. Two officers were talking to the argumentative couple, who now had their arms around each other. More police had managed to open the door to Sabatini's building and were heading inside, weapons drawn.

Sarac got slowly to his feet, brushing the grit and slush from his trousers as best he could. Jesus! He wiped his eyes with the back of his hand.

Someone took hold of his arm.

"You saw the whole thing, didn't you?" A female police officer, she couldn't have been more than twenty-five. No one he recognized. He saw her looking at the bloodstains on his trousers and coat. "We'd like you to accompany us to the station."

. . .

Sarac's been arrested, what should I do? /Natalie

Natalie was standing by the cordon, watching as Sarac was put in the back of a police car. He seemed okay, which was at least of some comfort. But what did the rest of it mean?

She received a reply to her text less than a minute later.

Hold back for now! /R

Okay, so what did that mean? How long was *for now*? His texts were even more abrupt than his phone conversations. She hated people who couldn't even be bothered to write their whole name.

So what was she supposed to do now? If Sarac could just look at the pictures and confirm that they were of the man he was looking for, she could complete her mission. But instead she watched him being driven away in a police car.

. . .

The car journey only took a couple of minutes; the nearest police station was just a few blocks away. While they were waiting
for the gate to the custody unit to open, the female officer's
phone rang.

"Nineteen forty-seven, Andrén," she said curtly. Then listened to the person at the other end.

"Okay," she said. The gate was now open, but she gestured
to her colleague to wait.

"Understood, we're on our way." She ended the call.

"We've been outbid," she said to her colleague. "We're to
take him straight to headquarters in Kronoberg."

The driver put the car in reverse and pulled back into the
street. He did a U-turn and set off into traffic.

"Who was it who called?" the male officer said when they
had reached Hornsgatan. "The duty officer at Crime?"

"I'll tell you later." The female officer gave Sarac a quick
sidelong glance.

The drive to Police Headquarters took barely ten minutes.

Sabatini's blood was still all over Sarac's hands and clothes.
He couldn't stop crying, and each time he sniffed, the female
officer looked at him in a way he didn't much like. As if she
thought he was pathetic for crying over a stranger. But Sabatini
hadn't been a stranger.

They drove into the underground garage and stopped by the
elevator leading up to the custody unit. They were met by two
people, a man and a woman, both wearing suits.

"We'll take it from here," the woman said.

"Okay," one of the uniformed officers replied. "You'll sign him
in as well?" She took her notebook out from her trouser pocket.

"We already have all the details," the woman in the suit
interrupted. "Thanks for your help, 1947."

She took Sarac lightly by the arm and led him over toward
the elevators. But instead of getting the elevator that went
straight up to the custody unit, they carried on, toward a smaller
elevator further inside the garage.

"Where are we going?" Sarac asked, hearing how flat his voice sounded.

"You'll see," the woman said, pressing the button for the top floor.

The corridor they emerged into looked deserted. Only half the lights in the ceiling were lit, there were rolls of paper and plastic piled up along the corridor, and the whole place smelled of paint.

They led him into one of the small rooms. Two office chairs facing each other, one window, blinds drawn. Nothing else.

"Would you like something to drink?" the woman asked.

Sarac nodded. He suddenly noticed that he was terribly thirsty. The woman left the room while her colleague stayed behind. In the distance Sarac heard the sound of running water. Then the woman came back and handed him a glass.

"T-thanks." He raised the glass, shut his eyes, and took some big mouthfuls. He tried to erase the image of the dying Sabatini from his mind's eye. When he opened his eyes again the pair who had escorted him were gone. Instead there was a man was sitting on the chair opposite him. A fair-haired, well-dressed man with a boyish appearance. Sarac recognized him at once.

"Hello, David," the man said. "My name's Oscar Wallin, but you already know that. We're old acquaintances."

THIRTY-FIVE

"Shame about Sabatini." Wallin leaned forward toward Sarac. "I've had CIs who've died. It gets to you, doesn't it? It makes no difference what they put in the handbooks or teach in courses. All that stuff about not getting too close, not getting involved." Wallin shook his head.

"CIs put their lives in our hands. We persuade them to cooperate, use all sorts of psychological tricks to snare them. And once they've taken the bait, as you know, there's—"

"No way back," Sarac muttered.

Wallin nodded slowly.

"You look awful, David. I almost wouldn't have recognized you. The last time we met was when I approached you with a proposal, if you remember?" Wallin leaned back in his chair.

Sarac shook his head slowly. "I've had a stroke, in case you haven't heard. I basically can't remember anything."

"From the past few years, yes, so I heard." Wallin smiled, a boyish smile that made him look even younger, if that was actually possible.

"I was working at National Crime at the time, where I too was involved in handling CIs. We even trained together, you and I, David. 'The twelve-step model for source recruitment,' I'm sure you remember," Wallin said.

Sarac didn't answer.

"One of my sources had told me something interesting," Wallin went on. "There were rumors that the Stockholm Police had managed to place a top-secret infiltrator at the heart of the criminal community. A person with the code name Janus. The Roman god with two faces."

Wallin threw his arms out. "Of course I didn't believe him at first. CIs are one thing, but infiltrators, people expressly placed inside criminal organizations, are, as you know full well, not permitted here in Sweden. It all gets a bit too complicated from a purely legal perspective, seeing as an infiltrator sooner or later has to commit crimes in order to maintain his or her credibility. And of course the police mustn't condone or, worse still, assist someone to commit crimes. Because how would that look?"

Wallin smiled even more broadly this time, but without the smile reaching his eyes. "But my source was insistent, told me that this Janus had caused a lot of damage. That it was down to him that a whole chapter of a biker gang had been broken up, and that the Russians had lost almost forty-five pounds of heroin. And even though they knew about the infiltrator, and there was a price on his head, and the bosses had even managed to find out his code name, they still didn't know who it was. So we at National Crime decided to take a closer look. And we discovered that Peter Molnar and his special operations team were responsible for most of the best arrests in Stockholm. And of course Molnar himself used to run his own informants." Wallin shook his head.

"I know Peter. He wouldn't have any problems breaking a few rules, and he's smart. But running such an advanced operation as this isn't really his style. The person we were looking for had to be smart, talented, motivated, and definitely not risk-averse. In other words, not exactly your average police officer. And if you looked at the officers working with CIs in Stockholm at the time, there was really only one obvious candidate." He held out his hands. "Top of the class, David Sarac. One of the few people who has ever got the better of me."

Sarac didn't answer, but it all sounded very familiar. Like an old story you'd suppressed but that came back the moment someone started to tell it.

"So we had an informal meeting, you and I," Wallin went on. "I told you what I knew about Janus. That he was an infiltrator, and that you were breaking a whole load of rules. That you might even be guilty of misconduct in public office."

"But that you weren't about to give me away," Sarac interrupted. "Not if I shared Janus with you. Giving you a chance of glory up at National Crime, to help build up your own reputation."

Wallin sat there in silence, tapping his fingertips together in his lap as he carefully studied Sarac's face. Sarac looked up, trying to keep his gaze steady.

Wallin was an asshole, a prime example. But he was smart as well. Sarac wondered where this conversation was heading.

"Memory is a remarkable thing, isn't it, David?" Wallin said thoughtfully. "You didn't remember our meeting, did you? Not until I told you about it just now. And then you had enough detail to find a path through the mist."

Sarac said nothing, fighting to keep his appearance as neutral as possible. Wallin seemed to see right through him.

"You really have lost your memory," he said. "I wasn't actually entirely sure, I suspected that the whole thing might be a smoke screen. A way for you to get out of the mess you'd got yourself into."

"You mean the fact that you were trying to blackmail me." The sharpness in Sarac's voice surprised even him. He saw Wallin squirm slightly in his chair.

"You wanted to share Janus," Sarac went on. "Or rather, you wanted to share the information but leave me to take all the risks. If I didn't agree to it, you'd uncover the whole operation. And make sure I was fired."

Wallin's mouth narrowed.

"And you were thinking of repeating your offer now, weren't you? That's why I'm here. Because you want to know who Janus is, and how to contact him? And what my hold on him is."

Sarac straightened up.

"Listen very carefully, Wallin. I can't actually remember anything about Janus, not a fucking thing. And even if I did, I wouldn't hand him over to you. You said it yourself a short while ago. Our sources put their lives in our hands. Trust us to do the right thing."

Wallin studied Sarac.

"You don't get it, do you?" he eventually said.

"What?"

"That if I can work out who's working Janus, so can other people. You just have to be smart enough to want to get to the bottom of the problem. You bribe an amenable police officer to get hold of the name of the best handler in Stockholm, and voilà!"

Sarac gulped unconsciously.

"We've been keeping our eyes and ears open, David," Wallin went on. "And a few weeks ago we got confirmation. Just days before your crash, in fact."

"What?" Sarac repeated. But this time he had already guessed the answer.

"Someone's looking for you, David. Someone's reached the same conclusion I did. That the only way to find Janus is through you."

. . .

The little room suddenly felt airless. The air-conditioning was probably switched off to stop it from spreading dust and paint fumes to the rest of the building. Sarac took his jacket off. The front was covered in Sabatini's blood.

"As you might have heard, I've changed jobs," Wallin said. "On paper I'm running an inquiry for the Ministry of Justice. Looking at the potential savings to be made from pooling resources among public bodies. But in practice I'm working under the direct orders of Minister of Justice Stenberg. Jesper has asked me to identify the best police officers in the country.

The ones worth investing in for the future." He paused to let his words sink in.

"It would be very easy to add your name to the list, David. You could be responsible for the way CIs are handled throughout the country. You wouldn't have to deal with tired old fossils like Bergh, or ass-lickers like Kollander. But you're not the sort of man who can be bought, David, I've worked that much out. That's why I'm not going to offer any enticement. But the fact remains." He pulled a face that was difficult to read. "As long as you are the only link to Janus, you're in danger. Regional Crime has already washed its hands of you, so you're pretty much on your own, without backup. But if, on the other hand, you were to start working for me . . ." Wallin threw his arms out.

"You'll see to it that I get protection," Sarac muttered.

Outside they could suddenly hear voices. Then there was a knock at the door and the woman who had given Sarac his water popped her head in.

"Bergh is here," she said curtly. "He's got Molnar with him. They're demanding to be allowed to see Sarac."

Wallin looked at Sarac.

"Show the gentlemen in."

But before the woman had time to turn around the door was thrown open and Peter Molnar pushed into the room. Bergh followed behind him.

"Peter, how nice." Wallin smiled. "And the head of the Intelligence Unit as well, my word! I was almost starting to wonder when you were going to appear."

Molnar seemed slightly taken aback by Wallin's reaction but quickly recovered.

"What the hell are you up to, Oscar?" he growled.

"Sarac and I have just been having a little chat, between old friends. Isn't that right, David?" Wallin nodded toward Sarac.

"Come on, David," Bergh said. "You don't have to sit here,

we'll take you home so you can have a wash and change your clothes. I've spoken to the duty desk, and they're happy to take a statement from you over the phone."

He gestured to Sarac to stand up.

"Stay where you are, David," Wallin said. "We didn't have time to finish our discussion before these two gentlemen barged in."

"It doesn't matter what rank you are, Oscar, you're not David's boss," Molnar said. "The way I see it, you have absolutely no authority to give any orders here."

Wallin met Molnar's gaze. Then he threw his arms out.

"How typical of you, Peter. You turn every situation into a cock-measuring contest." Wallin shook his head. "The truth, David, is that both Bergh and Peter here want to get hold of Janus just as much as I do. Maybe even more. You see . . ." Wallin leaned closer to Sarac. "If it turns out that either of them knew that Janus is an illegal infiltrator, then they'll be in a very difficult situation. Bergh is your boss and, at a guess, also your controller. He shouldn't have authorized an operation of this sort."

Wallin gestured vaguely toward Bergh, and Sarac saw him look away.

"And as far as Peter and his specialist team are concerned . . . well, perhaps you remember how sensitive the district commissioner is about subgroups that don't follow the rules, particularly very male groups?"

Molnar's eyes narrowed slightly, but he said nothing.

"As long as the results keep coming in she doesn't care," Wallin went on. "She's more than happy to hold a press conference and present their results as her own. But if the slightest little difficulty occurs, something that might put a spoke in the wheel of her plans to become our next National Head of Police, then . . ."

Wallin smiled again, the same cold, impersonal smile as before.

"Well." He nodded to Bergh and Molnar. "These two gentlemen want to make sure there are no loose ends, at any cost. No unnecessary risk factors."

Wallin paused, then looked directly at Sarac. "Such as you, David."

THIRTY-SIX

"Wallin's a slippery bastard," Bergh muttered as he maneuvered the car through the traffic. "Seriously ambitious, almost certainly aiming to become National Head of Police. This inquiry for the Ministry of Justice has given him the perfect platform. A chance to keep an eye on the competition."

"You mean the district commissioner in Stockholm?" Sarac said.

Bergh nodded.

"There are plenty of people who'd like to see a woman in the top job. Eva Swensk is a strong candidate, and she's strengthening her grip on the largest police district in the country. Which simultaneously means there's less room for mistakes, to put it politely."

Sarac said nothing for a while. Wallin's words were still bouncing around inside his head. He had broken the rules, he knew that already. He had actually known all along that Janus wasn't just an ordinary informant but an infiltrator. Someone he controlled, gave orders to, missions. Someone who even committed crimes with his tacit consent, as well as that of the police authority, indirectly.

But the feelings of guilt Sarac had been having trouble shaking off weren't the result of professional misconduct. An infiltrator who was managed well was an excellent asset. The question was rather: How well had he handled Janus? Or himself, for that matter? He still couldn't explain why his apartment had looked as if it belonged to a junkie, and he had no desire at all to go back there. Bergh seemed almost to have read his mind.

"The apartment's been cleaned up," Bergh said. "Must have been that girl, your care assistant, who did it. I think you've got a bit of new furniture as well, and the locks have been changed, but Peter knows more about that."

Sarac nodded, then suddenly remembered that Natalie had said she'd cleared up. He wondered where she was. And whether she was still sitting and waiting in the car over at Högbergsgatan.

"Listen, David." Bergh turned toward Sarac, and both his expression and tone of voice told Sarac what was coming.

"I know, I know," he said. "Obviously I should have called you or Peter rather than just going off to see Sabatini."

Bergh shook his head. "That wasn't actually what I was going to say, David, even if you're right. No, I actually wanted to apologize to you."

Sarac was taken aback and tried to work out which way the conversation was heading now. He failed completely.

"I shouldn't have put pressure on you the way I did up at the hospital," Bergh went on. "Not to mention the whole business of pretending to transfer you to the property store." He shook his head.

"Wallin's well informed. I'm not just your boss but also your controller, the one who should have been keeping an eye on you. But I allowed myself to be persuaded to ignore the rules. Janus insisted that only one police officer knew his true identity, otherwise he wasn't going to cooperate. So I wrote my own name on the form, even though you were actually entirely on your own. Kollander gave the whole thing his unofficial blessing. We let the possibilities blind us and didn't realize the risk we were exposing you to." Bergh shook his bald head.

"After your accident I panicked. Forty years in the force, mortgage on the house and the country cottage, Jonas's course fees, everything. I'd promised myself that I wouldn't end up like the Duke. Bribed and dishonored."

The name brought Sarac up short. A memory appeared but

disappeared before he managed to grab hold of it. Eugene von Katzow, that was the name of Bergh's predecessor, although he was usually known as the Duke. He was long gone by the time Sarac joined the department, after a lengthy internal investigation and a lot of media attention. But there was something else there, something that involved him personally. Another piece of the puzzle for his growing collection.

Bergh pulled into a parking space a thousand feet from Sarac's building. Then turned to face him.

"But then I spoke to the wife. And realized that it really wasn't the end of the world. To be honest, I'm sick of all the crap. I'm sick of arguing with officious assholes like Kollander who don't understand police work and kick up a fuss every time we have to pay a source more than the embarrassingly low standard fee. He doesn't give a damn about the benefit to society or how many crooks we catch, as long as the budget balances. Not to mention men like Wallin, only interested in their own careers." Bergh shook his head again.

"As you already know, the backup list of your CIs was missing from the safe. An internal investigation is under way up in the department, under the leadership of our old friend Superintendent Dreyer. I could probably have ridden out the Janus problem, but a serious security breach in my own department is another matter."

Bergh made a resigned gesture.

Sarac frowned. The name Dreyer felt familiar as well. Molnar had mentioned him before, but he hadn't reacted then. Now the name filled him with anxiety.

"Management has to make a show of force," Bergh said. "Kollander has already come up with one proposal, full salary up to retirement if I cooperate. Stick to the script and make sure nothing lands on him or the district commissioner. My lawyer says it's a good offer, and in the end it always comes down to money, doesn't it, David?"

Bergh shrugged and leaned closer to Sarac.

"You're a good police officer. A damn good one. But I've been involved in several cases where a handler has got too close to his contact, almost forgot who he was and where his loyalties lay. It's not really so strange. The job is all about dissemblance, assuming a role and making truth and lies sound exactly the same. But if you carry on for too long, in the end no one knows what the truth is—not even you yourself. We all have to calibrate our own moral compass, keep things tidy, if you know what I mean? Keep our own house in order."

Sarac's mouth had gone dry and he swallowed a couple of times.

"Right now the internal investigators are focusing on me," Bergh went on. "But it's only a matter of time before Dreyer comes knocking on your door, and you need to be prepared."

He reached into the backseat and pulled out an old blue bag.

"I've been going through my old things. Getting rid of stuff I no longer need. Maybe you should do the same." He passed the bag to Sarac. "There's some things in here that I think you might need. But don't open it until you're on your own, okay?"

He leaned across Sarac and opened the passenger door.

"Once again, David, I really am very sorry."

THIRTY-SEVEN

The apartment still smelled strongly of disinfectant. All the blinds were open and the wrecked sofa had been replaced with a new one.

"The boys sorted that out," Molnar said. "They took a trip to Ikea. We thought it made sense to change the locks as well and get you a proper security chain, so you can stay here for a couple of nights if you don't feel up to going back to the island. The internal investigators seem to be taking time off over the holidays; it's been pretty quiet for the past few days. What have you got there?" He pointed at the bag Sarac was holding in his hand.

"From Bergh," Sarac mumbled. "Some personal belongings of mine he managed to salvage down in the property store." Lying came surprisingly easily.

Sarac went into the bathroom and shoved the bag into the cupboard under the basin. For a moment he was tempted to open it, but he could hear Molnar's footsteps outside the door. So he took off his bloodstained jacket instead and threw it in the bath. He sat down on the toilet seat and began to fumble with his trousers. He realized that he'd left his stick somewhere, either in Högbergsgatan or in the police car. No matter, he seemed to be able to manage fine without it.

"David," Molnar said on the other side of the bathroom door. "What Wallin said is pretty much true." His voice sounded strained. "The whole Janus affair is a gray area, we were all aware of that." Then silence.

"But the possibilities outweighed the risks," Sarac said.

Molnar's sigh was audible through the door.

"Janus was something quite unique, a chance to change the game completely. We got fantastic results, in total almost seventy pounds of narcotics. Doping drugs worth millions, stolen luxury cars, weapons," Molnar said.

"But if anything went wrong, the damage would be limited to me. One single police officer who had exceeded his authority." Sarac could feel himself getting angry.

"That wasn't actually my idea, David."

"So whose was it, then?" Sarac opened the bathroom door and found himself staring into Molnar's sad eyes. His anger vanished instantly, he suddenly realized.

"Mine," he muttered. "The whole thing was my idea?" Sarac gulped, suddenly feeling rather sick. So that was what Bergh had actually meant. That he should have protected him from himself. "What you really want to know, Peter, is if I'm still planning to keep my word? If I'm going to take the blame when all hell breaks loose?"

"For fuck's sake, David!" Molnar looked pained and seemed to be searching for the right words.

"Bergh's wavering," Sarac said. "The head of Regional Crime's offered him a deal. Full salary to retirement if he takes the blame for the theft from the safe and keeps the other bosses out of it. It's probably part of the deal for him to talk about Janus, say he's an illegal infiltrator and so on."

Molnar pulled a doubtful face. "Kjell Bergh would never agree to anything like that. He'd never hang any of his own officers out to dry."

"No?"

Sarac suddenly realized that he was standing in the hall wearing just his underpants, socks, and a T-shirt. He went into the bedroom. That too had been tidied up. There was a new mattress on the bed and he found all his clothes in the wardrobe, washed and neatly folded away. It must have been Natalie. For a brief moment he found himself wishing she was there. The way things had been going recently, she was the only person he dared trust.

He heard Molnar shut the bathroom door, dug out a pair of jogging trousers, and pulled them on. Then he limped back out to the living room. His right leg was working better and better. The sofa was empty, and he heard Molnar running water in the bathroom. He sat down. The padding was hard but would presumably give a bit over time.

"Wallin said someone was after me," he said, loudly enough to be heard in the bathroom. "That someone had worked out that Janus is working for me, someone who might even have tried to kill me in the Söderleden Tunnel."

The bathroom door opened and Molnar came out.

"And you believed him?" he said. "I'm guessing that Oscar also offered you protection, right? That's what I'd have done in his shoes. First outline the threat, then offer protection. A classic way to recruit someone."

"So you think he's lying?" Sarac said.

"I didn't say that," Molnar said.

Sarac suddenly clutched his head, shut his eyes, and leaned back. Sabatini was back in his head. The blood, and his gasped whisper: *This wasn't supposed to happen. He promised . . ."*

"Sabatini . . . you knew him, didn't you?" Sarac said.

Molnar nodded. "I recruited him, once upon a time. You inherited him from me when I changed departments. A small-time crook, shame it had to end like this. You haven't said what happened, or what you were doing up at Högbergsgatan."

"I realized I wanted to ask Sabatini about something. But I was too late," Sarac said.

Molnar sat down on the sofa.

"Did he say who did it? Who stabbed him?"

Sarac took a deep breath. The words *It's all his fault* were echoing in his head.

"He was muttering loads of things, only half of it was audible." Sarac tried to keep his voice neutral. Why was he lying? Why didn't he just repeat what Sabatini had said?

"Brian Hansen, Selim Markovic, and Pasi Lehtonen," Sarac

went on. He saw Molnar stiffen. "They all worked for me, didn't they?"

Molnar nodded. "So you know?"

"That they're dead, murdered, just like Sabatini? Yes, I found out, all on my own. Without anyone telling me."

"The notebook." Molnar's eyes narrowed. "I had a feeling that was why you showed up at Sabatini's. You cracked the code and got hold of a name, yet you still didn't call me." His voice sounded cool, nowhere near as friendly as before. "Don't you trust me, David?"

Sarac shrugged.

"Do you trust me, Peter? Why didn't you tell me that someone seems to be trying to get rid of my sources? Besides, there are other things you're keeping from me, aren't there?"

Molnar looked at him, ran his tongue over his teeth, and seemed to be considering how to respond.

"Okay, David," he said. "You're quite right. There are things I chose not to mention." Molnar squirmed slightly, once again looking for the right words.

"At the hospital, after the crash. Your blood tests."

"Go on," Sarac said.

"You tested positive for both THC and methamphetamine."

Sarac's stomach clenched. He thought about the sticky meth pipe in his apartment. The smell, the feeling that it was a junkie's home.

"And I'm sorry to say that I wasn't exactly surprised," Molnar continued. "I'd had my suspicions for a while. I suppose I should say that I was thinking of raising the subject with you, but to be honest, David . . ." Molnar sighed. "You were working night and day with Janus. Delivering fantastic results, making us all look damn good. So why try to fix something that wasn't broken?" Molnar looked down at the floor.

"But I should have realized. The pressure of running such a big project, alone, without any backup. Knowing that you were running the risk of getting fired, maybe even prison. That's like balancing on a high wire without the slightest margin for error.”

Molnar held his breath for a moment before going on.

“Sometimes we end up getting too close to a CI, David. Share information we shouldn’t. Janus was the only person who was in the same situation as you, the only person who knew what you were going through. Maybe he suggested taking a little something, just to help you cope? Amphetamines to stay focused, dope to come down? Either way, it’s history now. We fixed the test results so there’s no mention of anything in the report. And after three weeks in the hospital you were clean, so I decided not to say anything about it to you. Obviously in hindsight that was stupid, but the fact is that I was ashamed of not offering you more support. And of letting you get too close to Janus.”

It’s all his fault, Sarac thought.

Molnar was staring at the floor, then he straightened up.

“What do you actually remember about him, David?” he said. “Things ought to be getting a bit clearer now, shouldn’t they?”

Sarac shook his head. “Still not much. To recruit such a serious criminal I must have found a good way in. It couldn’t have been money, the police force pays peanuts. So it was something else, something important, probably some kind of secret.”

“That’s what I’ve been thinking too,” Molnar said. “Go on, do you remember any details of his appearance?”

“Hardly anything at all. Just a dark-clad figure with a hood pulled up over his head. Nothing about how to contact him, no meeting places, but I’m sure I’d recognize him if I saw him.”

“I understand.” Molnar thought for a moment. “So how would you have gone about it, if we try to be less specific? You’re recruiting a heavyweight criminal source, someone whose identity absolutely mustn’t get out. You know you’re breaking the rules but that your boss will tolerate it as long as you do it discreetly. What’s the first thing you have to focus on?”

Sarac considered this. He tried to set his brain to neutral. He thought about the room in his dream, the whiteboard, the photographs, the spiderweb. He thought about mentioning it to Molnar but thought better of it. Not until he knew more.

"Funding," Sarac said, and Molnar nodded.

"I need money, to pay Janus. Travel, expenses, money to fund any deals he has to do. All expenses have to be approved by both Bergh and Kollander, so that's no good. I might be able to come up with some of it myself, fabricating travel receipts or claiming it's for other sources. But that won't work long-term."

Sarac fell silent and reflected.

"I probably need a backer," he finally said. "Someone who's prepared to cough up the money without asking any questions." A name popped into his head, a name he had heard Bergh mention that same evening.

"Do you remember who?" Molnar said.

"Von Katzow," Sarac said before he had even finished the thought. "Eugene von Katzow."

Molnar gave him a long, critical stare.

"Are you really sure about that, David? Involving the Duke would severely complicate things. His name is still mud for some of the bosses. You know he was hung out to dry in the press and all that."

Sarac tried to think, tried to sort out small fragments of the information that was starting to swirl about inside his head.

"I might well be wrong, of course," he said after a while. "Bergh mentioned von Katzow in the car, that could be where the name comes from. As you know, the connections up here aren't working too well right now." He tapped his forehead.

Molnar nodded. "Okay, let's skip that for the time being. Let's say you've sorted the funding, what would the next step be? How would you sort out contacts and meetings?"

Sarac tried to get back to his train of thought. Then he shook his head. "Sorry, it's completely blank."

"A car, maybe?" Molnar suggested.

"No, this type of source wouldn't like that. It would have to be somewhere that appealed to his ego. Showed how important he was to us. A good restaurant or a club. Cars . . ." He threw out one hand.

"Are for small potatoes." Molnar grinned, running his tongue over his teeth. "Good to hear that you remember what I taught you. You're almost certainly right. Meeting someone like Janus would require a very specific type of place. Discreet but still appealing."

Molnar fell silent and seemed to be waiting for Sarac to say something.

"How much do you know about Janus?" Sarac asked instead.

The question seemed to surprise Molnar.

"Basically no more than Bergh. In other words, practically nothing. Just that he's an extremely well-placed source and that he presumably isn't to be messed with. But, like I said, I'd worked out that you used a secret of some sort to recruit him."

Molnar ran his tongue over his teeth again. Was that an expression of nervousness, or just a tic he'd always had? Sarac wasn't sure.

"Okay, David, let's go back to the funding. Like you said yourself, you needed money. You must have used at least one secret account, if not more? That occurred to me when we were out on the island. Was there anything in your notebook about money or payments?"

Sarac shook his head. "Nothing at all, at least nothing that I've been able to work out."

"Shame," Molnar said. "The way I see it, the money's the only trail we've got that leads directly to Janus. I'm sure you see that, David."

He paused. He repeated that gesture with his tongue.

"There's only one way to regain control."

"Finding Janus," Sarac said. "Thanks, that thought had occurred to me."

Molnar didn't seem bothered by his sarcastic tone.

"Listen, David. The business with the safe is Bergh's problem, it doesn't affect us. If he's prepared to take the fall for that, fine. But seeing as neither Bergh nor Kollander know any details about the Janus affair, it's difficult for them to pin anything on you, at least without any concrete evidence. Do you see how I'm thinking?"

Sarac nodded.

"Without Janus and without any other documentation, they haven't got much of a case, have they?" Molnar went on. "They can't prove that you or I have broken any rules at all. All we have to do is make sure that Janus never existed. Do whatever it takes to . . ."

Protect the secret, Sarac thought.

THIRTY-EIGHT

Atif had a fever. Probably a pretty bad one. His body felt sluggish and his head was throbbing. There was only one chemist in the whole of the inner city that was open all night, and he didn't dare take the risk. Instead he popped out two more acetaminophen from the blister pack and swallowed them with some tepid tap water as he bent over the cracked little hand basin.

After what had happened in Högbergsgatan he was in an even worse position than before. He had made sure that the two vultures filming what was going on only managed to get his rear view. But that red-haired girl on the side street had tricked him, whistling and getting him to turn around instinctively, then taking a picture of his face. She was gone before he worked out what was happening. Very neatly done!

Janus was still one step ahead of him. He was getting rid of all the loose ends. He had already worked out what must have happened in Högbergsgatan. There had been a knock on the door and Rico had answered. That meant that Janus was either someone Rico knew or believed to be so harmless that he let him in. Someone delivering flowers, a postman, someone who wasn't any sort of threat.

No gun this time, no loud noises that might alarm the neighbors. Two well-aimed knife wounds to the gut, probably inflicted the moment Rico opened the door. A long, thin blade, to judge by the wounds. The perfect choice if you were aiming for internal organs. In ninety percent of cases a deep abdominal injury causes either severe bleeding or deep shock. After being stabbed twice Rico ought to have collapsed and bled to death in his hall while Janus walked calmly away. But Rico evidently belonged to the ten percent of people whose bodies reacted differently. People whose adrenal glands pumped out so much adrenaline that they managed to stay on their feet in spite of the severity of the injury, and even managed to walk a fair distance.

He stuffed all his clothes in a plastic bag, tied the handles, and threw it over toward the door. Then he got in the bath and turned the shower on. He let the water stream down his head and shoulders and scrubbed the last traces of blood from his hands and arms. After a while he crouched down. His body was aching badly, a six, maybe even a seven.

He needed to rest for a day or two and draw up a new plan. He had actually managed to find out something from Hög-bergsgatan. The film sequence had already been uploaded to the Internet. You could clearly see Rico dying in a pool of blood on the pavement. His own face wasn't visible, thank goodness, but the other man's was. You could even see his tears.

He hadn't been able to shake the impression he had got when he was there, and the video online had only made him more certain. The way he moved his head, the watchful look in his eyes, a few other barely noticeable aspects of his body language. The man was a cop. He had asked Sabatini about Janus and seemed to know what it was all about. As soon as the penicillin started to work and his body felt better, Atif was going to try to track him down.

• • •

Sarac locked the door, using all the new locks. He was exhausted and simply couldn't talk anymore. All he wanted to do was collapse in bed and close his eyes. Try to convince himself that everything he had been through recently, everything he had found out, was just a bizarre dream. When he woke up in the morning in his old bed, life would carry on on the other side of the chasm in his head. And this whole nightmare would be over.

Sure enough, the message on his bedroom wall was gone; Janus had probably wiped it off. He'd done such a good job that you couldn't see the slightest trace of it with your bare eyes.

Why hadn't he told Molnar the truth? That Sabatini had mentioned both Janus and Erik Johansson? Why hadn't he told him about the room in his dream, or the fact that he could remember an alarming amount of detail about Brian Hansen's death?

The explanation was simple. Somewhere deep inside he was still trying to protect Janus and preserve their shared secret. Even though the person he was trying to protect was probably a murderer. As soon as he shut his eyes he saw Sabatini's ashen face in front of him and heard his rattling breathing.

Five men on his list, a list crowned by a Janus symbol. Now four of them were dead. Why? That question was still waiting for an answer.

But everything that had happened had at least done something to his brain. It was probably the conversation with Molnar that had helped most. Ever since he found his office empty, Sarac had had the feeling that he was missing something. That he was interpreting things wrongly. And now he was certain of it. He had emptied his office himself; he even thought he could remember being there in the middle of the night, carrying out boxes. Moving everything to a safer place, away from prying eyes. Which meant that the room in his dream really did exist. That had been his base, the place where he had managed the whole Janus operation. It was somewhere out there in the winter darkness, maybe just a few blocks away. Guarding its secrets as it waited for him. That room was the corner piece he needed if he was to make a serious attempt to put the puzzle together. The only question was whether he really wanted to find it.

He slipped slowly into sleep and for a brief while was floating in a gray limbo. In the distance he could hear a siren. He didn't know whether it was outside or just in his head—sounds from the apartment upstairs. Someone was walking with heavy steps across the floor up there. An image appeared in his mind's eye. A dark silhouette in a hood, facing away from him. The silhouette slowly turned around, so slowly, almost in slow motion. The light fell on the man's shoulder, then the hood. But just as the light reached his face, just as he imagined that he recognized the man, another thought occurred to him. And suddenly he was wide awake. He had forgotten something, something he needed to check before he could sleep.

He got out of bed and limped into the bathroom. He opened the cupboard under the basin and pulled out the bag Bergh had given him. The zipper was stiff, but after a bit of fiddling it reluctantly opened. At the top of the bag was a blue bulletproof vest, similar to the one that had saved his life in the crash. Beneath the vest was a shoe box, and on its lid was a note with a short message. Big, jagged letters that reminded him of the ones he had seen in the hospital.

Everything begins and ends with Janus.

The box contained a snub-nosed revolver with its serial number filed off.

THIRTY-NINE

"In summary, we can say that the combination of these measures will result in an entirely new Swedish justice system. A justice system with consolidated management, control, and clear goals. A justice system for the future.

"That's all I wanted to say," Jesper Stenberg added after letting his words sink in properly. There were a few moments of silence in the room as the lights were turned back on. Stenberg took the opportunity to smile at the small group around the conference table.

"Well, thank you, Jesper." The prime minister gestured to Stenberg to sit down. "An exemplary presentation, I must say. Short and concise, not like so much that one has to endure. 'Death by PowerPoint,' have you ever heard that expression?" The prime minister smiled at the people around the table and was rewarded with the expected chuckles. Everyone laughed at the boss's jokes, no matter how many times they had heard them before.

"You've got some fairly radical proposals there, Jesper," Carina LeMoine said. "A reduction in sentences for people who give state's evidence, harsher sentences for organized crime."

Stenberg nodded. This lightly concealed criticism wasn't unexpected, nor indeed was its source. LeMoine was one of the boss's favorites. Legal training, a bit too young to be eligible for his job. At least for the time being. She was also very attractive, actually looked a bit like Sophie. He pushed the thought aside and concentrated on giving an appropriate response.

"That's right, Carina, I'm glad you've raised that." He used his most professional voice. And took her trick of using his first name and lobbed it back over the net. Fifteen–all, game on. "But I've studied the methodology very thoroughly. And looked at the results achieved in other countries. And I know from practical experience how much easier it is to get someone to cooperate if they have something to gain from it."

Thirty–fifteen to him, for his studies and practical experience. He looked her in the eye and raised the stakes with a smile.

"You're not worried there'll be problems when it goes out for consultation? The Bar Association is unlikely to be pleased." He thought he could detect a hint of uncertainty in her voice and seized the initiative.

"I have a very good relationship with the Bar Association, Carina, and I can assure you, and everyone else, that if my proposals are presented, they will be very well supported."

Forty–fifteen, match point.

He smiled again, raised his eyebrows slightly, and turned his head almost imperceptibly, as if he was waiting for her next question. But Carina LeMoine just looked down at her notes instead.

Game to him. A walkover. Karolina would have been proud of him.

For a couple of seconds he almost felt disappointed, as if he had been denied victory. But he quickly recovered. He smiled his very best television smile at the small group. The boss gave him a nod of approval. He looked like a big, happy toad.

· · ·

"Jesper, wait!" The elevator doors were about to close when Carina LeMoine called to him. He thought about ignoring her and letting the doors close in her face. But before he had time to decide the elevator doors opened again. She must have managed to press the button.

"We can go down together." She smiled at him as she

stepped into the elevator. She stood slightly too close to him, making him take half a step back without realizing it. The smell of her perfume brought him up short. Narciso Rodriguez, the same as Sophie's. That only emphasized the similarities. For a millisecond he thought he could hear a noise. A faint, rhythmic knocking against the metal walls of the elevator. He swallowed a couple of times.

"Are you all right, Jesper?"

"Hmm." He started and was forced to get his mind back on track.

"You look a little pale."

"Oh no, I'm absolutely fine. I was just thinking about something."

The elevator began to make its way slowly downward. Carina LeMoine made a little gesture with her hand, tucking a lock of blond hair behind her ear. Her skin was white, almost like porcelain.

"There was something I wanted to tell you, Jesper. In relation to our little discussion up there." She tilted her head toward the ceiling. "I didn't want to say anything in front of the others."

She smiled, revealing a row of tiny, pearly-white teeth.

"No?" he said. He regretted it at once. *No? Pull yourself together!*

"I happened to run into John Thorning the other day. We ended up talking about you, which isn't really that surprising."

She smiled again, and he smiled back automatically. What the hell was going on?

"I mean, he was your mentor, after all."

Stenberg nodded as he felt the elevator slowing down.

"That's why I asked about the Bar Association earlier. John's general secretary, of course, so we talked a bit about your plans for restructuring the justice system. Just as you mentioned upstairs, I was assuming that you had already sounded him out."

"Yes." Stenberg kept smiling, trying to work out where the

conversation was going. He didn't like the way she said *John*. It was too intimate, as if they were more than fleeting acquaintances.

"Obviously I wouldn't want to give you any advice," Carina LeMoine went on. "As Minister of Justice, naturally you have a broader overview."

She brushed something from the shoulder of his dark overcoat.

"But if I were in your shoes, Jesper, I'd probably make an appointment to see John Thorning, as soon as possible."

• • •

Sarac had put the key on the table in front of him. He had removed it from his key ring and thrown the other three away, the ones that fit his former office in Regional Crime and the old locks in his front door.

One key remained. A perfectly ordinary, flat key that fit a lock with seven tumblers. There was no number on it, no clues of any kind. He couldn't remember it, had no idea what lock it might fit or what the door looked like. It was the very absence of any memories that convinced him. He had emptied his office himself, he knew that now. He had kept it a secret from Molnar and Bergh so that they could both claim ignorance if anything went wrong. He had become the "lone cop acting on his own initiative," just as they had decided. So it seemed reasonable to assume that this key belonged to his new premises, the base from which he had single-handedly managed the entire Janus operation.

He leaned over the key, examining it as closely as he could. An uneven saw blade, with seven jagged points of varying lengths. He picked it up, held it in his hand. Shut his eyes. Waited . . .

Nothing happened.

He opened his eyes again. Of course nothing happened, he wasn't a fortune-teller, for fuck's sake. He had been too exhausted to take in what Molnar had said. But now, after a couple of nights' sleep in his own bed, after a shower, breakfast, and not least a change of clothes, he was in a much better state.

He had taken drugs, he had smoked both dope and meth-amphetamine. Maybe it had been a way of dealing with the constantly growing pressure. Living twenty-four hours a day with his work and with Janus, without anyone to confide in, and without anything resembling a safety net.

The drugs explained the terrible state of his apartment, and possibly even some of his hallucinatory memories. He had care-fully examined the things Bergh had given him. Trying to work out exactly what his boss had meant by giving him the bag. Not to mention the message on the lid of the box.

Everything begins and ends with Janus. What did Bergh mean by that?

A hardened criminal commits a murder at the same time as working as an infiltrator for the police. If something of that sort got out, the media would go crazy. Any police officer who could be linked to the case, no matter how distantly, would be fired instantly, and maybe even prosecuted. It was hardly surprising that he had sworn to keep a secret like that.

So what should he do? Tell Molnar everything? Ally himself to Wallin and hope that he didn't cut him adrift the moment the secret got out? Or had Bergh tried to imply an entirely different solution to his problems? Getting rid of Janus for good, before he was uncovered. Murdering the murderer?

He shook the thought off. Bergh was feeling guilty about pushing him out into the cold. Leaving him unprotected. Wallin was probably right, and if there was someone out there trying to get at Janus through him, the gun and bulletproof vest would come in handy.

The fact was that he had no evidence at all that Janus was responsible for Hansen's death, just his own fragmented mem-ories and assumptions. And he still didn't know anything about the man concealed behind the code name. The answer was in that room, in his secret base, he was convinced of that, and that was why he had to devote all his energy to finding it.

He got up and went over to the window. A curtain was fluttering opposite, drawing his eyes to it. There was no one in sight. The street was full of parked cars. About half of them had snow on their roofs, so they must have been there a couple of days. One of them was a Golf, which reminded him of Natalie's car, and he suddenly got the idea that she had come to see how he was. Then he realized that this one was newer, and in better condition. He actually felt a bit disappointed. But at the same time he felt ashamed. Natalie was a civilian, but he hadn't hesitated to drag her into this mess as soon as he had worked out how to make use of her. He had got her to exploit her personal contacts to get hold of information he needed, without any thought of what he was getting her involved in. Ruthless, that's what he was. Once Natalie realized what her assistance had helped him find, including the time and location of Sabatini's death, she was bound to ask to change patients. That was probably just as well. If Wallin was right, and there were people out there looking for him, he would do best to keep her well out of it.

He shut his eyes and closed his fingers over the key. Then he changed his grip and held it as if he were going to open a lock. He tried to imagine the key sliding into place, how the ridges matched up with the tumblers inside the lock. He turned it, feeling the lock click. He raised his left hand to where the door handle ought to be. He thought he could almost smell the metal against the palm of his hand. Slowly he pushed his hand down, pulling the door toward him. Then he slowly opened his eyes . . .

The clatter from the door of the apartment made him jump. For a moment he thought someone was trying to get in, that the events of the night he left the hospital were repeating themselves. Then he heard a gentle thud followed by the metallic clatter of the mail slot closing. He waited a moment as relief spread through his body, then went out into the hall to get the mail.

Two window envelopes and one small, brown, padded envelope with his name on it. He put them all on the kitchen table. He opened the bills first, then the brown parcel. It contained a small, cheap cell phone. On the screen was a yellow Post-it note.

Pin 9595.

He stared at the phone, then switched it on and tapped in the code. The keys were so small that he had to concentrate hard not to let his fingers slip. The start-up screen lit up, then the phone connected to a network. In one corner of the screen the message icon started to flash.

Move away from the window.

Then ring the last number called.

Sarac hesitated, but curiosity got the better of him. He went into the hall, then pressed the Redial button. The phone was so small that it almost vanished into his hand. The call was connected and he heard it start to ring. Then it rang a second time. He could feel his heart beating faster.

"Hello, David, good of you to get in touch," a hoarse male voice said. Sarac's pulse began to race. He recognized the voice: it was the tobacco man, the man with the gold tooth, the one who had visited him in the dark room at the hospital.

"We didn't have time to finish our conversation in the hospital," the man said, confirming his suspicions.

"W-who are you?" Sarac's voice sounded hollow.

The man let out a low laugh.

"Don't tell me you don't remember me?! And we were such good friends."

Sarac gulped. *Janus,* he thought. But for some reason the conclusion didn't feel as satisfying as it should.

"I'd like to meet you, David, preferably straightaway," the man said.

"I-I . . ." Sarac looked into the kitchen. He could see his own cell phone on the table.

"You're thinking about calling your friend Peter Molnar, aren't you?" The man emphasized the word *friend* in a way that Sarac didn't like.

"Do you know what, David, go over to the window. Stay tucked behind the curtain."

Sarac did as he was told. His heart was pounding so hard that he was having trouble breathing.

"You see the yellow building in front of you? Fourth window from the left," the man said.

"Hmm . . ." Sarac swallowed. It was the same window where he had seen the curtains fluttering a little while ago.

"There are two men in there watching you. Two of your so-called friends. Did Molnar tell you that?"

Sarac gulped again.

"Look farther down the street. Do you see the black Volvo, the one with no snow on the roof? There are two more police officers in there, working for Superintendent Wallin. I don't suppose Molnar mentioned them either?"

Sarac shook his head, then realized that the man couldn't see him. Peter should have told him, should have asked him to be careful, unless . . . He shut his eyes, trying to get past the thought that had just crept into his head. Unless . . .

"Your friends are lying to you, David, or they certainly aren't telling you the whole truth. They're scared of you, scared of what you might reveal. Maybe there's even some surveillance equipment in your apartment. In which case it won't be long before your phone starts to ring."

Sarac glanced at the cell phone on the kitchen table.

"Like I said, David, I'd like to meet. Preferably—"

Sarac ended the call. He slowly lowered the hand holding the phone. In the window on the other side of the street he thought he could see a slight movement. But that could be just his imagination. All of this could be his imagination. A fucking nightmare. Maybe he was actually still lying in his bed in the hospital, stuck in a coma, a world where his brain could do as it liked? In which case he'd dearly like to wake up. At once.

He turned and looked around the living room. The sofa was new, but everything else looked the same as usual. Or at least how he thought it should look. The leather armchair, the battered teak coffee table that he had brought from his parents'. The television, the rug, the bulbous lamp above the coffee table. His eyes followed the cable up to the ceiling. Did he really have a smoke alarm in the living-room ceiling, so close to the kitchen? When he looked closely, he could see the little light flashing. But he couldn't remember ever changing the battery.

He dragged a chair over and, with some effort, climbed onto it. He reached carefully toward the smoke alarm. But the ceilings in the apartment were a fair bit over ten feet high and he couldn't quite reach them. The white plastic covering of the smoke alarm was gray with dirt, but he couldn't work out whether that was because someone had made it dirty on purpose. Sarac remembered the stepladder in the basement. He'd be able to reach if he used that. But first he tried to stretch up once more. He wobbled but regained his balance. His fingers nudged the plastic, fumbling for the edge.

A dull buzz from the kitchen table interrupted him. The screen on his cell phone was lit up and the vibrations were making it rotate gradually on the tabletop. He climbed down and looked at the screen. Then he answered, trying to make his voice sound normal.

"Hello!"

"Hi, David," Molnar said. "I just wanted to see how you were feeling. You haven't been in touch."

"Hmm . . ." Sarac glanced up at the smoke alarm.

"Is everything okay? You sound a bit . . ."

"Are you watching me, Peter?"

"How do you mean?"

"I mean exactly what I said. Are you watching me?"

The line was silent for a few seconds.

"Don't go anywhere, David." Molnar's voice sounded dry. "I'm on my way over now."

The call ended.

Sarac took a deep breath, trying to collect his thoughts. Then he looked at the time. Molnar would be there in fewer than ten minutes. Time to make a decision. He glanced up at the smoke alarm again, then took the little plastic phone into the bathroom and pressed the Redial button.

"Okay," he said when the man answered. "What do we do?"

FORTY

Sarac went downstairs as fast as he could, clutching the cell phone to his ear. He had turned the shower on and clattered about in the bathroom, then rushed for the front door and crept out as quietly as he could.

"I'm down now," he said as soon as he reached the ground floor.

"Good. Now go over to the front door, but stay just inside so you can't be seen," the man on the phone said.

Sarac did as he was told and glanced at the time. Six or seven minutes left until Molnar showed up.

"So what do I do now?" he said.

"Wait for a bit. Do you see that bus stop about thirty feet to the right of the door?" the man said.

"Yes."

"In two minutes a bus will arrive. I'll tell you when to go out."

"Got it." Sarac took a couple of deep breaths, trying to keep his pulse down. Oddly enough, he almost felt a bit elated. He peered out cautiously into the street. The Volvo was pointing the wrong way; it would have to do a U-turn to follow him. But it would only take it a minute or so to catch up with the bus.

"Okay, now!" the man said.

Sarac opened the front door and walked straight to the bus stop, forcing himself not to look up at the window opposite, or toward the Volvo. From the corner of his eye he saw the bus approaching. He came to a halt at the bus stop and heard the bus's brakes squeal. He got on board without even looking at the driver. When the bus started to move he looked up. The Volvo had already pulled out into the street.

"Okay, so what do I do now?" he said into the phone.

"Press the button and get off at the next stop."

Sarac did as he was told. The bus swung around a corner and stopped right next to a flight of steps leading down to a shabby-looking hairdresser's. He got off and looked around. The Volvo still hadn't caught up.

"David!" The door to the salon opened and a woman stuck her head out. She was in her fifties, had fair, eighties-style permed hair, and a wrinkled, solarium-tanned face. "Quick, get inside!"

He obeyed, went down the four steps and on into the basement as quickly as he could. The salon was empty, apart from two barbers' chairs and a little trolley with various hair-care products.

"Keep going," the woman said, pointing to a bead curtain at the far end of the salon.

The room beyond it was tiny, probably no more than twenty-five square feet. A small folding table, two rib-backed chairs, a few sun-bleached posters advertising hairstyles that hadn't been fashionable for at least thirty years. A tall man in a suit, in his sixties, with a lined face and small round glasses was sitting on one of the chairs, but when Sarac came in he stood up.

"So good of you to look in, David," he said, smiling in a way that showed the gold tooth in his lower jaw. Sarac hesitated as his alarm bells went off. He had suspected several times that the tobacco man from the hospital might be Janus. But for some reason it had never felt quite right. And now he knew why. This man was a policeman, and his name was . . .

"Detective Superintendent Jan Dreyer," the man said, holding out his hand. "From the Internal Investigations Department, in case you'd forgotten. I'm sorry about the cloak-and-dagger stuff, but it's for your own good."

He gestured to Sarac to sit down.

"Coffee?"

"No, thank you." Sarac's head was spinning. Dreyer worked for Internal Investigations. He was the man leading the investigation into the theft from the security safe. But in the darkness up at the hospital it had sounded as if they already knew each other. Dreyer sat down on the chair opposite him. The smell of his eau de cologne almost knocked out the mixture of hair-care chemicals that otherwise dominated the air in the salon.

"You came to see me in the hospital and talked about an agreement," Sarac said, trying to fit these new pieces of the puzzle into place.

"Ah, you see." Dreyer smiled. "And I thought you were too groggy to remember. Do you remember anything else?"

"Sorry." Sarac shrugged his shoulders.

Dreyer looked at Sarac intently, apparently trying to work out whether he was lying.

"Well," he went on. "As I said, my name's Jan Dreyer, and I'm in charge of the Internal Investigations Department. You know what our job entails?"

"You investigate police officers who are suspected of committing a criminal offense," Sarac said.

"That's right. For the past couple of years we've been a separate organization that reports directly to the National Police Committee. In other words, we're entirely independent of everyday police work, but I'm sure you know that already."

Sarac shrugged his shoulders. Tried to remain as impassive as he could.

"And what do you want with me?"

"You really don't remember anything, do you?" Dreyer fell silent as he looked at Sarac, then he smiled. Something about the smile made Sarac's tongue stick to the roof of his mouth.

"I'm your handler, David," the man said with a smile. "And you're my CI."

FORTY-ONE

"Hello, this is Tindra." Her voice on the phone made Atif smile.

"Hello, Tindra, this is Uncle Atif."

"Amu, where are you? I miss you!"

"I miss you too, sweetheart," Atif said. "Are you having a nice time out in the country?"

"Really nice! Are you coming to visit us soon?"

"Soon," Atif said. "I just need to sort some things out first. But then I'll come and visit."

"Do you promise, Amu?"

"I promise, sweetheart. Is your mom there? I need to have a word with her."

"Okay." Tindra sounded disappointed. A clattering sound followed.

"Hello?" Cassandra said. Her voice was curt but not un-friendly.

"It's me, I just wanted to see how you were both doing," Atif said.

"It's okay, but to be honest I'm starting to get cabin fever out here. When can we go back home?"

"Not quite yet," Atif said. "There are still a couple of things I need to deal with first. I need to know that you're safe. As soon as it's done I'll be in touch. Until then you're going to have to lie low. Don't make any calls, do you understand? Especially not to Abu Hamsa."

The silence on the line told him she had already disobeyed his instructions. Shit.

* * *

"I recruited you to provide information about Peter Molnar and his specialist team," Dreyer said. "But also about your boss, Kjell Bergh, and the other officers handling CIs. Not least their former boss, Eugene von Katzow, aka the Duke."

Sarac felt his throat contract. He struggled to keep the expression on his face blank. The room had suddenly started to rotate anticlockwise, and he was forced to hold on to the seat of the chair to keep himself upright.

"As you might recall, the Duke left the police force a number of years ago. He had built up a system of informers and infiltrators who weren't registered, and who were paid through secret accounts. A lot of his sources weren't even criminals, just ordinary taxpayers who happened to work in key posts in private companies or public bodies. Telecom businesses, hospitals, property firms, councils, or the Tax Office—even the odd television celebrity."

Dreyer put his hand in his pocket and pulled out a pack of cigarillos.

"The Duke accumulated a stock of people who all owed him something. Who couldn't say no when he called to ask for a small favor. Lists of calls, maybe, someone's medical notes, whatever."

Sarac gulped, thinking about what Molnar had said about his own blood test.

"An informal system that bypassed all the rules," Dreyer went on. "But unfortunately we were never able to link him to any serious crimes, just a couple of disciplinary offenses. I suspect very strongly that the Duke called in some favors in both the prosecutors' office and the Ministry of Justice so he could get off lightly."

He took out a little blue plastic lighter from his other inside pocket, tapped a cigarillo out of the pack, and gestured toward Sarac, as if offering him one.

"I don't smoke," Sarac mumbled.

"You don't?" Dreyer smiled. "Are you absolutely sure about that?" He lit the cigarillo and took a deep puff.

"Well," he continued. "After the Duke had slipped out of the back door, Bergh took over his old job. But most of the work was actually done by von Katzow's protégé, Peter Molnar. Molnar's smart, he keeps his cards close to his chest and surrounds himself with extremely loyal cops. Basically, it proved impossible to check exactly what they were getting up to, and whether or not they were carrying on in the Duke's spirit."

He waved the cigarillo toward Sarac.

"But then you appeared, David Sarac, a rising star. When Molnar changed jobs, you took over most of his sources. You seemed able to fit in everywhere, to get almost anyone to trust you. A true chameleon. And you never seemed to stop working."

Sarac gulped. He wondered about getting up and walking out. But he realized he had to stay and hear the rest of the story.

"Over time it became clear that it was taking its toll on you. If you play that number of different roles, sooner or later you end up losing yourself. You forget who you really are. What you stand for."

Dreyer tapped his fingers gently on the tabletop.

"You were spending more and more time in the pub. But you didn't seem anywhere near as interested as you had been in setting up new contacts. Instead you mostly just got drunk, you even blacked out a couple of times. There were rumors that you were on the brink of collapse, and it was fairly obvious that none of your friends were interested in helping you."

"So you got in touch with me, and tried to get me to report on what Molnar and the others were doing?" Sarac's voice was trembling slightly. It reflected the uncertainty he was feeling fairly well.

"Is that what you think happened, David?"

Sarac didn't answer. His right hand was still clutching the seat of the chair.

"Come on, tell me. You're the expert here! Put yourself in my place. What would you have done to recruit yourself?"

Sarac took a deep breath. His headache made its entrance, right on cue. He was suddenly feeling nauseous. But he had to play along, he had to hear what Dreyer had to say. Collect more pieces of the puzzle.

"You got something on me," he muttered. "A blood test, something along those lines. Explained that I was in trouble. That I could lose my job. You fixed up a meeting."

"Go on!" Dreyer gestured with the cigarillo.

"You probably chose a discreet location, so discreet that the fact that we were even meeting there looked suspicious. Then you got someone to take some surreptitious pictures of us there together."

Dreyer took another deep puff.

"As soon as I showed up, the moment I sat down opposite you, you'd have me. Even if I turned you down, anyone who saw the pictures would get the impression that I'd talked. My credibility would be ruined."

Sarac leaned back, let go of the chair, and rubbed his eyes. He could suddenly remember a closed restaurant. A meeting of some sort, uncomfortable feelings that suggested he really didn't want to be there. It could very well be the truth.

"Was that how it happened?" he went on. "Was that the agreement you mentioned in the hospital? Talk, otherwise we'll destroy your career? Ruin everything you live for?"

Dreyer smiled.

"Just like you would have done, wouldn't you, David? You do what it takes to recruit a source."

Sarac leaned his head in his hands.

"And now, just like everyone else, you want me to give you Janus, don't you?"

"Janus," Dreyer snorted. "A ghost everyone talks about but

no one's ever seen." He shook his head. "Don't try to confuse the issue, David. You promised me something else entirely. Something considerably more interesting."

Sarac opened his mouth, but his brain had seized up and he couldn't think of anything sensible to say. Not after Janus? So what was their agreement about, then?

"Your task was to expose a mole up in Regional Crime," Dreyer said.

Sarac slowly shook his head. His brain was fumbling frantically for something, anything he could connect with what Dreyer had just said.

"I have no idea what you're talking about," he eventually said.

Dreyer sighed.

"Still loyal to your friends, I see." He stubbed out the half-smoked cigarillo, crushing it so hard that his cup almost tipped over.

"Someone up in your department has been selling information to the underworld, David. Everything's done through an intermediary, a lawyer called Bengt Crispin. Several major operations have failed because of this mole. Serious criminals have got off scot-free. But, strangely enough, never any operation in which Molnar and his team have been involved. When we finally managed to identify a couple of calls made from Regional Crime to Crispin, we began to realize what was going on. The theft of your backup list from the security safe has removed any trace of doubt, even among the bosses. They've given me a free hand to do whatever it takes to find the leak. The backup list is only an excuse, a reason to question everyone up at Regional Crime. A way to smoke the mole out of its hole."

Dreyer pulled a face that was probably supposed to look like a smile.

"We recruited you in October. We gave you until Christmas to come up with the name of the mole. We didn't hear from you at all for a month. Then, one evening toward the end of

November, I got a phone call. You sounded stressed, said you wanted to meet as soon as possible, and promised to hand over all the evidence I needed. And give me the name of the mole."

The man leaned over the table, so close that Sarac could see the delicate tracery of veins at the end of his nose.

"I've read the preliminary traffic report about your crash. In contrast to the later version, it mentions the fact that there was another vehicle right behind your car. And that minor damage was found on your rear bumper."

Dreyer smiled, once again revealing the gold tooth. Sarac's mouth suddenly felt dry as dust.

"I went to our meeting place, David. Waited over an hour."

Sarac held his breath.

"But one of your so-called friends made sure that you never made it."

FORTY-TWO

Sarac took the long way home, both to give him a chance to collect his thoughts and to make sure no one was following him. His head was aching and his brain was struggling to make sense of what he'd just found out. What Dreyer had told him turned everything upside down and left him in an even worse position than before.

Wallin was after Janus to boost his career. Molnar and Bergh wanted to get rid of incriminating evidence. That was why they were watching him, hoping that sooner or later he would lead them to Janus.

But if Dreyer was right, there was someone else with good reason to keep Sarac under observation. Someone in the group who was leaking information, and someone who presumably could earn a lot of money by revealing Janus's true identity.

In the end it always comes down to money, doesn't it? Bergh had said. Was that really some sort of confession? Was that why his boss had given up without a fight, because he knew he was in line to be questioned by Dreyer? That he was going to be uncovered?

And, once again, Molnar had withheld information from him. Maybe he had even been responsible for cleaning up the traffic report, the same way he had sorted out Sarac's test results? Just as Bergh had hinted in the hospital, someone had forced his car to stop. And made sure he crashed, in the worst possible way.

Sarac had no desire to go back to his apartment. Molnar would be waiting for him and would demand to know where he had been. Force him to lie, again. He didn't need any more smoke screens, half-truths, and retrofitted explanations. What he needed was clarity. The problem was that he had no idea how to reach it. The pieces of the puzzle were piling up, more and more of them. He was still looking for a corner piece, something he could work from, where he had his back covered.

Four men had placed their lives in his hands, with varying degrees of willingness. Now they were all dead. Who had killed them, and why? Could it be Janus, as he suspected? He hadn't got anywhere near to being able to uncover the man's true identity.

And who was the mole in the police who was presumed to have stolen his backup list from the safe, the person he had agreed to identify for Dreyer? Who was the fifth man on his list, the practically anonymous Erik I. Johansson?

The pieces didn't fit together. The drugs, the crash, Bergh, Molnar, Wallin, Dreyer, the mole, the list . . . Four dead men, a notebook whose code he had only half cracked, the secret base that had to be out there somewhere. Everything was spinning, turning into a maelstrom of information that he had no hope of sorting out.

There was only one common denominator. Janus. Everything began and ended with him, just as the note had said.

He glanced quickly over his shoulder before going into a 7-Eleven to buy some headache tablets. He found himself looking up at the cigarettes. When he inserted his bank card to pay, the machine bleeped.

Wrong PIN number!

He frowned and tapped the number in again: 3941.

The machine protested again, and Sarac stood there staring into space. Suddenly he could see a coded lock in his mind's eye. A shiny metal box mounted on a wall.

Three-nine-four-one, he thought once more, and all of a sudden he could the see the door next to the box. The same door as in his dream.

"Three, nine, four, one," he muttered out loud. Then he could see the building, then the sign with the name of the street on it.

"Wait, you forgot your card!" the shop assistant called after him.

. . .

The front of the building was partially covered with scaffolding, and there were two large containers outside, but he still had no difficulty recognizing it. This was the right place. His heart felt as if it were going to burst out of his chest, and he forced himself to slow down.

The door was locked, but the code 3941 made it click open at once. Sarac pushed the door and went inside. His pulse was racing in his ears.

He looked at the names on the board in the entrance hall. No company names, as far as he could tell, but on the fourth floor there was an E. I. Johansson.

Erik I. Johansson, the fifth name on the Janus list!

He walked slowly up the dimly lit stone stairs. The lighting didn't seem to be working properly so he had be careful where he put his feet. He was walking much better now, but he probably wouldn't be able to recover his footing if he tripped. It would be ironic if he were to fall at this point, ending up at the bottom of the stairs with a broken neck now that he had finally made it this far. For some reason that High Wire song and the image of the tightrope walker came into his head again, but he shook them off. Concentrate!

E. I. Johansson's door looked exactly the same as his neighbors'. He paused for a few seconds while he collected himself. The stairwell was quiet; not even the sound of traffic reached up there. All he could hear was the sound of his own heavy breathing.

Sarac crouched down and carefully peered through the mail slot. The room inside was almost pitch black. All he could see were the white outlines of some envelopes on the floor. It smelled musty. Sarac stood up and got the key out of his pocket. He looked over his shoulder, then slid it into the lock. It fit perfectly, and he turned it without any difficulty.

Once he was inside he realized why the room was so dark. Just a yard or so inside the hall was another door, considerably more solid than the one he had just come through. He looked around the small lobby and found two letters on the floor, which he picked up and slipped into his back pocket. They were both addressed to E. I. Johansson.

He fumbled with the key, then realized that there was no keyhole in the inner door. Instead he discovered a small recess containing a gently glowing red glass plate just above the handle. Without even thinking about it he pressed one thumb to the glass and held it there until the red light had turned green.

The room inside looked almost exactly like his dream.

Two covered windows to the right, with bars on the insides, and below them a small desk. The whiteboard covered with photographs was hanging on the wall in front of him, and by the left-hand wall, next to a stack of moving boxes, was a small, neatly made cot. Right in the middle of the room, a yard or so from the whiteboard, was a shabby, revolving leather armchair. He looked around and discovered a bathroom door and a small kitchen alcove. A faint smell of tobacco smoke hung in the air.

All of a sudden Sarac felt overwhelmed, almost faint. He took a couple of steps and sank down on the leather chair. He shut his eyes and tried to get his pulse rate down. It was difficult.

He'd done it! At least, he had found his corner piece. The location from which he had run what might have been the most successful infiltration operation in Swedish criminal history. And he had done so entirely on his own, which filled him with an odd mixture of horror and delight.

This was OP1, his hiding place, the black hole in the police system that neither his bosses nor his colleagues knew about. Not even his best friend.

Ideally he would have liked to throw himself at it all. But he forced himself to hold back. To enjoy the discovery, to sit for a while gathering his strength. His memories were coming back, one by one. He could see himself there in the room. The way he had organized everything, putting up the photographs, drawing the lines, making notes of different numbers.

He slowly stood up and went over to the whiteboard. It looked almost exactly as it had in his dream, just slightly more detailed. At the bottom of one side were four faces he recognized at once. The dead men: Hansen, Markovic, Lehtonen, and Sabatini. The pictures were all old, glossy police mugshots, with names and dates of birth along the bottom.

In the middle of the whiteboard was a row of other photographs inside a circle, but these were all relatively recent surveillance pictures. Next to each picture their names had been written in with black marker-pen. The handwriting was neat, not as aggressive and jagged as it had been in the hospital.

Beneath each name was a row of numbers that were probably cell phone numbers.

Abu Hamsa, he read next to a picture of a fat little man in his sixties with a fake-looking quiff. A red line led to a muscular man with cropped hair named *Eldar.*

The next picture was of a typical biker. Leather waistcoat, thick neck, long hair in a plait, gold necklaces, and plenty of rings on his fingers, as well as a pair of thin glasses. *Micke Lund.*

The red line from Lund led to another man in biker gear, but different colors this time. *Karim,* he had written, omitting the surname for some reason.

The remaining pictures were of two men in tracksuits, *Zimin* and *Ivazov.* At a guess, they were Russians, and below them was a photograph of a bald, hook-nosed man with unpleasantly sunken eyes whose name was evidently *Sasha.*

All the photographs, both the dead men at the bottom of the board and the gang inside the circle, had a blue line leading toward the center of the whiteboard. The red and blue lines crossed each other, making the whole whiteboard look like a spiderweb. In the center of the board was a familiar symbol. Two curling *J*s with their tails facing each other. Two faces in one, turned away from each other.

Sarac stood still in front of the whiteboard, waiting for the buzzing in his head to stop, and hoping that the spiderweb would help things to fall into place. But nothing happened. He tried closing his eyes for a few seconds, then opening them quickly. Still nothing. The men in the photographs just went on staring at him. Making no effort to make themselves known to him.

Disappointed, he walked over to the desk and started pulling the drawers open, one by one. In the first one he found more or less what he was expecting. Pens, paper, a dog-eared phone book, some other office equipment. In the second drawer a laptop and a bundle of dollars. In the third—a pistol.

He recognized the weapon almost immediately. A nine-millimeter SIG Sauer, in all likelihood his own service pistol. He picked it up, pressed a button with his thumb, and released the cartridge from the base of the handle with a practiced hand. Then he clicked it open and caught the small brass bullet that had been in the chamber.

He sniffed the weapon gently, breathing in the familiar smell of powder and gun grease. He found himself thinking once again about Brian Hansen and the bullet that had ended his life.

He put the gun down on the desk, then emptied the cartridge and lined the bullets up in a row. He felt the anxiety in his chest grow as he counted them in his head. Fourteen in total. Fourteen brass bullets in a shiny little row. There was just one problem. The cartridge had space for fifteen bullets.

FORTY-THREE

Natalie was slowly turning her coffee cup. Rickard's instructions had been crystal clear: keep an eye on the notebook and report everything Sarac did. Not particularly difficult, actually rather exciting, especially since they cracked the code together and managed to identify the five men. Sarac reminded her of a patient she had had while she was training. A woman with cancer who had been utterly furious with everyone and everything. She had even thrown a bedpan at the oncologist. Just like Sarac, she had refused to give up, refused to let people feel sorry for her.

But the murder in Högbergsgatan had left Natalie feeling wary. She had called Rickard from the ferry and had told him whom they were going to see and what the address was. And just before they got there Sabatini had been murdered.

The thought troubled her more than she wanted to admit. Rickard was hardly a killer, he was a cop. Wasn't he?

That was also something else that was worrying her. Rickard's appearance and the way he talked reeked of cop, but she couldn't recall his ever showing his ID. But he had to be a cop, surely, because how else would he have access to the police database? Maybe she should ask to see his police ID the next time she saw him.

He had called her a little while ago. He had sounded even more stressed than the previous time. He told her she still hadn't delivered what he was looking for, that he had expected more from their collaboration. She hadn't objected, hadn't wanted to let on how much the murder in Högbergsgatan had frightened her, and had made her question what she was doing. Instead Rickard had persuaded her that she had to work harder. Stay focused on her goal, do whatever was required. It had worked. She still had a chance to get back everything she had thought was lost. She just had to grit her teeth and get on with it.

First and foremost, she had to find Sarac and get him to confirm who the man in the pictures on her cell phone was. Sarac wasn't back in his apartment, wasn't answering his phone, and according to the helpful neighbor out on the island, the house there was silent and deserted. It was almost as if Sarac had vanished off the face of the earth. And that bothered her on more than one level, she reluctantly admitted to herself.

• • •

He dreamed he was lying at the bottom of a deep hole. Little threadlike roots stuck out of the dark, earth sides, narrow, hairy fingers writhing in pain. The sky high above was dark. In the distance was a snatch of music. The High Wire.

The four men were standing up above, around the edge. They were looking down at him with dead eyes. Hansen in his leather waistcoat, Markovic in his yellow padded jacket, Sabatini with his T-shirt soaked in blood, and Lehtonen in a bomber jacket with a dragon on the back. Two dogs were panting at his side. Their tongues were long and pink.

"Why?" Hansen said. His voice was surprisingly high.

"We trusted you, man," Markovic said. Water was seeping out everywhere, from his clothes, nose, and mouth. It was trickling over the edge of the hole.

Sabatini remained silent, just held his bloodstained hands in the air. The water was running faster now, Sarac could hear it, could feel it getting deeper around him. He tried to get up, but his body wouldn't do as he wanted, leaving him lying on his back. He felt the water cover his legs, then his chest. He tried to hold his head up as high as he could. One of the dogs was whimpering but fell silent when the water reached his ears, his cheeks. Washing darkness into his eyes.

Sarac woke up in a cold sweat. The room was dark, the only thing visible was the pale rectangle of the whiteboard. The photographs formed dark shapes on its surface. If he looked carefully, he could just make out the outlines of the faces.

He sat up in the armchair and reached for the light switch. He felt something rustling in his back pocket. The letters he had found on the mat in the hall. He opened the first envelope. A bank statement from a foreign account in the name of Mr. E. I. Johansson. There was another one in the other envelope, but for a different account.

He got the thinking behind the name now. Erik I. Johansson—with the English sense of *I*. Erik I. Johansson wasn't an informer but his own alias. One that made it possible to do things that couldn't be traced back to him. Like getting hold of this apartment, for instance. He wondered who had sorted out an ID number for him. Favors given, favors received.

He sat down at the kitchen table, smoothed the statements out, and put them down side by side. It didn't take him long to see a pattern. The first account seemed mostly to deal with in-payments. At the start of the period covered by the statement there had been more than a million dollars in the account, and four new payments had been made, amounting to almost the same again. There were only three withdrawals, although they actually seemed to be transfers. One for three hundred thousand dollars done at the beginning of the period, one for one hundred thousand in the middle, and finally one more at the bottom of the page. That transfer was for almost two million dollars and had emptied the account, leaving just one cent in it.

The account detailed in the other statement had an opening balance of twenty thousand dollars. There followed a number of small withdrawals, all marked *cash,* for even multiples of a hundred dollars, all withdrawn from various bureaus de change in the city center. The sums varied between five hundred and thirty-five hundred. They seemed to be cash withdrawals, suggesting that there was a debit card linked to the account. This theory was confirmed when he found the names of different well-known restaurants further down the statement. In the middle of the page was an in-payment of one hundred thousand dollars. He checked the date and reference number and saw that the money had been transferred out of the other account. Several more cash withdrawals followed, interspersed with more restaurants. At the bottom of the page he found a transfer that, just like on the other statement, left the account practically empty.

Sarac frowned. One account for income, another for expenses; that seemed to fit with what Molnar had said. But where did all the money come from? Two million dollars, that was about fourteen million Swedish kronor and, to judge by the activity in the expenses account, far more than was required. Every in-payment was identified only by a transaction number, so there were no clues there.

And someone had pretty much cleared out the accounts on the same date, in fact with an interval of just a couple of minutes. Who? Clearly someone with access to the right program, with the codes and passwords. Which raised the question— why? Why withdraw all the money and close what appeared to be a perfectly functional system? He studied the dates again and realized there was something he had missed.

The accounts had been cleaned out on Saturday, November 23. The same night as his crash.

• • •

The car was parked more or less where Atif had expected to see it. In the street, barely three hundred feet from the unprepossessing little door marked *Istanbul Hamam.* He opened the door and found himself in a courtyard. He carried on toward the building on the far side and went in through a shabby door. *"Best Turkish sauna in town, boys, I come here every Tuesday."*

He ignored the receptionist and walked toward the men's changing room. The moisture and heat from the various saunas could already be felt outside. His top began to stick and his heart was beating alarmingly fast. He opened the door, slipped inside, and grabbed a spray can of deodorant from an open locker.

Eldar, the thickset bodyguard, was sitting on one of the benches fiddling with his cell phone. He didn't see Atif until he was almost upon him. He flew up, fumbling for his gun. Atif sprayed a serious dose of Irish Spring directly into his eyes. Then he kicked him in the crotch as hard as he could. But his timing was off; Eldar managed to twist out of the way and the kick didn't have the full effect. Instead the man threw himself backward over the wooden bench and off the other side. Atif had to go around the bench to follow up his attack, giving Eldar a few seconds' respite.

The man pulled out his gun and aimed it at Atif as he rushed toward him. He was rubbing his eyes hard. Atif knocked the arm holding the pistol aside and butted the man right in the face but didn't manage a clean strike. The two men stumbled into the shower room. Eldar's legs crumpled and he fumbled for something to hold on to, and managed to pull off one of the shower hoses. Hot water began to spray around the room.

Eldar was taking wild swings around him. Atif ducked and then aimed a solid left hook directly at the man's liver. He finally landed a blow as he had intended. Eldar fell as if he'd been struck by lightning. Water was still pouring from the broken shower, soaking the prone man's clothes.

Atif staggered back into the changing room. His heart was pounding against his rib cage. He rubbed his forehead and found the back of his hand covered with a mixture of water and blood. His shirt was drenched, sweat was dripping down his back, and the humid air was hard to breathe. He sat down heavily on one of the benches. Eldar's gun was lying on the floor and he picked it up. Another Zastava, but in considerably better condition than Bakshi's. Atif stood up with an effort, released the cartridge onto the floor, and kicked it away. Then he dismantled the gun and flushed the pieces down the toilet.

Eldar was moaning feebly in the shower room, trying to curl into a ball but not really succeeding. Atif knew it would be a while before he was back on his feet. A heavy punch to the liver was astonishingly painful, nine, maybe nine and a half. Not the sort of thing anyone could shrug off quickly.

He opened the door with the word *Hamam* on it. He walked down the tiled floor of a corridor and emerged into a large room with a vaulted ceiling and tiled walls. His pulse was still racing, and he could taste blood and adrenaline in his mouth.

Abu Hamsa was lying on one of the stone benches while a sinewy little man massaged his hairy back. When the masseur caught sight of Atif he backed away in horror, holding his hands up. Atif nodded toward the door and the man immediately made himself scarce.

Abu Hamsa sat up.

"You look bloody awful, Atif," he growled, without seeming particularly surprised.

Atif shrugged his shoulders.

"Eldar?" Abu Hamsa raised his eyebrows.

"He'll live." Atif sat down on the next bench.

"That's just as well. Otherwise I'd have hell to pay," Abu Hamsa said.

"Why?" Atif picked up a washcloth and wiped the blood from his eyes.

"He's engaged to my daughter," Abu Hamsa said.

"Which one, Yasmina?"

"No, no, Yasmina's at university. Studying to become an engineer. Susanna, she works for me. Looks after my bureaus de change. That's how she and Eldar . . ." He gestured toward the changing room, then fell silent and looked at Atif.

"You know I can't just let this pass," Abu Hamsa went on. "Not even for the sake of old friendship."

Atif shrugged again.

"Okay, my friend." Hamsa sighed. "I'm guessing you didn't come here just so you could beat up my staff. So what is this about?"

Atif spat some bloody saliva toward the drain.

"I want help with something," he said. "The address of a police officer."

"You have a very odd way of asking for help, my friend." Abu Hamsa chuckled. "Explain to me why you think I should even consider such a request."

"Because I'm proposing a deal. You give me the address, and I give you something in return," Atif said.

"And what might that be, my friend?" Hamsa smiled. "What can a man who's as good as dead possibly offer me?"

"I can give you Janus," Atif said.

FORTY-FOUR

Sarac leaned over the battered old leather armchair. He had spent almost twenty-four hours in the room, with just a short outing to get supplies from the closest 7-Eleven. The packing crates over by the camp bed had turned out to contain his files. So he had emptied his office himself, just as he had suspected. Probably not long before the crash. Something seemed to have happened, something which had raised the stakes, making him even more paranoid. But what? Was it something to do with the mole Dreyer was hunting, or the threat Wallin had mentioned? Or was it something else entirely? The puzzle he was trying to put together kept growing the whole time. It was well on its way to becoming a five-thousand-piece Ravensburger with no picture to show what it was meant to look like.

He had written his thoughts down on a fresh piece of paper. He had divided everything into columns in a fairly understandable way that might help make things clearer. He certainly hoped so, anyway.

> *Problem number one:* four men had been murdered. Four men who had given him information and whose names were listed on the first page of his encoded notebook. Presumably their names had also been on the missing backup list.
> *Theory:* Whoever killed the men wanted to stop them from revealing something they knew. Something to do with Janus.
> *Conclusion:* The murderer was someone the men knew,

or at least were aware of. Someone who had a lot to lose. He believed he had a strong candidate already, Janus himself.

Weakness: The Janus project was top secret, so how could four minor-league informants have known anything that important?

Problem number two: Erik I. Johansson, aka Sarac himself, had access to two foreign bank accounts and secret premises. Up to the day of his accident the accounts had contained large sums of money. A number of small withdrawals had been made from one account, with large in-payments made to the other.

Theory: Erik I. Johansson didn't exist. He was an alias that Sarac himself used to be able to manage the project. So the accounts were his as well. The small withdrawals were mostly cash payments for the various CIs or used to settle bar and restaurant bills.

Conclusion: Running the Janus operation under a false identity, with murky funding and eventually from external premises, broke every conceivable rule. If it got out he would be fired and would probably end up in prison. So he had chosen to move out from Police Headquarters and turn himself into the solitary scapegoat.

Weakness: There was no obvious weakness here but plenty of questions. If the accounts were his, where was the debit card? And, even more pertinent, where did all the money come from?

Problem number three: Peter Molnar blamed both his stroke and his car crash on extreme stress in combination with drug abuse. And claimed that the confused car journey was part of his breakdown.

Dreyer, on the other hand, claimed that he had
been on his way to a meeting with the Internal
Investigation Department, ready to reveal the name
of the mole in Regional Crime, but that someone
had stopped him very literally by forcing his car
into a concrete wall. Bergh and Wallin seemed to be
working along the same lines as well: that someone
wanted to see him dead.

Theory: One or more of the men were lying, or
withholding important parts of the truth. Possibly
even all four of them.

Conclusion: No one could be trusted, they were all trying
to manipulate him for their own ends. Even his best
friend.

Weakness: Sadly there was no obvious weakness here
either.

And finally, where he had ground to a halt:

Problem number four: the same night he suffers his
violent accident, a violent gang member, Brian
Hansen, is found dead in the passenger seat of his
own car in Gamla stan with a nine-millimeter bullet
in his head. During the preceding hours someone
also empties Erik I. Johansson's bank accounts of
about fourteen million kronor. His own service pistol
is locked inside the premises belonging to Erik I.
Johansson. The gun is missing a nine-millimeter
bullet from the cartridge. And he also has a number
of disturbing memories of Hansen's death, to put it
mildly.

Theory: The fact that these three events took place on the
same day couldn't be a coincidence. Nor the gun and
the missing bullet. His service pistol had probably
been used to kill Brian Hansen.

Conclusion and weakness: Impossible to work out without more information. At least that's what he tried to convince himself.

The events of Saturday, November 23, all had one common denominator, and this time it wasn't Janus. *He himself* knew Hansen, *he* had access to the gun, the bank accounts, and the premises. It was *he* who suffered some sort of meltdown, and then, either with or without anyone else's help, had a violent crash. So what did that mean?

Why did he seem to remember the meeting with Hansen in the car, the shot hitting the back of his head? What had he actually been doing during the hours before the crash? He had been entirely certain that Janus was behind Hansen's death. But after finding the gun he was no longer so convinced. Could he have murdered someone without realizing it? Or was that precisely what he had done?

He pushed the sheet of paper away and went and stood by the whiteboard.

The laptop had been a disappointment. The browsing history had been deleted, all the document folders were empty, and the desktop showed nothing but a default blue background. The hard drive seemed to have been reformatted, so if there were any secrets left in the computer, they were buried so deep in its memory that he could no longer find them, which felt pretty fucking ironic.

He poked about in the drawers for a bit, more or less at random. Apart from the pistol and bullets, he also found the gun's belt holster and two other small leather pouches, one containing a spare cartridge and the other a pair of handcuffs. Right at the bottom he also found the little wallet containing his police ID. Why had he left it there? Another question lacking any sort of answer.

He was actually starting to get cabin fever. He longed to have someone to talk to. Someone he could trust, someone who—unlike Wallin, Bergh, Molnar, and Dreyer—had no agenda of her own and didn't manipulate the facts and mix up truth and lies to suit herself.

Someone like Natalie. Sarac realized that he was missing her, while simultaneously feeling guilty about dragging her into this whole business. On one level he was pleased she hadn't turned up at his apartment. On another he actually felt quite disappointed.

He slipped his ID into his pocket and pulled out the top drawer again. A few loose sheets of paper, a collection of pens, a dog-eared phone book, and, beneath it, a half-full pack of Marlboros. He tapped a couple of the cigarettes out onto the desk to check that there was nothing hidden inside the packet. Then he discovered a little red matchbook squeezed between the cellophane and the card. The words *Club Babel* were printed on the front. He seemed to recognize the name and pulled out the bank statement again. He found a number of payments marked *Babel Restaurant, Kungsgatan 30*. Fairly large amounts as well.

He pulled out the phone book and tried to find the restaurant's phone number, but without success. Perhaps the book was too old, and anyway, who used phone books these days when everyone had smartphones?

He thought about the discussion he had had with Molnar, about where he might have chosen to meet Janus. *Somewhere that appealed to his ego. Showed how important he was to us. A good restaurant or a club.*

· · ·

Number 30 Kungsgatan turned out to be one of the pair of tall towers, the one on the north side of the imposing street. The entrance was on one corner of the tower, five stone steps up from the sidewalk of Kungsgatan, and guarded by two enormous statues that seemed to bear the whole of the grand 1920s building on their shoulders.

Once he was inside, Sarac only needed to walk ten feet

across the stone floor of the lobby before the sound of the evening traffic faded away. He stopped in front of the elevators and read the sign. He found Club Babel on the sixteenth floor and pressed the button to summon an elevator.

The carpet inside the elevator was thick, and his sneakers sank into it. The restaurant consisted of a long bar and a few chairs, all in art deco style. A weary-looking bartender dressed in a shirt, waistcoat, and sleeve garters was polishing glasses, but otherwise the place was almost empty, except for a few Japanese tourists posing in front of the impressive view over by the big windows.

Sarac sat down on one of the chairs at the bar.

"How can I be of service, sir?" The bartender's voice and his slightly stiff phrasing made something click inside Sarac's head.

"I'm a member," he said, without really knowing why. His voice sounded different. As if he weren't quite himself.

"And your name is . . . ?"

"Johansson," he said. "Erik I. Johansson."

The man tapped at a screen that was hidden behind the bar.

"Of course," he said. "I didn't recognize you in your hat, Mr. Johansson. Welcome back." The man put a metal token on the bar in front of Sarac and gestured lightly toward a red velvet curtain in the far corner.

Another elevator. This one was smaller, with room for no more than four people. On one wall was a little metal screen with a slot in it, below a small makeup mirror. Sarac put the token in the slot and briefly caught a glimpse of his reflection in the mirror. He noticed that he looked different. It was something about his eyes.

The woman who met him outside the elevator doors was beautiful. Short, dark hair cut in a 1920s style, dark eye makeup, a small headband with feathers in it, and a straight, silk dress that stopped just above her knees. The little catches of her suspenders were faintly visible through the fabric. The spacious premises on the top floor matched her outfit perfectly. A check-patterned floor, with thick rugs here and there. Chrome, leather, and hardwood furniture, whose straight lines were picked up in the square patterns that had been painted on the walls just below the ceiling.

The tall windows faced south and east and showed a magnificent view of Stockholm, only interrupted by the equivalent floor of the south tower some sixty feet away. It was so close that the Roman statuary on its facade was clearly visible.

Roman gods, Sarac thought. Hardly a coincidence.

Just like the floor below, the bar and decor exuded the style of the 1920s, down to the smallest details. It was an art deco fantasy.

"Good evening, Mr. Johansson," the woman said. "We haven't seen you here for a while. Your usual table is already taken by another regular client, but of course you're good friends."

She gestured toward the far end of the room, where there were a number of separate booths. Sarac walked slowly toward them. He could feel his pulse getting faster. Who was sitting at the table? Could it be the man he was looking for? He glanced once more at the statues outside the windows, thinking about Roman gods.

But for the second time that day he was disappointed. The suited man in the cubicle wasn't Janus, he was sure of that the moment their eyes met. This man was in his fifties and had long, back-combed gray hair that was thinning on top. A pair of round glasses was perched on the end of his nose, and as Sarac approached he pushed the newspaper he had been reading to one side.

"Ah, there you are, Erik!" The man stood up and held out his hand. "I've been trying to get hold of you for weeks, but all I get is your voice mail." He took off his reading glasses and waved them in the air. "Sit yourself down!"

Sarac nodded and did as the man suggested. He recognized him very well and was searching frantically for a name.

"I was just reading about our new Minister of Justice." The

man moved his hand toward the newspaper. "He's going to be making some fairly comprehensive proposals, at least if the papers are to be believed. That's going to make my work more difficult. But fortunately there are ways around most problems, aren't there, Erik?"

The man smiled, showing a row of chalk-white crowned teeth.

Lawyer, Sarac was thinking. This man was a lawyer, and his name was . . .

"So, how have you been getting on?" the man asked, leaning forward across the table. "As you know, my clients are extremely eager and would like news of your progress."

Sarac didn't answer.

"Since we last met the situation has become more tense. Some of their business contacts abroad have chosen to start up an independent investigation. They've even sent over an external consultant whose presence has aroused a degree of anxiety."

He smiled again, the same crocodile smile as before.

"But I've told my clients to calm down. Assured them that you'll be able to deliver what they want."

Sarac nodded stiffly. He was trying to take in what the man was saying at the same time that his brain was working at top gear.

"So, how is it going?" the man said, then raised his hands. "I mean, of course I don't want to know any details, only anything that might serve to reassure my clients a little. Make them feel comfortable about what was, after all, a fairly considerable investment."

"Fine," Sarac muttered. "Well . . ." He looked around, then took a deep breath.

"You see, I haven't really . . ." He pulled his hat off and pointed at the plaster on his head. "I was involved in an accident. Things are a little confused."

The man was looking at him, and all of a sudden he didn't look so friendly.

"I mean," Sarac went on. "Could you just remind me about the terms of our agreement?"

The man straightened up slightly. He was staring at Sarac as if he were trying to work out whether he was joking.

"You're not trying to trick me, are you, Erik?" he finally said. "That would be extremely unwise, considering our previous dealings."

"No, of course not!" Sarac shook his head. "I just need to get things sorted out a bit."

He was making an effort to sound convincing. He suddenly discovered a little metal plaque along one edge of the table. Presumably the names of the regulars who had priority at that table. *Erik I. Johansson* was at the top. Below was another name he had heard Dreyer mention only a day or so before.

Someone up in your department has been selling information to the underworld, David. Everything's done through an intermediary, a lawyer called Bengt Crispin.

Sarac felt his stomach tighten.

"We've been working together for almost a year now, Erik," Crispin went on. "The results have been most satisfactory up to now."

Sarac nodded and ventured a smile even though the room seemed to be swaying. The statues on the other side of the street seemed to be hanging in midair, firing accusing stares at him.

He read the ornate lettering once more, trying to absorb what it meant. The true identity of the mole Dreyer was hunting, and whom he had been forcibly recruited to reveal.

"But what we've been paying you handsomely for, Erik," Crispin went on, "is to reveal the true identity of the person behind the code name Janus."

FORTY-FIVE

"Hello?"

"Good evening, Abu Hamsa. This is Bengt Crispin."

"Ah, our legal friend, how nice."

"I thought I should let you know that I have met my contact, just now, in fact. I'm afraid the situation is as I feared. It seems highly likely that he won't be able to deliver. At least not for the foreseeable future."

"I see. That's a great shame."

"So what do we do now?"

"Well, fortunately we have a plan B. An offer from a new player. Or an old friend, depending on how you choose to look at it."

"Do I want to know the details?"

"No, Mr. Crispin, I don't think you do."

. . .

Sarac remained where he was for a good while after Crispin had left. Drank the drink that had been brought over without his having ordered anything. Then another. One mystery had at least been solved. Now he knew where all the money had come from. Earlier during the evening he had started to suspect that he himself might be a murderer. Now he could add corrupt police officer to the list as well.

He straightened up and was just about to raise his hand to request a refill when the bartender placed another drink in front of him.

"Thanks, Noa," he mumbled. He surprised himself by managing to remember the bartender's name.

His mind was in a state of total confusion. Pretty much like his life. The more he dug about for the person he had been, the less he liked the results. The list of people he had betrayed was getting longer and longer. Bergh, Molnar, the guys on the team, himself, his sources, even Janus. Why the hell couldn't he have lost his memory completely? A total reformat, like the laptop in the desk drawer? Or, possibly even better, why hadn't he died on the spot? Both alternatives felt more appealing than the inferno in which he found himself right now.

What the fuck had he been up to? Had he started the whole Janus project simply in order to sell out his infiltrator to the highest bidder when the price rose high enough? *In the end it always comes down to money, doesn't it, David?* Or was his name really Erik these days?

The room was gradually filling with people. Most of them were men, and apart from him there wasn't a single one under forty. But more and more women started to appear, all of them in their twenties, which seemed to suggest that they worked for the club.

He recognized several of the men. Business leaders, politicians, even a television presenter. A couple of them nodded in his direction and he returned the greeting. The music that had been whispering in the background was turned up. Club jazz of some sort. Soporific hypnotic tunes that were making him sleepy.

The woman who had met him at the elevator appeared at his table.

"Excuse me, Mr. Johansson, I just wanted to let you know that we have a free massage session available, if you're interested. Rio has had a cancellation, and you usually . . ."

Without knowing why, Sarac nodded mutely. He allowed himself to be led through the room to a row of doors on the far side of the elevators. He stepped through one of them and found himself in a room with heavy velvet curtains covering the window. Scented candles were spreading a smell of sandalwood around the room. Sarac took off his clothes and sat down on the massage table in the middle of the floor. He wrapped a thick white towel around his waist.

He hadn't drunk any alcohol since the crash. The smell, the music, the subdued lighting, everything merged together to form a pleasant, numb daze. He lay down on his stomach and closed his eyes. He heard the door open gently.

"I was starting to think you'd forgotten me, Erik." The voice was soft, familiar, in a vaguely erotic way.

The warm oil made him start. Her hands were soft but firm at the same time. They soon found the tension in his neck and shoulders. And eased it, little by little. She seemed to know exactly how much he could take, skillfully keeping him balanced on the boundary between pleasure and pain.

He gulped and tried to gather his thoughts. He failed. He felt his erection creeping up on him. The music continued, then formed familiar words.

I owe everything
Debts I can't escape till the day I die.

He realized that he was groaning with pleasure, gently pressing his hips into the table.

"Turn over," she said in a low voice.

He did as he was asked but kept his eyes closed. He only opened them when she gently ran her hands over the scars on his chest. She was beautiful, more beautiful than he had remembered. His erection was straining under the towel, uncontrollably.

"I . . ." he murmured, making a halfhearted attempt to lift himself up.

"Shh . . ." she whispered, pushing him back down. "You know the rules, Erik, no talking." Her fingers were moving in slow, teasing circles over his stomach. Getting closer to the edge of the white towel.

He shut his eyes again, and the alcohol and music gradually encouraged his mind to slow down. He focused on enjoying the sensation of her touch, almost as if he were in a trance.

I am Erik Johansson, he thought as she slowly loosened the towel. He noted how the voice inside his head changed tone.

Erik I. Johansson, the man who doesn't exist. Suspected murderer, corrupt police officer, treacherous friend. Junkie, liar, john.

I live on the edge, balancing on the high wire. And I love it.

• • •

"John, it's Jesper Stenberg."

"Jesper, how nice of you to find time for me at last."

Stenberg considered maintaining the mask, going through the usual pleasantries before approaching the subject. Then he decided to abandon protocol.

"What the hell are you playing at, John?"

"You mean my informal little chat with Carina LeMoine? Yes, I thought that might get your attention. She's a smart woman, she'll go far. And she's a lawyer."

Stenberg could almost see John Thorning's self-satisfied smile at the other end of the line.

"You've been avoiding me, Jesper. You haven't returned my calls."

"Well, John, I did explain to you how sensitive this is."

"Exactly, Jesper. It's all very sensitive, and that's why the easiest option for you is to lie low. Wait a few months and hope that I get tired. So I thought I'd save us both time and energy by letting you know in simple, unequivocal terms that that isn't going to happen. In fact I'm actually starting to doubt that you've done anything at all for me and Sophie. That your promises aren't worth very much, and that I might have actually backed the wrong horse."

John Thorning paused, leaving his words hanging in the air. Stenberg didn't imagine he was serious. That he would sacrifice his own Minister of Justice just like that. The problem was that Stenberg couldn't afford to call his bluff. Sure, he could carry on regardless. Ignore the opinion of the Bar Association. But that would make everything much more difficult. The Association would pull all the strings at its disposal to stop his ideas, write articles, put pressure on its contacts in parliament, not to mention when the proposal was put out to review. There was no doubt that John Thorning had enough muscle to make his life seriously difficult. And the old man seemed to be back on form now.

"John, you've got the wrong end of the stick entirely." Stenberg shut his eyes, trying to make his voice sound calm. "Like I said, we put one of our best detectives on the case. Trained by the FBI—she's done service abroad. We chose her to get an entirely fresh pair of eyes."

He pursed his lips. Realized he shouldn't really be saying any of this but that he didn't exactly have much choice.

"She identified a few things that seemed strange. Among other things she found a tiny fragment of glass with blood on it. We're still waiting for the test results."

Stenberg took a deep breath.

"The reason I haven't wanted to say anything is that I didn't want to raise your hopes. In all likelihood the blood is Sophie's own." He fell silent and realized he was holding his breath.

"Where?" John Thorning said after a brief pause.

"Sorry?"

"Where was the piece of glass found, Jesper?"

"Under the island unit in the kitchen. It had got stuck in one of the cracks in the floor."

Stenberg could see it all before him. The way he had stood on the piece of glass, then pulled it out of his foot. The way it had bounced a couple of times, sliding over the shiny floor, under the kitchen unit, and finally slipping into the crack. He took a deep breath and started again. He put Sophie in his place. Imagined that she was the one who stood on the glass as she rushed after him. That helped a bit.

"How long?" John Thorning said. His voice was milder now, less aggressive.

"The glass fragment is at the National Forensics Laboratory now, and we have to wait for them to follow their usual procedures," Stenberg said. "If we put pressure on them to prioritize this particular sample . . ."

"We'd arouse unnecessary curiosity," Thorning concluded.

"Exactly." Stenberg did his best to sound detached. "A week or so more, John, I can't imagine we're talking about any longer than that. But I promise to get in touch as soon as we hear anything."

There was silence on the line, and for a moment Stenberg wondered whether the old man had hung up. Then he heard noise again.

"Okay. Let's say that, Jesper."

The call ended. Stenberg put the phone down and resisted the urge to go and wash his hands.

John Thorning wasn't going to give up until he saw a written report about the new investigation. Proof that they really had tried to do as he wanted. The forensic test was actually perfect, because it showed that they really had looked under every stone. The problem was that the result had to prove with one hundred percent certainty that the blood was Sophie's. But, as with so much else, it was all a matter of focusing on the ultimate goal. Not letting thoughts of failure enter your head.

The test result wasn't a problem. It would come back with a clear indication that the blood belonged to Sophie, and then his old mentor would owe him a large favor in return. Speaking of which . . .

He leaned across the desk and pressed the intercom. "Jeanette, can you send Wallin in, please?"

* * *

Stenberg leaned back in his chair and looked up at the Bobby Kennedy quote. He thought about Karolina, and all the sacrifices she had made in order for him to be sitting behind this desk.

"I can't shake the feeling that Stockholm is trying to get one over on us," he said as soon as Wallin had shut the door. "That all this business with David Sarac and his memory loss is just a smoke screen. A way for them to sweep things under the carpet. To send their infiltrator abroad and get rid of all the evidence before either we or the internal investigators manage to find anything."

Wallin nodded. "Yes, I've been thinking much the same thing. There are rumors suggesting that District Commissioner Swensk is prepared to sacrifice Bergh, and probably Sarac as well, in order to limit the damage. Of course you know that she and Carina LeMoine are close. They studied law together, and they're both on the board of the Women's Network in Stockholm."

Stenberg stood up and went over to the window.

"What do you think about the chances of bugging Sarac's phone?" he said.

Wallin shrugged his shoulders. "His official cell phone's gone, and we haven't got a current number for him." He thought for a moment. "But Sarac's very close to his former boss, a man called Molnar. If anything were to happen, he'd probably get in touch with him."

Stenberg said nothing, just raised his eyebrows in a pointed way.

"Phone tapping would require authorization by a prosecutor. We'd have to set up a preliminary investigation," Wallin said.

"But of course there are always less formal solutions to that problem," he added. "Although of course those involve an element of risk."

Stenberg looked out the window, his eyes resting on a seagull that was hovering against the backdrop of gray cloud. The bird was using the wind to hang almost motionless between heaven and earth.

"Have you tried tightrope walking, Oscar?" he said, without turning around. "The trick is not to look down. Not to even entertain the possibility that you might fall."

FORTY-SIX

"Hello, it's Atif."

"Atif, how nice to hear from you."

"Is this line secure, Hunter?"

"Of course."

"Two things," Atif said. "One: I accept your proposal. I'll take care of everything as soon as you've questioned Janus. Make sure he disappears for good."

"Excellent! And the second thing?"

"I need a car, and a gun," Atif said.

"We've actually already thought of that," Hunter said.

. . .

When Sarac slipped out the door night had long since fallen. The traffic on Kungsgatan was sparse and there were only a few people about. A sudden impulse made him turn right and head up the flight of steps leading to Malmskillnadsgatan. He kept stopping to catch his breath but found he could move more easily than he expected. His right leg felt almost completely okay. As if the alcohol, massage, and what had happened after that had changed him. Turned him into someone else.

He felt ashamed, of course, but considerably less than he ought to. Part of his brain was still enjoying the fleeting sensation he had experienced up there. The feeling that he could do almost anything, without having to worry about the consequences.

He could recall much more now. He remembered plenty of nights spent up there among the clientele of the exclusive club.

Friendship through secrets, invisible contracts. Life as Erik I. Johansson had been a game, a balancing act on a high wire that he had mastered for months, possibly even years. Until he had looked down and become aware of the abyss awaiting him beneath his feet.

The role had suited him perfectly, he just had to look at the bank statement to see that. Going through money like water. Drinks, dinners, and the other more discreet pleasures available in the private parts of the club.

There must have been a purpose to the role-playing at first. Recruiting new sources, key people in senior positions who could be useful—if not now, then at some point in the future. But as time went on he had lost his focus. Gradually erased the lines between right and wrong. Teamed up with Crispin so he could carry on living as Erik Johansson. Presumably he had started small, handing over discreet tips about people and addresses that were under surveillance. Then he had found himself on a slippery slope. He had become a mole, an infiltrator with conflicting loyalties. The handler who was being handled.

Police officer, snitch, mole, junkie, and evidently also a john. What a fantastic combination! It was hardly surprising that he kept feeling guilty, in spite of the chasm running through his brain.

Was that why drugs had come into the picture, to subdue his conscience? Or had the drugs been the reason why he needed more money? If Crispin was right, he had been prepared to commit the ultimate betrayal. Giving them Janus, his very best source. Could he have been that desperate?

Reality and performance, truth and lies—everything was blurring. Forming a web he didn't seem able to escape from. And right at its center the spider was waiting for him. Nursing its secret.

Sarac reached St. Johannes Church and began to cut across the churchyard. He followed the snow-cleared path between the graves without really knowing where he was going. He needed air, he needed to clear his head before he returned to his lair.

The sound of a car door made him start. Probably a curb crawler dropping off one of the few prostitutes who hadn't yet migrated to the Internet and was therefore still hanging around Malmskillnadsgatan. He turned around and saw the rear lights of a car as it drove off.

A faint movement off to the right caught his attention. It looked as if there were someone standing among the trees about three hundred feet away. Sarac felt his heart start to beat faster. The figure was standing there motionless and could easily have been a statue or a tall headstone that his brain had turned into something else.

But then he saw a tiny point of light. It vanished as soon as it appeared, but Sarac was still sure he had seen correctly. The glow of a cigarette.

Sarac turned around and started to walk toward the steps leading up to the church. He had to make an effort not to run. A new sound, a bird crowing. Sarac glanced back over his shoulder. The figure among the trees was gone.

He pricked his ears, trying to make out any other sounds. But apart from the distant rumble of traffic all he could hear was his own labored breathing as he struggled up the steps. The big, gothic brick church rose up in front of him. It had to be at least a hundred feet high, more like a cathedral than an ordinary church. Or a Carpathian castle from a vampire film.

He reached the top of the steps, stopped, and turned around. The churchyard seemed deserted. But he was still convinced there was someone there among the shadows. Someone who was watching him.

Fear was clenching his stomach and he forced himself to take some deep breaths. Then he started to jog toward the far corner of the churchyard.

Only when he emerged into the little street did he realize that he was in a dead end. To both the right and left his way was blocked by tall buildings, and behind him was the dark churchyard.

But right in front of him a narrow path led between the buildings and ought to lead him down to the considerably busier Regeringsgatan. He'd be able to get a taxi there.

He glanced quickly over his shoulder, then set off as fast as he could. He was aiming for the light of the streetlamps some three hundred away. He turned around again. A shadowy figure with a hood over its head was emerging from the darkness of the churchyard behind him.

Sarac began to run. His body protested at once. He couldn't stretch his right leg out properly and his breathing felt strained after just a dozen steps. He looked back again. The hooded man was gaining on him. Running with steady strides, just fast enough to avoid the risk of slipping on the icy ground. Sarac sped up, forcing his arms to help. His brain was trying to find a logical explanation for his panic. He tried to get his flight instinct under control but failed.

The little path came to an abrupt end. In its place was a sixty-five-foot drop, down which a flight of steps zigzagged toward Regeringsgatan.

Sarac tried taking two steps at a time. He felt tempted to jump the last of the first flight of steps but stopped himself at the last second. His shoes slipped on the loose grit on top of the ice and he almost lost his balance. He grabbed one of the iron railings, swung himself around to the right, and set off down the next flight.

The hooded man was about one flight behind him. Sarac lengthened his stride, taking three steps at a time. His right leg was wobbling badly, forcing him to keep one hand on the railing. He swung left and set off down the next set of steps. Not far to go now. But the hooded man was getting closer. Just before the last flight Sarac slipped, his right leg buckled, and his knee hit the ground.

He struggled to his feet, forcing his legs to obey. He could see the man clearly out of the corner of his eye now. He thought he could see a face. His lungs were burning and he could taste blood and adrenaline in his mouth.

The man was close now, right at his heels. Sarac took three steps at a time, not caring whether he fell. A car drove by on the road, just thirty feet away.

Sarac tried to call out, but all that emerged from his lips was a dry croak. He thought he could feel the man behind him reaching out for him, a hand brushing his shoulder.

He summoned the last of his strength and shot across the sidewalk and straight out into the road. He saw the headlights and managed to spin around. Blue, white, some lettering. Such a familiar word. The lights dazzled him, the studded tires shrieked on the tarmac. He held up his hands as the front of the car headed straight for him.

He shut his eyes.

·   ·   ·

Atif tapped in the code and opened the locker. Inside was a small, beige Fjällräven rucksack. He glanced quickly over his shoulder before pulling the zipper open. The angular shape was unmistakable. A nine-millimeter Glock, the model with a seventeen-bullet magazine. A decent gun, better than he had been expecting.

The car key was in the outer pocket of the rucksack. The consultant's men worked fast. Atif closed the zips, slung the rucksack on his back, and shut the door of the locker. The little white van was parked in a loading zone a short distance away, exactly as he'd been promised. A few blue, peeling company logos on the front and sides made it blend into its surroundings perfectly.

He unlocked the door, slid in behind the wheel, and put the rucksack on the floor in front of the passenger seat. He had almost everything he needed. The cop's address from Abu Hamsa, weapon and van from Hunter. And no hassle. As long as both Abu Hamsa and Hunter thought he was working for them, no one would bother him. And with a bit of luck Cassandra and Tindra would be safe as well, at least as long as no one worked out he was playing a double game. He was close now. Just one thing left to do, then he'd be ready for a meeting with a certain detective inspector.

. . .

"David Sarac, it is you, isn't it? Jesus! I hardly recognized you. Are you okay?" the police officer said.

The lights were still blinding Sarac. The patrol car had stopped just an inch and a half from his knees.

"Fucking idiot! You can't just run out into the road like that!" The driver of the police car was out of the vehicle as well now. The first officer held his hand up.

"Calm down, Jocke. This is David Sarac, he's a cop."

The driver stopped. "Oh, okay."

"Sarac," he went on. "Weren't you the one who crashed in the Söderleden Tunnel? We saw the wreckage, you must have had a guardian angel."

Sarac looked around. "Where did he go?" he panted.

"Who?"

"The guy in the hood, he was right behind me."

The two police officers exchanged a glance.

"We only saw you. It's a stroke of luck that we managed to stop in time. You came tearing out like you had the devil himself after you."

. . .

He gave them his address, then sat in the backseat of the police car and closed his eyes. Almost at once he felt that they were going in the wrong direction. When he opened his eyes he saw the officer in the passenger seat fiddling with his cell phone. But he was too exhausted to start arguing.

They headed east along Valhallavägen and turned left at the

Swedish Film Institute, then right, across the empty parkland of Gärdet. Snow had drifted across the road in several places, but the four-wheel-drive Volvo had no trouble sticking to the almost invisible little road.

The black 4x4 was waiting in the cul-de-sac among the patch of trees at the top of the hill. The police officers stopped the car and got out. They were hardly visible in the darkness. Sarac could see a number of shapes outside. He already had an idea who they were.

Less than a minute later the door beside him opened.

"Get out, David," Molnar said abruptly. "It's time for us to have a serious talk."

FORTY-SEVEN

They pushed Sarac into one of the seats in the back of the big 4x4. Molnar got in beside him, with Josef in the driver's seat as usual.

No hugs this time, Sarac thought as he watched the taillights of the patrol car disappear into the snow swirling over the field.

"You don't trust us, do you, David?" Molnar said. His voice was dry, neither friendly nor hostile.

"First you cracked the code in your notebook and found Sabatini, without telling me."

Sarac didn't answer.

"And now you've talked to Jan Dreyer. Let me guess . . ." Molnar frowned. "He told you that you worked for him. That you were on your way to see him when you crashed."

Sarac didn't answer.

Molnar exchanged a quick glance with Josef in the rearview mirror. Then he took a deep breath.

"Dreyer's smart, he's trying to manipulate you, David. Trying to implant things in your head that never actually happened. Did he say anything about a traffic report, and damage caused by another car?"

Sarac still kept quiet.

"That was floating around at the start, but closer examination couldn't find any proof, except for what looked like some much older damage to your car. But I bet you Dreyer said someone tried to make you crash. Maybe even one of us?" Molnar shook his head. "Dreyer's crazy. Properly mad, I mean.

Why do you think he works for the Internal Investigations Department? Josef, you tell him!"

"Because he's made himself impossible to work with anywhere else," Josef muttered from the driver's seat.

"Exactly! Once upon a time, before he became the most hated man in the force, Dreyer was a damned good cop. He and Eugene von Katzow set up the whole CI handler program. In those days every detective had his own contacts, there was no coordination at all. But the pair of them began to structure the whole thing. Started using systems to evaluate the reliability of different sources, all the sort of stuff we take for granted these days.

"But something went wrong. I've asked the Duke what happened, but he won't talk about it. Anyway, Dreyer ended up with a serious drinking problem. His wife left him, they had to sell their house, and it messed with his head."

The police radio crackled, but Josef switched it off.

"Dreyer got paranoid, got it into his head that the Duke was building up a secret intelligence service that was spying on everyone and everything." Molnar looked up at the roof with a sigh. "After that he was on sick leave for a long time. And got a transfer to Internal Investigations, who were stupid enough to take him on."

Sarac squirmed in his seat. A gust of wind showered some loose snow against the window.

"Dreyer set off on his crusade against von Katzow and managed to get a miserable old prosecutor on board. Secret operations, unaudited accounts, all manner of accusations. The fact is that they conducted over fifty interviews. They got warrants to search our offices, even the Duke's apartment in Gamla stan. But the only thing Dreyer managed to get him on was a few cases of inadequate record keeping. The sort of thing you could find in any police department. Complete nonsense."

Molnar shook his head, more forcefully this time.

"The Duke was suspended for six months and was hung out

to dry in the media. The papers wrote no end of articles about it all, the Duke running his own private intelligence service, recruiting celebrities, politicians, and businessmen, paying them from secret accounts. The whole thing was made up, gossip without a shred of evidence to support it. Then it all came to an end with two pathetic charges of professional misconduct and a few lines hidden away on page twenty-five. Dreyer was taken off the case and given strict instructions to stay away from us. Ever since he's been waiting for a chance to get revenge. To ruin, once and for all, what he helped to put together long ago. Your accident and the missing list gave him the opportunity. Not to mention your memory loss."

Sarac looked up. He remembered the whole story now, almost every detail. But there was something else there, something to do with Eugene von Katzow. Molnar's words interrupted his thoughts.

"The Duke realized he couldn't carry on. He'd become a burden to the department, so he left. A lot of people interpreted that as an admission of guilt. No smoke without fire and all that. The bosses all competed to distance themselves. The Duke's name is still like a red rag to a lot of people," Molnar said.

"And that's why you don't think he's involved in the Janus operation?" Sarac asked.

Molnar nodded. "Eugene was something of a mentor to me. We talk regularly, he can be a bit secretive, but I can't really believe he wouldn't have mentioned something like that to me. And, like I said, Eugene isn't well."

Sarac tried to think. Molnar's explanation sounded genuine, and Dreyer had certainly seemed a bit erratic up at the hospital. Not to mention all the cloak-and-dagger stuff before their meeting, the alcoholic tracery of veins in his face, the overdose of aftershave, and all that nervous, compulsive fiddling with the cigarillo. Everything suggested a man who wasn't entirely stable but was trying hard to hide it.

"You don't have to trust me, David," Molnar said. "To be honest, you're one of the best police officers I know. The idea that you could be an infiltrator, a rat . . ." Molnar pulled a skeptical face.

Sarac swallowed and tried to maintain his poker face. Suddenly the feeling that he had done something unforgivable was back, this time twice as strong as usual. But neither of the other two men seemed to have noticed anything.

"Dreyer's desperate," Molnar said. "He's prepared to do whatever it takes to get the whole lot of us. Lying, manipulation, all manner of promises and threats. The most important thing is for us to get hold of Janus. To limit the damage he's done. If we can do that, no one will have anything on us. Not even Dreyer."

"Hansen," Sarac said, without really knowing why.

Molnar nodded. "What do you remember? Be honest, David."

"I remember meeting him in his car on Skeppsbron. And that he died."

Molnar exchanged a glance with Josef in the rearview mirror.

"That's what we suspected but didn't want to say anything. Not until we knew more."

"My cell phone, the calls you said couldn't be traced?"

Molnar nodded slowly. "You called Hansen. Probably just an hour or so before . . ."

"I shot him!"

"Is that what you believe?" Molnar said.

Sarac shrugged. "I honestly don't know what to believe anymore, Peter. Everything's just one big mess of theories, blurred memories and pieces of a puzzle that won't fit together."

"I'm not going to pretend I can imagine what things are like for you, David. But the team and I are doing our best to help you. You're one of us."

Sarac swallowed again and looked down at the floor, thinking about the secret accounts and all the money.

"Brian Hansen was a total bastard," Molnar went on. "He had his own little sideline that the rest of his biker gang knew nothing about. Methamphetamine, sometimes heroin, not much, but more than enough. We found out about it and raided his home. Didn't find any drugs, but a computer full of pictures. Little girls, ten years and younger."

"So I approached him with a proposal," Sarac said. "No charges if he agreed to work for us, was that it?"

"Yep, a fully paid-up gang member owned by us, one who didn't even dare go for a piss without calling you first. Pure gold," Molnar said. "We used him to break up an entire chapter down in the Southern District. But I think Hansen gradually realized that you were taking drugs. He was terrified of being uncovered as a rat and ending up in some gravel pit with his cock stuffed down his throat. So he changes tactics and threatens to expose you, see to it that you get fired from working as a handler, maybe even chucked out of the entire force."

The high-pitched voice was suddenly echoing through Sarac's head. *I was thinking of suggesting a deal. Your secrets in exchange for mine.* So that's what the meeting had been about. Hansen trying to bargain his way to freedom.

"You and Hansen agree to meet at Skeppsbron," Molnar went on. "He's scared, so he chooses somewhere public. But he's got that wrong. It's dark, it's snowing hard, and there's no one around. You meet in the car and he tries to blackmail you into letting him go. But Janus knows about the whole thing. Maybe you'd even confided in him. If you get fired, his secret is in danger. So he follows you, and halfway through your meeting he jumps into the backseat. And gets rid of the threat to both you and him."

Another gust of snow lashed the windows, but Sarac was listening so intently that he hardly noticed.

"But instead of being grateful that the problem is solved, you're badly shocked by what's happened," Molnar continued. "One of your informants has died, right in front of your eyes.

Murdered by someone you've promised to protect. Your most important source. So you shoot yourself full of drugs, then you call me, babbling about something unforgivable happening. We arrange to meet but you drift through the streets in your car instead, high, stressed out, and paranoid. Until you end up in the Söderleden Tunnel. And just as we catch up with you the pressure in your head gets too much."

"And I have a stroke and crash," Sarac muttered. His headache had been quiet for a while, but now it hit him like a sledgehammer. His vision started to flicker.

"Hansen was already one of the living dead," Molnar went on. "His so-called brothers would have got rid of him if they found out he was informing on them. Not to mention his disgusting sexual preferences." He pulled a revolted face. "You don't have to worry, David. In my team we take care of one another. The test results of the blood sample are gone, as is your list of calls. We've just got a couple of more loose ends to sort out, then everything will be under control."

Sarac slowly shook his head. Back and forth, as if the movement could help keep Molnar's words at bay. Everything made sense, the details matched up with his memories. But there were still plenty of pieces missing.

"Hansen, Markovic, Lehtonen, Sabatini . . ."

He was about to say Erik Johansson's name as well but stopped himself at the last moment. He wasn't ready to talk about his base, let alone the money he had been receiving from Crispin.

"What's the connection between them?"

"We don't know yet," Molnar said. "Markovic had been in the water for about a month. I knew him, he was small potatoes, the sort who liked to shoot his mouth off about nothing. Someone strangled him with a piece of wire, then dumped him in Lake Mälaren sometime over the days following Hansen's death."

Molnar's mouth narrowed.

"Lehtonen took off to Thailand the day after your crash. He got back the day he was shot. His duty-free bags were just inside the door, so it looks like someone was waiting for him. He did a bit of dealing in performance-enhancing drugs, gave us a few tip-offs about his competitors. Which leaves Sabatini, but we've already talked about him. Four dead men, pretty much four different types of death."

He shrugged.

"With the exception of Hansen, they were all small-time crooks. They may have moved in the same circles to an extent, but there's no direct connection between them apart from the fact that all worked for you."

"You mean apart from the fact that they're all dead?" Sarac said somberly.

Molnar ran his tongue over his front teeth. "Here's what I think, David. The pay-as-you-go cell numbers you called just before you crashed—my guess is that they belonged to Markovic, Lehtonen, and Sabatini. You were probably trying to warn them about something, or someone."

Molnar paused, as if he was waiting for Sarac to take over. But when Sarac didn't say anything he carried on.

"Lehtonen bought his plane tickets that same evening, and one of Sabatini's credit cards was used in Italy a few days later, so he probably went by car or possibly train. Markovic, on the other hand, never made it. We found a filled-in passport application form on his computer."

Sarac was trying to gather his thoughts. But it was almost impossible. Flashes of memories, fragments of conversations, faces. It was all flying around inside his head, a wildly spinning maelstrom.

"Leave, get out of here! Right away!"

"But I've got the dogs, I can't just . . ."

"Fuck, Erik, I haven't got a passport."

"I'll go and stay with my family in Italy for a while until this blows over."

It all fit. He had told them to run for their lives. But why? Who did they have to run from? There was something else, one last secret. Something conclusive that he still couldn't get hold of. Something to do with Janus.

Something that meant that all of them . . .

Without exception . . .

Had to die.

"You asked me the other day if we were watching you. The answer to that question is yes," Molnar said in a low voice.

"But not for the same reason as Wallin's gang," he added. "They're using you as bait. Hoping that Janus is going to show up at your door so they can pick him up."

Molnar shook his head.

"Wallin was on the right track when he said you were in danger, David. But what he hasn't worked out, what no one seemed to have worked out"—he looked at Josef in the rear-view mirror again—"is that Janus has an entirely different plan. He's watching you, trying to work out if you're likely to keep his secret. If the answer is no, he'll disappear for good. And get rid of all the evidence."

Sarac looked up. He realized what Molnar was about to say.

"Including you, David."

FORTY-EIGHT

Molnar went with him up to his apartment. He even asked whether Sarac wanted the spare keys he had to the new locks. Of course Sarac ought to have laid all his cards on the table. His secret lair, the gun, the bank accounts, the whiteboard with all the pictures. He probably would have done so if it hadn't been for that visit to Club Babel. Molnar and his team weren't the enemy, as Dreyer had almost managed to have him believe, but his friends. Loyal friends at that, who were looking out for him. They were prepared to overlook his shortcomings and were taking risks for his sake. Protecting him from Wallin, Dreyer, and Janus.

But all that would change if they found out the true source of the money in those accounts. That he himself was in the pay of organized crime. Erik I. Johansson, a corrupt police officer, a CI. A rat.

So he had to go on keeping his mouth shut. Pretend he couldn't remember anything while he tried to figure out some way of escaping from the infernal labyrinth he found himself in. If there was a way out, of course. He was beginning to doubt that more and more. The pieces of the puzzle were starting to fit into place, but the problem was that he was finding the pattern they were forming increasingly unappealing.

"We're right across the street," Molnar said. "Press the alarm once if you want us to be discreet. Twice if it's urgent, okay?" He handed Sarac a small gray box with a button on it.

"Sure, no problem."

"And don't hesitate to call, David. No matter what the reason, okay?"

He nodded and attempted a smile. It worked better than he expected it to.

"Thanks for everything, Peter. I really am . . ." Sarac was momentarily lost for words, then couldn't bring himself to say them.

"Like I said, you'd have done the same for me, David. We're almost there now. All we have to do is get hold of Janus, and this whole nightmare will be over."

And what do we do then, once we've found him? Sarac thought. He realized that he already knew the answer. Bergh had given it to him along with the bulletproof vest and the revolver with the filed-off serial number.

·   ·   ·

Atif discovered the police officers almost immediately. All he had to do was work out where the perfect place to park would be if you wanted to keep an eye on the door, and then look for an anonymous Volvo. He walked closely past the car, chewing some gum very obviously and swinging the Nordic walking sticks he had bought from Stadium. Inside the car sat a man and a woman, both wearing dark clothing. The red diodes of the police radio in the middle of the dashboard removed any lingering doubts. The police officers in the car gave him no more than a cursory glance. They assumed he was yet another of the early-bird, sourdough-kneading spandex phantoms that seemed to have taken over the whole inner city.

Atif estimated the distance from their car to the door, trying to work out how much the van would block the view if he parked right in front of the door. He realized that it might work.

When he went around the corner of the street beyond the Volvo he spat out the chewing gum and stabbed it with the point of one of the walking sticks. He pulled a little cluster of spikes he had cut from a barbed-wire fence from his pocket and fixed it firmly to the chewing gum. When he walked back past the unmarked police car he carefully held out the walking stick and attached the spikes to the grooved pattern of the rear tire. He gave them thirty feet max before the spikes punctured the tire.

Atif carried on down the road toward his parked van. He saw the front door open and quickly slipped out of sight into another doorway, so he could watch what happened without being noticed. A large, blond man emerged onto the street, reeking of cop.

The man crossed the street and went around the corner without so much as glancing at the Volvo. He looked back over his shoulder briefly before going into the building on the corner. Atif waited for him to come out again, and stood there for almost half an hour before he was reluctantly forced to admit that he had a problem. The cops in the Volvo weren't on their own. There were others there too, and they'd been smart enough to conceal themselves properly. That meant he'd have to change his plan.

• • •

The man on the roof was standing perfectly still. Below him on the other side of the street he could see the dark windows of the apartment. If he took a couple of steps forward, stepped out of the shadows, and looked over the edge, he would see the police officers down there. For a moment he toyed with the idea of doing just that. Neither of them would see him, they were too busy focusing on the apartment. Hoping that the man asleep inside was going to reveal his secret at last. Their secret.

For a while he had been worried, actually more worried than he was prepared to admit. But he had done what was required and had got rid of all the risk factors. All but one.

The man turned around and pulled a half-smoked cigar from his inside pocket. He lit it between his cupped hands and took a deep puff. He was going to stop, he promised himself once again. But not just yet.

. . .

Sarac is dreaming he's back in the car. Hansen is in the front passenger seat, and he himself is behind the steering wheel. But there is someone else there too. A figure in the backseat wearing a hood, someone whose face Sarac can't see. A man, he's sure of that. Roughly his height and age. He knows who it is, but he still can't bring himself to say the man's name. Hansen is talking, trying to sound tough. But the anxiety in his voice is clearly audible even though he's trying to drown it with words.

"I was thinking of suggesting a deal," he says. He turns to look at Sarac and grins, trying to keep both his gaze and voice steady. But Hansen has sat in the front passenger seat for a reason. He's scared, he wants a backup plan. A quick escape route.

"We'll part as friends, no hard feelings." Hansen is still grinning, revealing a nicotine-stained row of teeth. Sarac looks at the man's pudgy hands and thinks about the girls in the pictures, no more than ten years old.

"So, what do you say, Erik? Have we got a deal or what?"

Sarac looks in the rearview mirror and meets the gaze of the man in the hood. Pale eyes, like his own. They're very similar, he and Janus, more similar that he likes to admit. They're both balancing on a high wire. They've chosen that for themselves, live for it. Love it.

The connection between handler and CI can sometimes become too strong. Is that what's happened with him and Janus? Have they grown too close?

"Well, what's it to be, Erik?" Hansen grins uncertainly.

Sarac goes on looking in the rearview mirror. He can see the other man smiling. Realizes what it means. He opens the door and gets out into the road. Takes out a cigarette and cups his hands around it to protect the flame of the lighter from the snow. Takes a deep drag.

A flash of light inside the car, then a bang.

The sound woke Sarac up, making him sit bolt upright in

bed. His heart was pounding in his chest, and his T-shirt was wet with sweat. His bladder was full, but he didn't bother to turn on the light and walked through the apartment toward the toilet in silence. As he passed the living room he glanced at the building opposite. The window was dark, but he knew that Molnar's men were in there. He wondered whether they would be so keen to protect him if they knew he was actually a lousy rat. And somewhere out there was Janus, perhaps waiting for the right moment to cut the last ties. Was Janus really prepared to go that far, after everything they had been through together? Had he actually created a monster, someone who would be the death of him? Was it now a matter of finding him before he himself was found?

Sarac shook off the feeling, turned, and took a step toward the toilet. He suddenly imagined he could see movement from the corner of his eye. He turned back and looked at the building opposite, then up at the dark rooftop.

But of course there was no one there.

FORTY-NINE

Natalie went up the stairs a bit too quickly. She stopped on the last landing for a minute or so to catch her breath. Didn't want to seem too keen. She fingered her cell phone. Hoped he was home this time.

Once she had collected herself she went up to the door and rang the bell. No answer. She tried again, with the same result. She opened the mail slot and called into the apartment.

"David, it's Natalie. Open up!"

She heard noises, shuffling steps. She glimpsed a pair of slippers and the bottom of a threadbare dressing gown. She quickly let go of the mail slot. The door opened slightly, with the security chain still on.

He looked terrible. Black bags under his eyes, his beard straggly and greasy, and the little woolly hat he was wearing could have done with a wash a long time ago. His shabby dressing gown was at least one size too big and hardly helped the overall impression.

"Are you going to let me in, then?"

He didn't answer, and just shut the door. A few seconds later she heard the chain rattle.

"Come in. Lock the door behind you." He shuffled into the living room ahead of her and slumped down on the sofa.

Natalie took a quick look in the kitchen. Clean and tidy, not so much as a dirty glass in the sink. She opened the fridge door. Full of unopened packets.

"When did you last eat? Properly, I mean?"

He muttered something she didn't hear. He was a complete

wreck, could hardly keep his eyes focused. Natalie took a deep breath.

"Okay, this is what we do," she said. "First, you need to have breakfast, or lunch, to be more accurate." She nodded toward the clock on the wall, which said half past eleven. "Then you need a shower, and then I'm going to give you a shave and cut your hair. Have you got the things here or shall I go down to the 7-Eleven?"

More muttering, something about the bathroom cabinet.

"Okay. And get rid of that dressing gown. You look like that guy in *The Hitchhiker's Guide to the Galaxy.*

"Toward the end of the film, not the beginning," she added.

● ● ●

He ate with a hearty appetite. Three eggs, a whole pack of bacon, two slices of toast. He washed it all down with orange juice and a cup of strong coffee. While he showered she dug out a pair of jeans and a long-sleeved T-shirt from his wardrobe. She also took the opportunity to have a poke about but didn't find anything interesting. With the exception of the new sofa, everything looked just as it had when she had cleaned the place up. She had been struck then by how impersonal the apartment was. No pictures, nothing that gave any clues as to who Sarac really was. The bookcase was full, admittedly, but it contained mostly English nonfiction. Natalie pulled out one of the books. *Influence,* by Robert B. Cialdini. She turned it over and read the back: *The classic book on persuasion, explains the psychology of why people say yes.*

Natalie put the book back in its place. A piece of paper fell out and she bent down to pick it up. A black-and-white photograph of a thin-haired man in a white shirt and black trousers balancing on a high wire. In the background was one of the towers of Tower Bridge in London, and beneath him, far below, the dark, swirling water of the Thames. But the man didn't seem bothered by the breathtaking view and was just staring ahead of him, toward his goal. She turned the photograph over, read the ornate handwriting, then put it back in the bookcase.

When Sarac emerged from the bathroom he was already looking a bit brighter. Seemed almost happy to see her.

Natalie nodded toward one of the kitchen chairs. "Sit down!"

She went into the bathroom to get shaving cream and a razor from the bathroom cabinet, and grabbed a towel. She found a pair of scissors in one of the kitchen drawers. She wrapped the towel around him.

"Chin up."

She trimmed his beard quickly, then soaked a kitchen towel in warm water and wet his chin and cheeks with it.

"Your bandage needs changing, it smells awful, and the tape isn't sticking properly anymore," she said.

She covered his face with shaving foam and carefully started to remove his stubble. Sarac moved his head slightly and she almost cut him.

"Sit still!" She grabbed his chin. She slid the razor blade carefully down his cheek and onto his neck. The blade scraped against the dark stubble. She noticed he was looking at her. There was something in his eyes she hadn't seen before. Not gratitude but something else. Something she liked.

"There," she said abruptly. "Wipe the rest of the foam off and we'll get your hair tidied up."

The transformation was complete. Freshly shaved, with his hair cut and wearing clean, intact clothes, Sarac actually looked very nice. The only sign of the wound in his head was a neat little plaster, no bigger than the palm of your hand, that she had fixed to his scalp. He was still pale and thin, but that would improve with time. He had cheered up and seemed more talkative. He had even made them both a cup of coffee.

"Look at this," she said, holding her cell phone up at him and trying not to show how eager she was. She would rather have shown him the picture straightaway. But she'd changed her mind when she saw the state he was in. She needed him focused so he could give her the answer she wanted. That Rickard wanted, she corrected herself.

ing new to give him. Nothing at all. Damn it! She looked down

"I took it over at Högbergsgatan," she said when he didn't react. "I saw this guy coming around the corner and thought about the description the police had given after that man was killed in Roslagsgatan."

Sarac looked at the picture and felt his stomach tighten. Then he realized that he recognized the thickset man.

"He helped me, or rather, he helped Sabatini. He ran across the street and used my scarf to try to stop the bleeding. He disappeared just before the police showed up."

"And you don't think he's got anything to do with it?"

Sarac slowly shook his head.

"Okay, shame." Natalie tried not to sound disappointed. She had been hoping this was the man Rickard was looking for. She had even toyed with the idea of how Rickard would react when she showed him the picture. Giving him exactly what he wanted, in color and everything. Whereas in fact she had nothing new to give him. Nothing at all. Damn it! She looked down into her coffee cup, trying to think of something else to say.

"How does it feel, David?" Fuck, she could have kicked herself. Classic sports journalist question, cliché number one. She ought to be able to do better than that.

"I don't really know how to describe it. Part of me wants to know everything, every little detail. And another part"—he shrugged his shoulders—"just wants to forget." He met her gaze and smiled rather wearily. "And I'm somewhere in the middle. Trying to stay up on the tightrope."

"Like the man on the bookmark." She nodded.

He nodded back, then frowned.

"The photograph of the tightrope walker," she clarified. "The one your friend Eugene sent you."

. . .

Atif saw the woman come out of the door. He had recognized her when she went inside a couple of hours earlier. The red-haired woman who had taken his picture up at Högbergsgatan.

He watched her as she jumped into a battered old red Golf parked on the other side of the street. She started the car, did a U-turn, and drove off. Without really knowing why, Atif turned the key in the van's ignition and began to follow her.

．　．　．

"No, no, it was only Natalie. She redressed my wound and patched me up a bit. She left a little while ago. Everything's fine, I'm going to get some rest, watch a bit of television. I'll call if there's anything."

Sarac ended the call and couldn't help gazing across at the windows of the building opposite. He looked at the time, then at the photograph. He turned it over and read the writing on the back. *To David, from your friend Eugene von Katzow.* Below the words was a familiar symbol. Two intertwined *J*s, forming a head with two faces, facing away from each other.

Twenty minutes left, time he got moving. The remote was on the table, and he surfed the channels until he found one with a lot of talking. He sat down on the sofa but got up again fairly quickly and lowered a couple of the blinds. He tried to make it look as if the light were bothering him.

After a while he stood up. He got out the bag containing the revolver and bulletproof vest that Bergh had given him and put his notebook inside it. He pulled on his jacket and boots and slung the bag over his shoulder before quietly sneaking out the door. When he reached the ground floor he turned right and emerged into the walled inner courtyard, then carried on toward the clump of bushes in the corner. He was relieved to see that Natalie had put the stepladder from his locker in the basement in just the right place. He tossed the bag over the wall, then carefully climbed up the steps and reached out his hands toward the tin plate covering the top of the wall. The steps wobbled but settled again.

Sarac took a deep breath and kicked one leg up. It went better than he expected. His body was reacting better with each passing day. He still ended up lying prone along the top of the wall as he gathered his strength. For a brief moment he felt ashamed; he had lied to Molnar again and tricked the men who were supposed to be protecting him. But he was a rat, a corrupt police officer, and possibly even a murderer. From now on he had to try to manage on his own. Try to sort out his mistakes. Clean up this fucking mess.

• • •

Atif was taking it easy. He let a few cars slip in between him and the Golf. The woman driving didn't seem to be in any hurry either. She drifted through the streets toward St. Eriksplan. Eventually she pulled over into a loading zone. Atif drove past slowly. He saw the woman reach across the passenger seat and unlock the door. He did a U-turn and parked on the other side of the street.

• • •

Sarac emerged from a door on the far side of his own block. He walked as quickly as he could toward the subway station. When he reached the platform he carried on and went up the stairs at the other end. He opened the doors and emerged onto St. Eriksplan.

• • •

Atif saw the man come walking across the square carrying a bag. He recognized him at once from Högbergsgatan. David Sarac, the man he was looking for. He smiled, started the engine, and put his hand in his pocket. He could feel the cold plastic handle of the pistol.

• • •

"Number 2, Själagårdsgatan, Gamla stan." Natalie put her foot down and pulled straight out into traffic, without waiting for a gap. Sarac looked behind them through the rear window but couldn't see anyone following them.

"He's got some sort of consultancy business, involved in training and lectures. Website and everything. Seems to be quite a big fish."

She tossed her smartphone to Sarac. The background picture of the website was the same as the photograph in his inside pocket. The tightrope walker above the Thames. The high wire.

He quickly scrolled through the text. *Eugene von Katzow is a former detective lieutenant at the Intelligence Unit of the Stockholm Police Force. He currently works as an international security consultant and lecturer. Among his clients are major organizations such as OSSE, ASIS, Interpol, and the ICC.*

"I didn't have time to read the whole thing. And there's loads of abbreviations. OSSE and ASSE or whatever there were." Natalie changed lanes again.

"They're both security organizations," Sarac said. "One's intergovernmental, the other's private. The ICC is the International Criminal Court in the Hague. Look out!"

Natalie forced her way in front of a taxi. The driver slammed on his brakes and blew his horn hard. Sarac turned around again. Apart from a few taxis, all he could see was a white van of some sort with a tatty company logo on the front. Everything looked fine.

FIFTY

Number 2, Själagårdsgatan was a beautiful, coral-colored, four-story seventeenth-century building with leaded windows, situated almost right in the middle of Gamla stan. It had to be one of the most beautiful residential buildings in Stockholm, and presumably also one of the most expensive.

Traffic was banned from the narrow alleyways and the snow that had settled between the cobbles made the street treacherously slippery, but none of this seemed to bother Natalie. She steered the car in between the old buildings and stopped right in front of the door.

Sarac sat in the car for a minute or so, studying the building. He remembered it clearly now, especially the beautiful, protruding stone porch. Pale sandstone with inlaid cherubs, and two statues on top. Roman gods again, that could hardly be a coincidence.

"You can park up there."

He pointed along the narrow alley to where it widened to form a small square. Then he opened the car door before she could offer to go with him.

For a moment he wondered about taking the bag containing the notebook and other things with him, but decided to leave it in the trunk of the car for the time being.

Some snow had caught in the building's doorway, leaving the door slightly ajar. He kicked it away and closed the door behind him.

E. von Katzow lived on the fourth floor. Sarac went up the stairs and stopped in front of the oak door. He took a few deep breaths, trying to lower his heart rate. Just as he was about to ring the doorbell he heard footsteps on the stairs.

"You could have waited," Natalie panted. "As luck would have it, a little old lady showed up and let me in." She winked at Sarac and for a moment he almost smiled. Instead he managed to turn the smile into an unhappy grimace. He didn't want to drag her any further into this than he already had. He would have told her to go straight back to the car if she hadn't already reached over and rung the doorbell.

The bell set off a familiar buzz inside Sarac's head and he closed his eyes for a few seconds. The door was opened by a straight-backed, desiccated little man.

"Yeees . . ." he said. The word almost vanished into his nose.

"Eugene von Katzow?" Natalie said.

"Who wants to know?" the man purred.

Natalie looked at Sarac and gave him a gentle nudge with her elbow.

"My friend here says he knows you."

"I don't think so," the man replied curtly. "You must be confusing me with someone else." He started to shut the door, but before it closed Natalie managed to block it with her foot.

"Come on, David," she hissed at Sarac. "Is this the right guy?"

Sarac slowly shook his head. The buzzing was getting louder.

"Excuse me, young lady, but would you be so kind as to remove your foot from the door?" The man's voice was just as dry as before.

Natalie gave Sarac a long look, then pulled her foot back. At the last moment Sarac raised his hand and stopped the door from closing.

"Arthur," he said. "Tell Eugene that David Sarac is here." His voice sounded different, softly spoken but firm. He let go of the door and it closed. Silence fell. Sarac noticed that Natalie was staring at him, but for once he said nothing.

The door opened again. "Please come in, Mr. Sarac," the little man said.

The man Sarac had called Arthur led them down a long corridor. Thick walls, a high ceiling, and a wooden floor that creaked beneath heavy, genuine antique carpets.

The room they walked into was more modern than Natalie had been expecting. A couple of comfortable sofas, a large film screen on one of the white walls. Lots of framed photographs and pictures on the other walls. The beautiful vaulted ceiling was subtly lit, making it feel even higher than it was.

A man in his sixties was sitting on one of the sofas. He was wearing a red velvet smoking jacket, and a pair of rectangular sunglasses covered his eyes. Beside him on the sofa, with its head resting on the blanket covering the man's lap, lay a large, brownish-yellow dog. As they approached the dog began wagging its tail slowly.

"Hello, Brutus," Sarac said. The sound of his voice made the tail wag faster, but the dog didn't bother to raise its head.

"You'll have to excuse us," the man on the sofa said. Clearly this was Eugene von Katzow.

"Both Brutus and I have a little trouble moving these days. Can Arthur get you anything? Coffee, tea?"

"Coffee, please," Natalie said.

Von Katzow gestured to them to sit down.

"You haven't introduced your friend, David." He nodded toward Natalie.

"This is Natalie, she . . . she's helping me out," Sarac said, pulling a slight face.

"I understand." Von Katzow nodded. "It's good to have helpful friends, isn't it? I couldn't manage without them."

Silence fell and Natalie took the chance to look around. Some of the pictures were actually old circus posters. He recognized the name Ringling Bros. on one of them, and Barnum & Bailey on another. They all depicted various types of balancing acts. The largest of them seemed to be for a film. She could see Britt Eklund's name down one side. *The Great Wallendas.* Where had she heard that name before?

"So, David, you found your way here in the end." Von Katzow's voice sounded more sorrowful than unfriendly.

"I'm glad you're back on your feet again," he went on. "But I'm afraid your visit here is in vain."

"How do you mean?" Sarac said.

Natalie couldn't put her finger on what it was, but his voice sounded very different. Sterner, more self-confident.

"You think I can fill in the gaps in your head. Explain what's going on. Somewhere deep inside perhaps you would even like to think that I am in some way behind it all," von Katzow said.

"And would that be wrong, Eugene?"

Von Katzow gave a wry smile.

"What do you really think, David?"

Sarac shrugged. "I'm not here to discuss what I think, but to find out what you know."

Natalie looked at Sarac, then at von Katzow. She saw that they were both smiling in similar ways. As if the trite discussion they were engaged in were actually something completely different.

"So typical of you, David." Von Katzow shook his head gently. "Straight to the point. Taking what you need, without any thought of the consequences. Of how your actions will affect other people."

Natalie saw Sarac's smile fade slightly. Von Katzow seemed to have noticed as well, because he leaned forward.

"I'm not the person you're looking for, David. Can we agree on that, at least? Perhaps you were hoping you'd come here and find the brains behind everything, but deep down you know that's not the case."

Von Katzow threw out one of his hands.

"I only have twenty percent of my sight left, I can't really go out without a guide. So I amuse myself by inviting people here, people I think might need a little push in the right direction. You were one of them, David, actually one of the more intelligent of them. Among other things, you share my interest in Roman deities."

Von Katzow paused as his servant came in with a tray bearing two silver pots and three cups and saucers. He put the tray down on the table and withdrew discreetly.

"I've met your old friend Dreyer," Sarac said as he poured Natalie some coffee. Now it was von Katzow's turn to look troubled.

"He claimed that I was actually working for him. That he had recruited me to spy on you and the others up in Regional Crime. What are your thoughts about that?" Sarac picked up his coffee cup and leaned back.

Natalie suddenly realized what was going on. She was watching a game, a sort of verbal chess match. She remembered the psychology books in Sarac's bookcase. They were all about influence, persuasion, getting people to do what you wanted.

Von Katzow sat in silence for a while, idly scratching the big dog's chin.

"I think Jan Dreyer is saying the sort of thing he thinks will work. The sort of thing that will fit somehow into the picture you're trying to put together."

Sarac put his cup down. "So you're saying he's wrong?"

"I didn't say that." Von Katzow went on stroking the dog.

"No, you didn't. You usually try to avoid plain speaking," Sarac said.

The two men were staring at each other. Neither of them said anything. They both seemed to be waiting for the other man's next move.

Natalie was already fed up. She needed answers, straight-away. Something she could take to Rickard that would restore his faith in her. She leaned forward and put the cup down hard enough to make it rattle.

"What's the big deal with the tightrope walkers?" she asked, looking at von Katzow. "That picture in David's apartment, now all these posters?"

Von Katzow turned toward her. His eyes were hidden by his dark glasses, which made his smile rather difficult to interpret.

"I've always been interested in the circus," he said. "When I was a child I dreamed of becoming a tightrope walker. I used to practice in the garden of our summer cottage, on a rope tied between two apple trees. But instead of a career in the ring, I managed to disappoint my parents almost as much by joining the police." He shrugged his shoulders slightly.

"But there are actually a lot of similarities between our work and a tightrope walker's." Von Katzow nodded toward Sarac. "Keeping your balance, no matter what happens. Not losing your concentration. Do you understand what I mean, Natalie?"

"And the guy in the picture, the one walking over Tower Bridge?"

"Karl Wallenda? He's actually walking beside Tower Bridge, not that that diminishes his achievement."

Von Katzow straightened up slightly, which made the dog start to wag its tail again.

"Karl Wallenda was the most talented tightrope walker in the world. He set up his own troupe of acrobats in the 1920s, and a lot of the records he set lasted long into our time. Karl's specialty was extreme heights. He would walk between skyscrapers, cross bridges. He rarely used any safety equipment. In fact he actually claimed that life only existed when he was balancing on the high wire, and that everything else was just anticipation."

Von Katzow shook his head sadly.

"Unfortunately that sort of hero no longer exists, my dear Natalie. Now everything is mostly about image. About being famous without actually doing anything to warrant it." He patted the dog's back gently. "Karl Wallenda died for his art, he fell when he was walking between two hotels in Puerto Rico in 1979. He had actually retired, he was over seventy by then. But for some reason he still decided to do it. Barely halfway across, the wind caught him and he fell to his death.

"Afterward his wife talked about having known him for over

fifty years. She had seen him prepare for hundreds of different potentially fatal challenges. But this was the only time she had ever heard him talk about the risk of falling. The possibility of failure."

He gestured toward the wall.

"I usually mention Karl Wallenda in my lectures. I use him as an example of how dangerous it is to allow the thought of failure to enter your head." Von Katzow smiled again. "I hope that answers your question, Natalie?"

"It does, but I've actually got another question, if that's all right, Eugene?" Natalie waited until both men were looking at her. Then she added her loveliest smile.

"Of course, my dear." Von Katzow raised his cup.

Natalie took a deep breath. She wondered whether what she was about to say was really such a good idea. But she had been lying low for several weeks now, not delivering anything that Rickard wanted. High time to take a few risks. Step out onto the wire.

"Tell me what you know about Janus. Who is he, for instance?" she said, and smiled happily when von Katzow's coffee caught in his throat.

.   .   .

Atif had lost the Golf for a while at Slottsbacken. He was taken by surprise when it turned left into Stortorget, and he had had to hold back. By the time he rolled into the square the Golf was gone. But as luck would have it there weren't that many streets to choose from, and even fewer parking spaces. After cruising around Gamla stan for almost ten minutes, he found it parked illegally just six hundred feet from Stortorget.

Unfortunately it was too narrow for him to squeeze the van in without blocking the whole of the street. So he parked the van around the corner, stuck one of his barbed-wire clusters to one of the Golf's front tires, and took up position in a doorway that offered a good view. All he had to do now was wait.

• • •

"The fact is," von Katzow said when he had recovered, "that I don't know who Janus is. And the reason is very simple." He cleared his throat.

"You never told me, David." Von Katzow turned to Sarac, who was still staring at Natalie. "We met here on a number of occasions, but mostly it was just me telling you things. About how everything had started, how we organized what the handlers did, our routines, rules. Various things we had learned over the years. The impossibility of fighting a linear war against an asymmetrical enemy. The importance of thinking outside the box."

The old man sighed.

"But you were almost as interested in the chaos that broke out later, when Dreyer and his internal investigators started their witch hunt. When we came close to destroying ourselves."

Natalie didn't really know what von Katzow was talking about but decided not to say anything.

"That was why you left. To save the department. Everything you'd built up," Sarac said, reluctantly taking his eyes off Natalie.

Von Katzow nodded slowly, suddenly looking rather tired. He leaned back on the sofa.

"What I know, David, is that we sent you on a course in the USA. I say we, because even though I no longer had any official standing, I was still able to pull a few strings on the other side of the Atlantic. Shortly after you came back you started talking about a secret project that you called Janus. You asked me for help with the initial funding. I helped you with that, and showed you the Janus symbol that I remembered from a book I'd read. But you didn't tell me anything else, and naturally I didn't ask. Now, in hindsight, I'm extremely glad about that."

Brutus suddenly sat up on the sofa, sniffing and pricking his ears.

"He does that sometimes. Arthur says that Brutus can

hear ghosts. Lost souls." Von Katzow stroked the dog's back. "Hardly surprising, really, seeing as we're in Själagårdsgatan, named after a charitable institution that cared for the souls of the poor." Von Katzow waited for the animal to lie down again before he went on.

"David, I'm afraid you're not the only one of my former adepts who's trying to get hold of Janus."

"Molnar," Sarac said.

Von Katzow nodded. "Peter's one of them, but there are others. I've tried to make it clear that I'm neutral in this matter. Peter sees me as his mentor. For that reason I asked him to keep me out of it as much as possible. Partly because I don't actually know anything that can help you, and partly because I don't want to risk any misunderstandings. You see, David . . ."

He nudged Brutus aside and leaned forward across the table.

"The people who want to get at Janus are prepared to do whatever it takes to find him. Nothing is off-limits." He turned his head to face Natalie. "I think I've said enough. Come with me, my dear, and I'll show you a picture of David here, when he was younger and happier."

Von Katzow stood up and invited Natalie to go with him over to one wall bearing a row of framed photographs.

"He's there somewhere. I'm afraid I can't see well enough to be able to point him out to you."

Natalie looked at the photos. They were all of different groups of people lined up in front of the camera. There were foreign flags in a couple of the pictures, whereas others seemed to have been taken somewhere inside the apartment. In the white border beneath the photographs the names and titles of the participants were listed. Most of them seemed to be police officers or prosecutors.

The photograph that von Katzow was pointing at seemed to have been taken abroad, seeing as the participants were flanked by the flags of both the EU and UN. She ran her finger along the row of faces without finding Sarac. Suddenly she stopped at one who seemed familiar. A blond, well-built man with a broad smile. She looked down and read his name. She stiffened when she saw that it was a different name than the one he had said to her.

"That's me." Sarac pointed at the next photograph. His voice sounded cold. Natalie straightened up quickly, smiled, and tried to make out that she hadn't seen anything. As soon as she met his gaze she realized that she'd failed.

FIFTY-ONE

They walked down the broad stone stairs together. First Sarac, then Natalie a couple of steps behind. Just before they reached the front door he stopped.

"Who told you about Janus?" Sarac said. The suppressed anger in his voice was unmistakable. "Was it the man in the photograph?"

"Why, what do you mean?" Natalie said, trying to buy herself a bit of time. They had talked about Janus out on the island, she was pretty certain of that. Or was she? She shrugged her shoulders. Did her best to sound completely nonplussed, while her brain was working at top speed.

"You've mentioned the name a few times, don't you remember?" She did a better job of striking the right note this time, and even managed a hint of the sort of sympathy he hated. But at the same time she was cursing herself inside. Sarac was right. She had been far too eager, trumpeting a name she wasn't supposed to know anything about. Mixing up truth and lies. Old von Katzow had seen the look on Sarac's face when she mentioned Janus and immediately suspected something was wrong. And he had set her up for a test. A test she had failed.

"Who are you working for?" Sarac said quietly.

"Adelfi Care, I've already told you that, David."

"And how long have you been working for them, Natalie?"

"A while. Why?" She pushed past him to open the door.

"How long?!" Sarac held the door shut. His eyes were black, and she actually felt a bit scared.

"Since November." Her voice was trembling slightly, enough for him to notice.

"What date, Natalie?"

Natalie bit her lip. "The twenty-eighth," she said in a low voice.

"Five days after my accident. When it was pretty much clear that I was going to survive and would need a care assistant," Sarac said.

The look in his eyes was burning into her head and Natalie had to look away.

"Who are you really working for, Natalie?"

"David, you're starting to sound a bit paranoid now. It's the stroke, it's making—"

"Stop that!" he snapped. "I saw you recognize someone in those pictures, so tell me who he is!"

"N-no one, I just thought one of them looked like an old friend." Natalie could hear how false it sounded. Shit, she didn't usually have any trouble lying. The photograph had taken her by surprise. Admittedly, the picture was a few years old and he was in uniform, but she had still recognized Rickard immediately.

"An old friend?" Sarac was still staring at her. "What's his name?"

Natalie hesitated. "Rickard," she finally replied.

"Surname. What's his . . . ?" Sarac stumbled and put a hand to his head.

Natalie seized her chance. She pushed him aside and opened the door. She walked quickly toward the car. Fucking idiot, giving her the third degree in a hallway. Who the hell did he think he was, anyway? After all she'd done for him, she'd practically saved his fucking life.

"Wait!" Sarac stumbled out the door. His head was throbbing badly, making his vision flare. He stopped and tried to find something to focus on. He caught sight of a man walking away farther down the street.

Natalie jumped in the Golf and locked the door, then put

the key in the ignition. Her face was burning with equal parts anger and shame. Her cover was blown, she'd been exposed, and she wasn't about to stay a second longer in this damn place. David and Rickard could both go to hell.

"Natalie, wait a minute!"

Sarac took a few steps toward the car but stopped when he heard an engine approaching. A white van with peeling blue lettering on the front was slowly coming around the corner. It stopped for a moment, as if the driver were waiting for something. He took a couple of quick steps toward the Golf. The door was locked. He tugged at the handle, then leaned over and banged on the windshield.

The van was getting closer. Sarac stared at the driver's seat and thought he could make out a bulky, dark figure. His heart was pounding. He should have followed his gut instinct and put the revolver Bergh had given him in his pocket instead of leaving it in the trunk of the car.

The Golf's engine started with a roar. Sarac banged on the windshield again, harder this time, but Natalie looked away.

"Natalie, open the door, for fuck's sake!"

The van put its headlights on full beam, dazzling him. He heard the Golf's transmission crunch. She was going to drive off and leave him there.

"Natalie!" he yelled, tugging one last time at the handle. This time the door flew open so abruptly that he almost lost his balance.

"Get in!" Natalie shouted. He obeyed instantly.

The Golf shot off with its wheels spinning, bouncing and sliding over the cobbles. It missed a protruding doorstep by a matter of an inch before Natalie managed to get control of the steering and aim the car straight down the narrow street.

The van was right behind them, its headlights lit up the whole of the inside of the car and Natalie had to knock the rearview mirror aside to avoid being blinded. The two vehicles raced through the narrow street, the noise of their engines echoing between the old buildings. Sarac looked over his shoulder, then at Natalie. She opened her mouth to say something but changed her mind. She decided to focus on the driving. Everything else could wait.

A junction was approaching, and Natalie slammed on the brakes and wrenched the wheel to the left. But the car didn't turn fast enough. The wall of the building was coming up fast. They were going to crash straight into it.

Natalie grabbed the hand brake and pulled it as hard as she could. The back wheels locked, making the car slide to the left.

The right side of the Golf slammed into the wall, then the car rebounded into the street. The next junction was only ten feet away.

"The car isn't responding like it should," Natalie yelled. "I think we've got a puncture."

She turned right, tugging the wheel as far as she could and repeating the trick with the hand brake. By the smallest possible margin she managed to squeeze the Golf into an even narrower street. The wheel was vibrating wildly in her hands, making it almost impossible to keep the car straight.

A heavy jolt made the Golf lurch. It hit the wall on the right, then the left. The van had rammed them and was about to do it again. A second jolt made the Golf leap forward out of control.

The buzzing was back in Sarac's head. Engine noise, headlights, lurching movement. This was all very familiar.

Suddenly Natalie slammed on the brakes, twisted the steering wheel to the left, and yanked the hand brake for a third time so that the Golf ended up sideways across the narrow street. The air inside the car filled with the sound of crumpling metal, then the bang of the air bag inflating.

The van was too close to have time to brake. The collision shook the Golf, shoving it forward another yard or so and wedging it between the buildings. For a brief moment everything was quiet.

Sarac was gasping for air. His seat belt was pulled tight
across his chest and a thin, white powder was swirling in the
air, stinging his throat. A loud, shrieking sound in his head
was blocking out all the noise, making the world move in slow
motion. He could see Natalie fighting with the fabric of the air
bag. Her lips were moving slowly. Then faster. Things suddenly
sped up again, throwing him back into real time.

"Run!" Natalie was shouting.

She pointed through the passenger window, toward the end
of the street.

"Get moving, he can't get past! Run, for God's sake!"

Sarac got his seat belt undone and pulled at the door handle.
The door was jammed. He spun around in his seat, raised both
feet, and kicked. He heard the sound of metal protesting.

"Hurry, he's getting out!" Natalie was still fighting with the
air bag and her own seat belt. Sarac pushed as hard as he could,
pressing down with his heels. The door flew open.

He tumbled out onto the street, then took a few staggering
steps before looking back. He saw that the man was out of the
van now. Thickset, with a hood over his head. Janus!

Janus had been watching his apartment and had seen him
shake off the police officers who were supposed to be protecting
him. And now he was here, to cut the last tie. Sarac was almost
paralyzed with terror, but somehow he managed to get his legs
to move. He already had a thirty-foot advantage. By the time
his pursuer had clambered over the Golf, it would be at least
double that.

He sped up and aimed for the street corner. One of his feet
slid on the icy road and he almost fell. But at the last moment
he managed to regain his balance.

Behind him he heard a car door slam shut, then the warning
alarm of a reversing vehicle.

Thirty feet to the junction, fifteen . . .

His feet slipped again; the cobbles were like glass. His right
leg almost gave way. He found himself on a steep slope and

turned left, heading downhill. Thirty feet ahead of him the road turned sharply right and carried on toward Järntorget. In front of him was a metal railing, and beyond that a sheer drop down to the street below, Österlånggatan.

Sarac slipped again and very nearly fell this time. Behind him he could hear the sound of an engine revving hard as it got closer.

His legs were moving automatically; the slope and the icy road surface made it impossible to stop. The van emerged at the top of the slope behind him. The beam of the headlights reflected off the windows on the other side of Österlånggatan. Sarac leaned right, trying to take the corner as sharply as possible. His right leg gave way and he slipped and fell to the ground.

He landed on his back, just a few yards from the metal railing. The fall knocked the air out of him. The back of his head hit the cobbles, and the night sky high above began to spin slowly.

He heard the shriek of brakes, tires crunching on the frozen cobbles, and tried desperately to get to his feet. But he was still groggy and couldn't get any grip on the slippery road surface; he merely managed to push himself backward, up against the railings.

The van was lurching toward him, its rear end sliding out until the vehicle was almost moving sideways. Sarac tried to get out of the way but realized he wasn't going to make it in time. He pushed back against the metal railings and closed his eyes.

The front and rear wheels on the left side of the van hit the edge of the sidewalk at almost the same time. The right wheels lifted slightly from the ground, and for a moment it looked as though the vehicle was about to roll on top of Sarac.

But the swaying van fell back onto all four wheels and came to a complete standstill. The driver's door opened and the man in the hood got out.

Sarac's heartbeat was racing in panic. He made a fresh attempt to stand up. This time he succeeded rather better. He cast a quick glance over the railing. About twenty feet down to Österlånggatan.

"Don't even think about it!"

Sarac spun around and found himself staring straight into the barrel of a pistol. The driver of the van raised his hand and pulled back the hood that was obscuring his face. In spite of the gun, Sarac almost felt relieved for a moment. It wasn't Janus but the man from Högbergsgatan. The one Natalie had photographed. The man who had helped him try to save Sabatini. What the hell was he doing here?

"Jump in!" The man slid open the side door of the van with his free hand.

Sarac didn't move. He turned his head, looking for options. In the distance there was the sound of sirens. Slightly closer he could hear a rattling car engine. The man lowered the gun a fraction.

"The alternative is that I shoot you in the knee and put you in the van myself. Your choice!"

Reluctantly Sarac took a couple of steps forward and put his hand up onto the roof of the van, but stopped in the doorway. He caught sight of the filthy mattress and cable ties that were already in there. He realized what was going on. He turned to face the man.

"Look," he began.

At that moment a hoarse-sounding car engine roared above them at the top of the slope.

• • •

Natalie swore through her teeth. Poor bloody Golf. The warning lights on the dashboard were lit up like a Christmas tree and the air stank of chemicals from the air bag. But at least the plucky little car was still moving.

There were lights on in half the windows lining the street, and she could see the silhouettes of people peering out. She didn't care. For a few brief seconds she had considered abandoning Sarac in the street. But she couldn't do it. She had lost face and been uncovered as a liar. But not just that. Rickard had lied to her, making her feel like an idiot twice over. She was angry with herself, not Sarac. Besides, no matter how you looked at it, she had an agreement with Adelfi. Sarac was still her patient, her responsibility.

The steering wheel was pulling badly, and there was a scraping noise from one of the wings, but that stopped when something fell off and ended up under the tires. The van had quickly reversed and gone back the same way it had come, to take the parallel street after Sarac. She should really have walked away from the whole thing. She should have abandoned the car, called Rickard, and explained that her cover was blown. But Sarac was still out there. Alone, and without much chance of defending himself.

She reached the junction and pulled out at the top of the slope. She could see the white van parked below, right next to the railings. She changed down to a lower gear and revved the engine. She grinned.

Payback time!

* * *

Sarac glanced quickly across the roof of the van. He saw the Golf careering down the slope. Natalie's hands were clutching the wheel, and her eyes were fixed on the van. He looked at the man with the pistol and saw his eyes open wide. Then he leaped through the open door.

* * *

Natalie rammed the van squarely in the middle of its side. The collision made its right wheels lift from the ground and it toppled slowly onto the other side. But Natalie didn't have a chance to see what happened. For the second time in the space of just five minutes she hit her head on the steering wheel, and this time there was no air bag to cushion the blow.

• • •

Atif saw the car coming but only managed to take one step toward the railings before the collision. The van tipped up and then began to fall toward him. The roof was only less than an inch from his head when he leaped over the railing and fell headlong toward the pavement far below.

• • •

Sarac crawled slowly out of the overturned van. The base of his spine and the back of his head were still aching after his earlier tumble, but he was pretty much okay. The Golf was standing just a yard or so away. Its engine was clicking and hissing, and a plume of steam from its radiator was rising from the hood. He went around it as fast as he could and managed to yank the driver's door open.

Natalie was leaning forward with her head resting on the steering wheel. When he gently pushed her back he saw blood on her face. Damn!

"Natalie?" He moved her shoulder.

"Natalie, can you hear me?" He looked down, checking for other injuries. The steering column was pressed against one of her legs, making it impossible to pull her out. He could hear sirens in the distance.

"Did I get him?" she said.

Her eyes were still closed, but he saw the corners of her mouth twitch.

"That bastard wrecked my car. Just tell me I got him, and I can die in peace."

"Natalie, I think you're probably going to be okay," Sarac mumbled.

"Of course I am, you idiot." She opened her eyes, wiped the blood from her forehead, and grimaced with pain. "I've cracked my forehead, probably got a concussion. Throw in a few mangled ribs." Natalie coughed. "Did he get squashed?"

Sarac shook his head. "I think he jumped over the railings," he said.

"Shame." She cleared her throat. "I got a quick look at him just before I hit. It was the guy in the picture, wasn't it, the one from Högbergsgatan?"

Sarac nodded. The sirens were getting closer, echoing between the buildings.

"Get out of here," she said. "I'll be fine."

Sarac looked around.

"Are you sure?" he said.

"Get the fuck out of here, David." Natalie coughed again and spat at his feet.

Sarac nodded but didn't move for a few seconds.

"Thanks," he said. "Thanks for helping me, Natalie."

The impact had thrown the trunk open. Sarac grabbed his bag and began to walk up the slope. He stopped after a few steps when he heard Natalie call after him.

"Oscar!" she shouted. "Oscar Wallin, that's his real name. Rickard's, I mean."

FIFTY-TWO

Sarac was walking up and down in front of the whiteboard. He was wound up, the adrenaline kick still hadn't subsided. The van driver wasn't Janus but the man who had helped him try to save Sabatini up in Högbergsgatan. The man must have heard him ask about Janus. And a couple of days later he shows up with a van and tries to kidnap him. Conclusion? The man in the van was looking for Janus as well.

What puzzled him was how van-man had managed to find him? His address was protected, his phone number was unlisted. But there were probably police officers who were prepared to sell all manner of information, if the price was right. Officers like him. No matter how the man had found him, he was someone else to add to the growing list of people who were searching for Janus.

The lawyer, Crispin, was trying to buy Janus for his clients. Molnar wanted to cover his tracks. And then there was Oscar Wallin, another of von Katzow's adepts, who wanted to take over control of Janus and pressure him into carrying on his work. Wallin had been one step ahead and had actually managed to infiltrate his own immediate network. Natalie must have reported everything that had happened to Wallin. The notebook, the breakthrough with the codes, the names. He was probably the one she had called from the ferry when they were on their way to see Sabatini in Högbergsgatan. Natalie was tough, she wasn't easily persuaded about anything, suggesting that Wallin was a considerably more skillful player than Molnar had believed.

He thought about Natalie and wondered how she was. He

suppressed an impulse to call Södermalm Hospital to check. Natalie was a closed chapter. He had trusted her, she had betrayed him. But she had also saved his life, which made it much harder to be angry with her. Fucking hell!

Then there was Dreyer and his internal investigators lurking in the background. Dreyer may have said he wasn't interested in Janus, but an infiltrator who murdered a police officer was exactly the sort of weapon he needed to sink the whole Intelligence Unit once and for all. Possibly even the whole of Regional Crime.

The last name on the list of people chasing Janus was his own. Why was he so keen? It had long since stopped being about any desire for revenge, or regaining his position on the team. He had let them all down; he'd never be able to look them in the eye again after he had sold himself out to Crispin. No, there was something else.

Did he want Janus to answer for what he had done? Probably not, he was pretty much caught up in it all just as badly himself. Was it about getting hold of the final pieces of the puzzle of who he had once been? That was certainly part of the motivation, but far from all of it. So what was it, then, what was left? Why was he still chasing a truth that kept getting more and more unpalatable? He still didn't really know.

Janus had been his infiltrator, his responsibility. Maybe, on some unconscious level, he still wanted to try to save him? Compensate for his betrayal, the money he had taken from Crispin to hand him over?

Sometimes handlers and sources get too close to each other, far too close.

It was all fairly clear to him now. Things had unfolded more or less as Molnar had said. Janus had killed Brian Hansen in the car. He could practically describe how it had happened. How their eyes had met in the rearview mirror, a tacit understanding of what had to happen. It wasn't a surprise, as Molnar had believed, but premeditated murder. Janus had killed Hansen, had done it for his sake, to save Sarac from ruin, but just as much to save himself.

The murder became their shared secret, tying them together forever. The gun to the head that made it impossible for either of them to betray the other. Was that why he had had a breakdown? Had he realized he had got himself into a situation it was impossible to get out of?

He had promised Dreyer the name of a mole that was actually himself, and in his role as Erik I. Johansson he had already taken Crispin's money to reveal Janus's identity. And Bergh and his bosses were demanding more results, the sort of thing that would allow them to go on looking the other way from his rule-shredding operation. And on the sidelines lurked Wallin, eager to get hold of Janus's secrets.

But after Janus killed Hansen for him, he was trapped. He had got himself caught in a mantrap that was impossible to escape. Was that why he had driven into the tunnel, pumped full of drugs, driving as if the devil himself were after him? Because he couldn't see any other way out?

Even if he tried to keep that thought at bay, the logic of it was undeniable. The stroke that almost killed him actually may have saved his life. Saved him from himself. Although in fact it had only given him a temporary reprieve. He was back in the mantrap without any possibility of escape.

Sarac put his head in his hands. He had allowed himself to be blinded by the excitement, crawling so far inside Erik I. Johansson's skin that eventually he had lost sight of himself. And had committed the ultimate betrayal of a source. Selling him out for money.

What had he told Lehtonen, Markovic, and Sabatini that evening that had made them flee for their lives? Was it as he and Molnar both suspected, that Janus was methodically ticking off all the names on a list? Killing everyone who posed the slightest risk of revealing his identity, all apart from one? Erik I. Johansson. Sarac himself.

Janus ought to have had plenty of opportunities to kill him if he wanted to. So why was he holding back? The only way to find out for sure was for them to meet, face-to-face. To find Janus before Janus found him. But he was still missing the last piece of the puzzle. The one everyone was looking for. The man's true identity.

There was one thing at least that he was completely sure of. What he was looking for was in that room. Somewhere in there was the clue that could help him find the right path, clear an overgrown path in his mind and give him what he needed.

He emptied the desk drawers and lined the contents up. The gun, the two cartridges, the handcuffs. Then the reformatted laptop, the phone book, various pens, a few coins, and the cigarette pack that had contained the matchbook from Club Babel. Finally he laid out the notebook, which he hadn't found in there, admittedly, but it definitely belonged there.

He opened it again. The first page with the five coded ID numbers, preceded and followed by the remnants of the torn-out pages. Then page after page of dates and coded messages, presumably meetings with various sources and contacts who had been listed on the two missing pages. He wondered whether one of them had been the lawyer, Crispin? Without the missing pages he would probably never know the answer.

He looked at the codes again. The system seemed fairly simple. A combination of numbers that could somehow be changed into an address. Addresses. He leafed through the phone book at random. He had wondered before about its purpose when he had clearly had access to the Internet. But now he suddenly suspected he knew why it was there. He picked the same sentence he had looked at several times before.

Meeting with Jupiter, 14.00 at 781216.

He didn't know who the source Jupiter was; his encrypted ID number had probably been on one of the missing pages. But he tried looking up page 78 of the dog-eared phone book. He picked out the first column and counted down to the twelfth row. It was the address of a bicycle shop at number 4 Skeppar-gatan. Neither the address nor the shop rang any bells at all. But he still had two numbers left of the code. He tried replacing the four with the number sixteen. Then he swore out loud when he realized he didn't stand a chance of finding out what was at that address, at least not without turning on his cell phone. He thought for a while, then risked it and called directory inquiries.

The address belonged to a restaurant.

He repeated the same procedure with a couple of the other codes and came up with a small hotel, then another restaurant. He compared the dates with the payments on the bank state-ment. It all fit; he had used the bank card to pay for dinner at each of the locations.

So the phone book itself was the key to the code for the meeting places. The breakthrough ought to have delighted him, but his joy at the discovery was tainted by the fact that it didn't get him anywhere. Janus's name wasn't on any of the pages; he'd already checked that, so once again he had come to a complete halt. But he was close now, closer than he had ever been.

With the cigarette pack in his hand, he slumped into the armchair facing the whiteboard. Almost without looking, he pulled a cigarette from the crumpled pack and lit it, using a match from the little red matchbook. As soon as he smelled it, he realized that the cigarette didn't just contain tobacco. He stared at it and only now noticed that it was hand-rolled, in contrast to the straight, smooth Marlboros that were left in the pack.

Smoking dope just a month or so after a stroke wasn't a particularly smart move. Especially not if you also happened to be a police officer. But, on the other hand, he had nothing better to do. He took a deep drag and held the smoke in for a few sec-onds before letting it out. Then he leaned his head back and felt a familiar sense of well-being slowly spread through his body.

He thought about Natalie again. Even though he had found her out, she had saved his life. She had put herself in extreme danger, even got herself hurt in the bargain. Natalie could hardly have been expecting him to reveal any more secrets to her. Yet she still hadn't hesitated to save him. He wondered why. She probably had a good reason, far better than any he could come up with.

He took another toke. The faces on the whiteboard were staring at him and were slowly beginning to move. They were drifting through the spiderweb, in from the edges toward the center. Toward the symbol that looked both like two faces looking away from each other and a huge spider. *The answer was there*, he thought. On that board.

"Which one of you is sitting on it? Come on, out with it!" Sarac said out loud. He grinned to himself. Realized he was already starting to get stoned.

"Is it you, Abu Hamsa? Or your muscle-bound friend Eldar?" He grinned again.

"Micke Lund, what do you know about the gods of antiquity? Do you know about Uranus?"

He tipped his head back and cackled at the ceiling. He was laughing so hard that tears were running down his cheeks. *Fucked up beyond all recognition*, he thought.

He pulled himself together, took another toke, and then forced himself to go back to the whiteboard. Four people left. The other biker—Karim with no surname. Then the Russian tracksuit mafia, Zimin and Ivazov, and finally bald Sasha with the hook nose and scary eyes.

Sarac leaned back. Tried to focus on Janus. To conjure up a picture of the face he had glimpsed in the rearview mirror in the seconds before the shot was fired.

Who are you? he thought.

Where are you?

The feeling came out of nowhere. There was something about his way of thinking that didn't make sense. That was . . . wrong.

The photographs were still moving through the web, merging into the room in a single big, circular motion.

He was back in Gamla stan. Running along a cobbled street lined with high, windowless walls. The only sound he could hear at first was his own heavy breathing. Then came the voices. Deep, high, strong, and weak in turn. They interrupted and drowned out one another, then blurred into a single maelstrom of words.

"What sort of police officer?"

"Keep the secret!"

"We have an agreement."

"I was starting to think you'd forgotten me, Erik."

"In the end it always comes down to money."

"No loose ends."

"Destroy ourselves."

"Someone's selling information."

"It's all his fault."

"The hooks are turned to face each other."

"Everything begins and ends with . . ."

. . .

The voices stop the moment the street shrinks and comes to an end, turning into a well-trodden path through the snow. Night sky and dark trees all around him. His pulse throbbing in his ears. In front of him on the white ground is a large black rectangle. A grave. He looks down. Sees the man lying down there, his face still covered by the hood. Jumps . . .

He knows that the landing will hurt. That the pain in dreams is unlike any other. But it still overwhelms him, making his sight flare. Blue lights on tunnel walls, fluorescent lights flickering, a spiderweb of red and blue lines leading toward the center.

In toward the poisonous spider waiting in the middle.

Janus.

Unless it was actually the opposite? Could it be . . .

The opposite?!

Hooks facing inward.

The realization hits him like a punch in the chest. Truth and lies have merged together, nothing is what it seems, everything is . . . wrong!

He crawls up into a sitting position and leans over Janus. He's holding his breath, doesn't know whether that's just in the dream. Slowly he reaches out his hand to the hood and pushes it back. At last he sees Janus's face, exactly as it looked in the rearview mirror. He sees the pale eyes, the familiar, tormented expression. He recognizes it, all too well. The man with two faces.

Janus smiles at him. The night sky reflects blackly, mournfully, in his eyes.

"Life only exists when you're up on the wire," Janus whispers softly.

"Everything else, David.

"Everything . . .

"else . . .

"is just anticipation!"

FIFTY-THREE

"It's about David Sarac, Minister." Wallin looked over his shoulder as if to make sure that Stenberg's door was closed. "Something seems to be going on."

"Really?" Stenberg tried to show just the right degree of interest.

"Approximately twenty minutes ago Peter Molnar received a text message from a pay-as-you-go cell phone. We're sure it was from Sarac." Wallin handed over a piece of paper.

The island, 20.00. He's coming.

"The island?" Stenberg said.

"Skarpö, in the Vaxholm archipelago," Wallin said. "Sarac has a house out there, registered in his sister's name. That's where he's spent the past few weeks hiding."

"And you think he's going to meet this infiltrator, Janus?" Stenberg said.

"Of course we can't be sure, but that certainly could be the case." Wallin nodded.

Stenberg sat without saying anything for a while, trying to look as if he were thinking. This was the chance he had been looking for. The repaid favor that would set him free, once and for all. But he had to get Wallin to back off slightly. And make it sound as if it were his idea.

"What do you suggest we do, Oscar?" he said.

"Well, obviously we could watch the house. The problem is that Molnar's men are smart. They'll do their homework. We'd need winter equipment, night-vision binoculars, and a whole lot more. Ten, fifteen people in total, experienced officers. An operation of that size, at short notice and managed with the utmost discretion . . ." Wallin shook his head slightly. "It'll be difficult, I'm afraid, Minister."

"I see," Stenberg said drily.

He noted that Wallin looked worried. People with ambitions like his weren't keen on disappointing the boss. But today Wallin's shortcomings played right into his hands. He forced himself to quell the beginnings of a little smile.

"Is there any other option?" he asked, in the same measured tone as before.

Wallin nodded.

"The island is served by two different car ferries. One from Vaxholm, and one from Värmdö. I can have people at both points on the mainland where the ferries leave from, and take pictures of everyone coming and going."

Stenberg nodded, then switched to a suitably disappointed tone of voice.

"Well, if that's the only suggestion you've got, Oscar, I suppose it will have to do. Now, if you'll excuse me."

Stenberg stood up to indicate that he had more important things to be getting on with.

As soon as Wallin left the room he got out his own pay-as-you-go cell phone and walked over to the little sink. He turned the tap on, then dialed the number and held the phone between his cheek and shoulder as he washed his hands. He made up his mind to ditch the phone in the lake in Ösby when he was taking Tubbe for his evening walk.

• • •

Sarac got dressed, did thirty push-ups in a row, followed by the same number of sit-ups. Then he pulled on the bulletproof vest Bergh had given him and taped the little snub-nosed revolver around his ankle with black insulating tape. He strapped the holster containing his service pistol to his belt and adjusted it so it was just above his right hip. He closed his eyes, then practiced drawing the weapon in front of the mirror. It went better than he had expected.

When he was done he took down all the photographs and Post-it notes from the whiteboard and put them in the kitchen sink. He put his notebook on top of them and used the last of the matches from Club Babel to set light to the whole lot. The fire quickly took hold, and the heat made the photographs curl up, reversing the colors for a few seconds. Turning black to white.

As soon as the flames had died down he pulled on his leather jacket and checked the room one last time. He found himself staring at the Janus face that was still in the middle of the whiteboard. He went over and wiped it off.

       •   •   •

"Vaxholm," Hunter said in Atif's cell phone. "I want you to be in position by six o'clock. Text me when you get to the ferry."

"Sure," Atif muttered. "No problem." He ended the call without saying good-bye.

He leaned back in bed. His body felt terrible. His right foot had swollen up like a football, and he would have to bind it uncomfortably tightly to get it into his boot. His knee was bluish-lilac, and his ribs, left arm, and left hand hadn't fared much better from falling from a height of twenty feet. But it could have been worse. If he hadn't landed in a snowdrift he'd have broken his legs, no question. And would have been lying on a wooden bunk in prison now instead of this creaking bed in his hotel room.

He got up, staggered into the bathroom, and swallowed down a handful of pills. He glanced in the bathroom mirror and concluded that he looked pretty much the way he felt. It was half past nine, plenty of time to have something to eat and get hold of another vehicle.

He pulled out his cell and dug out the right number.

"Hello?"

"Abu Hamsa, it's Atif." He sat down on the bed again with effort. "Something seems to be going on. This evening, out near Vaxholm," he said.

"Really? Good. You'll keep me informed, I hope?"

"Of course," Atif said. "I always keep my promises."

"Excellent. Well, make sure you're properly dressed, my friend. Apparently there's going to be bad weather out in the archipelago."

Atif remained seated on the bed, thinking hard. There was something about the conversation that didn't make sense. The tone of voice, and that talk about the weather. As though Abu Hamsa knew more than he himself did.

* * *

The boat from the city out to Vaxholm only took an hour. Ice had started to creep out from the shores, but the swell from the big Finland ferries was keeping it a long way from the shipping lanes. The car ferry hadn't arrived, so Sarac had time to find a tobacconist and buy a fresh pack of cigarettes. He pulled up the hood of his jacket, then stood on the car deck and smoked two cigarettes during the short journey out to the island.

He had a stroke of luck when they got there: a woman who lived fairly close to him had been on the ferry and gave him a lift to the end of the drive.

"There's supposed to be really bad weather tonight." The woman nodded toward the dark horizon. "The shipping forecast warned we might get thunder."

"Thunder in winter?" Sarac said.

"It sometimes happens out in the archipelago," the woman said. "Every ten years or so. Something to do with the difference in temperature between the sea and the air. My grandfather used to call it Janus thunder. Said it was a bad omen."

* * *

356 Anders de la Motte

Natalie's cell phone rang just as she had managed to open her front door. She dropped one of her gloves in a puddle on the floor and swore out loud to herself.

"Hello, this is Natalie." She bent down to pick up the glove, grimacing at the pain in her rib cage.

"Rickard here," the man on the other end said.

A short silence followed.

"You mean Oscar Wallin," Natalie said. "That is your real name, isn't it?"

"Something's going to happen out on the island this evening," the man said, without taking the slightest notice of what she'd just said. "I need you there to keep an eye on things."

"Oscar, did you ever really think about fixing my criminal record? Is that even possible?" she said.

"What do you think, Natalie?" the voice over the phone said, and she was immediately reminded of Sarac and von Katzow's verbal duel.

"I think you say whatever it takes to get people to cooperate, Oscar. Things they don't really believe, not deep down, but want so fucking desperately that they're prepared to do practically anything if there's even a tiny chance of it happening."

To her surprise Natalie heard the man laugh.

"You've learned quite a lot from spending time with Sarac, I see." He fell silent, and when he opened his mouth to speak again the amused tone had vanished.

"There'll be a car outside your door in five minutes. The police officers in it will either arrest you on suspicion of aggravated fraud or drive you to the ferry. Your choice, Natalie."

Natalie opened her mouth to say something, but the line had already gone dead.

FIFTY-FOUR

"Atif here, I'm in position."

"Good. How's the weather over there?" Hunter said.

"It's snowing pretty heavily, looking like it's getting worse," Atif said.

"Okay. Now take the boat across to Rindö and wait there. It's the yellow, open-decked car ferry."

Atif looked out through the windshield. He could see lights approaching some way off in the sound. He started the engine and rolled over to join the line of cars. He wondered if he ought to call Abu Hamsa and give him an update. He decided to wait. The plan was still working; neither Hunter nor Abu Hamsa appeared to have realized he was playing them both. Not yet, anyway.

• • •

Natalie was the last one up the steps to the little waiting room. She stopped briefly to peer out through the snow. Just as she had hoped, she could see the taillights of the dark Volvo pulling away from the harbor. Perfect.

Neither of the policemen in the car had uttered a word on the way there, which had given her plenty of time to think. She had long since cleared her computer of any possible evidence. She had got rid of anything that might link her to the fake kidnappings the day she agreed to work for Wallin. She hoped that would be enough, and that all he could do to her was lock her up for a few days. But there was obviously no way she could be certain. She was planning to play along for a bit longer. Pretend to cooperate, catch the ferry out to the island, then travel back as quickly as she could. She could blame the concussion she had received in the collision with the van. Wallin could hardly come down hard on her if she had been willing to go all the way out to the island. At least that was what she was hoping.

Off to one side of the staircase the car deck had already been emptied and new vehicles were starting to drive on board. There weren't many, maybe ten in total. A blue van with plenty of rust on it went past her. It had a tiny set of Christmas lights inside the windshield that caught her attention. Only after the van had driven past did she realize that she recognized the driver. She stopped abruptly and turned to look at the van.

"Probably best if you go into the waiting room," a member of the crew shouted at her. Natalie nodded and took another couple of steps up the staircase. She fished out her cell phone and tried Sarac's number.

"The number you have called cannot be reached."

She swore to herself and tried again. The cold was making her fingers stiff.

Natalie looked over at the van again. It was parked more or less in the middle of the car deck. The driver was staying inside.

She carried on up the staircase and tried to call again as soon as she was inside the waiting room. Still nothing. The snow was falling more heavily now, forcing the captain to use the foghorn.

Somehow she had to find a way to warn David that the man was on his way out to the island. She tried once more with the phone but still couldn't get through. The foghorn blew again, making the windows of the waiting room rattle. Natalie thought for a few seconds. Then she took her scarf off and wound it around her head and face, so just her eyes were visible. She opened the door and went slowly back down the steps.

It was snowing hard now, covering the van's windows. To start with Atif kept the windshield wipers running but switched them off after a while. He couldn't have his engine running on the ferry, and he didn't want to risk draining the battery. Besides, the snow-covered windows gave him a chance to go through his equipment in peace and quiet. He took the pistol out of his pocket and opened it to check that there was a bullet in the chamber.

There wasn't actually any need to look; he'd checked only an hour ago and there was no way anything could have happened to the gun since then. It was more about how he felt. The need to feel he was prepared.

He turned his head and looked into the back of the van. Crowbar, spade, axe, saw, duct tape, and a roll of black trash bags. And, right at the back, a long, heavy chain. Everything he needed to make Janus disappear for good.

He leaned back in his seat, shut his eyes, and thought about his little garden at home, and the starry sky high above it. But for some reason the memory was getting harder to conjure. He found his thoughts wandering to Tindra. As soon as this was all over he was planning to go up to Leksand and take her back home. Maybe he could even persuade Cassandra that they should all go to Iraq together and visit his mother. He tried to imagine the look on his mother's face when she saw her first and only grandchild in the flesh rather than in photographs. The way she'd look at him and silently thank Atif for making it happen.

· · ·

Natalie crept across the open car deck, holding on to the walls beneath the waiting room as she blinked in an attempt to get rid of the snowflakes that were swirling around her face. Approximately halfway to the van was a small door marked *Crew only*.

She opened it cautiously and peered inside. A flight of steps led down, presumably to the engine room. There was a large toolbox hanging on the wall above it. She lifted the lid and found what she was looking for.

The ferry turned slightly, meaning that the snow was blowing straight at her when she reemerged on deck. She blinked hard a couple of times and pulled the scarf lower over her forehead.

Her body was protesting, but she did her best to ignore the pain. She crept slowly over toward the van.

Fifteen feet left.

Ten.

Five.

One.

* * *

Atif put his coffee cup down. It felt as if the van had just rocked. Were they already there?

He switched the windshield wipers on. They moved back and forth a couple of times, pushing the snow aside. But all he could see in front of the bow was dark water and swirling snow. Must have been the wind.

He swallowed his pills with the last of the coffee, then screwed the plastic cup back on top of the flask. He looked at his watch. It was almost six o'clock.

"Not long now, Adnan," he muttered.

* * *

Natalie was huddled up next to the right rear wheel of the van. She felt in her pocket and took out the awl she had stolen from the toolbox. She felt frozen already. Her fingers were stiff and wouldn't grasp the plastic handle properly. She ended up using both hands. A blast from the foghorn made her jump. The awl fell onto the deck and rolled away under the van. Fuck!

Off in the distance she could see the lights of the little harbor on the island. It wouldn't be many more minutes before they arrived. She thought about getting up and hurrying back to the waiting room. But she had to delay the man and get a chance to warn David.

She lay down on her stomach with an effort and looked under the van. Her cracked ribs complained but she blinked the pain away. The awl was only a yard or so away. She stretched out her arm as far as she could and nudged the plastic handle. The sound of the ferry's engines eased a couple of notches. They were almost there.

She crept a bit further under the van. Her chest was protesting louder now. She reached out . . .

*   *   *

The jolt was very noticeable. They must have docked. Atif turned the key in the ignition and put the wipers on full, front and back. Then he lowered the side windows halfway so he could knock the snow away. He glimpsed something in the right side-view mirror. He turned instinctively and saw the back of a light-colored coat and covered head. A member of the crew, probably. Pretty awful job to have on a day like this.

The ramp was lowered and the cars in front of him began to roll slowly off the ferry. Atif set off slowly after them in the van. As soon as he was on dry land he realized that something was wrong. The rear tires weren't getting a proper grip on the snow, and the van was pulling to the right. A growing rhythmic thudding increased his suspicions. A puncture.

He pulled over and jumped out. The right rear tire was completely flat. When he crouched down to inspect the damage he discovered three neat holes in the side of the tire, right next to the rim. He frowned, then looked around him slowly.

*   *   *

The other passengers in the waiting room had already left down the staircase at the other end by the time Natalie climbed back up. She had to wait a while to try to thaw out her frozen hands on one of the radiators. She wished she'd kept her thick Lovika mittens instead of swapping them for the thin leather gloves that may have been dry but didn't stand a chance against the cold. Once her fingers had warmed up a bit she tried calling Sarac's cell phone again. Still no answer. She didn't have much choice, then. She had to get to the villa before the man in the van got there.

She went down the steps and crossed the ramp. The van was parked at the side of the cul-de-sac, right where she had to walk. The man from Gamla stan was crouching beside it, inspecting the punctured tire. Beyond him the taillights of the last cars were disappearing into the snow. Shit, she'd been hoping she could get a lift! The house was a mile and a half away. If she walked fast she could still get there first. Warn Sarac and get to safety with a neighbor. There was just one problem with that plan: she had to cross the cul-de-sac and go past the man with the van.

Natalie lowered her gaze, pulled her scarf lower down over her forehead again, and started walking.

FIFTY-FIVE

The black 4x4 was standing in the drive. Sarac found Molnar and Josef in the kitchen.

"Did you come via Värmdö?" he said as he pushed his hood back and brushed the snow from his clothes.

Molnar nodded, then removed his unlit cigar from his mouth and spat a strand of tobacco onto the floor.

"And the others?" Sarac said. He pulled out a chair and sat down opposite Molnar.

"I've put them to work sweeping the terrain," Molnar said. "Want to make sure Wallin's people aren't hiding in the bushes. By the way, is your cell phone turned off, David?"

Sarac nodded. "I switched it off before I caught the ferry back into the city."

"Good, we'll stick to short wave, our own kit, not the force's." Molnar put a small communication radio on the table.

"So when's he coming, David?" Josef said. His voice sounded tense.

Sarac looked at the time.

"Soon," he said. "Very soon."

•   •   •

Atif saw the woman walk past ten feet away. She had a scarf wrapped around her head and wasn't even looking in his direction. She was probably on her way to the parking lot a bit farther on.

He turned around and held his hand up to keep the snow out of his eyes as he stared at the rear tire. This was no ordinary puncture. If it was, the hole would be in the tread of the tire rather than the side. And there were also three holes. Conclusion: someone had sabotaged his van, most likely on board the ferry.

He thought about the person he had glimpsed in the side-view mirror and tried to conjure the image again. Light-colored coat, head covered. Could it have been a scarf?

He turned around and looked in the direction the woman had gone. But she had already been swallowed up by the falling snow.

· · ·

Natalie's heart was pounding hard as she passed the van. The man was big, almost seven feet tall. He made her feel even smaller than she actually was. She fixed her eyes on the ground, pulled the scarf tighter around her head, and concentrated on putting one foot in front of the other.

The road ran along the north side of the island, right next to the sea, without any trees or bushes to give shelter from the strengthening wind. There was a faint rumble from off to the north, suggesting that the storm wasn't yet at full strength. Natalie swore silently to herself. Jeans and a raincoat were completely the wrong sort of clothes for a task like this. But her padded jacket was both smeared in blood and covered with powder from the air bag. Besides, she'd hardly expected to have to go for a hike through a fucking snowstorm. She turned around, looking for car headlights, but couldn't see any. She was already freezing; the cold was making her already stiff limbs even harder to control. Unless she wanted to return to the ferry, the nearest house was on the other side of the little bridge that connected the two islands. And that was at least three thousand feet away, if not more.

This was a bad idea, Natalie, really fucking stupid! Why the hell couldn't you just stick to the plan and go back to Vaxholm?

• • •

"So, are you planning to explain or not?" Molnar said as soon as Josef had gone out to move the 4x4 from the drive. "How did you crack it, David?"

"Guess," Sarac said.

Molnar gave him a long look, then leaned back in the kitchen chair.

"You managed to find the place you'd been using as your base," he said.

Sarac nodded.

"It was only a thousand feet from my apartment."

"Jesus," Molnar said. "Did you find any account numbers?"

"Better than that. I found a whiteboard covered with photographs. A big web featuring everyone involved in the operation. Abu Hamsa, a guy called Eldar."

Molnar nodded. His voice was eager. "Hamsa's quite a celebrity. He's got a finger in all sorts of pies. Money laundering, bureaus de change, and plenty more. Eldar's his bodyguard slash crown prince."

"There were others," Sarac said. "A couple of biker-gang thugs. Micke Lund and someone called Karim, then two Russians. Zimin and Ivazov."

"Lund's Hells Angels, Karim Bandidos," Molnar said. "Despite all the talk of them being enemies, they look out for each other and share a number of business deals with those Russians. Anyone else?"

Sarac nodded.

"A bald guy called Sasha. Head like a skull. I've got a feeling he's a Yugo?"

"Serbian, to be precise. A real psycho, if it's the man I'm thinking of. Have you got the pictures with you?"

"No," Sarac said. "I cleared the room of evidence. Burned the pictures and notebook."

"You did *what*, David?" Molnar straightened up.

"I burned the notebook."

Molnar ran his tongue over his teeth a couple of times, and a little vein throbbed in his temple, but he said nothing. The radio crackled and broke the strained atmosphere.

"Why?" he said after a pause.

Sarac shrugged his shoulders. "No loose ends, just like you said."

"But what about the rest of the information?" Molnar said.

"Just a load of meetings with encrypted sources, people I no longer remember," Sarac said. "Worthless without the pages that were torn out."

He leaned across the table. "The pages you tore out, Peter."

The radio crackled again, no voices, just white noise. A dull rumble could be heard in the distance.

"What makes you think that, David?" Molnar was frowning.

"Because you wanted me to focus on the Janus list, and those numbers. Everything else was unimportant."

Molnar raised his eyebrows slightly. "I thought we were agreed on that?" he said.

"Yes, that's true," Sarac said. "I was just as keen as you to find Janus. To *not trust anyone*, to *protect the secret*, just like it said on the note up at the hospital, and scrawled on my bedroom wall."

"Sorry, but what are you talking about, David?" Molnar said.

"I'm talking about the fact that someone's been manipulating me. Trying to steer me in a particular direction. Messages, whispers, notes, phone calls."

"You're starting to sound like a nutter now, David," Molnar said. "If you've got something to say, I suggest you come right out with it."

"What really happened on the night of my crash?" Sarac said.

"We've already been through that several times," Molnar said. "You and Janus met Hansen. He tried to blackmail you, Janus got rid of him."

"So it was Janus who killed him, you're sure of that?" Sarac said.

Molnar shrugged. "It must have been. You realized you'd lost control of him, of the entire operation. You called the other three sources. Told them to get out of the city, that Janus might be after them as well. Then you took a load of drugs and called me. After which . . ."

"I had a stroke and crashed in the tunnel. Right in front of your eyes," Sarac said.

"Exactly." Molnar slowly shook his head. "Look, David, I'm sorry, but I don't think this is getting us anywhere. You still haven't told me who Janus is, or when he's going to show up. The boys are on standby, we're ready to roll."

He nodded toward the radio on the table. "We're here for your sake, David, to help you clear up all the loose ends."

"To get rid of Janus before he gets rid of me," Sarac said.

Molnar took a deep breath.

"We do what has to be done, David. You know that better than most people."

Sarac said nothing, just observed the other man. Then he pointed at the radio.

"Can you call them all in, Peter? I'd like to talk to them before we get going."

Molnar shook his head. "I'd rather have them out there, to make sure we don't suffer any unpleasant surprises. Wallin's gang, for instance."

"Okay, that seems logical," Sarac said. "How about calling them up, then? Make sure everything's okay?"

"I've ordered radio silence," Molnar said. "They'll be in touch if anything happens."

· · ·

The shaking that had been bothering her for ages had suddenly stopped. Natalie knew that wasn't a good sign. She had underestimated the weather and overestimated her own abilities, and she was rapidly coming to the end of her strength.

The bridge was there ahead of her in the darkness, maybe

just a few steps away. It was going to be a struggle to reach the other side. For the past six hundred feet or so a patch of woodland had given her some protection, but once she was out on the narrow bridge she would be at the mercy of the wind sweeping in off the sea. The sound between the two islands would act like a wind tunnel, making it hard even to stay upright. But she didn't exactly have any better options.

The thunder was much louder now, and soon the storm would hit the island with full force. A shape appeared in front of her, railings on either side of the narrow roadway. The bridge.

Natalie got impatient and took a couple of quick steps, but tripped on something under the snow. She tried to get her stiff legs to react, to get her balance back. Instead she toppled backward into the ditch. The hard landing knocked the breath out of her and she gasped. The snow swirled up around her, little dancing flakes, slowly melting. They gradually formed a fixed white glow. Natalie covered her eyes with one hand and tried to use the other to get back on her feet.

A car, a car had stopped to help her! She caught a glimpse of a driver's door opening, then a dark silhouette framed by the headlights. She got to her knees but couldn't stand up. She felt hands lifting her out of the ditch. The headlights were still dazzling her. The man who picked her up was strong, and he carried her back to his car as if she were a small child.

She noticed that he was limping slightly.

"So, how are you?" a deep voice said in her ear.

At that moment she saw the vehicle that had stopped. A blue van with patches of brown rust, and little Christmas lights in the windshield.

FIFTY-SIX

"You wanted me to focus on the money, didn't you?" Sarac said. "If I could just find out how Janus was paid, we'd be able to find him. *In the end it always comes down to money,* that's what Bergh said the last time I saw him. He was right, wasn't he? The whole thing's about money, isn't it, Peter?"

Molnar let out a low laugh and leaned over the kitchen table. "You're probably going to have to explain what the hell you're talking about now, David."

"I'm talking about almost fourteen million kronor. Money that was paid into the two foreign accounts I had at my disposal. Money that I transferred the same evening I almost died in that tunnel. Money that's the only reason why I'm still alive, Peter."

More silence. Ten seconds passed. Twenty. The thunder rumbled. It seemed to be getting closer. Sarac leaned back in his chair.

"It's going to be a fuck of a relief to get shot of Janus," he said. "Ever since I woke up in that goddamn hospital bed people have been trying to get me to say who he is. To start with Bergh and Wallin were the most persistent, but they're actually only incidental characters. It struck me that the ones who really want to get at Janus, the ones who are literally prepared to walk over dead bodies to find him, are the thugs in my pictures. Abu Hamsa, Lund, Karim, Sasha, the Russians. They're all terrified that Janus might be someone inside their own organizations."

Sarac took a deep breath.

"So I started to ask myself, how come they're so petrified? What do you think, Peter?"

Molnar just shrugged. He looked almost amused.

"How could senior figures in organized crime know that we have a secret infiltrator among them, how could they even know his name?" Sarac said, tapping his forefinger on the edge of the table to underline the importance of what he had just said.

"Presumably because someone told them," Molnar said.

"Yes, presumably. So the question is, who? And, not least, why?"

"The police force is full of leaks, it could have been anyone," Molnar said, throwing out his hands.

"You said yourself that Janus was a top-secret project," Sarac said. "That I was running it entirely on my own, specifically to stop anyone leaking information."

"Okay, but Bergh and Kollander both knew about Janus," Molnar said. "Or at least they knew he existed. Kollander even told the district commissioner everything."

"So you're suggesting that someone sold us out?" Sarac said. "A mole?"

Molnar pulled a face that was difficult to interpret but seemed to mean yes. But Sarac merely shook his head.

"I know who leaked news of Janus's existence," he said. "And I also know why."

. . .

The big man carefully put Natalie down on a mattress inside the van and closed the sliding door behind them.

He helped her take off the stiff, frozen scarf and then her cold gloves. He fiddled with something she couldn't see, then passed her a cup of hot coffee from a flask.

"Drink this," he said curtly.

Natalie did as she was told and felt warmth spread through her body.

"T-thanks," she shivered.

"Don't mention it," The man sat down on the floor beside

her and leaned back against the side of the van. He seemed to be studying her intently.

"It was you who punctured the tire," he said. A statement rather than a question. She didn't reply and took refuge in the cup of coffee.

"You know him, don't you? David Sarac?"

She looked up, then gave a short nod.

"Then you know where I can find him." The man nodded slowly. "But naturally you won't help me. After all, you were on the point of freezing to death for his sake." He gestured toward the door. Natalie didn't respond.

"You could at least tell me what your name is. I mean, I have just saved your life."

"N-Natalie," she said. "You?"

He pulled an amused little face, as if the question surprised him.

"My name's Atif, Atif Kassab."

"And what do you want with David, Atif Kassab?"

"Nothing, not anymore."

"B-but yesterday, you tried to . . ."

Atif looked at her carefully, and a little smile crept into the corner of his mouth.

"It was you driving the red Golf, wasn't it? That's how you got that." He nodded toward the surgical tape on her forehead and looked almost impressed.

Natalie didn't say anything.

"Yesterday I thought David Sarac was the only way I was going to find someone else," Atif said. "Today it's different. I know they're going to be meeting out here, I just don't know where, exactly. Not yet. But I'm expecting to find out very soon."

He got up and climbed through to the driver's seat.

"But seeing as you were on your way toward Skarpö, it wouldn't be too foolish an idea to drive a bit farther."

He put the van in gear and slowly steered the van out onto the narrow bridge.

• • •

"To begin with, Janus was probably mostly just a rumor on the street," Sarac said. "But as time went on, even the bosses would have started to see the signs. Arrests, seizures, plans that went wrong. But they couldn't be completely sure, not until they got a second opinion. Someone whose information couldn't be doubted. In short, they needed . . ." Sarac tapped his finger on the table again. "A bent police officer.

"So they turn to that lawyer, Crispin," Sarac continued. "He finds a well-placed police officer who needs the money. Meets him by chance at a private club in one of the Kungsgatan towers. When the police officer confirms that Janus really does exist, paranoia spreads like wildfire. All their efforts are focused on finding the traitor, as they frantically try to cover their own backs. The flow of money up through the chain slows down and soon the bosses' bosses start to complain, threatening all manner of things."

Sarac paused for a couple of seconds, laced his fingers together in front of him, and swallowed.

"So they start showering more money at their bent policeman," he went on. "Fill his foreign bank accounts with millions of kronor, to get him to reveal Janus's true identity. Maybe some of them even give the policeman small tip-offs about their competitors' activities. After all, everything can be blamed on Janus."

The radio on the kitchen table crackled for a couple of seconds, then fell silent again.

"But the corrupt officer never had any intention of surrendering Janus," Sarac continued. "In actual fact, he is exploiting Crispin for his own ends. All the policeman has done is confirm that Janus exists and pass on information about some relatively unimportant police operations, and he gets showered with money and tip-offs. Money that he uses to pay other CIs without having to go through any bureaucracy or checks. He pays out large enough amounts that more and more people are prepared to consider becoming informants. Because almost all of us have a price, don't we, Peter?"

Molnar didn't answer, just stared hard at Sarac.

"In this way the police officer quickly builds up his own secret, self-financing organization," Sarac went on. "He's able to deliver more and more tip-offs, better and better, all of them ascribed to the astonishingly skillful infiltrator, Janus. His bosses and colleagues are delighted. They all want to share in the glory. The police officer knows what he's doing is wrong. That the ends don't justify the means. But he doesn't care. The excitement is driving him on, the thrill of balancing on the high wire."

Sarac fell silent for several seconds, loosening his laced fingers slightly.

"Up to that point, the whole thing has been an almost perfect intelligence operation," he continued. "The enemy is busy destroying itself. The distrust among them is now almost total, and they're all informing on one another. And the most elegant part of the whole scheme is that they're actually funding their own demise.

"But then the policeman gets a new idea," Sarac added. "Eventually the money starts to dry up, which perhaps isn't too surprising. After all, despite his promises, the police officer hasn't delivered Janus. But instead of winding down the operation, he decides to do something else. Something that strengthens his credibility and buys him a bit more time. Another couple of months on the tightrope."

Sarac paused again and took a deep breath. Thunder was rumbling ominously in the distance.

"He picks out three CIs," he said in a low voice. "Three small-time crooks who have never really delivered anything useful, people he can easily do without, and he leaks their identities. He sells them out for money, to raise his credibility as a mole. The police officer realizes he's condemning the men to death. They're a small sacrifice for a greater cause, at least that's what he tries to convince himself. An asymmetrical war against an asymmetrical enemy, as the Duke would have put it."

The radio on the table crackled again, a static hiss from the approaching thunderstorm.

"But at roughly the same time the police officer encounters a problem," Sarac went on. "Another CI has been stupid enough to try to blackmail him. Threatening to shake the wire, make him fall. In a moment of desperation, the policeman does something unforgivable. And suddenly, when he comes to his senses again, he realizes that he has actually already fallen off the tightrope, has fallen farther than he could ever have imagined. That he has transgressed against everything he once held sacred."

Sarac shut his eyes and tried to keep his voice calm.

"So, in a moment of regret and clarity, the policeman calls to warn the three informants, tells them to leave the country at once if they want to live. Then he empties his accounts of the bribe money, moving it somewhere no one else can get at it. He decides to confess everything he's done and take his punishment. But then he makes another mistake, a particularly fateful one."

Sarac leaned forward toward Molnar. He could hear the sorrow in his voice.

"He calls his best friend, the only person apart from the police officer himself who knows all the details of the operation: the double-crossing, the bribes, the men who have been condemned to death, everything. The police officer wants to warn him, tell him that everything is about to collapse. But then the story takes an unexpected turn. A scenario that the police officer could never have imagined. His best friend tries to kill him."

A powerful clap of thunder made the windowpanes rattle. A moment later all the lights in the house went out, plunging the room into darkness.

FIFTY-SEVEN

"Seeing as we're telling stories," Molnar said. His chair scraped as he stood up.

"Once upon a time I had a friend, maybe we could even call him my best friend." He took a couple of steps out into the hall.

"He and I shared a secret. You know what secrets are like, David. Some of them bind people together, bind them very tightly. Our secret was one of those. It made us feel a bit smarter than everyone else."

There was a faint creak as he opened the door at the top of the cellar stairs. Then the sound of the fuse box being opened.

"It was my friend who came up with it all," Molnar went on. "His brilliant idea, and, if I'm honest, I was envious of his intelligence, his talent. Even though I was his mentor, I found myself admiring the skill with which he mastered the game. How he could get people to do exactly what he wanted."

Only the light of a pocket flashlight was visible from the cellar stairs.

"But then something happened. My friend played the game too well. He lost his way, and eventually made an unfortunate decision that threatened to reveal our secret. At first I felt disappointed, and pretty miserable. Then I felt angry."

A few seconds of silence followed.

"But then I started to think about what would have happened if our roles had been reversed. If it had been me who had lost my way."

Molnar closed the fuse box, shut the cellar door, and came

back out into the hall. Apart from the light from the flashlight, the house was still in total darkness.

"So I decided to do everything I could to help my friend. Help him find his way back to himself. Help him to keep our secret."

He shone the flashlight directly at where Sarac had been sitting. The kitchen chair was empty.

• • •

Atif had crossed the narrow bridge. Lights appeared on both sides of the van, outdoor lamps and light from windows. He carried on through the small settlement, following the road deeper onto the island.

Natalie sat silently in the back. Her chilled body was gradually warming up, making it ache much more than before. She had briefly considered pulling the side door open, jumping out, and running to the nearest house. But she could hardly stand up straight, let alone get her stiff fingers to work the lock.

Atif drove on for another thousand feet, then stopped the van at a point where the road was slightly wider. The snow didn't seem to be falling so heavily now, as if the powerful thunderclap had marked the zenith of the storm.

He turned toward Natalie. Then he pulled out his cell phone. The screen was dark.

"You're still not thinking of helping me, Natalie?"

She didn't answer.

"See that house over there?" Atif pointed to some lights a short distance away. "All I have to do is go over and ask where David Sarac lives," he said.

Natalie shrugged her shoulders. "Go ahead."

Atif opened his door. "Don't go anywhere, Natalie."

• • •

"Come on, David." Molnar turned the flashlight off. He walked slowly into the dark little library, then on into the living room.

"We haven't got time for this sort of game. Janus . . ."

"Is on his way." Sarac was standing over by the window, looking out at the garden. Outside it was still snowing, albeit not quite as heavily as before.

"Janus was the perfect intelligence operation," Molnar said. "The sort people could write books about. But all you had accomplished wasn't enough for you, you wanted to make the operation even better. Instead of winding it down as planned, you tried to surpass yourself. You lost contact with the ground. I tried to warn you, tried to get you to realize that once you go past a certain point there's no way back. But you didn't listen. You were high on a cocktail of drugs and your own abilities. You thought you could pretty much do anything. Hansen's death brought you up short. Made you realize the cost of your actions. And all of a sudden you didn't want to play anymore.

"But by then it was too late. Just as I'd tried to tell you, there was no way back . . ."

"So you tried to stop my car in the tunnel? Tried to kill me to stop me from meeting Dreyer?" Sarac said.

Molnar pulled a pained face.

"I just couldn't let you do it, David. Hand over all the fantastic work you'd accomplished to someone like Dreyer."

"That *we*'d accomplished, Peter," Sarac said. "You and me. Janus was our project. Apart from Josef, we're on our own out here, aren't we?" Sarac pointed at the radio. "You must have let him in on the whole thing the moment I hung up that evening. Maybe you offered him a share of the bribes, unless he agreed out of loyalty alone? I'd guess it was a mixture of both. But no one else in the group knows what's going on. I daresay they're all sitting at home watching television right now?"

Molnar didn't answer.

"You must have been seriously fucking surprised to find the bank accounts empty," Sarac said. "Almost fourteen million, vanished without a trace. No clues at the office or in my apartment, even though you tore the furniture apart. You hadn't reckoned with the fact that I'd got so paranoid that I'd got hold of other premises. A secret base only I knew about."

Molnar kept silent and merely moved his head slightly.

"That was why you didn't finish the job up at the hospital," Sarac said. "Without me the money was gone for good, so you had to get me out of the hospital before I confided in anyone. So you wrote those messages, to make me think I was being hunted. That I wasn't even safe at home."

Sarac pointed down toward the garden.

"It was you standing down there," he said. "You were secretly keeping watch on me while I was stuck out here in isolation. Cut off from the outside world, with my head full of fragmented memories, lies, and half-truths, exactly the way you wanted. Was the money really that important, Peter?"

Molnar cleared his throat.

"Would you believe me if I said I was actually hoping to get my friend back?" he said. "Get back the David Sarac I used to admire."

Sarac pulled a face and slipped one hand into his pocket. His fingers closed around his cell phone and found the button that switched it on.

"You thought that the Janus list in the notebook was about money, and that the numbers were bank accounts," he said. "But I'd actually listed the ID numbers of everyone who was involved. Hansen and the other three, and Erik I. Johansson, my own secret alter ego. In your hunt for the money you managed to put me on the right track. The money's gone. Save the Children, other charities, I haven't really got a clue." Sarac carefully got his phone out and turned away, holding it close to his chest so Molnar wouldn't see the glow of the screen. He pulled up the message he had written and saved earlier.

Molnar ran his tongue over his teeth a couple of times, then shook his head.

"No, you're wrong there, David," he said. "You quoted the

Duke a little while ago. You clearly listened very carefully to what he had to say. Eugene always says how important it is to have a way out. An emergency exit of some sort, so you can quickly get out of an operation if things go wrong. I'm sure you followed his advice. Somewhere you've got an emergency exit, a hiding place where you've got a bit of money stashed away. You might even have some other things there. Fake passports, account numbers, bank card readers. You should have taken that emergency exit when everything fell apart. But instead you decided to get yourself a conscience."

Molnar shook his head gently.

"We can still turn this around if we work together. All that's left is tidying up a few loose ends."

"Like Markovic, Lehtonen, and Sabatini, you mean?" Sarac interrupted. Molnar didn't answer.

"You saw the list of calls from my phone, Peter. Maybe you even recognized the numbers. Either way, you immediately worked out who I'd called, and that I'd warned them all," Sarac said.

"But you couldn't know what I'd said about you, or Janus. You couldn't feel safe."

Molnar still didn't say anything.

"Lehtonen and Sabatini managed to get out of the country. They'd probably have stayed away longer if someone hadn't called them and said it was all a false alarm. Someone they knew and trusted. Someone they'd worked with before. The very person who actually wanted to see them dead."

Molnar was slowly moving toward Sarac.

"I only did what I had to to protect the secret, David. Our secret, yours and mine, just like you said. Even Bergh had no idea how it all worked, he thought it was just a matter of digging out your backup list and carrying on. When it went missing he panicked, thought someone had stolen it. Whereas in actual fact . . ."

"There was no list," Sarac muttered. "I'd replaced it with an empty envelope to protect our secret. To conceal the name that was missing, that couldn't be there."

He moved his thumb over his phone and closed his eyes. He thought about Janus's face in the rearview mirror. His own smile, the smell of Hansen's fear.

Debts I can't escape till the day I die, a familiar voice whispered in his head.

Janus—the Roman god with two faces. Just like him.

He pressed the Send button. Twice, just to make sure. He saw the message leave the outbox. Now there was no way back.

"So what happens next, David?" Molnar said. "Now that you know everything, now that I know that you know?" He lowered his hand and placed it on his holster.

Sarac looked at his watch. The luminous hands said it was two minutes to eight.

"We wait," he said.

. . .

As soon as Atif had gone, Natalie tried to sit up. She felt her pockets, looking for her cell phone, but quickly realized it wasn't there. Either she'd lost it when she fell or Atif had taken it without her noticing. She crawled over to the side door and started to pick at the lock. Just as she'd thought, her fingers wouldn't do as she wanted. Suddenly the inside of the van was lit up by headlights. A large vehicle was approaching at top speed. Natalie crawled over to the little rear window and reached her hand up in an attempt to wave at the driver. But the vehicle sped past, large and black, so close that it made the van sway. Its taillights headed off down the road, getting dimmer and dimmer. Then they suddenly got brighter again as the brake lights lit up a thousand feet farther on.

The driver's door of the van opened and Atif jumped back in. He had his cell phone in his hand.

"No one home, but it's all sorted anyway. Looks like we're almost there." He waved his phone.

More headlights approached and another vehicle drove past, a van this time. Atif sat and watched it. His eyes followed the lights until they turned off the road at the same place as the previous vehicle.

Atif started the van and pulled out gently into the road, following the thick tire tracks through the snow.

"Can you explain something to me?" he said. "Why did you do it? Risk your life for him? Are you together?"

Natalie shook her head.

"So why?" He sounded genuinely interested.

"You wouldn't understand if I told you." *I'm not sure I do myself,* she thought.

• • •

The radio crackled again, but this time there was an agitated voice at the other end.

"Peter, it's Josef. A car just stopped down on the main road. Now it's heading this way at full speed, and it sounds as if someone's approaching on foot from the other direction, through the forest!"

"What's going on, David?" Molnar was fighting to keep his voice calm.

"We got it wrong, Peter," Sarac said sadly. "We broke our own code of honor, we revealed secrets we'd promised to protect. I tried to fix it, but some things are just too broken to mend."

He held his cell phone up to Molnar.

"I did what they've been paying me for," he said. "I told them Janus is here on the island tonight. I didn't want to give them the address until we'd had a chance to talk. I wanted to be completely certain that we're both equally guilty. And now they know where Janus is."

Molnar spun around and walked quickly into the hall and

382 Anders de la Motte

over to the front door. An engine was roaring, and the drive was lit up by headlights.

"Who are they?" he yelled over his shoulder as he drew his pistol. "Who did you tell, David? The Yugos? The Russians? The bikers?"

"All of them," Sarac replied. "I contacted all of them."

FIFTY-EIGHT

Security consultant Frank Hunter had planned the operation down to the smallest detail. Four men in total, plus him. Two for Sarac, two for Janus. Bulletproof vests, military harnesses, stun grenades, and light weapons.

In just a couple of minutes Janus would be lying tied up in the car. The trunk contained all the equipment that was needed to make him talk, mostly drugs. Violence only paid off when you wanted simple answers like yes or no. His employers wanted more than that, much more. They wanted to know absolutely everything. Who Janus was working with, for how long, what information he had handed over, and so on. And once they'd got that, and Janus's entire story was recorded, his new "friend" Atif Kassab would take care of the rest. An unpleasant sort, that Kassab. A man who had long since crossed all imaginable boundaries. Predictable in his desire for revenge, but also exploitable.

The engine of the 4x4 was roaring, and adrenaline was pumping through his body. Even though Hunter had done this plenty of times before, he still enjoyed the rush. This was what it was all about, the result of his sacrifices. The Sophie Thorning job had demanded a degree of improvisation, but it had still been one of his best. As close to perfection as you could get at such short notice. The body, the apartment, the car—everything had been taken care of. He had done what was required.

And now that improvised operation was paying off at last. Favors offered, favors repaid. His employers would be pleased, the way they usually were. Frank Hunter always delivered.

"Alpha team, go!" he said into his radio, and two of the men clinging to the outside of the jeep leaped off while it was still moving and started running toward the back of the house. The car was rushing forward, powerful lights blazing in all directions, drenching the driveway in light, for maximum effect. It braked sharply in front of the porch.

"Go, go, go!" Hunter yelled into the radio, although there was really no need. The third man who had been clinging to the side of the 4x4 was already halfway to the front door. The driver ran after him, battering ram at the ready. In a couple of seconds they'd be inside, and in less than half a minute it would all be over. And he wouldn't even have to get out of his seat.

Suddenly he detected movement at one corner of the building. The headlights were shining on a large man who was holding a gun in both hands.

Hunter pressed the button on his radio, but before he had time to call out a warning his man up on the porch had opened fire. Shit, that better not be Janus.

Hunter opened the car door and jumped out. He drew his pistol and aimed toward the corner where the large man had disappeared.

"Enemy down, breach the door! Go, go!" Hunter yelled into his microphone. The door gave way as the battering ram smashed the lock. At that moment he heard another powerful engine roaring up the driveway toward the house.

• • •

Sarac saw the two men go around the corner of the house, heading for the unlit veranda. White camouflage clothing, protective goggles, and balaclavas. They were clutching their weapons with both hands. As shooting broke out at the front of the house the men began to run straight at him.

Sarac drew his pistol in a single, smooth movement and fired off two shots. He realized instantly that he had aimed far too high. The sound of the pistol going off was deafening and made his ears ring.

The men threw themselves down on the snow and returned fire. The bullets shattered the old veranda windows, showering him with razor-sharp shards of glass.

Something hit Sarac's forehead. He put a hand to his face and felt blood, and quickly retreated into the hall. Molnar was yelling from the staircase and he stumbled in that direction. There was a crash from the front door, the sound of wood splintering. Then two shots from Molnar's gun. In the background came the roar of another car engine.

• • •

"This is Leader, heads up!" Hunter yelled into his microphone. "We've got company!"

He spun around as headlights lit up the driveway behind them and the sound of the engine got even louder. Hunter realized that his plan was in serious danger. But he wasn't about to give up now, he wasn't going to let the thought of failure enter his head.

A dark van careered into the turning circle in front of the house. Its headlights dazzled Hunter. He hesitated for a couple of seconds, then fired two shots directly at the vehicle's windshield. The van kept coming. Hunter fired again, peppering the windshield with little white holes. The sound of the engine was still getting louder, rising to a howl.

Hunter threw himself aside, straight into the snow. A moment later the van smashed into the back of the 4x4.

• • •

"Upstairs!" Molnar yelled. Sarac obeyed at once. From the living room he could hear glass crunching under heavy boots, then several small thuds as something bounced across the floor.

"Stun grenade!" Molnar roared from the foot of the stairs.

Even though Sarac was prepared, even though he was facing away from the hall and had his eyes screwed shut, he was almost knocked off his feet when the stun grenade exploded.

The blast sucked the air from his lungs, and the flash of light dazzled him through his tightly closed eyelids. He tripped on the top step and fell flat on the landing. He rolled over and aimed his pistol at the stairs.

Molnar forced his way past him and staggered into the corridor. Sarac thought he could see a white silhouette on the stairs and let off a couple of shots. The ringing in his head meant he hardly heard the sound of his own gun going off.

He tried to snake backward into the corridor, then got to his knees and blinked hard a few times. Even before he looked around, he knew where Molnar's gun was pointing. Straight at his head.

. . .

Hunter rolled over in the snow, aiming his gun at the crashed van. The engine was silent now, and a column of white steam was rising from the hood. The collision was so hard that the 4x4 had been shunted forward almost seven feet, and its front bumper had gone through the wall of the little outhouse.

Hunter could hear shouting from inside the van, then the sound of a sliding door being opened. Several burly men jumped out. At least two of them were carrying rifles. Hunter fired but only managed one shot before his gun clicked. Out of ammunition. Fuck!

He released the empty cartridge as he tried to pull a new one from his belt. A man in a bulletproof vest holding a pump-action shotgun in his hands was heading straight for him. It was one of the Russians from the meeting at the gym. Hunter rammed the new cartridge into place, released the safety catch, and fired, all in the same fluid movement. The man staggered backward but still managed to fire one shot at Hunter. Burning pain flared up in one of Hunter's legs and he rolled sideways, beneath the 4x4.

There was more shooting from the direction of the van. Hunter couldn't see exactly where the shots were coming from, but they seemed to be aimed at the porch. He could see feet, heavy boots, moving from beneath the vehicle, and tried to take aim at them. His hands were shaking and his heart was pounding hard. Failure was not an option.

"Man down," someone yelled in his earpiece. "Man down!"

He felt for the microphone. This whole operation was rapidly going completely to . . .

 * * *

Hell! Detective Inspector Josef Almlund was crawling through the snow, pressing his hand to his gut and feeling the blood running between his fingers. The bullet had hit him just below his bulletproof vest and must have caused a fuck-load of damage to his intestines before exiting through his back. He slumped back against the wall of the house, fumbling in the snow for his gun, but couldn't find anything. A few moments later he realized that he must have pissed himself as well. Fuckfuckfuck . . .

Five men came charging out of the forest in front of him, rushing across the snow. They were all wearing green and beige camouflage outfits that made them stand out clearly against the white background. In their hands they were clutching heavy assault rifles, all pointing at him.

One of the men went up to Josef, kicked some snow at him, and said something to the others in a language that Josef thought was probably Serbian. Then he put his assault rifle to Josef's head.

Josef shut his eyes, thinking that this was one hell of a shitty way to die. None of this would have happened if he hadn't listened to Peter Molnar. Hadn't let his greed get the better of him.

When he opened his eyes the men had gone around the house toward the turning circle. He felt his chest for his radio but discovered that the pocket on his shoulder was empty. The ear-shattering clatter of assault rifles made him cover his head with his arms.

 * * *

Hunter looked out from beneath the 4x4. He could see the men's backs as they rushed around the van. Blue bulletproof vests, tracksuits, a long plait of hair. He could hear the sound of their shotguns firing, followed by a pistol as someone up on the porch returned fire.

The clatter of assault rifles came out of nowhere. The sound was deafening, bringing down snow from several of the nearest trees. One of the men from the van crumpled as the others threw themselves down and sought shelter.

Hunter twisted to his right and could see heavy boots and camouflaged legs between him and the house. He fired almost without aiming, emptying his entire cartridge. He heard a cry as one of the men in camouflage slumped to his knees. Then the man turned his assault rifle toward him.

A moment later one of the men from the van shot the man in the head. The shower of shots almost blew the man's head from his shoulders.

Pain suddenly broke through the veil of adrenaline. Hunter rolled over onto his back and looked down. On his left shin he could see blood and broken flesh clearly visible against the white of his trousers. He shut his eyes and almost threw up.

"Man down!" someone was still yelling in his earpiece. "Man down!"

The men with the assault rifles started firing again and seemed to be concentrating their fire on the men crouched behind the back of the van. Their bullets riddled the soft metal, turning it into a sieve. Hunter could hear the men behind the van howling in agony. He realized he had to get out of there, right away.

"This is Leader," he hissed into the microphone. "Abort mission. I repeat, abort mission!"

A bullet punctured the tire next to him, and another drilled through the metal just an inch and a half away. He'd been spotted. Hunter tucked his arms in toward his body, kicked off against the underside of the vehicle with his intact leg, and rolled away from the house.

The ground fell away beneath him as he tumbled out of control down the slope and in among the trees. He fell head over heels a couple of times, actually leaving the ground before hitting a tree trunk. The collision knocked the air out of him. He coughed and slowly tried to sit up. His nose and mouth were full of snow, and one side of his head stung like hell. He crawled up to a sitting position and took shelter behind a tree, then put a hand up to feel his ear. His fingers didn't find what they were looking for. With an icy wrench in his gut, he realized that most of his outer ear was missing.

The shoot-out up at the house was still going on. Protracted bursts from the assault rifles, growing more and more intense. Then a bang, so powerful that he felt it in his chest. It took him a few seconds to work out what it was. A hand grenade.

Hunter fumbled for his radio but discovered that his pocket had been torn from his vest. A fresh sound made him look up.

A thickset man with a ponytail was rushing down the slope, just thirty to fifty feet away. He was taking long, stumbling strides, lost his balance, and tumbled over, before landing feet-first in a snowdrift. But instead of rolling away the man sank into the snow almost up to his waist and just sat there. Hunter recognized him as another of the men from the meeting at the gym, Micke Lund, one of the bikers.

Lund looked around and started when he saw Hunter pressed against a tree. Their eyes met.

There were shouts from up at the house. In Serbian. "The fat bastard's down there! Kill him!"

The bullets from the assault rifles cut right through Lund's bulletproof vest, going through his body and throwing up little bursts of snow behind him. The man's eyes opened wide for a few seconds, and he stared at Hunter as if he were trying to say something. Then he slowly slumped forward.

Hunter leaned his head back against the tree trunk and closed his eyes. His stomach clenched and for a few seconds he felt as if he were falling.

FIFTY-NINE

Sarac stared at Molnar. Then at the gun pointing at his head. His ears were still ringing and he was blinking hard to shake off the aftereffects of the stun grenade.

He heard steps from the staircase and spun around, and just had time to see a camouflaged figure before Molnar fired. The man cried out and tumbled backward down the stairs.

Sarac got to his feet and began to walk slowly down the corridor. Molnar was still aiming right at him. Sarac raised his own gun and pointed it at Molnar. He stopped so close that their barrels were almost touching.

"You fucking idiot!" Molnar's face was white. "What the hell have you done?"

"Markovic, Lehtonen, and Sabatini," Sarac interrupted. "You killed all three of them. At first you tried to make it look like there were three different killers. Then you tried to blame everything on Janus."

"You hardly gave me any choice," Molnar snarled. "Someone had to clean up the mess you left behind. Hansen got what he deserved, you couldn't let him blackmail you and took appropriate action. I was only doing the same as you, protecting the secret."

"Janus," Sarac said. "Everything begins and ends with him. But the hooks of that symbol face inward, not out."

Molnar nodded. "So you've finally realized. I was actually starting to wonder."

He raised his radio without moving his gun from Sarac's head.

"Josef, can you hear me? We have to get out of here."

The radio crackled.

"Josef, are you there?" Molnar said.

More static, then a deep voice with a faint accent.

"Your cop friend can't talk right now. He's not feeling too good."

Molnar grimaced and waited a couple of seconds before replying.

"And who are you?"

"Sasha," the man said. "I have no issue with you, cop. All I want is Janus."

Molnar glanced quickly at Sarac.

"Who?" he said.

"Very funny," the man replied.

There was more noise downstairs now, footsteps approaching through the hall.

Molnar took a deep breath, then lowered his gun. Sarac did the same.

"There are three or four of them," Molnar said. "All armed with assault rifles. As far as I could tell, sounds like AK47s."

Sarac nodded and took the chance to change his cartridge.

"This isn't over, David," Molnar said. "Do you get that? As soon as we get out of here . . ."

"I get it, Peter." Sarac released the safety catch. Then nodded to Molnar.

More noises from below, whispers, then movement.

"Can we get out that way?" Molnar nodded toward the veranda behind them.

"Yes," Sarac said. "But it's at least a fifteen-foot drop."

Molnar turned and opened the door to the veranda. He stepped cautiously out among the building material. Sarac followed him.

Behind him he heard quick footsteps, then the sound of something rolling across the floor of the corridor. Sarac spun around and saw a green metal cylinder with a yellow stripe down the side following them out onto the veranda. It stopped right next to the gas cylinders.

His legs started to move by themselves. Sarac opened his mouth and shouted. Roared!

• • •

Atif opened the door of the van. The noises from the house had gone quiet.

"Sorry I have to leave you like this," he said.

Natalie pulled a face. The parcel ties he had used to tie her to one of the cargo hooks in the floor were cutting into her wrists. But as long as she lay still it was okay.

Atif closed and locked the door behind him. He assumed the neighbors must have called the police already, but it would be more than an hour before anyone got there. But at least she wouldn't freeze to death.

As soon as the van door closed Natalie crept backward over her hands so they were in front of her, then shifted position so she could reach the front pocket of her jeans with her fingers.

Atif walked up the narrow track. The weather seemed to have changed completely, switching from tempestuous storm to silent, beautiful snow.

The turning circle in front of the house looked like a war zone. He had heard the sound of the hand grenade a short while ago, and the sight that confronted him was pretty much as expected. Two bullet-riddled wrecked vehicles in front of the porch. The snow was covered with brass-colored empty bullet cases and he could almost taste the gunpowder and TNT in the air.

Atif walked around the rear vehicle, a van that had been pretty much turned into a colander. He saw the dark-rimmed crater where the hand grenade had gone off. There were several bodies on the ground and he heard someone whimpering in Russian but didn't stop to find out who it was. The front door to the house was open, jagged splinters of wood sticking out from the frame. He could hear noises inside, someone screaming.

· · ·

"Hand grenade!" Sarac roared as he rushed for the far end of the veranda. Molnar seemed to have realized it already and was two steps ahead of him. He'd raised his gun and was emptying the magazine into the windows in front of them, knocking out several of the old panes of glass.

Sarac did the same, firing once, twice . . . then he raised his hands in the air and jumped. The pressure wave hit him while he was in the air, hurling him through the old windows and out across the snow-covered grass. He landed on his stomach, catching his left arm beneath him. He heard it snap. He gasped for air and tried to roll away. His ears were howling, his whole head aching.

A big piece of glass was sticking out of his lower left arm. He pulled it out and got to his knees. There was less bleeding than he expected. He checked the rest of his body for further injuries with his right hand. The bulletproof vest seemed to have saved him from the worst of it, but when he touched the back of his neck his hand felt wet with blood. Strangely enough, he couldn't feel any pain.

On the ground in front of him, half-buried in the loose snow about a yard away, was a familiar object. His pistol. He picked it up and got to his feet. Then he started to stagger across the grass, away from the house and toward the old fruit trees.

"David!" Molnar's voice cut through the roaring in his ears and made him turn around. "Where the hell are you going?"

Molnar's gun was pointed straight at him.

"That way," Sarac said, gesturing toward the edge of the forest. He heard how strange his voice sounded. Then he noticed the man with the assault rifle who had appeared in the doorway about ten feet behind Molnar. And saw him raise his weapon.

• • •

Atif carefully pushed at the front door. The fresh explosion had left his ears ringing, but the smell was even stronger than before. Gunpowder, smoke, TNT—and some other more subtle smells beneath them. Adrenaline, blood, fear, death.

The air inside the hall was full of dirt and sawdust and he had to squint in order to see anything. He stepped inside and discovered a body impaled on the banisters of the imposing staircase. Camouflage clothing, bulletproof vest, military boots. A flickering light from the upper floor was growing stronger. The sound of fire greedily attacking old wood.

He peered into the living room and beyond, through a glazed veranda. There were two figures on the snow-covered grass, both with their backs to him. He recognized one of them, David Sarac.

On this side of the two figures, in the middle of the doorway, stood a man with an assault rifle, taking aim at them.

• • •

The bang was abrupt, and nowhere near as loud as Sarac had been expecting. When the man in the doorway collapsed he didn't understand what was going on at first. Then he caught sight of another figure silhouetted on the veranda. He recognized him almost at once. The man from Gamla stan.

• • •

Atif shot the man with the assault rifle right in the back of the head, didn't even have time to think about it. The body fell without a sound. He stood there for a moment, looking down at the lifeless body as blood pumped out of the hole in his head. He had done it again, killed someone without a second thought. Admittedly to save someone else, but still.

The unknown man out on the grass had turned toward him and fired a shot in his direction. The distance was too great, but

Atif ducked instinctively. He saw David Sarac run toward the edge of the forest. The other man went on shooting toward the house. Atif raised his gun and took aim.

A tiny flicker in one of the panes of glass made him change his mind and throw himself to one side. The hail of bullets from the assault rifle missed him by a hairsbreadth and shattered almost all the remaining windows.

Atif ducked behind the sofa, fired two shots blind, and threw himself into the next room, a small library with beautiful built-in bookcases, just like the ones he had at home. He got to his knees and took aim at the doorway. And waited . . .

He heard the sound of footsteps, whispering, then someone clearing his throat.

"I was wondering when you were going to show up, Atif," a familiar voice said. It was his old friend Sasha. "I presume old Hamsa sent you, then? Because he's *helping* you find the man responsible for your brother's death?" Sasha let out a low laugh. "Hamsa uses that gym as a money-laundering operation. The moment Adnan ran in there waving his gun, he was finished. But because he was your brother, none of them wanted to take responsibility for getting rid of him. So they came up with a smarter solution."

A crashing sound from upstairs interrupted Sasha, and judging by the smell the fire had seriously taken hold up there now.

"Think about it, Atif. Whose idea was the raid on the security van? Who knew all the details and could tell the cops everything? Who had taken a fancy to Adnan's girlfriend?" Sasha laughed again. Atif licked his lips.

"They ratted on Adnan to the cops so they could get rid of him," Sasha said. "Then blamed it all on Janus. Whereas the dirty work was actually done by that little rat Bakshi. After all, as you know, he's good at that, he's on the payroll of a whole load of different cops. All it took was one phone call."

Atif could make out movement in the next room and heard

someone whisper in Serbian, then footsteps. He turned and looked out toward the kitchen. They could take him from two directions at once, trap him like a rat.

"So you're actually working for the man who killed your brother, which is pretty ironic, don't you think, old friend?" Sasha said.

Atif looked at the nearest window. It was high up and looked solid. Jumping through it wasn't a particularly appealing prospect. Instead he glanced toward the kitchen. He saw a reflection in one of the pieces of glass still hanging from the kitchen window. Saw a very familiar movement.

"You see, Atif," Sasha went on, but Atif was no longer listening. He took three quick paces straight out into the kitchen and almost ran into the other man, who had just pulled out the cartridge from his assault rifle.

Atif shot him in the middle of the forehead, then carried on past him, out into the hall. The salvo from Sasha's assault rifle slammed through the walls, sending splinters and ricochets all around the room.

Atif took cover behind the staircase. A sudden burst of pain struck him in one side. A six, maybe a seven. He felt the injury with his hand and discovered dark blood. Not good.

"We don't have to do this, Atif," Sasha called from the living room. His voice no longer sounded so confident. "I can help you get revenge for your brother, all I want is Janus. We can work together, the way we used to."

Atif was breathing hard. On the stairs the heat from the fire on the floor above was palpable. His eyes started to water, and the smoke was making him cough. In a few minutes it would get hard to breathe. The only possible ways out were through the front door or back through the kitchen, but that would give Sasha an easy line of fire with his assault rifle. He thought for a moment.

"Okay!" he said, then got slowly to his feet and peered inside the living room.

Sasha was standing there with the rifle in his hands. When he saw Atif he held the gun up, its barrel pointing at the ceiling.

Atif walked into the room, doing the same with his pistol. He saw that Sasha had a bloody bandage around one thigh. That explained his sudden willingness to cooperate.

"Look at us, Atif." Sasha smiled. "Neither of us looks in particularly good shape." He gestured toward his bandaged leg, then at Atif's jacket, one side of which was now red with blood.

"They headed off toward the forest. I know the terrain, there's nowhere for them to go," Sasha said.

Atif nodded, still looking at Sasha. In the past five minutes he had killed two of Sasha's men. But the other man didn't seem remotely bothered. Abu Hamsa, the treacherous little bastard, had been right about one thing: there was no longer any honor. The only question was whether there ever had been.

"By the way," Sasha said. "I'm sorry about that message to your niece. It was Abu Hamsa's idea, I just helped him carry it out. Children should be off-limits."

Atif nodded mutely, feeling pressure building up in his head. He thought about Tindra, and how she had happily taken the Christmas card home in her little schoolbag, not realizing what it meant. Tricked into thinking that Santa had sent a message to her and her uncle. Then he remembered what he had promised to do to the people who dared to get at him through his only niece.

Sasha turned and walked toward the doorway. The same Sasha who had once sworn to kill him. Outside the sky was still dark, not a glimpse of any stars.

"Are you coming, or what?" he said over his shoulder.

Atif closed his eyes and saw Tindra's little face in front of him. He opened his eyes and stared at the back of Sasha's death's-head skull. There really wasn't any honor left. Not anymore. He raised the pistol and squeezed the trigger.

· · ·

Natalie grimaced with pain as she massaged her wrists. She had managed to get her trusty ChapStick out of her pocket and had greased her hands, enough for her to be able to pull them through the cable ties with a bit of wriggling and a fair degree of force.

The shooting up at the house had fallen silent now. She looked around for her cell phone and found it on top of the dashboard.

Six missed calls, all from Rickard. She had no intention of calling back. Rickard, aka Oscar Wallin, could fuck right off. What she ought to do now was get out of there, knock on one of the neighbor's doors, and wait there until the police showed up.

She got out of the van, looked up toward the house, and noticed the thick column of smoke above the roof. She thought about the gunfire, explosions, and cries that she had heard down in the van. About the people who had to be lying up there injured, people who would bleed to death before help could arrive. David Sarac might well be one of them. Maybe she'd never get to be a qualified doctor, but at that moment, out there on the island, she was probably the closest thing available.

Natalie clambered back inside the van and gathered up everything she could find. A roll of duct tape, a blanket, some cable ties. In a compartment marked with a red cross she found a surprisingly well-stocked first aid kit. She shoved everything into an old plastic bag, jumped out of the van, and started to make her way cautiously up toward the house.

SIXTY

Sarac reached the orchard and had just got in among the trees when Molnar shot him. The bullet hit the back of his thigh and his leg gave way beneath him. He fell and rolled over. He managed to get his pistol out and fire off a shot. It missed.

The gun clicked and he automatically released the empty cartridge. His left hand was useless, so he held the pistol between his legs while he fumbled for the spare cartridge with his right hand.

Molnar stumbled toward him and fired a shot that passed just above Sarac's head. Sarac managed to get hold of the cartridge and pushed it into his pistol. He spun the weapon around, aimed it straight at Molnar's body, and released the safety catch. He pulled the trigger.

Nothing happened.

He hit the butt against his thigh and felt the cartridge click into place. He repeated the bolt action by pressing the top of the gun against his belt.

Molnar shot him from just ten feet away. The bullet hit him in the neck. His head fell to one side and blood gushed into his throat, leaving him gurgling for air.

Molnar was standing right above him.

"And where do you think you're going, little David?" he slurred as he kicked Sarac's gun away.

Half of Molnar's top lip seemed to have been torn off in the explosion, transforming his expression into a macabre grin of perfect white teeth. Sarac spat out a mouthful of blood and tried not to glance toward the edge of the forest. He failed.

Molnar saw him looking. At first he stared up at the tall trees, then realized what Sarac had been looking at.

"Toward the exit!" he slurred triumphantly. "Of course!"

He walked past Sarac, toward the old concrete gateposts that marked the end of the garden. He squatted down between them with an effort and scraped away the snow. At the bottom of one of them a small, barely visible symbol was carved into the old concrete. Two ornate *J*s facing each other, forming two faces looking away from each other. Molnar pushed the snow aside and found a canvas flap that the cold had pushed up from the ground. He pulled at it, then started to laugh out loud.

"You followed the rules, David," he said. "Obviously I should have realized. Hell, I've stood down here for hours keeping watch on you. And the answer was right under my nose the whole time. Janus, the god of transitions. Of doors, gates, portals." Molnar leaned his head back and laughed again. A disconcertingly shrill sound that echoed between the trees.

The god who starts and ends all wars, Sarac thought. His head and body were aching, and his throat kept filling up, making it hard to breathe. He really ought to try to get to his feet and make a last attempt to stop Molnar.

But he realized that he'd never make it. Instead he slowly pulled himself up into a sitting position and leaned his back against one of the old apple trees, spitting out yet more blood. The exertion made his vision blur.

In just a few minutes he would be dead. Oddly enough, the thought made him feel something like relief. But he had one last thing to do. A mission to complete.

He clenched his right hand a couple of times, then carefully felt down his trouser leg.

Molnar was scraping the snow away between the gateposts and uncovering more black canvas. Then something that looked like a handle.

"You and the Duke and your fucking Roman gods." He

grinned. "Shall we place bets on whether I'm going to find a bank account number in the bag? Maybe even a card reader?"

. . .

Atif was walking slowly across the grass. He was treading carefully, as if he were trying to make sure he didn't fall. He was following the tracks through the snow, just like Adnan had done when he was little.

His clothes were wet and he could feel blood running down one side.

"Nearly there, Adnan," he muttered.

He saw David Sarac leaning against a tree. His face was white, his head was hanging at an odd angle. There were patches of red in the snow around him.

The other man was standing about thirty feet away. Atif recognized him now; it was the man he'd seen coming out of the door of Sarac's building. Was he Janus? If Sasha was right, he wasn't guilty of Adnan's death. But Atif wasn't about to take any risks. A psychopath like Sasha was capable of saying anything and making it sound believable. He hadn't come this far only to abandon his mission.

Atif raised his pistol, feeling the pain getting steadily worse. An eight, close to a nine now.

The first bullet missed Atif by three feet or so. He carried on walking, waiting to shoot until he was sure of hitting his target. The man fired again, using one of the gateposts as a support. Another miss, but this time so close that Atif could feel the rush of air as it passed. He raised his gun and aimed.

The third bullet hit him below his ribs, making him stagger. Atif kept walking, forcing himself to hold his pistol hand up. The man's weapon clicked and Atif saw him fumbling desperately for a fresh cartridge. He took a step, then another. The man clicked the new cartridge into place and raised his arm.

Atif shot him twice, in the center of his body. The man dropped his gun and slumped beside the gatepost. Atif carried

402 Anders de la Motte

on staggering forward and didn't stop until he was holding the barrel of the pistol against the man's head. He realized too late that it was a mistake. A millisecond before the blow hit him he noticed that the man was wearing a bulletproof vest.

Atif tumbled backward but managed to grab hold of a branch at the last minute and stay on his feet. The man kicked him in the thigh, making his leg buckle. Then he aimed a rock-hard right hook at Atif's ear that brought him to his knees, and followed through with an elbow to his shoulder. Atif fell forward and ended up on all fours. He felt the ground lurch.

An arm tightened around his throat as a hand pushed hard at the back of his neck. He tried to break free and keep his airway open.

But it was too late. The man already had him in a stranglehold. Atif could hear the other man's breath panting in his ear. He could almost smell the adrenaline coursing through his body. The scent of victory.

Atif twisted his head, trying to buy himself a few more seconds. His fingers felt along the outside of his shin, and he reached into the back of his boot. His fingers closed around the switchblade he had taken from Bakshi, and he pulled it out and opened the blade. At that moment his field of vision began to shrink and turn black. He tried to raise his arm but realized he didn't have enough strength left.

* * *

Sarac rested his right hand against his knee. He drew as much air as he could into his lungs and closed his left eye before he squeezed the trigger of the revolver Bergh had given him.

There was still a bit of insulating tape stuck to its side, but that didn't bother him. He waited until the bead was right in the middle of the notch, then pulled the trigger the rest of the way and shot Peter in the middle of his triumphant, mocking grin.

For a moment Molnar stood there with his arms around

Atif's neck. A hole had appeared in his perfect row of teeth. His eyes stared blankly at Sarac, as if he still couldn't take in what had happened. Then he collapsed without a sound.

After a few moments Atif straightened up slightly. He took several gasping breaths, then slumped back against a tree, in the same posture as Sarac. On the ground beside him he found his pistol. He picked it up and closed his fingers around the butt. He found that it had got very heavy.

"Is that him?" Atif gestured with the barrel toward Molnar's body. "Janus?"

Sarac shook his head, then cleared his throat and spat another mouthful of blood onto the white snow.

"So where is he, then?" Atif's voice sounded weary.

"Everywhere." Sarac waved his revolver in the air, then back toward the house.

Atif raised his pistol and aimed it at Sarac. Sarac immediately did the same to Atif. For a little while they just sat there, staring at each other above the barrels of their guns.

"One of the others," Atif mumbled. "Which one?"

"You don't get it." Sarac coughed and spat out even more blood. "Janus isn't *one* of them."

"Who is he then? Tell me, for fuck's sake!" Atif waved his pistol angrily. He noticed it was getting harder to hold. He stared at Sarac, then looked over toward the wrecked house; the flames were leaping from the roof. High above them the clouds had eased slightly. Leaving a gap through which the stars were visible.

The god who starts and ends all wars, a voice said in his head. It sounded like Adnan's.

And suddenly he understood, he understood how it all fit together. He realized to his own surprise that he was smiling. So smart, so utterly ingenious. And, at the same time—so incredibly cruel.

"You," he muttered. "Y-you're Janus. You, them, all of you—everyone. Together . . ."

Sarac smiled wryly. Blood was seeping from one corner of his mouth, forming little bubbles. The arm holding the revolver sank to the ground.

Atif lowered his gun, leaned his head back against the tree trunk, and started to laugh. A couple of seconds later Sarac joined in.

They were still laughing when Natalie found them. Hoarse, rattling laughter that had nothing at all to do with joy. They didn't stop until she told them to shut up.

EPILOGUE

"So, how do we handle this, Minister?" Wallin was sitting in the armchair on the other side of Stenberg's desk.

"Nine dead, another ten wounded, several of them police officers. The worst underworld shoot-out in Swedish history," he said.

"We turn it to our advantage," Stenberg said. "A sign of how organized crime is getting out of control. The police can't handle it, they need more resources, better leadership."

"And the police officers who were there, what about their involvement?" Wallin said.

"Well." Stenberg made a small gesture with his hand. "That's primarily the district commissioner's problem. After all, they were her staff. At a guess, Eva Swensk will do what she usually does: blame everything on a few individuals and wash her lily-white hands of the whole business. I'd say her chances of succeeding are fairly high. Bergh has already had to resign, and David Sarac looks like an excellent candidate for the vacant role of scapegoat. Besides, he'd have trouble defending himself, wouldn't he?"

"But Minister, surely you're not thinking of letting Swensk get off that lightly?" Wallin sounded anxious.

Stenberg smiled and gave a little shrug of his shoulders. "Sometimes one has to reevaluate one's position, Oscar. It's all about alliances. I had a good meeting with Carina LeMoine this morning. Eva Swensk has strong support inside the party. Besides, as Carina pointed out, a female National Police Chief would undeniably make us look forward-thinking and progressive. In many ways it would make everything simpler. Favors given, favors received, that's how things work."

Wallin nodded and appeared to think hard for a few moments. Then he opened the folder he had placed on the desk between them. It contained two apparently identical forms with official-looking logos at the top.

"Speaking of which, Minister," he said. "We've had the test results back from the National Forensics Lab. The blood found in Sophie Thorning's apartment."

"Oh," Stenberg said, trying to keep his voice calm.

Wallin looked at his boss. Waited until the other man's gaze wavered slightly. That told him all he needed to know. He took one of the forms out of the folder and pushed it across to Stenberg.

"The blood was hers," he said. "So there's no evidence at all to prove that anyone else was in the apartment when Sophie Thorning died."

He paused and looked down at the almost identical form that was still in the folder. He waited long enough for Stenberg to look at it before slowly closing the folder.

"You're quite right, Minister," Wallin said. "Alliances are important. But one should never forget who one's real friends are."

Stenberg sat and looked at Wallin in silence for a few moments, then looked up at the Kennedy quote above the man's head, the one his wife had given him. Finally he cast a quick glance at his Patek Philippe. For a brief instant he got the impression that the second hand was stuck.

"I understand," he said in a toneless voice. "Thank you, Oscar."

"Don't mention it, Minister."

Wallin stood up and walked toward the door.

"Oh, one more thing," Stenberg said, trying to sound unconcerned. "What happened with that infiltrator? Did we ever find out who he really was?"

Wallin shook his head.

"No one we've questioned admits to knowing anything about Janus's true identity. Nor anyone else, for that matter. He seems to have gone up in smoke. Almost as if he never existed . . ."

ACKNOWLEDGMENTS

There are always a lot of people involved in the creation of a book. Some are easy to thank: my family, editor, and agent. Or all the brilliant people who translate my stories into so many different languages. Others are more difficult to thank publicly, because I am unable to identify them by their real names for various reasons. But that doesn't in any way diminish my gratitude for their help.

I would like to say a special thank-you to the popular psychologist Henrik Fexeus, who has taught me a lot about how easy it is to fool the human mind. For someone who knows its secrets, at least.

Anders de la Motte
New York, 2014